THE EAGLE LEGACY

Mark D Richardson

To Frances

Love

Mark D Richardson.

ABOUT THE AUTHOR

Mark was born in Leicester in December 1961

Educated to A level standard and with a passion for writing, he designed school newsletters, produced many school plays; wrote articles in a teen magazine 'Look and Learn' and instead of the assigned English essay homework, created short stories on a regular basis.

After several writing courses and correspondence assignments, novel writing became a hobby. He started with a fantasy novel, followed by short story of a real life experience in the States, before constructing a rough draft of a thriller in the world of football.

But it was his passion for detective movies, spy thrillers, murder mysteries and whodunnits, that provided the material and inspiration for The Case Files.

The Eagle Legacy is the first of many in the series. High energy, explosive thrillers set in a world of constant threat, a continual tale of good against evil.

PROLOGUE

1944

Tyres cracked through the ice of the pitted track as the transporter made its way up the mountain. The Mercedes engine screamed in protest, the cargo forcing the axles to near collapse as the tired chassis tried to steady its course on its dangerous ascent. Three passengers bounced around in the cramped cab, rolling with each crevice and ridge.

Eric Ahlers shone his torch onto his wrist checking his watch, they had four hours of darkness left. It would be tight. The heater turned to maximum, blew barely warm air and fumes into the cab. A fruitless exercise as the damage the truck had sustained during its service to the Reich, had worn many of the seals. Even through his thermal socks and knee-high boots his feet were numb from the cold as it swirled around his ankles. He had lost all feeling in his knees hours ago.

"How much further?" He found the slow, uncomfortable journey frustrating, even though it was as expected. With the payload of four ton of gold secured behind, the slightest misjudgement would mean certain death.

"It should be only three kilometres Herr Ahlers, fifteen minutes at most." Jurgen Blatz kept his eyes fixed on the beams from the headlights. He was careful to avoid the worst ruts in the track while trying to keep the vehicle as steady as he could. It became increasingly difficult as large flakes of snow had hazed his view, doubling as they splattered against the glass.

"We should be able to see the others once we clear the next bend." Hans Breidle, wedged tightly between the driver and Ahlers, held a torch over the map spread across his lap. He pointed to the red mark showing their destination, a short way ahead from their current position.

"Good!" Ahlers stared through the glass at the white deluge smothering the windscreen after every sweep of the wipers. Relentless mounds of snow and ice pounded the vehicle as they crawled onward. But his eyes saw nothing, his thoughts fixed on the immediate task ahead, a task he repeatedly mulled in his mind. Germany was losing the war. The combined forces were advancing from the west at an alarming rate, the Luftwaffe was near to decimation, morale at an all-time low. To top it all, millions of countrymen with their entire families had fled the major cities, escaping to the hills, with more leaving every day.

It was why he, Eric Ahlers, had to double cross the Fuhrer.

As a double agent, a trusted member of Himmler's inner circle, he could plan ahead, avoiding suspicion. This trust was vital as he was about to effectively bankrupt the war effort along with any hope of victory. It was necessary for the greater cause, the true destiny of the Fatherland.

By the age of thirteen, he had been infiltrated into a surrogate family in England, nurtured, conditioned, thoroughly prepared for this moment. They had groomed him as a disciple amongst many to lay the foundations for the day of reckoning. A day when the world would bow at their feet. He had been taught well, pleasing his tutors with his natural intelligence and guile. His development had proven extraordinary.

Within his adopted country, with the help of influential contacts, along with his own natural ability, he advanced swiftly through the upper echelons of society. It allowed him to achieve his intended goal, to be recruited by the government's security agency. As a recruit in the growing intelligence corp, he soon became an expert in counterintelligence. From Germany, they closely monitored his advancement, until he became an integral part of the Hitler movement.

It was only a matter of time, as a trusted agent, before they posted him on assignments to gather vital information, missions of national importance to the war effort. It went exactly as planned. He had two nations, now at war, providing him with the training, development and the intelligence to bring either country to its knees. It was everything he needed to fulfil his ultimate goal. To serve only one nation, one ruler, his true allegiance to a far greater force, and to this his loyalty was beyond reproach. He could feel a rush of adrenalin course through his veins as he looked on at the blizzard hurtling towards them, seeing nothing, yet seeing everything before him. He had a clear route, a target, and he was relishing the challenge. He was part of the development of a new world. Building the foundation for a future that would change mankind forever. Now he was a few hours away. All the planning, all the risks, the deceit, had led him here. It was time.

The trip from London had been simple. As an agent for the Secret Intelligence Service, he had the perfect cover. When he presented the opportunity of contacting an SS defector, they made all preparations for him. They provided easy passage through Europe to his destination, Berlin. The meeting went ahead with an SS Captain, a Captain known to him by the name of Gerd Brandt, a lifelong friend and trusted companion. He, like Ahlers, had been conditioned by the Hitler youth before a greater calling took control of their lives. They had both been summoned to SS headquarters. Their mission is to move the gold reserve from the vaults across the border and into Switzerland. Eight trucks, thirty-two ton of gold, a carefully selected team chosen by Himmler himself.

They had guaranteed safe passage thanks to the political clout of Colonel Brust and his influence within the Swiss parliament. A cash injection into the local economy also helped to oil the wheels. It was too easy. As soon as they reached Zurich, the master plan took form. They ambushed the convoy as planned, disciples of the faith eliminated Himmler's crew, taking their place for the remainder of the journey. It was an easy kill, each disciple to a man, a knife to the throat, clean and simple. Routes and plans changed as they implemented new orders. Gerd Brandt took one truck to deposit the gold at the expected location, four ton of gold, no consignment note, no questions asked. Brandt remained behind with a small team to dispose of Himmler's crew. Ahlers rode with the remaining seven heading east into the mountains.

"We are here." After nine hours perched on the hard sprung bench seat, Eric Ahlers felt a sense of elation as Breidle indicated a small beam of light waving to and fro a few kilometres ahead. A lookout showing the way.

Pulling into a clearing, they parked next to the dark silhouette of a single truck. A silent sentry positioned alongside the entrance to a small cave. Killing the engine, extinguishing the lights, they jumped from the cabin into an ankle deep blanket of snow. As the wind buffeted them, ice cutting into their skin, they faced the lookout as he shouted something inaudible before gesturing for them to follow. Ahlers gripped his MP40 tightly to his body, keeping his overcoat wrapped around him as he pushed himself on. They followed the sentry, moving briskly past the rear of the truck, heading for the ominous dark hole cut into the mountain, offering shelter from the worsening storm. Their escort shone his torch into the rear bed of the silent vehicle as they rushed past, to show it was bereft of cargo. They were ahead of schedule. He was too cold to offer any response, instead, Ahlers zeroed in on the soldier's boots, keeping his head low to minimise his discomfort.

Being the chosen ones, he knew the disciples would carry out their tasks with military precision. With relief they stumbled into the cave entrance, the harsh elements died instantly. Ahlers felt his nose, ears and cheeks burn as his warm, oxygen rich blood raced to the surface of his skin. The sound of boots crunching on loose granite echoed in his head, his eardrums still ringing from the violation of the bitter cold air. He grimaced as the footfalls pounded like sledgehammers smashing against steel.

"You have done well." He shouted as he tried to control his senses. The volume shocked him as it bounced off the walls.

"Thank you, Herr Ahlers. The crew, have worked tirelessly. I think you will be pleased with our work."

"And the other trucks?"

"Gone, your comrades are on their way to Austria."

"Good… Good." The ringing in his ears had subsided, his voice quietened, echoing gently around them.

Following the tiny beam of torchlight, the four men stayed close, being careful not to stumble on the uneven floor.

Minutes later they were in a cavern illuminated by kerosene lamps. A fire burned at its centre offering a welcome warmth and more importantly, a coffee pot steaming on a stand straddling the flames. Lifting the pot, the lookout poured the contents into four tin cups, handing three to the new arrivals before taking a deep swallow from his own. Ahlers took a seat on a rotting beam close to the fire. Propping his rifle alongside him, he held the cup in both hands taking a tentative sip at the dark aromatic liquid. He gasped with relief as genuine coffee filled his mouth, warming his insides as he swallowed. He was grateful for the superior brew they had provided in recognition of his rank. Thankfully, not the grain-based Ersatzkeffee shit the troops and prisoners of war were forced to stomach. As he finished pouring a second cup, he sat watching as the disciples worked around him. They had knocked part of the far wall through, exposing a hidden chamber. Several of the team had formed a line, passing the ingots hand over hand like a human conveyor through the opening, out of sight. A second team worked methodically, transporting the gold from the last truck, piling it with the rest ready to be sealed away. They worked in silence, engrossed, almost mechanical as they tackled the job in hand.

After an hour the hidden chamber was sealed. Hardpan from the clay and soft soil were mixed and spread until the opening was hidden, smoothing crevices to blend in with the original wall. Once dry, it would remain undetected until the day of reckoning. Hans Breidle handed Ahlers a map of the cavern complex, crudely detailed, omitting the location of the hidden chamber. He was no cartographer, but there was enough detail there to find his way when he needed to.

"Well done, every one of you." Ahlers rose from his seat throwing the dregs from his cup onto the fire, it hissed a tiny plume of smoke into the air. He climbed onto the beam to address the troops.

"You have prepared the ground for a new world. You will be remembered throughout history by the names of your birth. Your families and family's family will look back with pride as every one of you will be forever engraved into the heart of the Immaculate Queen of Heaven." Ahlers took a small notebook from his tunic, flicking through to find the marked page. Looking down at the eyes staring back at him he spoke slowly.

"Let us pray as disciples of the faith and let us remember, whatever good things have been shown forth by the pious King, are more the most holy Virgin's honour and glory, who rewards all things."

Hans Breidle smiled as he sank to his knees, pride swelling in his chest. He could sense the others kneel around him as he closed his eyes, awaiting the words. It had been his first real mission, his first kill, he felt exultant. He knew he had proven himself and was sure Herr Ahlers had noticed his single-mindedness and commitment. He was determined to work his way to the top table, become a name amongst greats. He bowed his head settling into a peaceful state as Herr Ahlers began…

"Sweet Mother of Jesus and my Mother, how glorious was the Age of Faith! How strong was Holy Church to wean the hearts of her children from earthly glory to a Heavenly Kingdom!…"

As Ahlers read from his notebook, he crouched down from his vantage point. Grasping the barrel of his MP40 he carefully lifted it into his arms, cradling it as he continued…

"… As alas be how dark, how desolate and hopeless seem our times! When will return the glorious ages of faith, dear Mother?…"

He folded his notebook, pushing it back into his tunic, keeping his voice steady and true as he kept his eyes on the praying disciples. All were bowed, eyes closed, deep in prayer.

"… When shall the church once more crown her Emperors and Kings?…"

Being careful to retract the bolt in a smooth motion, he felt it lock into place with the tiniest of clicks. It could have been mistaken for a crackle of embers from the fire.

"… When shall Jesus and his truth reign supreme in the hearts of all mankind?"

Raising the submachine gun towards the throng he noticed one staring back at him, Hans Breidle. His face serene, innocent, at peace with the world. For what seemed like an age the young disciple looked from Ahlers' eyes to the muzzle and back again, he showed no fear, instead he smiled. Opening his mouth, he uttered a single word.

"... Amen."

The MP40 exploded into life, strafing through the young bodies before any had time to react. The explosion of rapid fire drowned their screams as it pumped thirty-two rounds into flesh and bone. Within five-seconds the last empty shell hit the stone floor, rattling to a stop by the ruined face of Breidle. For several minutes Eric Ahlers stared at the eleven fallen bodies of his comrades, watching as two struggled to breathe through shredded lungs. He waited for the desperate gasps and gurgles from blood filled mouths to cease, welcoming the silence as all life save his own left the cavern.

Further along the tunnel was a deep excavation of perhaps thirty feet, or so it seemed to Eric Ahlers as he listened to the final body hit the ground below. It had taken close to an hour to drag each corpse to its final resting place, a further thirty minutes to extinguish the flames and collect all the kerosene lamps.

Taking the last illuminated lamp to assist his exit, he caught sight of a glimmer amongst the blood-soaked floor. Stooping, he picked up a hinged brooch, an oval attached to a gold stickpin. It was open revealing a smooth gold pearlescent bowl. It was empty. Closing the clasp, he ran his fingers over the intricate design of a two-headed eagle. He guessed it had been a souvenir taken by a disciple as they transferred the gold. No matter, he had been judge, jury and executioner. Whoever had stolen it had paid the ultimate price.

Hiding it away in his tunic he took a final look around before making his way to the exit. She would love his gift, and with any luck, if he could wrap up quickly, he would be home in three days to pin it on her.

Light flecks spread across the Zurich sky as Ahlers walked along the Munsterbrücke. The smooth cobbles of the bridge shone damply through the early morning mist. They gleamed a dull orange from the low light of spherical lamps spaced at regular intervals.

All was quiet save for the ripples from the River Limmat as it brushed through the arches below. He welcomed the bracing air, cleansing him from the rigours of the past few days. Briskly walking the two miles after hiding the truck in the designated lockup, he was eager to complete his task as he wanted to get home.

It gave him time to run over the mission, checking in his own mind that he had been thorough. There was no room for error, no place for complacency; it had to be clean, precise and deadly. Dominating the skyline ahead was the impressive twin towers of the Grossmünster. The 12th century Romanesque cathedral was a fitting spot for the final leg of his journey. He felt as if it was watching his approach, studying him, testing him. Looking up at the twin-domed steeples he followed the smooth contours to the golden crown sitting on top of the spire. A rush of exhilaration coursed through his body, humbling him as its resonant power tugged at his very soul. His eyes remained fixed on the magnificent structure as he moved towards it seeking approval, imploring it to give him a sign. To reassure him after everything he had done for the Order, that he had fulfilled his destiny.

An explosion of light burst in front of him taking him by surprise. He covered his face waiting for the pops and sparks dancing across his closed eyelids to subside. A sharp pain coursed through his head momentarily. He took a deep breath. It had been an arduous journey, he could feel all the muscles in his body urging him to rest. Lowering his hands as the light dimmed he faced the flickering twin beams of headlights. Parked below the white equestrian statue of Burgomeister Waldmann was a Volkswagon Beetle. Its engine ticked gently as it waited for its passenger, a lone dark shadow sat motionless behind the wheel. The Furher's "people's car" had been provided for their safe passage across the Swiss border. It was an ideal cover for the clandestine operation, a car reserved for high-ranking officers and dignitaries.

Not long now and it would be over. He would disappear for a while, lie low, take a long needed rest, waiting for the end of the war. A war his homeland was sure to lose. The end of an era but the beginning of a new age.

"You have done well my friend." Gerd Brandt greeted his comrade as he slid into the passenger seat beside him.

Brandt could see the weariness in Eric as he slumped into the seat alongside him, the task had been punishing. In comparison, his had been simple. Once he had provided Himmler's crew with a watery grave within the meandering waters of the Limmat, he dismissed the two disciples who had assisted him. They had assigned them to other tasks for the cause.

He then only had to deliver the gold, switch vehicles and wait patiently for his friend. Having time on his hands, he had used it well, spending it on the riverbank. It had been a clear day and although chilly; the sun had provided a pleasing warmth. The pleasant ambience along with the wine had offered some much needed relaxation. The interlude also allowed him to think of Clarissa and his beautiful, beautiful son Fabian. His newborn whom he had seen for only three weeks in the four months since his birth. Those striking blue eyes, full of love and hope. His family were his life and shortly they would be together, safe and hidden from the world as the war ran its course. Until the calling, they would move them to a safe house, a new identity, a new life with protection and immunity to permit him to see his son grow. By the time he was fully grown, they could walk arm in arm together, comrades in the development of a perfectly ordered new world.

"It went well, my brother." Eric Ahlers settled himself into the passenger seat. He took a moment to sink into the foam filled padding, letting it ease his muscles from the brisk walk.

"Shall we go?" Gerd Brandt selected first gear, reaching for the brake.

Eric Ahlers placed his hand on Brandt's arm, pulling the gear lever back into neutral, stopping him from disengaging the brake.

"One moment Gerd…" Ahler's voice was monotone, devoid of emotion. Brandt looked at the hand on his arm, moving up until he was staring into the face of his comrade. He was greeted with a blank expression, eyes glazed, looking straight at him and yet straight through him.

"May God be with you." Ahlers spoke barely at a whisper. So quiet, Brandt took a while to register the words. The gunshot made him jump before it tore through his spleen, ripping through his lung and shattering the driver's window on exit. He had been betrayed. Pain racked his body as the trauma to his organs registered in his brain. He found it difficult to gulp in air, his senses became numb. He tried to fight for control, to clear his head and make sense of what was happening. But the pain… Oh God…the pain. He opened his mouth to scream, nothing came. He felt himself falling… falling… moving through the air, feeling his body lift away from the car, drifting. Suddenly his head crashed into something hard… then he was still.

Ahlers pushed Brandt from the driver's seat, out of the car. He felt nothing as the head of his childhood friend smashed onto the cobbled stones of the bridge. The crack sounding even more sickening in the still morning air. Facing straight ahead, eyes fixed on nothing in particular, Eric Ahlers pulled the door closed, placed the stick into first and drove away.

Birds called their first morning song as the Volkswagon ticked across the Munsterbrücke, through the winding city streets of Zurich.

CHAPTER ONE
Friday

Colin poured hot water onto his blend of instant coffee, sugar and milk and nonchalantly stirred the mixture. He stared at the swirl of white froth as it steamed to the rim of his mug, the rhythmic tinkling of the spoon soothing his nerves.

It was Friday 13th, the second one this year and it irked him as he would have to leave Derek in charge of business yet again. On the last occasion, it had taken over a week to put the books straight. He had to match cheques to accounts, clients to cases. Spending hours poring over expenses trying to hunt down and justify the expense receipts which would have taken him over a month or more to spend himself. To top the lot, clients would call for him, instead of taking a message, they would be 'helpfully' inconvenienced by his partner. That alone would take nearly a month to straighten out whenever he took time off.

It was 9.30, the office opened only an hour ago, and he was already staring at the phone, desperate to call in to check if everything was running smoothly.

Superstition, the bane of his life, had dogged him from childhood, building until it grew into what was now, acute paranoia. Black cats, magpies, ladders, broken mirrors, but the number 13 was the worst by far, good luck or bad it ruled his life. Today being the 13th meant he would spend the whole day as a recluse. The outside world did not exist and would remain so until after midnight. He was well stocked; he wouldn't starve. He had the TV to keep him company, books to keep him stimulated, food to keep him fed. Not that any of that mattered on a day like today. The TV reminds him at every news bulletin or daytime chat show of the dreaded Friday 13th. He can't concentrate on a book, and as far as the food, forget it, no appetite. Sipping his coffee, he stared through the window at his glorious garden.

Just short of a third of an acre of sumptuous well-kept lawns complimented by a beautiful rose garden to the east with a palatial gazebo at its centre. A beautiful Greek temple styled building complete with decorative Doric columns housed the heated pool to the west. The crafted meandering pathway led through the grounds connecting all the elements. It ended at a set of ornate gates cut neatly into the conifer hedgerow. He could see the red-tiled roofs of the stables beyond, where his wife spent most of her days with her horses. He should enjoy life, it had treated him rather well.

Thorn Paxton and Gant were flourishing, the client base increasing month on month. Marital and Corporate suits were growing, while Death and Probate always provided a regular income. The business had been thriving for eleven years, assuring their financial future.

The house, a sprawling ten bedroom mansion, was purchased shortly before they married. They paid for it outright from the proceeds of the practice and a sizeable cash injection from his father-in-law, Major Paxton. Part wedding present, part an inheritance from the death of his wife's grandmother, the Dowager. The running costs were easily managed. Colin had been able to increase his impressive portfolio. He snapped up eight reasonable properties in the village and several overseas dwellings in the Med. The income from the village investments alone created enough revenue to run the household as well as provide a salary for them both. Together with the stocks and shares in shrewdly managed funds, they were millionaires in their own right. Life should be good. But his superstitious paranoia was reaching OCD proportions. It began to prevent him from leading a normal life.

Moving the mug away from his lips he placed it onto the breakfast bar, his eyes fixed on a specific part of the garden. A chill coursed through his body, rippling through his spine. His cheeks grew warm, and he could hear his heartbeat in his ears as it pulsed rapidly in his chest. Taking a deep breath to slow it down only made it pick up speed. Beads of sweat poked through his hair follicles ready to run down his forehead. He swept his hand through his naturally fine blonde hair feeling the wetness between his fingers. The 'kakaka' call came well before he saw it… but he knew what to expect. At the highest point of one elm in front of the pool house, was the sharp features and rich black and white of a magpie. Its long rigid tail flicked as it called out a mocking jittery laugh. Placing his hand to his head, he pretended to doff his hat.

"Good morning Mr Magpie, and how is your lady wife and family." He whispered, an old traditional riposte to dispel bad luck.

Studying the garden for the second one, he whispered to himself 'where are you?'. One more and he could relax. One for sorrow, two for joy, three for a girl, four for a boy… It haunted him constantly. One magpie, it meant bad luck. Was it the firm? His portfolio? He paced the kitchen, crossing his fingers, reciting a mantra which sounded more like a moan as he tried to wish away bad karma.

'Please let it be ok… please let it be ok.'

After ten minutes passed, he had calmed down enough to think of a way of making the most of his day. He made himself another coffee before heading to his games room. Perhaps the TV would provide a welcome distraction. He settled into his Lazy-boy, switched on the fifty inch screen, and channel hopped, feeling soothed as the footrest rose and he reclined.

But, today Colin will die.

Annabel Paxton-Thorn rode Freddy through the High Street. He'd performed well this morning, a lot perkier today. He swayed his head as he strolled along the kerb; a sign of contentment. Being the first real excursion for him in the four months since the liver scare, she couldn't believe how well he had done. He'd endured several examinations recently, the biopsy in particular, really distressed him. But after plenty of rest, regular doses of antibiotics and polyionic fluids, he seemed back to his old self. She knew he would need to slow down, but with careful monitoring and the right care, he would live out a full and contented life. Freddy being the favourite of her four horses would always get her special attention.

As the sun broke through the clouds, birdsong filled the air as the steady clack of his hooves echoed through the street. It was going to be a beautiful day. She leaned forward smoothing the mane along his powerful neck.

"Good boy, that was better wasn't it." She cooed into his ear.

"Morning, Mrs Paxton-Thorn." She sat up in her saddle scanning the street.

It was Brian Bellham, closing the gate of a cottage garden after delivering the post.

"Nice morning." He smiled.

"Good to see Freddy out and about again. He looks great."

"Thanks, Brian. Yes, he's recovering well. He enjoyed the exercise this morning; it's his best day so far."

"Well, it seems to have done you both some good. You look great too." He winked at her before delving into his bag, fishing out a bundle of letters for his next delivery. Brian was in his mid-thirties, a member of the local football team. In all weathers, he wore his fluorescent jacket, baseball cap, combat shorts and hiking boots. He tanned all year round, his athletic body evident in the definition of his bare arms and legs. She flushed as she watched him walk away.

There were some good looking males in the village and being attractive for her age, she drew a lot of admiring glances from many of them. She even had a few flings, nothing serious, a few rolls in the hay, the occasional overnight stay. But none of her conquests lived in Mittand Burrow. Never one to shit in her own backyard. Well, except for one time. A total disaster she now has to live with every day. Never again!

She deserved the attention. She looked after herself and was proud of her body. Why should she not have a healthy sex life at forty-four? Just because her marriage to Colin had become a sham, with her husband more interested in the bottom line figure than her own. She was not ready to be the dutiful wife reserving sex for birthdays and Christmas. She had needs which if weren't met at home, she would seek elsewhere.

She should have left him years ago because the obsession with the practice had taken over their lives. She became a fixture of the house, an ornament called upon when required. But she could not risk losing everything, in particular, her self esteem and standing within the village. She also needed to maintain her relationship with her father. He loved Colin like a son, a love which brought with it an inheritance over and above her spinster sister and wayward brother. She would not jeopardise it.

Watching Brian walk along the path, she could feel herself grow warm in the saddle. She could see those powerful arms wrapped around her in a passionate embrace. It had been a few weeks since the body of a man had laid next to her naked skin; she was at the stage where she needed a top up. Sighing wistfully she pulled her eyes away from the postman, returning her attention to Freddie. The only ride she would get today.

She passed the newsagents as Linda Norwood appeared in the doorway.

"Morning Linda" Annabel greeted her with a smile, pushing any thoughts of pleasure back into the recesses of her mind. Linda looked up at the woman on horseback.

"Oh! Good morning Annabel." She looked over her glasses, trying to smile as best she could, but her sharp features and haughty expression only produced a grimace full of teeth.

"Will you be at the meeting tonight? There's a lot to get through."

She turned her back on Annabel as she put a notice in the shop window. It was to promote the fete next month. It was one of her many duties as chairperson for the Women's Guild, the reading group and Neighbourhood Watch. She was the matriarch, a fearsome woman with her own ideas of how the village should be run — her way.

"Yes, Linda. See you at eight." Linda was already on her way to her next stop, striding purposely along the High Street managing just a cursory wave as she dwelt on her next task.

"Cow" Annabel whispered as she kicked Freddy on towards the stables.

They had not seen eye to eye from the time she first took residence in the Manor House. Something to do with her father and Linda's late husband.

But she had never understood it. Her father dismissed it as folly from years ago and all Linda would offer was 'ask your father'. Whatever it was, Linda was unwilling to forgive, making it clear she would never be a friend of a Paxton.

They clashed on so many occasions at local meetings, whether at a reading group, Entertainment committee or Parish Council meetings, it was incessant. The organisers wondered if it was wise putting them in the same room together. But both women would not budge, vowing to be there again the next time. There were benefits, however. Most events oversubscribed as their appearance was a huge draw. The majority attended just for the entertainment value.

Allowing Freddy to trot on towards the Manor House she planned her day. She would muck out the stables, groom the horses and probably take Signet out this afternoon, leaving Moorland and Fin to graze. She would tend to them tomorrow.

Her stable hands were the best in the area, and they cared for the horses as if they were their own. As the relationship with her husband became increasingly mundane, the loneliness became more oppressive, they had got used to seeing her roll up her sleeves. She involved herself daily with so much gusto and enthusiasm even for the most menial of tasks. They now saw her as a part of their team rather than the Lady of the Manor.

Today she wasn't planning to enter the house until the evening. She had to stay away. Colin was having one of his Friday 13th days, and it drove her mad. She had loved Colin so much at the beginning even though he was one of her father's carefully vetted introductions. Something she constantly resented.

Once she had come of age, most of her dates had originated from Major Paxton's military connections. Good stock, excellent breeding and prospects was his description of her prospective dates. The same profile she looked for herself when selecting her horses.

When they inevitably failed, she was the one at fault. She hadn't given them enough time, didn't present herself well enough or had discredited the family name with her attitude. She didn't let it concern her as she had her father's steely reserve and felt total indifference until they introduced her to Colin. He was the Brigadier's son from the old regiment, and Major Paxton made sure she knew the importance of this.

She resented his attitude and set out to disappoint, but Colin turned out to be far from what she expected. He was not a military man, favouring law instead, and he had a determination to do what he wanted to do rather than be groomed. He wasn't sex on legs, but he was a good looking man, and kind. She spent most of her time in his company feeling like a princess, something very important to her.

What brought them together was the non-conformist way they both dealt with their parents' rules and regulations. They knew as a couple that they disappointed in so many ways and it became their mission to take control of their own lives, to fight against the regime. The collaboration turned into a love so strong that before they knew it, they were making plans for a life together. It delighted both parents when they announced their engagement. The Major and Brigadier even congratulated each other on the forthcoming union.

The wedding had been a lavish affair with more military personnel present than housed at the local garrison. They took over the village, holding the reception in the grounds of the Manor House in a marquee large enough to contain a football pitch.

Unfortunately, the pomp and ceremony caused them problems right at the beginning of their married life together. The local villagers resented the pretentious invasion. They made life difficult for them for several months. The whispers as they walked through the streets, the stares and the silence when they entered The Fleece for a quiet drink. They even had eyes boring into them as they shopped in the local stores. Some retailers would serve others before the newlyweds as if they weren't there. It wasn't easy, they began to see the Manor House as more of a prison at first.

They had the horses who Annabel spent most of her time with. Riding the fields and tending to them took up most of her day, returning through the rear of the house just as Colin arrived home from work.

She still had her friends in Oxford and once a month they would meet for shopping, lunch and a good gossip, but it became her only outlet which she resented. She missed the daily contact with like-minded people, making her feeling increasingly isolated.

The situation changed for the better once the practice moved from Oxford and opened in nearby Lysbie. It looked like they had turned a corner. The villagers noticed Colin's growing reputation, and he gradually took local work. Only small enquiries at first, but as news spread he gained their trust and represented some of them in probate and criminal cases.

Soon he became their local solicitor, becoming an integral part of the village within a short space of time. There were a few however who wouldn't accept them, mainly Linda Norwood. The rest were content to keep their feelings to themselves or at least keep away from them. It was mainly for fear of being ousted as part of the minority.

They began to receive invites to most functions, Annabel even joined local group meetings. She preferred the reading forums or the Women's Institute. It enabled her to meet with like-minded people. Before long they joined her for her lunch and 'girly' days, sometimes holding afternoon events at the house. Life became almost normal again, nearly idyllic.

Unfortunately, it was this acceptance that affected their marriage. Within two years Colin had changed. As the business flourished, he spent more hours at work. He sometimes arrived home just before midnight, then out the door again at 7 am leaving Annabel feeling neglected. His need for acceptance from the locals became an obsession.

They hardly saw each other during the week. At weekends Colin would pore over the accounts, snooze in the armchair or stare at the TV.

Sport was his thing, which she detested, not once would he suggest a film that they could watch together. Then there was the pub, playing poker with the Wilkies, two rugby playing old Etonians determined to rewrite the rules on bachelorhood. They swept Colin up in their festivities, trying desperately to relive their university days. The thought of spending the rest of her life with this man depressed her. Things would have to change, or she would go mad.

It was around the time his superstitions got out of hand, like avoiding ladders or breaking mirrors. Starting as a stupid quirk, it got so bad he even studied the whole ethos of superstition; its roots, its consequences, which in the end made him neurotic. It got even more out of hand — Friday 13th, lucky seven, black cats, magpies, mirrors, ladders, full moons. The list was endless as Colin lived his life through the influence of good and bad karma. His horoscope, the stargazers governed his rules for the day.

They became his heart and mind. Money and success were the catalysts. He had spent so long building the business, amassing a fortune and gaining acceptance, he became worried that he could lose it at any minute. She resented him, refusing to humour him as she had at the start until his paranoia became overbearing and the rows started. Being of strong character, far stronger than Colin, it would always end with her either throwing something at him or catching him with a right hook. Twice he had ended up with a black eye which distanced them even more until they eventually lived separate lives.

She now regretted the marriage, sometimes wishing they'd never met. But she could not lose her lifestyle, which she would if she called it a day. Her father would make sure of that as he had as much to lose as she did.

The aristocracy had ensconced the Major into the country set and the Rotary club. This acceptance was, in part, due to the Brigadiers influence. Father would let nothing get in his way as he elevated his standing within the echelons of the local gentry. A divorce would see an end to all he had worked for, the status, the kudos, the acceptance into the rich set.

The Major already had status in a small village where half the community either worked for or were reliant on the Paxton wealth. But it was a big world out there, and he was making inroads amongst the surrounding elite. She also had dreams of her own. Visions of grandeur and the high life far away from Mittand Burrow. One of the well to do, a name around the world. A place she belonged.

The only way she could be free and keep her wealth and position would be if Colin were dead. These thoughts appalled her to begin with. As bad as it was she still loved him or rather, loved the man she married.

But as time passed, she imagined car crashes or heart attacks, dreaming of the day when police arrived at her door to give her the bad news. She thought about her reaction. It would be a shock obviously, but would it devastate her? Could she cope without Colin in her life? After all, she would inherit the house, the business, the property portfolio; she could live her life again. She took the trail surrounding the Manor House and headed towards the stables.

CHAPTER TWO
History

Linda Norwood watched the horse disappear from view. A look of disdain etched on her face as she stared at the corner of Fallows Grove.

"You realise it's not her fault Linda, don't you? You should give her a break." George Caine had come to the doorway of his bookstore, The Good Read, after seeing Linda attach her poster to his window. He looked at her as she watched Annabel leave and by the look on her face she was still having issues.

"She's a Paxton, George." She continued to stare down the street preferring not to make eye contact.

"Yes, but she is also a Thorn, and you know Colin is a good man. He has helped a lot of residents out of all sorts." It ruined the poster in Linda's hands as she prepared to fix it to the bakery door, the last comment hit a nerve causing her to crush the top half.

"The man preys on the misfortunes of others, Death, Divorce, Bankruptcy; he's a vulture. Just like the rest of their kind." Her swipe at the gentry was a regular gripe. She hated the 'them' and 'us' categorisation. It fractured the community, particularly now the divide seemed to be edging in favour of the wealthy. George knew her real gripe was that she didn't have a foot in either camp, but if she had to choose, she was better suited to the group she disliked the most, 'them'.

She was a larger than life character, some would say matronly. Her austere clothing, haughty nature and lacquered silver blue hair made her look the part. But it was her eyes, the shimmering grey globes, peering through angular bifocals. They exuded malevolence. Her stare was more an interrogation of the soul once she locked on. She was normally intimidating, sinister at her worst. She was as hard as she looked, thriving on the fear, using it to good effect to create her self-appointed position of power.

Some, like George, saw her more as a novelty. Someone who was a part of village folklore, who would always be the queen bee. She was the organiser, someone who they could wheel in to represent the residents at a higher level. They feared her at regional council as she usually got her way. She, and she alone saved the Post Office, Library and Primary school from closure. She continued to work tirelessly to raise funds to ensure it would stay that way. Not through any charitable nature, not because deep down she had a kind heart. It was because she enjoyed fighting the establishment, a personal battle to get her own way.

George tried different reasoning.

"They've had a tough time Linda. Taking the Manor House had its own problems, you know what this village is like. Things seem to have settled down now, perhaps the time is right to move on and forget this silly squabble."

Screwing the ruined poster into a tight ball, Linda thrust it into George's hand. She met his eyes, staring over her bifocals, holding them steady for several seconds trying to unsettle him before she spoke.

"They killed my husband George, and there is nothing... NOTHING... that will allow me to do anything for any of them unless it is to attend their funerals. There!... Have I made myself clear? Good!" Turning tail she stormed off giving George no time to counter her argument. He called after her.

"Linda! Come on, you can't keep being like this. You know Annabel and Colin had nothing to do with it. Major Paxton could hardly be to blame for Roland's state of mind at the time either."

He regretted saying it as soon as it left his lips. She came to a halt with her back to him, his words bouncing around in her head. George tried to soften the blow, retract a little, add a little reasoning.

"Come on, old girl. It's been four years. Life goes on and as I have heard you say many times to others, time is a great healer." Linda turned to face him.

Even from twelve yards away he could see she wasn't happy. She walked towards him, slowly at first, but by the time she had reached halfway she was in full stride. George's smile faded as she picked up speed and by the time she reached him it had fallen away completely. Standing a yard away from him, she leant towards the shop window, ripping the poster away. She tore it to shreds, throwing the pieces at his feet. Moving closer she looked up at him, her eyes red with rage.

"Forty years of marriage takes a lot longer than four years to forgive and forget." The anger in her voice was evident as she spoke through gritted teeth.

"And murder stays with you for life." They said no more as she turned her back and strode away leaving George stunned by her verbal assault. He knelt, scooping up the scraps of paper as the morning breeze shuffled them along the pavement.

Linda could feel the blood pounding in her head, heating her cheeks and forehead, she knew she had flushed red. She was so angry right now and needed to get home before bumping into anyone else, In her current mood, she would rip a hole in them. Leaving the High Street she passed by the village green, taking a fleeting glance at the old rectory. All the memories came flooding back. She pulled her coat tighter, averting her gaze as she strode on. It was the route she took regularly, it brought back the memories of Roland and the wonderful life they shared in their once marital home. It was when reminded of the tragic circumstances of his death, she suffered the flashbacks. They had haunted her for four years.

On leaving the army, Roland had enrolled as a constable with the County police force. After many years of pounding the beat from regional HQ, they assigned him to Mittand Burrow as the resident bobby. His transfer home was a reward for his dedication to duty, with only six years to serve before his retirement.

The old rectory, in disrepair since the war, was purchased by the constabulary and renovated, utilising a quarter as a sub-police station complete with office, interview room and two holding cells. The rest belonged to the Norwoods. It was their dream home. The house overlooked the green, along with the church, Post Office and two pubs, a real focal point.

For Linda, it provided the status she craved, a window to the world. Positioned centrally, she had an unobstructed view of the main thoroughfares. With the help of her binoculars, she could see the full length of the High Street. Whether or not Roland wanted it, he received a full activity report on the comings and goings daily over dinner.

The villagers loved and hated her because, although she was ideal for the position as head of the neighbourhood watch, she didn't care who she shopped. If they broke the law, the police would hear of it. Linda just thrived on the power. Roland, in contrast, was a quiet man who took his job seriously, taking pride in everything he did, always sympathetic, always there to help. He wasn't just the law; he was a counsellor, arbiter and sometimes just a shoulder to cry on. He loved every part of his role and most locals took to him immediately. There were some however who didn't give him a chance.

He had been in the Fifth Battalion of the Royal Engineers stationed near Oxford under the command of Major Reginald Paxton. The Major, being the son of Lord and Lady Paxton, had a smooth passage through the ranks. He was protected from the gruelling route the rest of them had to take to achieve even the smallest promotion. Roland progressed through the ranks to Warrant Officer and recommended for officer training.

But they knocked him back on every occasion for no apparent reason. Many years later it transpired that Major Paxton had blocked the application every time. There was no way he would allow a commoner from the village in the officers' mess. Once Roland took up his new post in the village, Major Paxton complained bitterly. But, as he was now just seen as a pompous assed civilian, his protests fell on deaf ears.

It was the day Roland issued a parking ticket that proved the catalyst for his death.

He ticketed a Bentley illegally parked on the main street. Some idiot had parked the car directly in front of the entrance to The Golden Fleece car park.

He faced angry punters unable to leave or enter the car park, and it took all of his resolve and personable skills to calm them down.

He set about issuing a ticket, calling a tow truck to remove the Bentley. He waited by the vehicle, in the hope the driver would return before he had to resort to such drastic action. The registration was PAX TON1. He knew who the car belonged to, and he knew his patience was being tested. But he had a job to do and he would ensure he followed procedures to the letter. With several witnesses present, some directly affected by the blatant flouting of the law, he felt comfortable they would see his actions as the only course available to him.

As the truck pulled up to tow away the vehicle, Major Paxton left the Fleece and immediately activated the remote to open the doors to the Bentley.

"I wouldn't do that if I were you, Major." Roland walked around to the driver's door, pulling out his breathalyser. The Major approached until he was nose to nose with the constable.

"I'd like to see you try to stop me Warrant Officer Norwood." He spat the words into Roland's face. The Army reference, a blatant dig at his failure to progress. Roland ignored it, remaining in control.

"I can smell alcohol on your breath Major, and I must prevent you from entering the vehicle. Once I am satisfied you can legally drive, you can be on your way." The Major's temper rose. He looked at Roland and then down at his keys. Without notice, Paxton threw the keys at the officer, storming back into the pub.

"You are finished in this village Norwood." He slammed the bar door as he disappeared inside. Roland wiped the blood from a small cut just below the eye. He collected the keys from the pavement and after handing them to the transporter driver, finished writing up the ticket.

It was apparent the Major had a problem with Roland's position within Mittand Burrow and the constable was careful to avoid conflict as much as he could. He turned a blind eye to the lock in's at the Fleece as he knew it was a card school arranged by Paxton. It was still a total disregard of the law, yet another way of making life difficult for Roland. But it was no big deal, he'd let it go.

On occasions when cycling along the lanes, the Bentley would overtake him at speeds well over the limit, again he would let it go. He should report it but it was traffic's problem, and it seemed the Major picked up speed when he was the only witness to it. All the misdemeanours were minor issues meant *to wind him up, but it would not bait him. He loved his job and had no intention of rocking the boat. He was confident they would soon forget the parking incident. He had even persuaded the transporter driver to deliver the car back to Paxton Hall, saving the Major the indignation of a visit to the pound. It only left the parking ticket as a reminder of his indiscretion.*

Within a month the constabulary hauled Roland in front of his superiors. He was made to answer a charge of victimisation towards the Major, presenting him with several incidents where it was claimed, Roland had singled the Major out for misdemeanours. He was alleging harassment and a vendetta against him and his family, all untrue. It had come down from the Commissioner, a fellow Rotary club member along with Major Paxton and Brigadier Thorn, he didn't stand a chance. They suspended him for thirty days pending a full investigation. Roland was distraught.

Linda walked past the pavilion keeping her emotions in check. She started to recall the aftermath of Roland's suspension and the struggle they had to gain support.

The villagers, who had all been very much on Roland's side, offered nothing at all. The Major was using his influence to get at them. Many employees at Paxton Hall were residents and fearing for their jobs remained tight lipped. The rest relied on revenue generated by the Paxton's and with the daughter taking up residence in the Manor House, the balance had shifted.

The Norwoods no longer provided the security and order for the close knit community; the Paxtons had taken control. A military style manoeuvre typical of the Major. A week after the suspension the Norwoods were treated as outcasts. The villagers didn't ignore them, they just avoided them wherever possible. Linda recalled how she would often have a shop to herself as fellow customers would quietly leave within minutes of her entering.

The force sent a stand in, an old timer called Bert Halford. He tried his best to reassure them that everything would pass and things would soon be back to normal. He had seen this many times before and in his experience, by letting it run its course, the suspension would be enough to satisfy the Major. However, the more she tried to reassure her husband, the more Roland sank into depression. He would position himself by the window staring out at the village, never speaking, hardly eating and on some occasions, not sleeping.

Then one evening it all changed. Linda returned from a neighbourhood watch meeting to be greeted by an over enthusiastic husband. He had prepared dinner, and as they ate, he talked through his day patrolling the village. His highlight was the rescue of Jane Horwicks' cat from the oak near the cricket pavilion. She listened intently, laughing along with him as he explained how, as soon as he reached the cat, it casually walked down through the branches, trotting away without a care in the world. She was still chuckling along with him as she collected the dishes and took them to the kitchen.

Once alone the tears came, and they wouldn't stop. Roland was wearing the same clothes he had been wearing all day. He had been in his armchair, people watching for at least 6 hours and he was still there when she returned. Her husband was losing his mind.

The following week Roland was dead.

That morning, he was fully dressed and preparing to leave the house for the first time in weeks. He told her of some chores he needed to catch up on and would see her soon. Before leaving, he hugged her and kissed her goodbye. She should have suspected something then. They had been married for over forty years and although there was the odd peck on the cheek, they reserved hugs and kisses for Birthdays, Christmas and New Year. He seemed like his old self, and she thought fresh air would do him good. She should have gone with him, but she just watched him leave with a skip in his step and a smile on his face. It was a smile she would never forget, a smile she would never see again.

Bert Halford was the one to break the news. They found Roland hanged in the barn at Croft End Farm. No note and no explanation. The verdict was suicide, but she knew it was down to the stress, the humiliation and the Paxtons.

The whole of Mittand Burrow observed the funeral, all turned out to show their respects, many gave their condolences in such a way that she knew they carried the guilt of his death on their conscience.

Whether through pity or genuine concern they welcomed her back into the fold. Linda knew the olive branch was an exoneration of any responsibility for Roland's death, but she needed them, so she grasped it and held on tight.

The constabulary sold the rectory, which forced Linda to leave. She bought a small cottage in a mews alongside the village green, directly opposite her old home. She watched with a heavy heart as they redeveloped it into a medical centre. But it was a reminder of her time with her husband, and she wanted to see it every day, and every day she thought of Roland. It took a full three years for her to rebuild her life. She struggled to take her place back in the community. Within the past year, she had regained control as the events organiser and head of the neighbourhood watch. She had just started to bring order to a village which had become fragmented.

But, she would never forget those who had avoided them in their time of need.

She didn't blame them entirely as the situation was forced upon them, but she felt they capitulated far too quickly. She became dismissive of them all and however hard they tried to make amends, the most they got in return if at all, was a monosyllabic grunt of gratitude. She had no friends but wasn't looking for friendship. She had Snowflake and Coal and liked the fact, like all cats, they showed affection when they wanted to and fended for themselves when they didn't. She would have made a good cat. What she craved was order, and she was so close to achieving it again. It was the only solace she needed to make her happy.

She entered the mews, her anger dissipating as the rows of thatched cottages softened her mood. Pushing through the gate of her cottage the fragrance of her blooming garden instantly surrounded her. The wisteria and clematis had come early this year, meandering along the walls, doorways and facias of her home. The pinks, blues and purples brightened the whole plot. It created a multi-coloured backdrop to the carefully manicured lawns and hedgerow. Had she not run into that bitch earlier, the entire sight and smell would have calmed her instantly.

But her thoughts were elsewhere, as they always were when she relived the worst day of her life. She had two wishes. She wished that one day tragedy would strike the Paxtons, a disaster that would rip their lives apart as hers had been. The second wish was to be there to witness it all. She walked the stepped paving and on reaching the front door, heard a rustle from the bushes below the window.

Snowflake leapt from cover and wound around her shins as she rummaged for her keys. The fluffy white Persian had been asleep under the roses waiting for her to return. Tiny specks of earth dropped from her coat as she continued to circle. The door had opened only a crack before the cat bolted inside — time for breakfast.

CHAPTER THREE
Stress

As the Porsche came to a stop at his designated space, Derek Gant checked himself in the mirror.

"You'll do son." He purred as he smoothed his hair back and admired his flawless complexion. He marvelled at his dreamy brown eyes and winked to himself.

Today was a good day. Not only was it Friday, he loved Fridays, but his partner wasn't here. He was having one of his turns. Derek would have his desk cleared in an hour, pick up Becky by three, and they would be off. A whole weekend of good food, fine wine and great sex, he couldn't wait. Becky was new, but he thought he might keep this one for a while. She was filth! Grabbing his briefcase from the front seat, he walked through the glass doors to the ground floor offices. The Porsche bleeped, locking as soon as he disappeared from view.

Eliza Winch watched him arrive, feeling her neck bristle as Derek left the car. It would be one of her bad days. Colin wasn't in today, so she would make it her task to ensure the place was clean and tidy, in perfect order for his return on Monday. But with Gant on the loose, it would be a challenge. He was a moron and disrespectful to most people he ran into. He had lost clients because of his attitude; she was forever getting complaints about his telephone manner. She closed her eyes, wishing he would turn around, get back in his car and drive away.

Having had a lie in this morning, she felt ready for him. She would not take any crap today. She usually rose at six, showered, dressed and carefully administered her makeup to prepare for Colin. Not that he insisted, he didn't even notice. He knew nothing of her feelings for him. But she would never stop trying to get him to notice her.

She had fallen in love with him two years ago, and it was now so bad she fantasised about them being together, a pipe dream as she knew he wouldn't leave Annabel for her, but it was a fantasy she couldn't let go. She was not unattractive, she knew that, and at thirty-six only eleven years his junior, an ideal age to look after him, be the younger woman on his arm and she would make him so proud. She had a body most women would die for, tightened three times a week in the gym. She was not short of admirers, but she only had eyes for one man, and she would save herself for him, just in case. The problem was, she lacked confidence, something she had suffered from all her life. She had always been shy, and as the years passed she developed a reclusive existence. Away from work, she would spend the evening curled up with a book or swept away by the TV, involved with the drama in the soaps. As her feelings for Colin surfaced, she tried to think of ways to boost her self esteem. She wanted him to see her as a strong woman, like his wife, but it would take some doing. She attended a few evening meetings, the reader's circle, the Women's Guild and the church group. It surprised her how easy it was to mingle with the other members. They allowed her to mix quietly amongst them without bringing attention to herself. Mind you, with Linda Norwood and Annabel Paxton-Thorn present, attention on anyone else was at a premium. The limelight was well and truly hogged. Eliza found her confidence flourishing, she could see the change as the weeks passed by, and eventually so would Colin.

The door swung open, bouncing off the doorstop as Gant bounded into the office.

"Morning, Lizzie." He strode past her into his adjoining room without even looking at her.

"Ellie!" She corrected him. She hated the way he made her sound like an old spinster.

"Any calls for me?" He stood at his desk checking the post, his door open to enable him to bark at her from there.

"Not for you, but Mrs Langfield is coming in at three. She wants something from her file and insisted on seeing Colin. She seemed frantic, so rather than tell her he is not here, I thought you could see her. If she only needs someone to open her file you can handle it, can't you?" Her sarcastic tone wasn't lost on him.

"Nope, no can do. Call the old man and get him to get his arse in here. She is his client." He finished ignoring the post and placed the letters unopened into his in-tray. They could wait until Monday, it was too close to the weekend to work.

"NO!" Eliza felt for Colin, and what he was going through today, it must be awful for him, she would not upset him for anything.

"She will only be here for a few minutes, but the information she has to relay is key to winning the case. I'm not interrupting him, particularly today of all days. You can see her."

"Oh, for fuck's sake!" Gant stormed from his office and stood over her. "No way! I'm going in ten minutes, I've got a meeting in Oxford for the Baron Case." Walking over to the coffee pot he poured himself a drink.

"You must postpone her until Monday." He took a sip from his mug, keeping his eyes on her as he swallowed the bitter liquid. He stood with his other hand in his pocket, legs planted in a macho stand of defiance. She hated the man. Why Colin had ever agreed to partner with this neanderthal was anyone's guess.

"No! You can postpone the Barons. You know it's a waste of time anyway, a lot of work for nothing. The Langfield case is a big fee opportunity, and he would expect you to cover for him." She was standing her ground on this one. Her loyalty was never in question. Putting his mug down he walked to his office. He returned in seconds having collected his briefcase and stood by her desk. He leant forward looming over her, causing her to sit back in her seat to look up at him. She could smell his overpowering aftershave as it stuck to the inside of her nostrils. She stifled a cough.

"I suggest if it's so important, why don't you call your boyfriend to deal with it. Because I am outta here love." He left the office leaving Eliza staring at the closing door, mouth open, wondering what to do next.

Colin bloody Thorn was a pain in the arse. This stupid paranoia made him a bigger dick than he was when they first met. His weekend was all planned, no worries, no stress, just a blonde with a penchant for good food, good booze and good head. Now he had to contend with a bollocking on Monday morning after the snitch bitch reported everything back to him. Derek Gant leant back in the driver's seat of his Porsche and pinched the bridge of his nose. He didn't start the engine as he took a few minutes to chill. He was meeting Becky in three hours, so he had plenty of time.

He had a good life and when he could be bothered he was a good solicitor. If he didn't need Thorn to keep him in the luxury to which they accustomed him to, he would have left years ago. But he was having too much of a good time to work for a living. They first met as graduate trainees at Grestons law practice in town. Thorn was the archetypical snotty nerd, taking to all tasks with relish and they soon realised his potential. Before long they made him a junior partner and everyone could see he was going places. They were chalk and cheese, but he could spot an opportunity when it presented itself and so set out to make Colin his best buddy. It worked a treat. They would socialise, hang out together until eventually, he had convinced him they were inseparable. He couldn't stand the weasel but needs must. He did just enough to keep himself employed, and if he needed to cover his tracks, Thorn was pleased to help. Then the day came when Colin broke away to set up his own practice.

He had the backing and the financial support of his father, the Brigadier. He had also built up a nice little property portfolio which would quickly provide the means to invest in a new business. And thanks to Annabel Paxton, Thorn's girlfriend, he got his meal ticket served on a plate. Their fathers, Brigadier Thorn and Major Paxton had introduced the two lovebirds. Gant found it challenging to get between them, they seemed to hit it off in no time, spending every waking minute joined at the hip. But, after putting Thorn through a guilt trip about leaving his best buddy behind, they soon became a threesome. At first, Annabel saw him as an intrusion, a leech who was hanging on to her fiancés coattails. She had seen through him straight away, and it took immense amounts of tact, charm and humility to position himself where he needed to be. Then they partied. Colin being near teetotal would be out for the count after only a few beers or glasses of champagne. It allowed him and Annabel to party on into the small hours. She could keep up with him most of the time, and their relationship grew into a solid friendship. His scheming worked so well he even got Annabel to sponsor him when they set up their practice. So after a substantial investment from the doting fathers, Thorn's investment and a small investment of his own, Thorn Paxton and Gant was born.

Things could not have been better, Thorn ran a tight ship. His dedication stretched to helping him to continue to do just enough to support his existence. It also filled his pockets with more cash than he had ever dreamed he would see in his lifetime. They all became rich, but Thorn strove for more. He was so focused on the business he hardly went home, leaving Annabel feeling neglected after a while. His idea to make amends was to encourage Gant to keep his wife entertained, take her out for the night, keep her happy, be a friend to her.

It was inevitable things would progress, and sure enough, within six months the affair started. It was pure sex to begin with, fuelled by alcohol, frustration and a physical attraction, borne from the need to feel wanted. Annabel was insatiable, calling him at all times of the day to satisfy her appetite. Who was he to neglect the needs of a woman? It was one job he would never shirk from. The problem, however, was he liked to share the love. Many women needed to benefit from the Gant charm and he wasn't ready to limit himself to just one. The one woman in question being the wife of his partner made it even less appealing.

He tried to slow things down a little, but it backfired when Annabel went ballistic. She threatened to expose him as a rapist, blackmailing him into continuing the affair. She promised to leave Colin and in one drunken, deranged rant, even offered to pay someone to bump him off so they could be together. That was the last straw.

He booked a holiday to Spain, flying out with no notice, no mobile, no contact details, he needed to get away. He was in turmoil at first, drinking heavily and partying to get out of his head. But after a couple of evenings with willing bar conquests out for a good time, he thought more clearly. He had a whale of a time, returning two weeks later with a deep tan and a new resolve to conclude his ties with Annabel and get on with his life.

He needn't have worried. Annabel visited him as soon as he returned home and made it very clear she regretted the affair. She wanted nothing more to do with him, and she would recommend they buy his share of the practice, allowing him to live his life elsewhere. She also threatened him, should he ever breathe a word of their affair, she would ruin him in more ways than he could imagine. It got to him. His persona was loud and overbearing, but he was a coward, and it scared him shitless. Her attitude was remarkable and still to this day he did not understand why the change of heart.

The reason he was still there, four years after her ultimatum, was partly through Thorn's guilty conscience. He was deluded enough to think he was to blame for his best friend's neglect. He had also knuckled down for a full year, winning some prestigious cases, which bolstered the coffers immensely. Luckily he hardly saw Annabel because when he did, she was venomous. His only regret about the whole affair was that he lost his only real friend, and he missed her.

Starting the engine, he reversed out of the car park when he suddenly remembered the Baron file on his desk. If he was to use it as a cover for leaving early, he should really have it with him. But he couldn't face another argument with Miss Goody Two Shoes as soon as he walked through the door. He reversed out onto the High Street. He would get a bollocking anyway, so it was pointless worrying.

"Fuck em!" He roared at the top of his voice as he rammed his foot on the accelerator and hurtled down the Copse Road.

The phone rang three times.

"Hello?"

"Hi, Colin? It's Ellie." The tiny voice echoed through the earpiece.

"Oh, hi Ellie, is anything wrong?" Nobody ever phoned him with good news on a day like this. He was already thinking the worst.

"No, not really Colin."

He flushed as he anticipated what was coming. What did she mean? Yes, there is something wrong, but it's not too bad or no, not as bad as you think, but bad anyway.

"Mrs Langfield called. She needs something from her file and is arriving here at 3 PM."

"Mrs Langfield. Are you sure?" This call was worse than he thought.

"Yes, Mrs Langfield and she sounded quite agitated. I didn't want to tell her you weren't here, so I asked Derek to see her…"

"NO!" He didn't mean to shout and tried to recover himself.

"No Ellie, Derek can't see her; it has to be me." He could feel the panic rising inside him, fluttering inside his stomach, rippling through his chest.

"Don't worry Colin…" The panic in his voice startled her.

She softened her voice in sympathy as she could tell he was struggling with the decision he had to make.

"Derek has left already. He said he had a meeting in Oxford, the Baron case, although the file is still on his desk so I'm not sure where he has gone." She would not leave that bit out. Gant deserved what he got. There was an eerie silence for a few minutes as Eliza waited for a response. She could sense Colin weighing up the options.

She was happy to turn Mrs Langfield away and rearrange for Monday as she knew he would be reluctant to leave the house today. She prepared to suggest this as a solution when Colin's voice came through the receiver.

"Ellie, please get the file ready and refreshments in my office. I will be there in an hour." The phone went dead.

Eliza stared at her handset. She could not see how this was so important to make him come in today of all days. Feeling a rush of excitement tempered with concern for her boss, she would make sure he had everything in place for his meeting, and once Mrs Langfield had gone, she might be alone with him. Perhaps she could persuade him to join her at The Badger across the road. Knowing he wasn't a big drinker, perhaps just a small one would help to calm his nerves. If she needed to, she would stay with him until midnight, until the 14th arrived. Now that would be nice, she couldn't help smiling. Then the realisation hit her, goose bumps appeared on her skin, and her cheeks grew hot. She looked awful!

She had dressed down, using minimal makeup just to feel human. She couldn't let him see her like this. She only lived ten minutes away so she had time to get back to freshen up and change, finish her makeup back at her desk before he arrived; she couldn't face him like this.

Hurrying over to the filing cabinet, Eliza withdrew the Langfield file and placed it in his office. Opening the credenza and removing the cafetiere and teapot, she put them on the tray and ran them to the kitchen for when she returned. She would do her best to impress him, hopefully he would finally notice her. It was a hope that surfaced every time she was alone with him, but he never did. This would be different she tried to convince herself. Although deep down, she knew it wouldn't.

Being irrational, which she always was where Colin was concerned, put her through the whole gamut of human emotions. The exhilaration of the chase which transferred into the fear of not being presentable enough. Then anger replaced the excitement at the thought of him coming in. It didn't matter a jot what she did, it would make no difference. She was just the receptionist who he knew by name, that's all. She had now reached the emotional stage, wiping away tears as she switched on the answerphone and grabbed her bag. Realistically, there wasn't a damn thing she could do to make him notice her; she might as well be dead. She wished she had never met him, let alone fall in love with him. He was ruining her life, it had to stop, she couldn't stand it. She was irrational and falling apart, never believing she would let a man make her feel this way. She loved him so much, but she hated him too, hated him with a passion.

Setting the alarm she pulled the door shut, locking the three point mortice. She rushed to her car and drove away.

Once Colin had replaced the receiver he leant against the table, closing his eyes.

Why was she here? There was a problem obviously, but how

serious wouldn't become apparent until they met. But first, he had something to do, part of his instructions for times like these. Walking into his study, he pulled the laptop from the bureau drawer and switched it on.

While it was booting, he ran up the stairs to the first floor landing and stood in front of a gilt-framed Monet. It was centrally positioned on the wall between the master bedroom and one of the guest suites; an impressive display for their guests.

He felt around its edge until he found a ridge. He pressed the release, pulling the hinged frame away from the wall. Tapping the code into the keypad, he swung the door open, taking a small flash drive from the shelf, he ran back to the computer.

Sweating from a mixture of exertion and panic he logged on and pushed the dongle into the USB slot. His fingers flashed across the keyboard as he typed in the code, stopping from pushing another key as an error message flashed across the screen. He needed to calm down a little as he only had three chances of entering the correct code before it locked him out. Negotiating through security protocols, he stared at the screen he needed. Gathering his thoughts, he closed his eyes as he thought of something appropriate. Then it came to him; perfect considering the date. He smiled as he typed the phrase. He looked at it for several minutes to ensure he spelt it correctly, reciting it to himself three or four times.

Satisfied, he input a linked second phrase and finished with the six digits it would reveal. His finger hovered over the return key as he checked and double checked his efforts before finally executing the file. The flash drive blinked as it confirmed a connection to the central server, sending it through the new data, encrypting it as it processed. The screen cleared and 'accepted' flashed at its centre. Relief flooded through him as he logged off and removed the dongle.

It was time to get ready.

CHAPTER FOUR
One for Sorrow

Holding his arm against the tiles with his head lowered, Colin let the warm spray from the power shower cascade over his shoulders and down his back. His brain was in turmoil as he fought to control his fear, trying to rationalise the reasons for the unexpected visit.

'I will only meet with you if absolutely necessary. However, in the unlikely event, this should happen, you MUST alter the code before our meeting. I cannot stress enough the importance of this instruction.'

They were specific orders given to him at their last appointment, well over six months ago. She was convinced someone was trying to affect the outcome of the probate over her mother's estate. One person, in particular, being her long-lost sister, Claudia. She had suddenly materialised after forty-eight years to contest the will. It was so shrouded in mystery, it caused Jayne Langfield to question the validity of Claudia Robertson, even claiming she was not her sister. There were things about the case that worried him, in normal circumstances he would have turned it down.

But he felt a sense of loyalty as Jayne Langfield's mother, Gloria Barth, had been one of his first clients as a junior partner at Grestons. There was also the tempting offer of a substantial retainer to take on the case, so he decided against his better judgement to accept it.

Now he had to meet her on Friday 13th it just added to the stress. He felt blocked in with nowhere to turn, a sense of foreboding he couldn't shake. He wished he could go to bed, curl up and stay there until tomorrow. It was an irrational fear that was taking hold of his life. It affected his psyche, and there was nothing he could do about it. He had sought medical advice, subjected himself to psychiatric tests. He suffered weeks of intrusive investigations, even regression to see if it had anything to do with his childhood, his upbringing. Colin had nothing to grab hold of, nothing to explain the terror he felt when a superstition hits. But after all he had subjected himself to, no matter how much money he threw at it, nobody had the answer.

His mind was going over and over what he should do. He could postpone, make Jayne come back on Monday. But she had already made it clear that meetings were not required unless it was absolutely necessary. Having built a reputation for reliability and trust, he knew he would have to go. The fact Derek had skived off again, probably to shack up with a girl somewhere for the weekend. It was of no consequence in the current circumstances, apart from adding a little clarity to a decision he needed to make.

Drying himself, he made plans to cease the partnership on Monday. It had gone on long enough. Although they had been firm friends in the early days, he consistently disregarded the importance of the practice. It had caused a few rifts over the last year or two. Even Annabel, who had been a great supporter of Derek, wanted him out. One minute they seemed fine, then almost overnight her attitude changed. She hardly had a good word to say about him these days. He put it down to Derek's lack of effort. He wasn't doing enough to bolster the profits, and his handling of some of his clients was way below par. It undermined the high standards he expected from his practice.

Throwing the towel towards the wash basket, he left for the bedroom.

He had a meeting to attend.

He knotted his tie in the Baroque mirror in the hallway, the only area in the house that kept the classic Georgian feel of the exterior. The rest was more neoclassical, extending to the rear, where ancient Greece influenced the pool house.

Grecian marble of white and gold covered the floors of every room. It portrayed a palatial ambience that displayed beautifully the upper-class image Annabel thrived on.

He felt more comfortable in the hall with its more traditional surroundings. His favourite was his man cave. He had installed most of his own choices; the plasma, Lazy Boy, games console and mini bar. It was the only room in the house that felt belonged in the 21st century.

Studying his face in the mirror, he saw a tired man. This situation was becoming a strain, but he didn't know how to slow it down. He was obsessed with the practice and everything about it. He had built it from scratch, growing it year on year. He was contemplating more staff, but as soon as he planned for it, he feared the business would dry up, so he took more work on himself. He saw an eighty hour week regularly which compared to Derek's eight made it even harder. He didn't want to turn work down, but he was not about to give any more new clients to his partner.

After Monday it would no longer be an issue. Even though he had dried himself thoroughly after his shower, his shirt was sticking to him. He was sweating. He could feel the panic rising in him as he contemplated breaking his self imposed curfew.

Opening his briefcase, he shut it in the same movement and opened it again; he was all over the place. He stared at the tan leather lining and the empty innards, his eyes scrutinised the lines of stitching. It was as if time stood still, feeling his heart thudding, his breathing laboured. The silence was deafening. Yelling at the top of his voice, he threw the case across the hall taking a Faberge egg with it. It bounced off the wall, coming to rest at the foot of the stairs. The egg was in a million multicoloured pieces scattered all over the floor with the stand upside down, dented and broken under the telephone table. It was a reproduction, still expensive but not the end of the world. Annabel wouldn't see it that way, but it would have to wait. There was a more important thing to do, like leave the house. Choosing the Range Rover keys from the cupboard, he took his jacket from the hanger and set the alarm as he entered the porch. Double locking the door he stepped onto the drive.

It was a warm afternoon with a bright blue sky. The sun hid behind a fluffy white cumulus, waiting patiently for it to pass, allowing it to spray the streets with radiance once again. He crossed the gravel drive towards the cars, concentrating on the black Range Rover, feeling calm. His outburst in the hall had released some of his pent up emotion.

He heard the gunshot crack in the distance moments before his legs gave way and he toppled onto his back. There was no pain, just pressure in his chest. He had stopped breathing and was sure that no air was filling his lungs, but he had no desire to breathe. He couldn't move, only stare into the blue void of sky. The silence overwhelmed him, feeling like a spectator as the world passed him by. The sky shrank as the edges of his vision became dark, slowly moving inwards, drawing towards the centre of his eyes. A bird flew across his view, a black bird with distinctive fanned wings, a thick band of white crossing from wing tip to wing tip. Its long tail flicked as it passed by, laughing a 'Ka-Ka-Ka' as it disappeared. One for sorrow.

Then all went dark.

CHAPTER FIVE
Venezuela

Jack Case looked out from under his camo blanket at the guard who had fallen asleep for the second time. He would give it another five minutes and then make his move. He checked his PDA. The tracker was still registering, the icon hadn't moved during the hour he had been hiding in the undergrowth.

He was relieved, as it meant the hostage was restrained, but alive. He only had ninety minutes to get her out and get to the boat before becoming stranded. He was 2000 metres above sea level in the Montane forests of Venezuela on the Cordillera La Costa. A 450 mile mountain range stretching from east to west on the northern coast of Venezuela. It was thick with vegetation and as damp as hell. It soaked his fatigues, which were already wet after the 2 kilometre trek from the jeep, left behind once the trail ended. The blanket did its best to protect him from the rain, but the mist replacing it was seeping through as if it wasn't there. It also soaked the thin latex wetsuit he wore close to his skin, but his body heat kept him relatively warm. He would need to move soon though, otherwise, he'd seize up.

All was silent save for the patter of drips rippling in the foliage as they rode on the slight breeze. The crickets had stopped their incessant chirrup five hundred metres ago. Jack was feeling the strain, something he had thought about during the last four missions. At 38, although still physically fit, it was taking its toll. His reaction times were slipping, his reflexes seconds slower each time, he needed a break. Perhaps a permanent break.

He took the call from the agency forty-eight hours ago. The mission was to rescue a hostage snatched from a busy market in Rio. She was a young student, visiting as part of a gap year from her studies at Cambridge.

Zabrina Rashad had been part of a volunteer humanitarian group teaching English in the repressed areas of Brazil. She had been snatched while out with friends on Saturday. One of the group had turned out to be a plant for a faction renowned for kidnapping prime targets and holding out for eight figure sums. On the last two occasions, the perps had received the ransom money only to have the hostages wash up on a beach off the coast of Venezuela and Brazil. The kidnappers had disappeared without a trace, melding back into their communities. They had no leads... until now. Thanks to the client's paranoia, he had found them.

Abdurrahman Rashad Bin Al Sharif, Abu to his friends, billionaire and chief broker for oil negotiations to the western world, had provided a contingency for all of his children.

It was his insurance against just such an atrocity. As with most super rich, their main concern was to stay that way. They publicly declare their families to be their most valuable possession. But they also want to protect against any member of the family costing them more than they should. Ransom was a word eliciting more fear than a drop in the exchange rate. At birth, each of his nine children had miniature tracking devices, no bigger than a grain of rice, implanted under their skin. It was a new technology in the 1980s and relatively untested. But with a few million pounds from Abu and the best micro technologists around, they had perfected it. Within five years they marketed it to those who could afford it, and the billionaire had recouped his investment ten times over.

The ransom requested was $20 million, Abu had arranged for staff to deliver the funds in used dollar bills. The drop, the next morning, was to be at a designated container at Puerto Cabello, six miles from his current location. There was a total media blackout. Every government had a vested interest in Abu's main business and had pressed the alarm bell when he approached them for help. It was more a demand to get his daughter back, and with the clout he had, they had no choice. The problem was, no government could afford to gnore Abu's demands, but they could not be seen to be directly involved. This was where Jack came in.

He was a wraith, part of a crack extraction unit employed by LARA - Land Air Reconnaissance Agency. The unit consisted of the elite from the armed forces, specialists in search and destroy missions. Their role, to assist in the fight for world peace and to support global security. They had no allegiances, self-sufficient and highly dangerous.

He had been dropped in the dead of night at La Guaira by Navy Seals from the US frigate patrolling the Caribbean. From the port, he made his way into Caracas to check in at his designated hotel. The Lidotel in the City Centre, a well known tourist trap, an ideal location to take delivery of the rest of his equipment. His Glock with spare magazines, hand grenades, night glasses and two KABAR knives. They had been delivered to the hotel in an everyday sports bag, handed to him by a reliable concierge on his arrival. He had managed a few hours sleep, but as usual, it was never enough.

His next stop was the Dama Antanona restaurant for a lunch of Pabellon, the Venezuelan national dish. A bowl of stringy beef; black beans, rice and fried plantain slices, washed down with several shots of Tequila. He hired a jeep for the trip into the Cordillera La Costa where he caught up on a few more hours sleep, helped by the Tequila.

At midnight he drove into the mountains, making good time until the road disappeared. Using the PDA for guidance, he made the rest of the journey on foot. As he climbed the vegetation grew thicker, small palms blocked many of the paths, and it became more and more treacherous as the mist descended. With visibility just a few feet, he slowed his ascent.

Two hours after leaving the hotel he arrived at a clearing containing two ECO observation huts. They were used by ecologists to monitor and observe the ecosystem of the Montane forest and the life within it. Inhabited for eleven months at a time, they were left vacant for a month to monitor the area remotely. The kidnappers knew the right time to strike.

He watched the guard change a few minutes after he arrived. This one had a few hours to go yet. From his vantage point, he counted nine hostiles. Eight in the larger of the buildings, easily visible through the full size windows from what he assumed was the observation hut. There was one sentry outside the smaller sparsely windowed cabin. He was unsure if there were more inside, but he would soon find out. Two jeeps parked in front of the larger building blocked the view of the seated man from the inhabitants. He had fallen into a deep sleep, his chin resting on his chest. He was wearing a waterproof hooded cape pulled tightly around him, the raised hood hiding his face. It was soaked and shimmered in the light from the small lamp positioned above his head.

This relaxed approach could work to his advantage. It made sense the kidnappers wouldn't expect a rescue attempt as they had agreed on the payment. The sentry was purely protecting the merchandise, making sure there was no escape. Moving his blanket aside Jack crawled silently from the scrub. A frog leapt into the air as he placed his hand on its slippery body. It let out a disgruntled croak as it bounced into the undergrowth thrusting through the fronds of fern. The leaves rustled, snapping loudly in the night silence. Jack froze keeping his eyes on his target, the dozing man snorted, moved his head slightly and recrossed his outstretched legs. Within seconds his shoulders slumped as he drifted back to sleep. Raising himself to a crouch, he carefully crept into the open, one eye on the building to his left and one on his destination. He could see no other movement, they had dimmed the lights as the rest of the hostiles settled down to sleep. This cover was all he needed to get the job done.

Reaching his target, he stood up to his full height and kicked the bottom of the sleeping man's boots. The sentry stirred, sleepily raising his head. It was too early to be relieved. Becoming more aware, he looked up at a white man dressed all in black; he was smiling.

"Hi." Jack continued to smile as he swept the knife across his throat.

The man's eyes stared widely at his attacker, he tried to shout but could manage only a gurgle as the blood pumped out of the jugular vein. He tried to struggle free, but there was a hand over his mouth, pressing his head back against the hut. There was also a knee pressing hard into his groin making movement impossible. He grabbed his attacker's arm trying frantically to push it back, but he was powerless as his strength ebbed away. As each pump of blood sprayed from his neck, he faded in unison. His hands were losing their grip, he couldn't feel his fingers as he looked into the white man's eyes, pleading for help. They were expressionless, cold. There was nothing he could do as his brain shut down and his arms flopped to his side. As he took his hand from the dying man's head, he felt life slip away. He carefully rested the chin back onto his motionless chest. The blood had stopped flowing from the wound; it had mixed with the rain on the already sodden cape. Once he had repositioned his feet carefully, it looked as if the sentry was still sleeping soundly. Feeling underneath the cape he found a set of keys attached to the dead man's belt. Snapping the cord he moved to the lock, inserting the first key. It rattled uselessly in the barrel.

Three keys later he felt a click as it worked the tumblers.

Pushing the door open he slipped inside.

A variety of charts and maps covered the walls. To the left, a large workstation filled with paperwork, a computer and a CB Radio station. The far wall covered by filing cabinets and three glass tanks housing several plants lit by infra-red lamps, giving the interior a warm glow.

Hundreds of Petri dishes on glass racks, some with tiny shoots thrived in the ambient temperature. They were neatly labelled on shelves covering the rest of the wall space. To his right was a single camp bed. Lying on top, bound and gagged, was Zabrina Rashad. Locking the door, leaving the key in position, he moved towards her. She watched him, eyes wide as he approached the bed. She struggled and moaned from beneath her gag. He stooped until his face was upon hers.

"Hi, I'm Jack, I'm here to take you home." He whispered as he went to untie her hands.

She continued to struggle, moving her hands away from him, her eyes still staring wildly. Had the gag not been in place she would be screaming at him by now. It is always the policy to leave the hostage gagged during a rescue to eliminate the risk of them crying out. By the look of this one she was feisty, so the gag seemed wise. She nudged her head towards him gesturing, trying to show him something.

He checked the edge of the bed for any signs of a trap, running his hand along its side. Zabrina moaned louder, raising her eyes in frustration, continuing to move her head vigorously. Taking the Maglite from his pocket he shone it over her, checking her pillow, her restraints and finally underneath the bed. Zabrina let out a moan of relief and flopped her head back on the pillow. She had been right to protest. Fixed to the springs of the bed was a small plate with a central bracket holding a test tube horizontally at its axis. Within the test tube was a large ball-bearing sealed inside by a cork through which poked two bare ends of wire. He followed the wiring until it ended at what looked like a car battery fixed to two large cakes of C4. It was a booby trap. A fine wire with a spring at its centre had been connected to the base of the tube. Pulled taut it held the ball-bearing at the domed end of the glass. It allowed small movement from the mattress without activating the mechanism. But if he lifted Zabrina from the bed, there would be nothing left of both of them. The line would snap, the test tube would tilt, and the ball-bearing would roll onto the wires completing the circuit. Looking up, he turned to her and mouthed an apology as he scanned the room. Turning away, he was sure he caught her raising her eyes in dismay.

Three things struck him as he searched the room for something to use. First, it was a crude trap that probably dated back to the second world war. Second, he couldn't understand why the captors would go to such lengths to restrain her. Third, how stupid were they? Had the bomb exploded, it would have been huge. The sentry would be obliterated along with the hut, and the explosion would have reached the larger building housing the others. There would have been nothing left of the entire area. Whoever had planned this had not expected the goons or the hostage to survive. He also felt for Zabrina. She would have spent the last three days fearing to move, leaving only her terror filled thoughts for company.

He lifted a bin then replaced it. Tried a chair, testing its weight then replaced it. Seeing a mobile drawer unit beneath the workstation, he tested its weight. Opening the top drawer, he removed papers and a hardback book and lifted it again. Satisfied, he went back to the bed. Zabrina watched him as he approached with the drawer unit, eyeing him questioningly. Putting the drawers down he pointed to himself, gesturing for her to watch him. Jack laid on the floor lifting his feet vertically. He shaped the letter L, dropping his calves horizontally to create the letter Z. Getting back to his feet he nodded for confirmation. She nodded back to signal that she understood. Positioning the unit near her feet, he cut her bindings, signalling for her to bring her legs up. She moved her feet along the side of the steel box in a walking motion as Jack pushed it towards her. He pushed gently, careful to ensure smooth movements to avoid snagging the corners on the bedclothes. Once underneath her, she bent her knees, resting her calves on the top of the unit. Jack signalled for her to hold her position and pushed. It forced Zabrina backwards, gradually sliding along the bedclothes until her head was free of the bed. By the time her shoulders reached the end, he stopped once he was sure the weight was over the trigger, and she was close to falling off. Walking back to her head, he gripped her shoulders and eased her gently from the bed.

Instinctively he closed his eyes, waiting for the explosion just in case he had misjudged her weight. There was silence save for the muffled sigh of the relieved hostage. Zabrina stood gyrating her hips, bending to and fro to ease her aching back. She pushed her hands towards him to untie them. He shook his head.

"Later." He mouthed.

She kicked him in the shin, thrusting her hands at him. Taken by surprise he stumbled, rubbing his leg. What was wrong with this girl? Shrugging in resignation he drew his knife, putting his finger to his mouth to tell her to be quiet as he sliced through the bindings. She ripped at the knot behind her head pulling the gag free and throwing it across the room.

"About fucking ti……" Jack launched at her and clasped his hand over her mouth spinning her around, pulling her into him. He whispered harshly in her ear.

"If you want to get out of here alive keep your mouth shut!" She held her hands up in submission as he released his grip, moving his hand away slowly, just in case she started again. She twisted out of his arms and slapped him across the face. She was breathing hard, staring at him with steely determination. Her hands clenched and unclenched by her side as she challenged him.

She was twenty-four years of age and beautiful. Her dark complexion, even after the last three days, was smooth and free from any marks. Her almond eyes and angular eyebrows shaped her face towards a cute button nose above sumptuous lips. She wore a loose fitting jacket over a cut away tee shirt exposing a diamond studded belly button twinkling in the light. Her tight fitting jeans emphasised her trim figure. He guessed that she was not a fan of middle eastern traditions. This mission would be no cakewalk he thought as he went to the only window in the building.

She liked him. He was special forces, probably SAS she guessed. He was strong, and the way he carried himself, confident. She liked what she saw. He had the looks too. His shaven head was close enough to leave only a blue shadow on his scalp. Together with his matching stubble following the contours of his square jaw, he exemplified the ruggedness of a powerful man. The irregular shape of his nose carried the battle scars of several breaks showing her he was not afraid of a fight. It wasn't misshapen enough to affect his good looks, however, in fact, he was striking. It was his eyes that left a lasting impression, piercing blue or green, she couldn't quite see in this light, but they scared and reassured her at the same time. They were the eyes of an assassin, and she was relieved she wasn't his target, but if he played his cards right, he could be hers. She joined him at the window.

"Can we go now?" She whispered as she followed his gaze.

Through the window he could see a jeep, a black panda logo emblazoned on its bonnet and doors, the symbol of the World Wildlife Fund. It was one of the ecologist fleet. There was a winch fixed to the rear stanchion, that could come in handy.

The window had no opening, the temperature controlled from a unit on the wall. He would not attempt to break through as it may wake the kidnappers, they would need to use the door. Turning the key, he stopped short of engaging the lock.

He heard voices outside, one goon was trying to wake up the dead man. It was mere seconds before there was a shout as he realised his comrade wasn't sleeping. The door handle turned followed by a crash as he tried to break it down. The frame splintered but held against the force, it wouldn't take much more punishment, he had to act fast. Grabbing the chair he threw it at the window; it bounced off.

"Shit!" He hadn't accounted for that. The window was reinforced to keep the temperature for the plant cultures.

"Here, try this." Zabrina hauled the CB base station into his arms, she was stronger than she looked. He threw it with all his might, the glass cracked but didn't break. They pounded at the door again, this time the frame cracked, the next hit would smash it. He could hear more shouts from outside as the rest of the kidnappers appeared. He had no real choice now, he pulled out his Glock and blasted the glass into smithereens.

"Quick, let's go." He helped her through the window before dropping behind her. He then doubled back, resting his gun on the sill aiming at the door.

"Get to the truck and look for keys!" He shouted back as Zabrina ran on. He hoped as it was a base car, the keys would either be in the glove box, under the visor or in the ignition. They were in the middle of nowhere, and he would wager incidents of car theft were zero.

The door exploded from its hinges and slammed into the centre of the room. The momentum caused the gunman to stumble and collapse on top, trapping his fingers under the ruined timber. He didn't get up again as a bullet shattered his skull. Jack downed two more as they rushed in, they were dead before they landed on top of the corpse. Two more ducked out of his line of fire, his two bursts passed harmlessly through the doorway into the forest beyond. He could hear footsteps heading his way as the captors ran around the building to trap him at the rear. Swinging around he checked both ways continuously, waiting for the first one to turn the corner.

Headlights shone into his face as a jeep hurtled towards him. It spun sideways, skidding to a stop six feet away. The door swung open.

"Hurry, get in." It was Zabrina. She had managed to get the jeep started. The hostage was now the rescuer. He ran, keeping his head down and dived into the passenger seat as bullets hammered into the side panel. A round hit his door slamming it shut.

"Let's go!" he screamed as he spun in his seat and returned fire.

CHAPTER SIX

Escape

The jeep accelerated away from the clearing, its rear wheels slipping erratically as the tyres struggled for grip on the wet floor. Crashing through a thicket it hit a dirt track, launching headlong into the forest. Sparks were exploding from the rear as gunshots pinged off the bodywork.

"So, where are we heading?" Zabrina asked, expertly throwing the jeep through the undergrowth and around the palms as they hurtled into view.

"I would say if we're going downhill, we're heading the right way." Jack was holding on for dear life, bouncing off the spongy seat. Thankfully, the lack of roof saved his head from a battering.

"No shit Sherlock" came the reply. Her Cambridge education had been worthwhile.

"I know that." She continued.

"I thought my knight in shining armour would have turned up with an escape plan."

He looked over at her. She handled the jeep well, and for someone restrained in such a way for the last three days, she had incredible powers of recovery. Either that or the adrenalin had kicked in, and she was on an artificial high which could end up getting them killed. He noticed there were no keys in the ignition. He smiled in admiration, she had hot-wired the car.

"My father insisted we were all trained in skills that could save our lives." She offered after catching him looking at the empty keyhole. It was true the Sheik provided his children with the self preservation skills needed to protect his billions. But he couldn't help thinking it was a dangerous way to live your life. It was still a concern that shock may overcome adrenalin and he needed to resume control. He decided on tact.

"Zabrina, let me take the wheel. You've been through a lot in the last few days." He offered.

"Call me Rina." She replied.

"And I have a feeling you will need both hands free." She was looking in the rear-view mirror.

He turned to see two sets of headlights in the distance. The goons were giving chase. Pulling out the PDA he reset the homing signal for Patrice and hung it from its lanyard around the heating control on the dash. It omitted a green pulse on the small radar showing northeast.

"Keep the light to the top of the screen. That's our route." She swung the jeep to the right at the earliest opportunity. A palm frond whipped his head.

"Hey, careful!" He raised his hand to avoid being hit again.

"Sorry…" She smiled.

"… Just lining up with the light."

The jeep bounced into a recess and leapt into the air landing with a sickening crunch on all four wheels. She floored the accelerator and continued on, this girl would definitely kill him! The rear-view mirror exploded. They were closing in and well in the range of the bullets. Swinging around he let off three rounds in quick succession. One headlight exploded, but the other kept pace with them. He was about to shoot again when the jeep hit a log and launched into the air. Jack flew higher; he had removed his seatbelt.

He fell headlong into a bush at the side of the road and rolled several times before coming to a stop, crashing into the sharp bark of a palm tree. Shaking his head clear he checked himself over. Thankfully, as only his pride had taken a hit, he scrambled to his feet. Rina skidded to a stop in the middle of the track and reversed.

"No!" He waved her on. "Keep going. I'll catch you up." Just before being thrown he noticed there was only one jeep in pursuit. They must have split up and were trying to head them off. He had to get back to Rina, but he needed to even the odds. A bullet hit the palm inches from his head showering him in wood chips. He scrambled into the undergrowth, staying low, pushing fronds aside to give him a clear sight of the dirt track. Just then he heard a vehicle slide to a halt. One gunman barked an order, and he heard consecutive thumps as two of the passengers jumped out, heading towards his location. He pinned himself against a palm out of their line of fire and waited. It wasn't long before he heard the swoosh of someone cutting a path through the undergrowth just feet from his position. He held his breath.

A man came into view sweeping the machete in front of him. Grass and leaves filled the air as he cleared his path, keeping his eyes trained on the ground expecting his target to be hiding amongst the foliage. He watched him move a yard ahead, then broke cover. He was on him in a flash, placing his hands on both sides of his head. Jack snapped his neck with a movement so fast, his quarry had no time to realise he was dead. He swept up the blade and turned to look for the other kidnapper. He didn't need to look far. Standing five yards ahead of him was a heavy set man in military fatigues. His features were typical of the area, greased black hair pushed away from his dark skin. Under his nose, he wore a moustache that Castro would have been proud of.

He smiled as he raised his AK47 to finish him. It was a case of fastest first, and his opponent had a distinct advantage. Jack had the blade in his hand, down by his side, no time to bring it up to use effectively. He had to think fast. Bracing himself, he threw the machete underarm, diving forward as it spiralled away from his grasp, banking on the rifle aiming at his torso and not at the floor. He covered his head instinctively as he slid to a stop, with only a palm leaf for protection. Shots rang out as he landed. They came nowhere near him, instead hitting the leaves high in the trees overhead as the gunman toppled backwards. The blade had sliced through his larynx, the hilt stopping it from passing straight through his throat.

Laying still for a few seconds he let out a deep breath. That was close.

Making his way back to the dirt track he could hear the shouts of the driver as he questioned the outcome. He couldn't grasp the lingo, but he could tell by the tone of his voice he was expecting a response. Edging closer to the vehicle he heard the two goons in the jeep arguing, probably deciding what to do next. He took the Glock from its holster and pulled a knife from its sheath. He would help them with their decision. With his gun in his left hand and the knife in his right, he ran from the forest. He threw the knife at the passenger standing in the vehicle's rear, training his gun on the crop of bushes to the left of his position. The blade buried deep between the man's ribs, sending him spiralling from the jeep. In one smooth movement, he dived forward, moved his gun from his left hand to his right and shot the driver. The bullet hit just below the back of his neck, and the upward trajectory took his forehead clean off. Brain splattered the windscreen as he slumped onto the steering wheel.

Running for the driver's seat, he hauled the corpse onto the track. He floored the accelerator heading after Rina. Blood and brain impaired his vision, but he cringed at the thought of having to wipe it off with his sleeve. He looked around for something to use; he could see nothing. He raised his gun and shot out the window. A cool breeze rushed around his face causing him to squint. The one headlight made visibility less than perfect, the thin slither of rain was like driving through a light fog. He kept his foot down, but as the undergrowth grew thicker, he was braking more than he would like, as rocks and foliage jumped out of the mist. Banking left he tried to picture the compass on the PDA and headed in what he assumed was the right direction. He had to close in on the second car before they got to her. It would not be worth killing her yet as the ransom was not due to be paid for a few hours, but they could not risk her raising the alarm. He was confident that once they had collected the money, they would not need her. If he lost her now, it could take days to find her without his PDA, and by then it would be too late.

He heard gunfire a little way ahead. Swinging the jeep right at a fork in the track, he saw the glow of rear lights in the distance. He was catching them. He urged the jeep on, he was gaining on them. Before he had time to react, he cleared the forest and launched into a clearing. Gunshots ricocheted off the frame of his shattered windscreen as he drove into a trap, his survival instincts forced him to dive from the jeep. He rolled behind a small outcrop of rocks and watched as the vehicle disappeared from view over the cliff edge. They were way off course. Risking a quick look at the situation, he poked his head over the largest of the rocks. A bullet blasted granite into his face from inches away, forcing him back into cover.

Rina had stopped her jeep close to the cliff's edge and was cowering behind the front wheels. The two goons were behind their vehicle a good way from her and with a clear view. They had peppered the vehicle from a safe distance, unsure if she had a weapon. One gunman was on a radio while the other covered the rock preventing him from moving. Jack bowed his head swearing under his breath as he heard the pulsing revs of an engine. They had called for backup. Peering carefully around his hiding place he gauged the distance between the goons and Rina. It was more than enough. Grabbing a grenade from the pouch, he snapped the pin changing his position to peer from the other side of the rock. He waited for the shots to come as they spotted his new position. He didn't have to wait long. Rolling backwards he jumped up from the opposite side, hurling the grenade in an arc, watching as it flew towards their vehicle.

"Rina! Cover your head!" He hoped she heard him before he ducked down.

The gunmen watched the grenade bounce towards them. Shock and surprise delayed their reactions for only a few seconds as it rolled, spun and came to a rest behind the rear wheels. But it was enough. They shrieked, scrambling into each other with legs and arms all over the place, trying desperately to jump clear of the vehicle. The blast took the lower limbs from one of them and catapulted the other eight feet into the air. Two somersaults later he landed in a heap, his head positioned at an impossible angle, his chin resting on his shoulder blades. The jeep flipped and landed on the hapless victim already without his legs. His screaming ceased as it came to rest on top of him. Looking back at the forest, tiny lights sparkled in the distance like fireflies dancing through the trees. They grew steadily brighter, accompanied by a steady hum, the hum turned into the sound of an engine. There were more of them heading their way.

Running to the jeep, he was hoping Rina had heard his shouts and braced herself for the explosion. Apart from being smothered in bullet holes, it was in the same position as it had been before the blast. He found her sitting with her back pushed against the front wheel, resting her head on her raised knees, held tightly by her linked hands. She looked up at him as he approached.

"You took your time." Her voice cracked as she bravely tried to make light of the situation, but her eyes gave her away. He put a hand on her shoulder and squeezed.

"Nearly home." He smiled. Although he knew there was work to do yet.

Grabbing the PDA from the dash, he activated the tracker before slipping it back into his pocket. Looking down from the cliff's edge and recognising the telltale ellipse of the Gulf of Trist, he knew they were directly above Puerto Cabello. Seven hundred feet above to be exact. Not only were they at least 20 miles away from where they should have been to rendezvous with Patrice, but they were stranded with no easy way down. He could see a platform cut into the rock. It was the maintenance shelf supporting the hundreds of floodlights lighting the port from above, surrounding the whole expanse, just short of a mile long. There were manholes positioned evenly along the shelf leading to steel stairways down to ground level. It was still a good hundred feet, but if they could reach it, they had a route to the port. Leaning into the jeep and releasing the handbrake he grabbed the wheel manoeuvring it until it was facing the forest. With Rina in the driver's seat, they reversed until it was a foot from the edge. He kicked out some fist sized rocks lying close by, jamming them behind the wheels. He then headed for the winch. He should have ninety-four feet of cable which would bring them close enough to the platform to start their descent to the ground. Taking off his belt he offered it to Rina.

"Hold your hands out." He beckoned her forward.

"Why?" She asked, eyeing him with suspicion.

"Just do it!" He commanded, probably harsher than he meant. He tried to soften his voice, but he was aware of the vehicles closing in on them and judging by the increase in volume, they would be here any moment.

"Rina, trust me, I want to get us both out of here alive."

Acting like a spoiled brat, she raised her eyes and huffed as she presented her hands to him. He wound the belt around her wrists, looping it twice before tying it off. Releasing the winch, he watched as he weight of the hook carried the unwound cable over the edge. The winch spun furiously until the empty spool jolted to a halt. He locked t off and removed his jacket. He called her over as he squatted down.

"Hook your arms over my head and climb on." He motioned the movement. She climbed onto his back, he pulled her hands down his chest until he was comfortable he had her before getting to his feet.

"Now try to keep your hands in this position, the belt is just to keep your hands together. If you slip, you'll strangle me, so pay attention!"

Grabbing the front of his shirt, she felt the firmness of his pectorals. They were solid, taut from the strain of the weight he carried. She could jam her fingers under those, it would be like gripping rocks. She placed her cheek against his and felt his jaw flex. He tilted his face away, looking at her from the corner of his eye.

"Ready?" He asked as he bounced her twice to get used to the weight. Rina felt he was testing her as you would a rucksack. Charming, she thought as she acknowledged him. Jack straddled the cable and wound his jacket around it. Placing his hands into the sleeves through the cuffs gave him makeshift leather gloves.

Gripping tightly he eased them over the edge.

CHAPTER SEVEN

Pursuit

It took time to get used to the extra weight of the girl as he descended the cliff face. His arms and legs objected, to begin with, he was finding it difficult to gather a rhythm. Some footholds crumbled away as soon as he set foot on them, which slowed them even more as he searched for solid protrusions. It was proving harder than he thought. Eventually, he gained a momentum which allowed him to abseil some of the way. Looking down he could see they were just forty feet from the platform, they would be there in no time.

A bullet ricocheted a foot above his head, and a second near his shoulder, stone chips stung his face, one hitting his eye. The shock caused Jack to loosen his grip, plunging them fifteen feet. He tried to pinch the cable tightly to slow them, but it slipped through his leather clad hands. He rammed his feet against the granite wall to try again, scraping chips loose and surrounding them with dust. Both feet caught a tiny ridge which stopped them with a jolt, he bent his knees to soften the impact, but it didn't prevent Rina from being thrown back. She lost her grip on his shirt as she slipped backwards, the belt around her hands caught at his neck, choking him. Bullets chiselled pieces of rock all around them. Thankfully, the irregular shape of the cliff face prevented a clear shot from above. It only needed one lucky bullet however, and it would all be over.

Jack held on, releasing his feet from the ledge. He kicked his legs in a circular motion, winding up the cable from below, wrapping it around his calves. Pushing his weight down into the tangle of wire, Jack could feel the entwined steel bite into his legs, supporting him. He pulled his jacket free, letting it fall to the platform below and pushed his upper body into the rock. Lifting his arms to his neck and grabbing Rina's wrists, he pulled the belt away from his skin, taking a few seconds to gulp in much needed air. What he did next was a risky manoeuvre, and it took Rina by surprise. She screamed. Leaning back, still holding her tightly by the wrists he swung upside down, his backside pressed into the rock as the cable supported his legs. Rina, still screaming as she dangled from his arms, looked down at the wooden platform beneath her. They were eighteen feet away, but with his six foot and her five foot six she was only six feet from safety.

"I am going to let you go now." He shouted.

"What! Are you out of your mind?" Rina squealed, kicking her legs as she tried to climb up his arms.

He could feel the strain on his shoulders as she struggled.

"Rina, stop! You'll get us killed!" As if on cue several shots ricocheted nearby. She stopped struggling.

"Bend your knees and fall onto your side. It will soften the landing." He didn't mention that she should be careful not to roll forward as there was a six hundred foot drop on the other side of the shelf. It would only worry her. She had been screaming hysterically anyway, so he knew it wouldn't make any difference.

"Right, after three…" He began.

"No… No… No… don't you dare." She screamed up at him.

"One…"

"Jack… DON'T!"

"Two…"

"JACK!"

"Three…" He let go.

She screamed all the way down. Remembering to bend her knees she fell onto her side. She lay still for several seconds relieved that she could feel solid floor beneath her. More gunfire forced her into action. Getting to her knees, she gnawed at the belt around her wrists until she pulled it loose, throwing it over the side. Dusting herself down she ran to the wall, pushing her back into it to gain as much shelter as she could. Seeing Rina was safe, he pulled himself back up the cable until he had straightened. He untangled his legs, one of which had gone dead.

He was thrown off balance as a bullet dislodged a rock above, glancing him on the shoulder as it fell. Out of control, he flipped upside down again. The cable snapped taut as it ascended rapidly. Rina screamed his name as she could see what was happening.

The kidnappers were winding the winch in and taking him back up towards them. His weight had pulled the cable tight around one of his calves as he was being pulled up by one leg. He could see the platform moving further away, now twenty feet from it, twenty-two, twenty-four. He frantically looked around the face of the cliff for a foothold he could use with his free leg, scraping his heel into the rock to try to slow himself. Hitting a protrusion, he jammed his foot against it. With his leg acting as a pivot he swung out from the cliff face, pulling himself upright. It gave him the seconds he needed to take the weight as he kicked and wriggled his leg free. The cable was still rising as he slid down, clinging onto the hook at the end.

He was at least twenty feet up from the platform, but he had no choice. He turned to face the rock and bracing himself; he let go.

Lumps of granite and stone cut into his hands as he tried to slow his descent. His boots tried to find purchase, keeping his legs moving as he scraped them against the brittle surface.

His knee caught on an outcrop, and he plummeted the remaining fifteen foot vertically, slamming hard against the platform. He felt his ankle crack as he landed and was thrown back against the handrail. Thankfully, it held firm. He sat there for a few seconds in a daze. His left ankle was painful, he couldn't tell if it was broken, but it would cause him a problem. His body was burning from the punishment of the rock wall, and he felt giddy.

A bullet ricocheted off the metal handrail bringing him back to his senses. Wincing as he moved out of the line of fire, he rested against the rock face. For the time being he was a difficult target to hit. Rina shuffled along the wall towards him, picking up his jacket as she came across it. Reaching him, she flung her arms around his neck.

"Thank god, I thought I had lost you." She kissed him on the cheek, nestling into his neck. She sobbed, her reliance on him was evident. He held her for a few moments before moving her gently aside.

"Come on, the last leg." He raised himself from the floor. Testing his ankle he winced, very painful, but it would have to do. He pulled on his jacket and moved to the nearest manhole. Turning the wheel latch of the metal cover, he pulled at the door. Lifting it easily he let it clatter onto the platform before calling her over. He helped her through the trapdoor, following her onto the metal steps. He leant through to pull the door shut, it would slow their pursuers for a short while, but they would need every second they could get. Looking up briefly as he swung the door towards him, he confirmed the need to get a move on, and fast. Four gunmen were abseiling down the cable, these guys would not give up. He slammed the door above his head and spun the wheel, locking it shut.

They were safe for the time being as they descended the metal stairs two, sometimes three at a time. It was a long way down, but he was hopeful they would make it. His ankle was swelling, he could feel it in his boot and pain shot up his shin as he put pressure on it. It definitely felt like a break. He needed some R&R desperately, he was out of shape and knackered.

He had just the place. His house on the Cornish coast. A place where Jack Case did not exist. A life of peace, normality, where he could fish, sail or just walk the beach, breathing in the clean air. A place where time stood still.

"Look!" Rina shouted as she pointed to a set of stairs a hundred yards parallel to their position. The door had opened, and a pair of legs materialised, descending the stairs at speed. A goon appeared, his back to them as he pumped down the first flight of steps. Once he turned for the second flight, he would face them with a clear shot. The stairs created a z pattern down to port level. They needed to make the next flight as it would provide cover and the steelwork was large enough to add protection of sorts. They ran down the steps as fast as they could, they made it just in time.

"Oh, no!" Rina looked straight ahead.

The trapdoor, a hundred yards in the other direction, had opened and a second gunman ran down the steps. They weren't as stupid as they looked, they were attempting to surround them on their descent. He took a shot which made the first goon stop, using the stairwell as cover. They descended another flight. As they rounded the next set of stairs a blast from the second gunman clattered across their path forcing them to stop. It would be cat and mouse all the way down, as they were taking it in turns to be the attacker and the attacked. Jack lost his temper and fired the rest of his bullets at both stairwells, knocking one gunman down, forcing the other to scamper for cover. Pulling another magazine from his pouch he snapped it in place, the spent one clattered down the stairwell and out into space.

They were still two hundred feet above ground level, and there were now four gunmen on each stairwell. This time he knew their luck had run out. There was no way to outrun them all, he would need to make a stand and fight it out. Rina pushed herself into the wall making her body a difficult target to hit, she hoped.

Firing at the left stairwell, two goons crumpled and fell from the steps, plummeting to the ground, it was a lucky shot. He fired at the other stairwell and two more collapsed. One dropped onto the steps while the other tipped over the handrail and fell screaming to the ground.

Another shot hit a gunman square in the chest, pushing him against the wall before collapsing onto the steps.

He hadn't taken that one.

Looking down, he could see the small boat bobbing steadily at the mouth of the harbour. A flash came from the deck and seconds later the sound of a gunshot reached his ears. Another man fell from the stairs.

It was Patrice; he had followed his beacon, arriving just in time. The last three gunmen scrambled back up the stairwell to get away. One wasn't so lucky, tumbling earthwards, bouncing off several flights before his mangled frame landed on concrete.

It took a further fifteen minutes before they felt the concrete beneath their feet. Rina helped him down the last few steps as his ankle had worsened with the stress of the steel. He sat on the bottom step, breathing a sigh of relief.

They were still a hundred yards from the fishing boat, an American Seiner that would not look out of place here, Patrice had done his homework. It was in the lagoon near the inlet to open waters. Patrice could not risk getting any closer because of the boats moored at the port head. The time and difficulty to manoeuvre around them would be too high a risk. Gunshots splashed around the boat as the gunmen continued to shoot from the platform, they weren't the best of marksmen. The distance made it near on impossible to guarantee a fatal hit, but they were peppering the area between him and the boat, making it difficult for them to make a break for it. Patrice occasionally returned fire which gave a few second's respite and at least ensured the gunmen remained where they were, but there wasn't enough time to get to the boat before the shooting began again.

"Can you swim?" He weighed up the options.

"Of course I can swim. I'm rich, not disabled." She said, looking down her nose at him. The transformation from the frightened little girl halfway down the cliff to the hard faced little rich bitch back at the hut was remarkable.

"Well, get ready to get wet then." He fired back. "I just hope your lungs are as powerful as your mouth." He left her with that as he took a running hobble and dived into the lagoon.

She stood wide eyed and open mouthed as she watched her rescuer dive headlong into the water and stay submerged. How dare he, he had no idea who he was rescuing! Scruffy common toe rag! Thirty metres later he emerged, swivelling around to face her, raising a hand beckoning for her to hurry. She felt like crossing her arms, refusing to move until he apologised. She was a princess, she was used to better manners. Just then, water sprayed all around him as he was spotted from above, he submerged sharply to avoid being hit. He had done it on purpose to draw fire away from her as she made her escape.

She smiled. That's better she thought, diving into the water.

It was warmer than the light rain continuously soaking them, and she cut through it with smooth forward strokes. She emerged to take on more air, but she knew she was well short. Jack's head appeared seconds later, he had covered the same distance as before. He was well over double her distance away and close to the boat. That was impossible, he must have the constitution of a salmon she thought as she gulped in a huge expanse of air and submerged for her second attempt. A bullet whooshed past her head, a spiralling tube of water cut through like a spear disappearing beneath her. She pumped her limbs hard to get away soon regaining her smooth strokes as she cut a swathe through the lagoon. The shooting had stopped. She took two more breaks for air before she gratefully grasped the metal steps and pulled herself up onto the vessel. A hand appeared before her face.

"Care for some assistance, madam?" Jack offered with a smile, which in any other circumstance would have won her over. She accepted it and let him help her on deck. Tilting her head to her left, she started wringing her long tresses through her hands, squeezing out as much of the salt water as she could. It was rather pointless without a towel, so she gave up. She walked towards him; he was still smiling. Their eyes met, but before he could speak, she stopped him with a right hook to the jaw.

"That's for dropping me onto that fucking platform!" Anger rising in her voice.

Jack regained his composure and waggled his jaw to check for damage. There was none. He caught her wrist in his hand as she swung another punch.

"Will you stop hitting me!" Ungrateful bitch. Not one bit of gratitude for saving her life. She kicked him on the shin. This time he went over as it landed on his good leg, leaving him on his damaged ankle.

"And that's for swimming off without me." She looked down at him with her hands on her hips.

"Why you ungrateful …"

"Now, now children let's all calm down shall we." Patrice walked towards them, cradling his high powered rifle like a baby in his arms.

He was sixty years of age, medium height, slightly heavier than he should be, compliments of good food and fine wine. His grey beard was well trimmed and shaped neatly around the contours of his chin. He was dressed like a deep sea fisherman. Black padded waterproof overcoat covered a thick white roll neck jumper. He wore knee length waders with the tops rolled to show the white lining over his black trousers. As a finishing touch, he sported a captain's hat with a badge depicting a trawler emblazoned above the peak. His neck length grey hair poked out from the back.

Jack burst out laughing at his old friend.

"Bloody hell. Its Captain Birds Eye." He roared.

Patrice propped his gun against a crate and faced Jack who

gingerly got to his feet to meet him. They moved towards each other and hugged tightly, slapping each other's back and laughing.

"Patrice, what the hell are you wearing?" Tears formed in his eyes and his ribs ached.

"What?" Patrice backed away with his arms wide. "I thought I would try to blend in."

"Patrice, we are three hundred and fifty miles from Trinidad and Tobago. Norway is five thousand miles the other way." He sniggered as he watched his friend's quizzical expression.

"Next time, get yourself a flowery shirt and a Panama hat."

"But I've used this stuff once before remember. When we took that guy... from Denmark...... Oh!" It finally registered, and he shook his head as he realised his cock up.

"Never mind, old friend." Jack smiled as he placed a placating hand on his shoulder.

"Ahem!" Rina intervened.

"Sorry to break up this touching reunion, but I could do with a towel." She was standing in her now familiar pose, arms crossed, knee slightly forward. Only this time she was tapping her foot impatiently.

"And I think we should get out of here". Jack observed the port from over Patrice's shoulder and saw several vehicles speeding along its length. They were either coastguard or guerillas. From above, climbing down the stairwell, the remaining pursuers poured through the manholes. They weren't giving up, they wanted their hostage back.

Patrice grabbed his rifle and headed to the bow, climbing the steps to the bridge.

"Get below!" He shouted back. "You'll find towels in the bathroom."

He fired the engine and swung the Seiner towards the Caribbean Sea.

Ten minutes later they were in open waters heading away from trouble.

CHAPTER EIGHT
Psych

The accommodation deck was basic but comfortable and well equipped, the small galley kitchen led through to a narrow corridor. A door led to a walk-in shower to the left and the four berth, two bunk sleeping quarters to the right. The tight walkway opened into living quarters, a padded bench seat covering all three walls with a low table fixed to the centre of the room. It was well lit and warm. Rina sipped coffee from a plastic mug wincing at the bitter taste.

"Sorry, no milk" Jack apologised as he took a swallow from his cup, grimacing himself at the concoction he'd found in the coffee jar.

Finding several towels in the tiny bathroom closet, he selected the one he thought was the softer and draped it around her neck. Rina relaxed on the bench seat opposite him, her legs curled up under her. He knew the tired dralon upholstery was a world away from the luxury she was accustomed to, but he was sure it was preferable to a sackcloth camp bed, complete with a booby trap. Under the light of the cabin, she radiated beauty. Her olive skin, smooth and unblemished, had a sheen like pure silk. A wispy silhouette framed her long black hair, the salt water causing a slight frizz that a photographer would charge a fortune to recreate. The way she tilted her head as she stared at the floor lost in thought made her look demure and vulnerable.

"Your father has a boat coming for you." He said, breaking the silence. "We rendezvous in fifteen minutes. Are you ready to meet him or do you want us to circle for a while?" It was a question he had to ask, to be sure she was in the right state of mind.

His mission was to deliver Abu's daughter to him unharmed, and that was his intention, but it was never as simple as it sounded. The emotional stress Zabrina had experienced could manifest as irrational outbursts, denial and in some cases, Stockholm syndrome. He had seen it many times before as the euphoria of the rescue fades, and the fear returns. The horror that sits within the recesses of the brain, waiting to pounce with little or no warning.

He had to be sure she was as strong as she seemed and a good rest was all she needed. She raised her eyes from the floor and looked into his. She appeared bright, alert and determined.

"I'm fine." She ran her fingers through the length of her hair, feeling for snags, checking for damp spots.

"What about you?" She gestured to his foot.

"I'm fine; I don't think it's broken. I'll be alright after a few day's rest." She deflected his question well. He took the conversation back to her.

"What do you plan to do now?" He was checking for any signs of stress.

"Oh, I'll have a few weeks at home, get pampered by the servants, showered with affection by my mother and lectured by father. Then I will return to England to finish my thesis." She replied, no hesitation, no embellishment, good.

"What about you?" She countered.

"Do you have a wife to go to? A girlfriend? What's your next mission? Another damsel in distress, perhaps? Tell me more about yourself, Jack." She was rattling off questions one after the other, deflecting from herself again.

"Not a lot to tell. No wife, no girlfriend and I have no idea what's next."

He wasn't sure whether she was playing him or if she was trying to avoid the questions for fear of bringing her demons out into the open. He needed to make sure she was ok, but she was making it hard for him. He tried once more.

"Are you close to your parents?" He leant forward, placing the empty cup on the table, watching her reaction

Rina returned his stare, following his movement as he settled back in his seat. This time she hesitated, studying him as if she was searching for the right thing to say. This could go one of two ways. She would either answer, choosing her words carefully or just babble. She could always keep talking until she was sure she had covered everything. She did neither.

She threw her cup at him. It bounced harmlessly on his shoulder, a small amount of coffee splattered his face, it was lukewarm.

"BASTARD!" She slid her legs from the bench and leaned forward, her eyes searing into his.

"What the fuck do you want me to say? Or, do you want me to curl up and blubber? I'm not some naïve tart who wants to please you and automatically bow to your handsome good looks because you are the great Jack whatever your name is! Nor am I one of your psychology experiments to be tested to see if I am sane enough to be put back into society." She stopped, sat up straight, narrowing her eyes. Her lips pursed as she thought for a moment. Her eyes widened, and she gasped incredulously.

"That's it, isn't it?" She spat the accusation at him.

"You're checking my emotional stability; you're psyching me out." She turned, picked up a cushion and made her way around the table towards him.

"You stupid wanker!"

Jack slid around the bench as she reached for him. She swung the cushion and missed. She followed him around and took another swing, but he continued to move out of her way. He caught his foot on the table edge, wincing in pain. This woman is a psycho, he thought as he held his throbbing ankle, waiting for the pounding to stop. Rina saw the pain etched on his face and stopped the pursuit. She threw the cushion at him, letting it bounce harmlessly over his head as he ducked.

They sat staring at each other for a moment, locking eyes and taking time to calm down, reflecting on the last few minutes. It was Rina who spoke first.

"How much background do you have on me?" She asked, keeping her voice level, devoid of emotion.

"Enough." He replied. He did have enough. He knew about her father, her schooling, her voluntary work, where she had been kidnapped. Everything he needed to succeed in his mission, as he had proven.

"Did you ever look into my studies at Cambridge? The subject I have spent the last three years perfecting?"

He continued to look at her.

"Psychology." He got there before she spoke and shook his head as he realised he had been out psyched.

"Exactly, Psychology, the study of the human Psyche, behavioural and mental processes of human emotion and the reasons why we do what we do." He blew out his cheeks and chuckled, he had read her all wrong. She was ready.

Rina was smiling, it had been quite an adventure.

She got to her feet, walked around the table and stood over him, her legs straddling him. She leaned forward and holding his shoulders, moved towards him, kissing him slowly and deliberately. He reached up to hold her waist, pulling her nearer. She pulled back and lifting her leg over his, turned around and sat down beside him.

"I'm sorry, I hit you." She said putting her hand on his.

"And thank you for saving my life." She rested her head on his shoulder. He moved his arm around her, allowing her head to nestle into his neck. Jack rarely found himself in a situation he couldn't handle. She intrigued him, and it disappointed him that he wouldn't have the time to learn more. But he knew it could never be.

It was a dangerous life, one he was destined to live alone. Too many organisations wanted him dead, and he would never willingly put someone in a position where they could become a target. They made the most of the respite, sitting together in a comfort zone they both embraced. A dreamlike state the steady rocking of the boat added to the sensation. It carried them away to a warm, comfortable place. Neither spoke, they didn't have to. It was a time when words were not required, leaving them with their thoughts.

The door to the upper deck opened, bringing the sounds of the sea into the cabin. Patrice called down from the top of the stairwell.

"Jack, I think you should come on deck and bring the young lady with you."

CHAPTER NINE
Reward

Sheikh Abdurrahman Rashad Bin Al Sharraff stood on the deck of the Seiner, with a bodyguard at each shoulder. They dwarfed their six foot boss by at least another foot. Both held M16s in their arms, fingers resting on the trigger guards. Their eyes followed Jack as he emerged from the cabin, his hand in Rina's as he helped her through the doorway. She turned to face him making sure she was side on from her father and with her obscured eye, winked at him. Bowing cordially she walked steadily towards the Sheik, stopping a few feet away to look at her father. Lowering her head in respect while keeping eye contact the whole time, then straightened. Her father continued to stare at her, running his eyes over her face. He showed no emotion as he surveyed the rest of her. He was checking for damage.

He was a handsome, young looking fifty-five. His clear olive skin enhanced by a neatly trimmed beard and a full head of jet black hair. His beard was trimmed around his chin, finishing with a sharp arrow point just below the centre of his mouth. His stunning amber eyes were mesmerising, oozing intelligence and guile, ideal in his role as the Middle East's foremost negotiator. He would be challenging to read in any situation. He was dressed impeccably for the evening in a tailored black dinner jacket, and highly polished hand made shoes. His eyes glistened with tears as he finished his inspection and opened his arms to her.

"My daughter." He beckoned, and she ran to him burying her head into his chest. Stroking her hair, he gently kissed her as he held her tight. The tears fell from his eyes as he closed them; she was safe. Time stood still as they embraced. Patrice eyed him quizzically from his position near the stairs. Returning his gaze, Jack gave a slight shrug of his shoulders. Who knows?

Moored on the Seiner's starboard bow was the Sheik's boat, The Esmerelda, a two hundred foot super yacht which towered over them and was three times longer. Lights along the deck and through the many windows bathed the smaller boat in fluorescence. This vessel would have been one of the smaller yachts owned by the Sheik and at thirteen million dollars, one of the cheapest. His Caribbean plaything, the deck of the Seiner being lower, meant the gangplank used for boarding had to be positioned at a less than perfect angle. It did not detract from its style, white with a carpeted walkway and luminescent handrails illuminated from within. It would not look out of place as an entrance to a Hollywood film premiere. The yacht, having eight bedrooms and nineteen staff quarters, was more like a small floating hotel. It was used to entertain clients around the millionaires' playground between Port of Spain and Port de France. For a business trip around the Caribbean Islands, it was a magnificent sales tool.

Placing both hands on his daughter's shoulders, the Sheik held Rina away from him.

"You have had quite an adventure, my daughter." The voice was soothing, sympathetic.

"Go now and rest." He gently moved her towards one guard who bowed to him, acknowledging his silent command.

Jack watched her climb the gangplank of the Esmerelda. As she was about to board, she stopped to look at him. She blew a kiss before the bulk of the bodyguard obliterated his view as he escorted her into the luxury she was born into.

"I am forever in your debt Mr…?" The Sheik enquired

"Jack." He replied "Just Jack."

"Yes, of course." He acknowledged with a bow.

"Jack, I have three million pounds ready to place in a bank account of your choice. Let me have the details, and it will be there by morning." He produced a gold cased notebook and Mont Blanc pen. Patrice gave a low whistle at the mention of the money, it was greeted with a contemptuous glance. Feigning a chore, he repositioned his hat and headed for the bridge, leaving the three men on deck. Jack looked at the proffered notebook and then back again.

"Thank you for your kind gesture, but it's unnecessary. The Agency will contact you shortly, and you can negotiate with them."

The Sheik smiled, continuing to hold the pad towards him.

"Believe me Jack, the Agency will be well rewarded. No, this is for you."

It could be the route to a new life. A way of leaving the Agency and the pain it brought with it. He had five years of excellent service behind him with a 100% record. He could lock the door on his Cornwall home and forget there was ever a life away from the tranquillity and clean air of his private life. Private life, that was a laugh he thought. He would never have a private life in the sense of living his life in private. He was a wanted man.

As Matt Collins, the pseudonym he used in his home town, his life in the safe house covertly patrolled by agency specialists and monitored 24/7. As Jack Case the wraith, number one in his field, he was wanted dead by governments, criminals, megalomaniacs and every other low life organisation. They had either been cleansed, obstructed or destroyed by the Agency and in particular by him. If he left, he would be dead within twenty-four hours. He also couldn't be sure if the Agency wouldn't see fit to remove him from existence if he ever resigned. He was a dangerous man. No amount of millions would ever give him back the life he once had. He led a life or death existence.

"I'm sorry sir, but I cannot accept." He knew there was a fine line between refusing and offending and he hoped he was not crossing that line now. Abu eyed the man before him. He liked him and could use a man like him to head his security force.

"I want you to work for me." He tried a different tack.

"Two million a year, total control of my security, full responsibility for hiring and firing. In fact, rewrite the protocol. It will be yours." This would get him the man he thought.

It made him smile. He was being hustled, and the Sheik was refusing to take no for an answer. After all, he was a proven negotiator. Once again he would not be swayed.

"Again, thank you for your kind offer, but I am an agency man, and I still have a role to play. Please accept my thanks but I must decline, and I mean no offence." Next time he might if the Sheik didn't stop. Sheik Al Sharraff placed the notebook and pen back into his jacket before withdrawing a business card from his top pocket.

"You are a remarkable man Jack, and I will never forget what you have done for my family. Here take this."

Jack took the proffered card.

"I have billions." He said casually.

"And more resources than most governments throughout the world." He dramatically swept his arm all around to demonstrate.

"You have my private number and mail. I am at your disposal. Whatever you need is yours, money, weapons, vehicles, anything."

Now that could be useful he thought, accepting the card.

"Thank you." He said as they shook hands. The Sheik held Jack's hand with his right and with his left hand, his wrist.

"Please use it as I want to reward you. No time limit, no monetary constraints, no conditions, oh, and another thing."

Now what? Hadn't he said no conditions?

"From now on call me Abu." He nodded to his guard as he turned away from Jack, walking towards the Esmerelda. They didn't look back as they boarded and disappeared inside.

Six crew dismantled the gangplank in no time. Within minutes the super-yacht was a shrinking silhouette in the backdrop of the new dawn, pushing aside the darkness of a memorable night. Jack looked up at the bridge.

"Patrice! Get us out of here!" The engines spluttered into life and the fishing boat, heading west by southwest, chugged steadily into open waters.

CHAPTER TEN
Goodbye

Warm afternoon sun bathed the memorial garden of St Peter's Church. The smell of fresh cut grass mixed with a variety of blooms filled the tranquil air with the sweet aroma of summer. Most of the residents of Mittand Burrow wanted to pay their last respects. Mourners lined the path leading to the Paxton mausoleum, each holding a single rose. Father Richards waited by the gates to the garden as they returned. He shook hands and thanked them for their attendance as they made their way down to the Manor House for the prearranged wake. Annabel Paxton-Thorn had asked for her husband's ashes to be housed in the family mausoleum within the beautifully tended garden. Both families readily accepted the request, and in the four weeks, it had taken to release the body, a section of the vestibule had been prepared in readiness. Colin's ashes were housed in an emerald and gold urn and placed in a small alcove within the marble walls. A brass plaque inscribed with the family name and the Thorn crest sat proudly below. Hanging from the walls on either side were two porcelain vases ready to accept roses from the mourners, by request of the widow. There was one other alcove alongside Colin's, and below it was a brass plaque bearing the name of Annabel Paxton-Thorn.

The cremation was a private ceremony held at the Lysbie crematorium.

The small cortege then returned to Mittand Burrow for a memorial service, open to anyone who wanted to pay their respects. There was no seat spare within the church, and they packed many more mourners into the nave, some even crowded in the porch to be a part of the ceremony. Colin had made many friends during his time in the village. Father Richards couldn't remember a service to match it for size.

"Great service, Vic." Derek Gant grabbed his hand and squeezed tight, grasping the priest's shoulder with his other hand as he pumped vigorously.

Not the best of form. But then again, that was Gant all over. He watched him as he walked away with Becky Willis clinging to his arm for dear life. She teetered down the stone steps to street level on five inch Jimmy Choos. It was a far cry from her usual daily choice of Wellington boots, a prerequisite for cleaning the cowsheds on Horley farm. Other mourners passed them on the stairs as Gant had to help her down each step, giving her enough time to steady her feet before she attempted the next one.

Gant, always a confident boy, had developed a definite spring in his step since the death of his partner and it hadn't gone unnoticed by the locals. He was spending more time in the area and as it was more convenient, had stayed as a guest at the Manor House as he attempted to keep the practice running.

This regularity had started tongues wagging. Gant made matters worse by spending far too much time in the Fleece. His approach was to splash more money than most locals earned in a month, to try to make a name for himself. The name he made was 'grave robber' as his attempts at drumming up trade had alienated many, including existing clients who had started to look elsewhere.

Father Richards had been a regular visitor to the Manor House during the last four weeks, providing comfort and support to the widow. He was more than sure Gant's arrangement was purely professional, although the villagers would take some convincing. It was not, however, his place to pass judgement. He continued to watch the young couple as they reached street level, walking the perimeter of the green as they made their way to the Manor House, Becky moving no better on a level surface than she had on the stairs. It could take them a while he thought, smiling to himself.

"Father?" Father Richards turned to see Annabel Paxton-Thorn standing before him. She looked beautiful, dressed in a black forties style flowing gown with the buttons of the bodice modestly fitted to her neck. She wore a pillbox hat with a full veil which misted her kohl rimmed eyes and deep red lips, giving her the look of Hollywood.

"Thank you for your kind words, it was a wonderful ceremony." She held his hand gently in hers.

"I think Colin would be pleased." He replied.

"He will be looking down right now, feeling comforted by the turnout today."

"Watching them eat and drink us out of house and home you mean." Major Paxton was standing behind his daughter. He moved a step back as he realised he had verbalised his thoughts.

"Father! How dare you at a time like this." Annabel spun and confronted him before sobbing uncontrollably. The Major went to her and took her hand to soothe her, but she snatched it away, moving down the stone steps to get away from him.

Eliza Winch, struggling to stem her tears with the smallest of handkerchiefs, stood underneath a willow which seemed to bow as if in respect. She watched Annabel approach and held out her arms. They collapsed into each other, gently rocking as the emotion of the day took hold. Their sobs of despair carried on the light breeze of the quiet afternoon.

Both women shared the grief for the man she loved. One had always loved him even though he had never known, and one had realised too late that he was her life. Annabel had lost the love for her husband. He became so wrapped up in everything else, he had forgotten about her. But it was only now, looking back over the last five years, realisation finally dawned that she was also to blame.

She longed for the attention Colin used to give her in the early days. But as he worked harder and longer to provide the lifestyle she was used to and expected, she sought affection elsewhere. She would avoid him as punishment, spending all her time with the stable hands; it was her way of getting back at him for his neglect.

He did nothing wrong; he was just working hard to provide her with everything she had ever wanted. She had come from a privileged background, but it was Colin who had made her wealthy. She would gladly give up all the wealth for a chance to turn back the clock. The last four weeks had taught her you never really know what you have until it's gone, and she missed him.

Eliza had lost nothing as she had nothing in the first place, but it hadn't stopped her from having the worst month of her life. Her dreams were shattered, her world crushed, and she felt like she had no reason to live. Remarkably, a week after the death of Colin, and when she was at her lowest ebb, she had a visitor who pulled her back from the brink, Annabel Paxton-Thorn. Annabel had known of Eliza's infatuation with her husband and had always found it sweet, in a way she was pleased. It seemed funny looking back, how proud she felt knowing her husband had such an attractive admirer. Eliza put her in the shade when it came to age, looks and figure.

But she had been confident and arrogant enough to know Colin would never stray. It resulted in a very dismissive attitude towards the whole notion. Annabel now envied Eliza for maintaining her love for him, all those years spent working alongside him, right up to the last day of his life.

She needed to feed off it during her time of remorse although it was difficult at first. Eliza could see no failings in Colin, and she carried his torch as a burden. But as they talked, to reminisce and get to know each other, Annabel realised how lucky they had been to know him. Blessed to have loved him and to remember him for the man he really was. They were now hugging unashamedly on the streets of Mittand Burrow in a union of friendship and pain. A union through the love of one man who had changed their lives forever. They were joined in their grief and pain; it helped in the healing and supported their resolve. They would overcome it together.

After a short while, they moved apart. Eliza placed her hands on Annabel's shoulders and looked into her swollen eyes.

"Are you Ok?" Eliza dabbed the widow's eyes with a new handkerchief taken from the plentiful supply in her handbag.

"Not really… You?" Annabel returned the favour with her well used handkerchief.

"No, not at all." Eliza's lip trembled again.

Annabel gently kissed Eliza on the cheek.

"Come on, let's go…" Annabel wrapped Eliza's arm in hers as they set off.

Father Richards and Major Paxton watched the ladies forlornly make their way to the house. Brigadier Warren Thorn joined them at the gate having stayed behind to help the warden seal the Mausoleum.

"Thank you, Gerald." Brigadier Thorn firmly grasped the priest's hand.

"Colin would have liked that." Warren Thorn, resplendent in full military dress, towered over the two men.

At seventy-two he had developed a slight stoop, although he carried himself as straight as he could and with dignity. But his eyes showed his desolation. He had always been a deliberate man, a 'why say ten words when three will do' matter of fact man. He did not suffer fools lightly and had a deep monotone voice which lacked emotion. It allowed him to gain attention as soon as he opened his mouth, ideal in his regimental career. But now it had lost its edge, he was subdued, broken, and had not been seen for the last month until today.

He suffered three weeks of police investigation. Guards posted continuously at his home and question after question about Colin, his friends and enemies, clients, anyone he had recently been in contact with, in the weeks leading up to the shooting.

By the time they finally released his son's body, having drawn a complete blank, the Brigadier had become a shadow of his former self. The killer had been hiding in the loft of the pool house. But apart from the smashed latch to gain access and the broken glass from the small circular porthole used to take the shot, there was no real evidence. The investigation was ongoing, but the crime appeared to have all the signs of a professional hit with carefully covered tracks. The house had been searched but not ransacked. Taking the keys from Colin's dead body they had entered and disabled the alarm. It appeared their purpose had been the contents of the safe on the first floor landing, behind a reproduction Monet. There was £5000 in fifties, a Rolex and a diamond necklace, handed down to her granddaughter from the Dowager. They remained untouched. Annabel was at a loss to think of what else had been in the safe. Colin must have put something in there unbeknown to her, but there were no clues as to what it might have been. As far as she was aware, there had been no strangers in the house in the previous month. The cleaners were residents known to them. Mrs Claridge and her two daughters, who had been cleaning for the Paxtons for years, were discounted almost immediately.

Police had set a mobile incident room on the green and one by one they questioned the residents about Colin. They investigated every avenue, his marriage, his relationship with his father, his business partner, his friends. But each time no new evidence came to light.

After ten days they dismantled the incident room. The noticeable police presence reduced to two officers posted at the Manor House, two at Paxton House and two with the Brigadier. A patrol car toured three times a day, morning noon and night, but there was a feeling amongst the locals that it was a wasted exercise. They were running out of ideas.

The police were still keen to maintain a presence for fear it may prove to be a vendetta against one or both of the families involved. The DI assigned to the case, Walsh, didn't give a lot away apart from the fact that they were continuing with their enquiries. He had said the pathologist's report had helped but wasn't prepared to elaborate. Even the Major's relationship with the Commissioner shed no new light on the investigation. He had the feeling they were not telling them everything.

"Come on Warren, we should get over there." Major Paxton gently placed a hand on the Brigadier's shoulder while gingerly negotiating the steps leading to the Manor House.

"See you over there, Gerald?" He called back to the priest who was watching the military men of yesteryear amble across the village green.

He waved in confirmation, turned and walked back into the church. He locked the heavy oak door preparing to finish up and join his parishioners in celebrating the life of Colin Thorn. The two long term comrades dawdled towards the Manor House in silence for a while, contemplating the consequences of the day.

It was a pleasant afternoon, the sunbathing the grounds with a golden warmth while the birds sang happy songs oblivious to the sombre mood. Usually on such a pleasant afternoon, the green would be full of families enjoying the sun. Children playing happily, sun worshippers sleeping or picnicking. The town's orchestra playing gentle sounds in the colourful bandstand, and the familiar aroma of hot dogs filling the air, while ice cream vans offered more cooling

:reats. A relaxed, happy time and a community in harmony.

Today all was silent as the village mourned.

"I wish we didn't have to do this damned thing, Reggie." Brigadier Thorn said as they approached the big house.

He remembered the day the young couple moved in. It was a similar day to today, the sun shining, a warmth in the air and a happiness he could touch. He could still see the proud look in his son's eyes as he realised he now owned this beautiful piece of history.

"I know what you mean." Major Paxton offered.

"But it is what Colin would have wanted, and it might help us all to get over these last few weeks." The Brigadier countered.

"That it may." Paxton agreed. "But once this is over I will not rest until they bring the killer to justice. This horror has destroyed my daughter." He tended to speak first and think later. The inappropriate timing of his last statement registered at the same time as it escaped his mouth and he turned to apologise. Thorn held his hand up to stop him.

"It's Ok Reggie, I know what you mean, but life goes on. We need to remember Colin but also understand that we are all experiencing a loss and perhaps this 'event' is what we need." He gestured towards the house as they approached the garden.

Major Reginald Paxton was a selfish man, and it would take one hell of a situation for his main concerns not to be about himself. The death of Colin had been an inconvenience to his elevation into the establishment. It was where he belonged, and Thorn was helping him get there. But it had been put on hold just as he was about to get his invitation. Justice Pickard had cancelled his ball out of respect for the Brigadier.

Delores Cranbourn had postponed the hunt, and they had forced him to cancel his dinner party to observe the mourning period. But he was running out of time.

The next meeting at the Masonic Hall in Winchurch was in four months, and he had an inkling, at last, that he was about to be proposed. Members included a Justice of the Peace, four barristers, three MPs the Commissioner and the Brigadier. They were only the ones already known to him. Most of the influencers he needed in his life were members. It was the final piece for his entry into the set to be assured. He had to be invited, be initiated and develop through the ranks. He was oblivious to the fact that he would never be invited.

He had to find the killer or be seen to be the one to have put it all together. The Commissioner had blocked him, and he could glean nothing from the DI.

He soon discovered his influence in all other areas of the investigation was non-existent, and it would not do. If he could be the one to put the wheels in motion and succeed, he would have Thorn in his pocket, forever in his debt. And he knew exactly who he needed to contact.

It meant calling in a favour and splashing a lot of cash, but money was the least of his concerns to win the ultimate prize. That was priceless.

Two officers stood guard at each side of the entrance to the gardens. One of them moved sharply to swing open the heavy iron gate, standing to attention as the two men walked through.

Instinctively the military men saluted and were pleased to see it returned as a mark of respect to their rank.

CHAPTER ELEVEN
Sombre Party

The cellos wove the soothing melody of The Swan by Camille Saint-Saens around the magnificent garden of the Manor House, providing a soothing atmosphere for the mourners as they arrived in their numbers. Waiters circulated amongst the guests with silver trays of champagne. It helped with the initial awkwardness, as locals mixed with the gentry in an unprecedented show of unity. They ranged from nearby farmers and local business people to the upper echelons of society. They included the Commissioner, the Chief Justice, two local MPs and Delores Cranbourn.

Today and for the next few hours, they stood shoulder to shoulder in memory of Colin Thorn.

"… And of course, she gets everything. That's all we need. Like father like daughter." Linda Norwood polished off her third glass and swiftly caught a waitress as she passed by, replacing her empty vessel with a full one.

"Of course I am sorry for the Brigadier and his son. He was a lovely lad and deserved better than that. Mind you, marrying into that family would always end in disaster." She looked over the shoulder of Janice Carrington as she spotted Muriel Corbett.

"Muriel … MURIEL!" She waved her glass in the air until her target looked her way. Then she thoughtlessly barged through the crowd making a beeline for her next victim, her glass spilling its contents as she passed.

"She never lets up, does she." Tom Carrington said to his wife as he wiped a patch of spilt wine from his sleeve.

"She'll never let it go, I'm afraid. She went through a lot when Roland died. I feel a little sorry for her." Janice Carrington watched Muriel Corbett trying her best to be cordial to Linda.

She winced at some things she was saying, no doubt regarding the Paxtons.

"Well, I don't. She brought a lot on herself with her attitude. It amazes me that some people have anything to do with her; she's an awful woman." Janice slapped her husband's arm playfully.

The Carringtons were the owners of the Golden Fleece and had been joint landlords for twenty years. They saw all the comings and goings and had an advantage over most. They were sober as the truth serum in the form of real ale, fine wine and quality liqueur was poured. The locals openly discussed the stories and rumours, voices becoming louder as the drink flowed. There was nothing hidden in the Golden Fleece, its walls had been soaking it all up for over two hundred years.

When Roland committed suicide over four years ago, the village became a hotbed of rumour and innuendo; gossip, lies and half truths. The Major had warned off many of the locals from casting aspersions on his good name. Most of the farms, stores and businesses local to Mittand Burrow were in deep with the Major. Due to his commercial agricultural enterprises, they could ill afford to lose the revenue. So they abandoned Linda Norwood, leaving her to grieve alone.

The Golden Fleece had been a haven for her. The Carringtons were not reliant on the Paxtons and would not be drawn into the situation. They had helped Linda as much as they could. She was even giving the use of one of their guest rooms after the loss of her home. Linda was not one to ask for help. She was also not forthcoming with any show of appreciation. But in her own way she was grateful to the Carringtons and would have nothing said against them. Janice became a close friend of hers. She often helped with the various group meetings Linda organised. They even offered the function room for the reading group once a month.

Tom didn't get such an easy time. It was like being married to two women, one he shared a bed with while the other controlled his life. She would lecture Janice on the error of Tom's ways and then criticise the way they ran the pub.

She attempted to change the menus for the restaurant, voicing her ideas on the decor. She even tried negotiating with the brewery. She complained that the ales were wrong for the area, the choice of optics were poor, and they needed a more varied selection of wines. This interference caused arguments when she wasn't around, leading Tom to try his best to avoid the woman. He loved his wife, and he hated rowing, they rarely did before Linda arrived, so he would always find a reason to remain out of the picture.

Funnily enough, they upgraded the ales, added new wines to the stock, and offered a wider range of optics. It riled Tom and hurt his pride, but he had to admit it had been a success. Trade was up by half.

She was a remarkable woman, but there were times, for which he now felt ashamed when he felt Roland was better off where he was.

Derek Gant left Becky with the Reynolds girls and went into the house in search of Annabel. It was vital that he was seen to be caring for the grieving widow, particularly with the Major around. He had to protect his investment. He also wasn't one hundred percent sure she hadn't played out her fantasy.

Colin was dead, and it seemed to have been a professional hit. Annabel had the inclination and the cash at her disposal to have easily arranged the murder. He was reasonably sure she hadn't, as she had been in a right state since his death. But then again, she was deranged. She could play the role of the devastated widow to cover her tracks. He didn't want to know and to be honest, didn't care. He would keep his head down and just rake in the pound notes.

He made his way through the kitchen, squeezing past the chefs as they prepared the spread of game, fish, entrees and pastries. He skillfully dodged the waiters as they buzzed around, collecting the prepared trays and discarding the empties. Passing through the hall, he spotted her in the drawing room talking to her father. She was sitting, head bowed, on a chaise longue dabbing at her eyes.

"But Daddy, I can't do this. I want Colin." She stifled her sobs in the now soggy handkerchief.

"Darling, this is what Colin would have wanted. We have to be there for our guests. Life goes on, and he would not want to see you like this."

"Life goes on. That is typical of you." She held the handkerchief in her lap as she lifted her head and looked him in the eye.

"Shall we tell Colin that life goes on? Oh, no we can't; HE'S DEAD!"

"Control yourself, girl!" Major Paxton stood to attention to give himself a few extra inches.

"Think of the family, we don't behave in this way. Now pull yourself together and get out there and greet your guests." He had lost his composure, he had to calm her down. Did she not understand who was out there?

"No father, YOU go out and meet YOUR people." She was shouting now. The Major rocked on his heels, taken aback at being talked to this way.

"I am not taking orders from you, and I won't do anything for 'The Family'" She waggled two fingers at him as she emphasised the reference.

"Just go away and leave me alone. And stop being such a pompous ass, at least for today." She finished.

"How dare you…"

"JUST GO!" Annabel screamed in his face as she stood to confront him, pointing at the door.

The Major huffed and mumbled as he left her and headed for the door, brushing past Derek as he moved sharply out of the way to let him into the hall.

"See what you can do with her, will you?" He spoke from the corner of his mouth as he stormed off.

Annabel screamed in frustration and paced the room as Derek entered.

"Oh great! Now I've got the leech visiting me."

"Whoa! Steady on old girl. I'm only here to see that you are OK." He said defensively holding his arms up in front of his chest. Annabel looked at him with a resigned smile.

"I know you are." She said as she walked towards him. To his surprise, she grabbed the lapels of his suit jacket and shoved him against the wall, pushing her weight fully into him. Her mouth was so close to his ear, he could feel the heat of her breath in his ear canal.

"You slimy little bastard!" She whispered through gritted teeth.

"Had he not been killed, Colin would've got rid of you, you bloodsucking piece of shit!" The venom was real, she had been waiting for this moment.

"You have a choice, and one week to make your decision." She eased off and stood apart from him.

"I want you gone from my life, this family and the business. You either resign, and I will pay you off with what I feel your miserable contribution is worth. Or make me an offer for my side of the business and ruin it on your own. Or, I'll sack you and tie you up in court for so many years, you will draw your pension before you get any money from me." Her eyes bore into his as she gave him time to let her words sink in.

His confidence had gone. It was a vicious onslaught brought on in part by the occasion and partly because her father had already wound her up. But her underlying feelings towards him were clear, and he could see he would need to take action. Derek adjusted himself, trying to press the crease marks from his lapels, giving him time to compose himself to speak.

"Annabel, calm down, please." It was all he could say to ease the situation. He would leave his charm and wit in his locker for another time.

"I wanted to check on you as I didn't see you among the guests. I just came to see if there was anything you needed."

"The only thing I need right now is for my husband to walk through that door and tell me that everything will be fine. Can you arrange that for me?" She looked at him questionably.

"Thought not." She stated. "So, the next best thing is for you to fuck off forever. I want you out of my sight, my business and my life. Got it?"He looked at her. She had lifted the veil, and apart from a slight puffiness around her eyes, she looked beautiful. The mascara was tsunami proof, and her scarlet lips added drama to her features, emphasising her perfect mouth. Lowering his gaze, he moved towards the door.

"I will ask my accountant to look at the books over the next week and come back to you with my decision. I'll make sure the outcome will be beneficial to both of us." He left the room.

"The best outcome for me would be never to have to look at your smarmy little face again." She said, following him out before turning and heading up the stairs to her bedroom.

"FUCK!" He thought it would be easier than this.

After Colin died, he should have been head of the practice. Annabel had no experience, he assumed that it would leave her high and dry with Derek as her only option to keep things afloat. Clearly, she had other plans. Could he afford to buy her out? He wasn't sure; it depended on the accountant. In the meantime, he would check on the viability of the current cases and look at the costs going forward, including staff. Lizzie was an excellent legal secretary, but she was Colin through and through and would have to go. Would his pay off be worthwhile if he resigned? Probably not, having only a 30% stake. It would last him a year or two, and he would be back where he started. Option three was not an option, he would not let her sack him.

On his way through the kitchen Gant grabbed a whisky bottle, he threw the screw top into the waste and scooped half a glass of ice from the bucket. Pouring himself a drink he entered the sunlit garden, wincing gratefully as it burnt down his throat.

Sauntering through the guests he found Becky with the postie, Bellham. Gant smiled to himself, taking another gulp of single malt.

"You've got no chance mate." Chuckling he walked towards them.

CHAPTER TWELVE
Unwelcome Guest

After thirty minutes, lightly seasoned by half a bottle of vodka diluted with a splash of soda, Annabel felt composed. She returned to the celebration of her husband's life, having changed into a stunning full length red dress from her Terani collection. Her hair had been pushed back to accommodate a dazzling diamond tiara that sparkled in the diminishing rays of the setting sun. She felt a million dollars.

All heads turned as she entered the garden, standing on the steps that led onto the lawn, where most of the guests were situated. The hum of conversation carried on the light breeze.

Taking a champagne flute from one of the passing waiters, she tapped the rim with her engagement ring, to bring all conversation to a lull, eventually to silence. She had used her time well since the murder to take stock of her life and had worked tirelessly to begin the process of change. This day was the first day of the rest of her life. She looked around at her guests before taking a deep breath and beginning her speech.

"Well, this is a wonderful turnout. Colin would have been thrilled." So far so good!

"I know it has taken a while for all of you to visit us. For some of you this has probably been a difficult trip to make." She scanned the crowd until she found Linda Norwood who was staring blankly at the woman in red.

"I would just like to say that although we felt like real outsiders when we first arrived, I feel very much part of the village and I know Colin did too." She choked a sob as she spoke his name taking a moment to compose herself.

She held her forefinger under her nostrils to stem the flow of emotion that was coursing through her body. It brought whispers of 'ah' and 'shame' from the guests.

After a short while, she dropped her hand and continued.

"I am staying." She stated, scanning faces for any signs of disdain. None came.

"And if you will let me, I would like to contribute to our community far more than we have in the past. Colin had wanted to for years but because of his tireless efforts with the practice, he could never find enough time."

That got their attention.

"So first of all, I will pay for the renovation of the village hall. I have arranged for work to begin in five days. Secondly, if I am allowed, I would like to build a new cricket pavilion in my husband's name." A ripple of applause began throughout the crowd, gaining momentum until all were in unison.

It was news to her father and breaking away from his group, which inevitably included Brigadier Thorn, he made his way towards her. What the hell was she doing? She saw him heading her way and hastily lifted her hand to bring those gathered back to silence.

"One more thing and father, stay where you are." Major Paxton stopped dead and with his trademark huff, placed a hand into his pocket while looking up at his daughter. He couldn't help but feel a sense of pride at how she had taken charge. Was she getting at him? Paranoia was now hugging the Major like a long lost friend.

She was in control now and would have no one spoil this moment. She opened her red designer bag and pulled out a small brown package. With careful grace, she unfurled it until it turned into a four page A4 booklet. She smoothed the creases with one hand, rubbing it up and down the front of her dress until, with a snap, she raised it in the air.

"I have bought the old rectory, and the good doctors have accepted my offer of a new practice by the Library, much more appropriate; I hope you would all agree." There were gasps from the crowd and a wail from the direction of Linda Norwood. Annabel descended the steps, moving deliberately through her guests. They watched in silence as she passed by them. That was apart from the sorry sobs of the lady who had once called the rectory her home.

She stopped in front of Linda, and their eyes met. Linda, looking up at the widow and with Janice helping her to stand, glared at the younger woman.

"I suppose you are here to gloat, huh? Haven't your family done enough, no, of course, you haven't, you just needed to add one more twist of that knife?" She spat the words out with a venom tempered only by the amount of alcohol already consumed. Spittle peppered Annabel's face. Some of it failed to make the journey and dribbled slowly down Linda's chin.

Annabel looked at Linda smiling sympathetically, she had learnt a lot about the locals over the last few weeks. The sincere well wishers, people she had never met before but who Colin had taken time to befriend. Annabel wanted to help make amends for some of the historical issues caused, in the most part by her family. Before she treated her to another tirade, she offered the booklet to Linda.

"These are the deeds to the rectory. They are yours Linda, Colin and I want you to have your home back." Again the crowd gasped.

Linda Norwood fainted.

There was a stunned silence as the guests watched the drama unfold. The Carringtons were reviving Linda while everyone else either looked on or looked at each other.

The loud squeal of the entry gate as it swung open diverted their attention. Accompanied by one officer on guard, was a new guest. He was a tall well built man in his mid fifties, wearing a black silk tie in honour of the occasion and a perfectly tailored black suit. He was well groomed with a full head of hair swept back to expose tanned chiselled features. He adjusted his cuffs as he scanned the crowd.

"Ed?" Commissioner Burrows frowned as he set eyes on him.

For a man of his condition, Major Paxton made the gap disappear between himself and the visitor in seconds.

"Good afternoon Ed, glad you could make it." He shook his hand vigorously.

"Hi Reggie, good to see you again, it's been a while." The American accent, totally out of place in the quintessentially English surroundings.

"Can I offer you a drink?" Reggie Paxton waved his hands toward a waiter who arrived with a full tray. The American helped himself and took a small sip, looking around the garden as the champagne livened his mouth.

"Nice place you have here." He said, taking particular notice of the pool house.

"Ed Ryker, good to see you." The Commissioner who had been following pushed past the Major offering his hand in greeting.

"Harry Burrows. Good to see you too." Ed smiled perfect white teeth.

Paxton noticed the handshake and felt surplus to requirements. Ed was on the square, he secretly boiled inside. It was all developing around him, making him feel even more of an outsider, and that would not do. He needed an invitation; he had to be included in this. He was hoping to use Ed Ryker to his advantage, and felt his confidence return, realising how this could be a blessing in disguise.

"Shall we find somewhere a little more private?" Major Paxton suggested.

"Sure." Ed replied.

"Lead the way."

"What are you up to Reggie?" Commissioner Burrows stopped them in their tracks. He was sensing someone was treading on his patch.

"Oh, nothing really, I just want to pick Ed's brains for a few minutes. We'll be back before you know it." Paxton waved his hands dismissively as he walked past.

Ed followed him but not before he glanced at the Commissioner, showing it was a little more than that. A look of concern and a slight nod towards Major Paxton as a sign to follow. Only slight, but enough to cause the Commissioner to look towards the rest of the guests.

Commissioner Burrows knew there was trouble if it involved Ed, worse still he knew nothing about it, which perplexed him. He searched the garden and saw the Brigadier helping Linda, settling her in the seat provided. He had just passed a glass of water to the stricken woman when Burrows grabbed him by the elbow and leant forward to whisper in his ear.

"Warren, we have a problem. Can I have a word?"

The Brigadier helped Linda take a few sips of the water, she couldn't manage it herself as her hands were shaking so hard she would have soaked herself. He passed the glass to Janice Carrington to take over.

"Ed Ryker is here." Burrows whispered, escorting the Brigadier away from the group.

"What! How?" Brigadier Thorn looked stunned.

"Reggie invited him. They are having a few minutes so he can pick Ed's brains, so they told me. But I think Ed wants us to join him." Thorn's eyes narrowed as he contemplated the news.

"Where are they?" He walked towards the house.

The Commissioner caught up with him.

"REGGIE!" Thorn shouted as he marched along the hallway, leaning into each room as he passed by. Enquiring eyes looked through from the kitchen as he slammed each door before moving on. He found them in the study.

The Brigadier stormed into the room followed closely by the Commissioner.

Ed Ryker was sitting on an Eames lounger while Major Paxton leant against the white ash desk. As they both turned towards the door, Paxton jumped out of his skin, standing instinctively to attention.

"Reggie, what's going on here?" Thorn towered over the Major forcing him back to lean once more against the desk. Throughout his fifteen years in the village, Major Paxton became accustomed to giving orders, well used to belittling people. He had confidence stemming from his wealth and the military, he was feared by those less fortunate which he thrived on. He now felt two feet tall and didn't know what to do.

"Hi Warren, long time no see." Ed approached the Brigadier, hand extended. Thorn turned and faced the American. He shook his hand, that handshake again!

"Hi Ed, good to see you, although it is somewhat of a surprise." He looked back at the Major to emphasise the point.

"I'm sorry to hear about your son, must have been a hell of a shock. I hear he was a fine boy, my condolences." Ed was defusing the situation.

"Thank you, and I apologise for barging in on your conversation. Been one of those days, I'm afraid and then when Harry told me you were here…" He paused as he looked him in the eye.

"What's going on, Ed?"

"I called him." Paxton had composed himself.

"I wanted him to help with the investigation."

"Are you mad!" Commissioner Burrows had been a bystander until now.

"What the hell would LARA want with a rural murder case? We have it under control."

"Do you?" Paxton had his chance to elevate his position, and this was the moment.

"You've investigated for a month. You've had every man, woman and child in the village interrogated, fingerprinted and dismissed. The pathologist has nothing, and you have been deliberately evasive when we try to get information. Are we expected to let them get away with this….He was our son!" The last statement was for effect, but once it was out, he realised it was true. He saw his daughter's husband as a son and had loved him as one.

Brigadier Thorn reacted by placing a hand on the Major's shoulder, squeezing gently.

"Thank you, Reggie. I know you meant well."

The Major lowered his head, 'that did it' he thought as he kept his head down, hiding his smile.

"Well, sorry to put a dampener on this, but I cannot allow it. This is a police matter, a LOCAL police matter." The Commissioner looked at each of them as he made his point.

"We will continue with our investigation. I have some of my best men on this, and I assure you we will have answers sooner rather than later. So I'm sorry to have wasted your time Ed, but this is way out of your jurisdiction."

Ed relaxed back into the lounger, looking up at Commissioner Burrows, studying him for a moment.

"I'm sorry to spoil the party Harry, but LARA has been assigned."

It was Thorn who reacted first.

"What, no… you can't, how much has he paid you." He looked at the Major.

"Whatever it is we will pay you 10% more to go away. Harry has told you he is handling this, I am confident he will come good. Ed, we cannot have this going outside the village, we have a community, a tourist economy and a damned good force headed by this man." He gestured toward the Commissioner.

"And a dead son?" Ed left it in the air and watched them react.

The Brigadier turned and glared at the American.

Ed Ryker, Head of LARA, an organisation hidden from the world and only recognised by officialdom on a need to know basis. A way for world governments to pass the buck and come away clean if it went wrong. LARA preferred this as it enabled them to complete missions their way, without red tape and protocols.

He remembered the first time they met over twenty years ago when as a Navy Seal he was posted to the UK under the Brigadier's wing, something neither of them wanted. Due to some unpleasantness during the conflicts in Panama, the US needed him out of the way. It was the British Army who ended up with him, which Ed always saw as punishment and after tours of duty in Greece, Northern Ireland and Germany, he went AWOL.

He gave himself up after a few years travelling, returning to the US to be formally court marshalled. He then disappeared, enrolling in LARA as a wraith, the seek and destroy team and it fitted him like a glove. He always brought trouble wherever he went, now trouble came to him. He proved to be lethal, as well as a born leader which helped him steadily move up the chain of command. Seven years ago, just as the Brigadier was due to retire, he received a call from LARA headquarters to be introduced to the new chief, Ed Ryker. The bad penny had returned. It was a short call as the Brigadier wanted nothing to do with LARA and in particular Ryker. He was retiring, so it was easy to dismiss him.

Now he was sitting here in front of him, a little older and perhaps wiser, but still a dangerous man.

"Sorry Ed, I can't allow it." It was the Commissioner again. He looked over to Major Paxton.

"Give Reggie the money back. We don't need this right now."

"He's not paying." Ed remained seated and drained his glass, resting it on a small side table.

"This is from high up, a national security issue and like it or not we are in this together." All three men looked at him as if he had just grown a second head.

Commissioner Burrows found a chair nearby and sat down heavily. Brigadier Thorn chose the Rococo bench seat, and Major Paxton froze for the second time in as many minutes.

"This is ridiculous." Burrows could feel his authority weakening.

"Where has this come from? Colin was a solicitor, not a spy. What has this got to do with him?"

"It's nothing to do with Colin exactly…"

"What do you mean by exactly?" The Brigadier interrupted.

"He was a bloody solicitor, didn't you hear the man? He wasn't involved in anything illegal, he was a quiet family man. He had never been in trouble in his life!"

"It wasn't why he was killed, it was how." Ed continued.

"He was killed with a Black Talon."

CHAPTER THIRTEEN
No Choice

Major Paxton looked over to the Police Commissioner.

"Did you know about this Harry?"

Harry Burrows looked perplexed. He knew nothing of this and wanted to know why he hadn't been given this information first. Ed stepped in at this point.

"Harry would never have been informed. The pathologist's report followed protocol and stated that a ten millimetre dumdum killed Colin. So we would base the investigation around the gun used by the shooter and not the bullet used to kill him."

"So how did you find out it was a Black Talon?" Brigadier Thorn leaned forward with his hands pressed firmly on his knees

"That was thanks to a very bright intern at the University of Oxford." Ed explained.

"Scott Mallion, a young student over here from LA, was on assignment in the lab with your guys when they did the autopsy. He recognised the talons from the extracted bullet and reported it to his tutor during one of the discussion groups."

"The tutor contacted a colleague in the Metropolitan police. It's something they encourage them to do if they uncover anything unusual. It was bounced to every department, shoved along like a hot potato until it landed in our lap."

Commissioner Burrows stood up and with his hands in his pockets paced the room.

"Ballistics is not one of my strong points I must admit. So perhaps someone can tell me why the Black Talon is so significant."

"It's a hollow point, taken out of circulation in the late 90s before being discontinued completely in 2000." Ed began.

"It was used primarily by law enforcement agencies in the US and the military as an enhancement to the standard dumdum."

Finally, he was getting through to them, having now gained their full attention.

"Instead of just mushrooming on contact as all hollow points do, the Black Talon, as it mushrooms, exposes razor sharp petals or talons that rip into the body. It grips onto the inner organs ensuring that it does not ricochet or exit the victim. It was known as the Cop Killer."

Ed looked over to the Brigadier as he bowed his head and sighed.

"I'm sorry Warren, I should have…" The Brigadier interrupted before he could complete his apology.

"No, it's fine Ed, go on…" his head still bowed, asking him to continue.

"The bullets were removed from public sale in 1993. They were issued to law enforcement officers and the military only until withdrawn completely." Ed continued.

"But who's saying that you can't still get the bullets? You can get anything on the internet these days." It was Paxton who made the point. He had bought many strange objects using e-commerce.

"That is true." Ed agreed.

"But they don't come filled with Curare."

The other three men looked at each other.

"A drug that causes paralysis to skeletal muscles." Ed looked over to the Brigadier.

"Are you sure you want to do this Warren?" Warren Thorn had joined the Commissioner pacing the study, his head still lowered, but more in despair than in thought.

"Keep going, Ed, we're here now." He said wearily.

Ed knew this would be hard for him to hear, but he could think of no way to dilute it without avoiding the facts.

"Curare is an old drug, an ancient drug. The first recorded reports were in 1596 by Sir Walter Raleigh of the natives of South America using poison-tipped arrows. It's a plant toxin indigenous to the area, used to paralyse the prey to guarantee the kill." Thorn raised his head and stared at the American.

"So they paralysed my son before he died?" He said it slowly and deliberately as each word struggled to leave his lips.

"No Warren, he would not have suffered as he was shot cleanly in the heart. It would have been instant." Ed tried to soften the blow even though he couldn't be one hundred percent sure himself. Had it not been instant, the drug would have paralysed Colin. The pain of the wound would have been excruciating as muscle reflex and reactions would be nullified.

It was more than he was willing to mention. Brigadier Thorn didn't answer, he nodded, either satisfied or appreciative that Ed had not elaborated further.

"No… wait, wait… that can't be right." Commissioner Burrows rounded on Ed, a deep furrow had developed on his forehead.

"I saw the pathologist's report. The autopsy said nothing about Curare or any poison of any description."

"It was classified." Ed explained.

"It was pure coincidence that at about the same time I received the call from the Major to invite me to this meeting, Colin's file appeared on my desk. We immediately cordoned off the whole investigation and our guys moved in. When we discovered the Curare, we left it out of the report to you. We changed it."

"You changed it!" Burrows looked at Ryker incredulously.

"I can't believe I'm hearing this. You have kept all my staff, the team, my whole operation in the dark this whole time? What gives you the right…"

"The Official Secrets Act, national security and powers far higher than you and I give me the right." He had to meet this head on Ed realised, otherwise they would waste time casting aspersions all night.

"Harry, the only reason you weren't told until now is that I was coming here anyway. I deemed it far better to speak to you in person than to have you read it in a memo. You of all people should see that."

A twitch appeared just above the Commissioners left eye as he deliberated on his next move. He reluctantly had to agree. In the same circumstances, he would have done the same. He returned to his seat.

"So where do we go from here?" He finally admitted defeat.

"I will put a man on the ground." Ed continued.

"He's one of my best, and he will blend in. There's something here, and until we find out what it is, we won't find the group involved."

"Group?" Major Paxton desperately needed to get involved in the conversation. He was trying to understand what was going on, having lost it when Black Talon was mentioned.

"This was an organised hit and with the use of Curare, we could either be dealing with South American, Asian or Eastern European origins. However, until we know, we have no idea what we are up against. All I can say is that someone, somewhere, is after something important. As yet we have nothing to go on, but we are working on it."

Ed knew the next question before it came out of the Commissioner's mouth, so he answered just as Burrows prepared to speak.

"We can narrow down the origin because Curare is ancient. It was refined later into a drug called Tubocurarine and used as an anaesthetic for medical surgeries in the late forties. It was replaced again with what we use now, Pancuronium. The latter would have been the obvious drug of choice as it is easier to get hold of; it's available in any hospital pharmacy throughout the world."

"It is mainly used today in the areas we have identified. South America, in certain parts of Peru, Bolivia and deeper recesses of Brazil. In Malaysia and other areas around the South China Sea and Eastern Europe, in particular, the Balkan states."

"So that's it then?" The Commissioner rose to leave.

"I guess I turn a blind eye and let you get on with it."

"Harry, wait… that's not what we want." Ed rose to stand with him.

"My agent will be one of yours as far as the public is concerned. We need to make it look like a normal police investigation. The only thing that will change is that my man will head it up and report to you, via me." He looked for approval.

Harry Burrows thought for a moment, analysing the information. He was in charge, it was his jurisdiction, but he also knew his men. They were just village bobbies, and the CID in Lysbie were not murder specialists, only having one in the past 15 years. He was in a no win situation. He would have the case taken from him anyway, as the city boys would have the manpower and they would edge him out. At least with LARA he would keep the case as the resources Ed could throw at this would dwarf the Met budget, let alone a regional force.

Resigned to his decision he faced Ryker.

"You've got my attention. Let's meet on Monday and put all the details together." He looked over to the other two men in the room.

"How do you feel chaps? Is this what we want?"

"Absolutely!" Major Paxton nodded enthusiastically. It wasn't quite how he planned it, but at least through his actions, he appeared to have set things in motion which would hopefully be to his advantage. Things couldn't have worked out better.

Brigadier Thorn sighed resignedly. It had all moved too fast, and he was finding it difficult to take in.

"I don't think we have much choice." It was the best he could manage, but his mind was racing.

CHAPTER FOURTEEN
Assigned

Jack kept his pace steady as he powered along the sandy Marizian beach. The Cornish air cleansed his lungs as he concentrated on his rhythm. His ankle had improved. No more sharp tweaks as his feet sank into the wet sand, just the occasional twinge, only a sprain, but an inconvenience during his training routine.

He had spent the first three weeks since returning from Venezuela pumping his upper body. It was the tedious side of fitness. Alone in a gym, surrounded by wood and glass and unless armed with an MP3 player, disco music from the PA system. After a week of 'Call on Me' drilling into his brain he succumbed to the new tech and settled for the manic riffs of Metallica and Slipknot to see him through.

He was looking at the beautiful Cornish coastline dominated by St Michael's Mount. It was a former Benedictine priory, a fortified castle and house. It was now an island full of life with its own microclimate that nurtured rare and exotic plants within the grandeur of its garden. The castle mount cast a glorious silhouette against the backdrop of the red and gold morning clouds streaking across the blue canvas.

The Bluetooth buzzed in his ear. He flicked the button on the earpiece.

"Case." He answered

"Hey Jack, how's the ankle?" It was from Ed Ryker.

He slowed to a walk to clear the breeze rushing through the speaker.

"Hi Ed, better thanks… can't do a marathon but I can dodge a bullet." His way of showing that he was ready to be reassigned.

"Hey, that's great!" Code for a correct answer because something's come up.

"There's a file at your station I need you to look at. It's a strange assignment, but it's based in a quiet English village, and I think you could do with the rest. Digest it, I'll see you at three, usual place." His earpiece beeped as they cut the call. Could do with a rest? This was intriguing.

He stepped back into his stride and jogged from the beach onto the roadside. He then started the punishing push up the tiny streets leading into town. Passing the picturesque terraced cottages stepped in uniformed rows, he contemplated the upcoming meeting with his boss.

Venezuela had been a total success. But throughout the mission he doubted himself, and he got sloppy. On too many occasions he could have got Rina killed, and that was not his style. He had thought about her often over the last few weeks. It was just another job, he knew that but there was something about her which had got under his skin. It concerned him that he might be showing signs of burn out.

He passed through the town and powered the last mile to the sanctuary of his home. A tiny village in Penzance containing one pub, one post office, and convenience store, with 100 residents spread over half a mile. Before heading for his cottage, he stopped off at the post office.

"Why Mr Collins, nice to see you up and about again" Hetty Granwick had owned the store for years and took great interest in all the residents.

She was a round cheerful old girl who always wore a floral apron when in the shop, she looked ready to bake a cake at any moment.

"Morning Hetty, yes the ankle feels a lot better this week." He replied lifting his foot, circling it to show her the movement.

"You wouldn't catch me on those ski slopes." She said as she went around the counter to fetch the post from his PO box. At her age, it was highly unlikely.

Jack was in a safe house. A location far enough away from major towns and cities to allow him the semblance of a normal life as Matt Collins, IT consultant. He travelled the world providing support to major blue chip companies worldwide. As he could be away for extended lengths of time, the post office held a PO box for his mail to be collected whenever he was passing. Upon his return from his last trip, he had been on crutches for the first week, a skiing accident to maintain his cover.

"I find it hard enough walking these hills in dry weather, add ice and I'm on my bottom in seconds." She laughed at her own joke as she passed him the small bundle of mail. His assignment was amongst it.

"Will you be staying for a while?" She asked after she had stopped laughing and wiped her eyes with a hanky produced from the pocket of her apron. She laughed at everything, and he couldn't help smiling along.

"No, I'm away again next week for a short while, another European assignment." He said as he felt the package containing the DVD.

"That company will be the death of you." She said, laughing again.

"Here, have one of these." Hetty passed him a small cherry lollipop. It was her routine and had been for years. He felt like a kid returning from school, calling in for sweets before going home. The school had closed over ten years ago, well before he had arrived. He found out from the locals that she always kept a box of sweets for the kids. Her way of maintaining life as it used to be. Everyone got a sweet, even the Jones's from two doors down, and they were in their eighties. He popped the lolly into his mouth and gave her the wrapper.

Wishing her a good day he left the shop, jogging the short distance home.

His home was a three bedroom cottage overlooking Mounts Bay. It was tidy, fully stocked by the agency with all the comforts he needed and more.

The living area was comfortable with a leather suite, dark oak furniture and shelves full of books he had yet to read. The kitchen, complete with Aga and pine country furnishings finished off the decor in keeping with the style of the property. He spent most of his time in the conservatory to the rear of the cottage. With an unobstructed view of the Bay and St Michael's mount, it was a perfect location for contemplation. Making himself an instant coffee he discarded most of the post apart from the jiffy bag containing the DVD and climbed the stairs.

Passing the main bedroom, he entered the study. It was sparsely furnished with a small shelf containing a few books on IT management. Under the only window in the room was a contemporary desk in walnut, complete with inset leather writing surface. An old leather swivel chair his preferred choice to accompany it.

He placed the coffee on the desk away from the leather inlay. Feeling under the front lip of the workstation he found the slight recess. Touching the fingerprint reader the inlay rose. He watched as the monitor came into view, fixed to a slimline workstation complete with DVD drive, keyboard and mouse.

Once the equipment came to rest, the screen sprung to life. He placed the disc into the drive, it crunched as it burnt data onto its surface. They were sent regularly through the post, always blank to maintain cover, keeping the pseudonym intact. The information on the discs had no relevance to any mission, just the means to collect fictitious work from his fictitious employer. Depending on what they revealed at the end, they were either stored in a rack or given to Hetty.

The screen showed an image of a man.

"This is Colin Thorn..." The voice he heard was Sara Moon.

She was central operations at HQ, an IT and logistics specialist, tactical operations expert and a damn good agent in her own right. Sara was brought inside a few years ago, proving invaluable throughout all missions.

She was the eyes and ears for all the agents, from the sky, the airwaves and the ground. She could track each operative, pinpoint targets, offering support when required. The PDA they all carried was their life support system, but it was Sara who kept them alive.

"The attack took place at the Manor House in a town in the southwest called Mittand Burrow." He punched notes into the PDA as she briefed him on the background to the mission. Twenty minutes passed before he had all the information he needed to get an overall feel for the case

"You have to become part of the investigating team already in place to uncover the group involved. Ryker is planning to arrive at the normal location by three pm today. He will add the meat to the bones. Oh… and don't be late Jack, you know it will be me who gets it in the neck. HQ out." As the screen went blank, he pressed the eject button to release the DVD. The drive again crunched, whined and after a few seconds the tray slid out.

The DVD had changed. On the front was a picture of two cartoon dogs, a spaniel and a mongrel eating a piece of spaghetti between them. Written on the disc was 'The Lady and the Tramp'.

Taking it from the drive he popped it into its sleeve, putting it on the shelf with his other movies. He would drop into the post office before he left and give them to Hetty. She saved them for her DVD library to lend to the kids when they called.

Leaving his desk, he moved to the master bedroom to shower and ready himself for his short trip across the bay.

CHAPTER FIFTEEN
Easy Money

Derek Gant was sweating.

Having spent the last few days sorting through paperwork, checking the viability of the clients, weighing up the options of buying or selling his rights to the practice, he felt mentally drained. He could see no way of coming out of this with more than two month's salary or up to his eyes in debt for more years than he could contemplate. But three days ago, out of the blue, he struck gold.

He received a recorded letter marked 'Private and Confidential Addressee only'. Inside was a beautifully handwritten note, a business card and a cheque.

Dear Mr Gant,

I would first like to offer my condolences on the untimely death of your partner Mr Thorn. He was a unique man who had been of tremendous help to our family over the years. We will miss him. I realise this is a difficult time for everyone associated with Mr Thorn and I felt I should wait a respectful length of time before sending this request.

I am writing to you to ask for your help in continuing the investigation of the Barth Probate case, that your partner has been handling for many months. All paperwork has been prepared, and I have issued representation by proxy to allow you full access on the family's behalf. It is imperative you take adequate identification to assist with this when you arrive.

Mr Thorn notified me he has left information at the location on the business card which will allow you to continue with the investigation. Please ensure that everything you receive is memorised and NOT written down in any form. Further instructions will be provided once you have completed this initial task.

I must stress that the intelligence gathered will have a major bearing on the case for the good of our family and will prove extremely rewarding to you and your business for many years to come. I have enclosed a cheque for you personally to cover your expenses in this matter and trust I can rely on your discretion at all times.

I will contact you in two weeks to arrange a meeting to discuss your findings and will provide you with further details which will help to progress the case towards its conclusion.

Yours

Jayne Langfield (Mrs)

At the Central Bank in the heart of the city of Oxford, he was sitting at a green baize table in a sparsely decorated room waiting for the manager to arrive. He couldn't believe his luck.

He had a personal cheque for £15,000 burning a hole in his pocket. It was more than enough incentive to persuade him to drive the 20 miles and arrive by the time the bank opened. He wasn't sure what was going on, but with an expense account like this, he was more than happy to see it through.

It had taken over half an hour to go through the paperwork and listen to the bank manager recite from memory the emergency procedures in case of fire. They made him leave his possessions with a brute of a man who, in his black suit, would be more at home on the door of a night club. He was allowed to keep the cheque, which he had removed from his pocket and admired several times in the last 20 minutes, counting the zero's, breathing in the perfect aroma of ink, print and paper, the smell of money.

George Wainwright entered the room. His pinstriped three piece suit was typical of a man who was a stickler for protocol and tradition in his role as manager.

"Ah Mr Gant, I apologise for the delay, had a few things to clear up."

He moved behind Derek and leaning forward, he placed a book sized thin metal plate in front of him, in the same way, a silver service waiter serves the main course. He moved it left and right, slightly forward and back a touch until he was happy that it was in precisely the right position. It was smooth with no discernible markings, just a slab of metal. Realisation dawned. He had seen this plate once before, at their offices a few months ago. Colin had arranged a meeting with the partners, something about security and new technology. It was a new way to offer the ultimate in protection for both the clients and the firm. He, Colin and Annabel was one of the first in the UK to register for this state of the art security system.

Only Colin knew what the plates were for, saying 'you'll find out when you need to' but he kept emphasising their importance. Moving to the front of the table, so he was facing Gant, Wainwright put his hands together and linking his fingers, rested them on the table. He leaned towards the younger man, eyes fixed on his.

"Now Mr Gant, I would be grateful if you would place your right hand on the reader in front of you." He nodded at the plate. Spreading his fingers, he placed his hand onto the cold surface and waited. Almost instantly it was surrounded by a luminescent glow, with a slight vibration which tingled through his fingers until it bleeped once and extinguished.

"If you could follow me, Mr Gant, bring the reader with you." Wainwright moved behind him and holding his card over the keypad, led him into a steel lined corridor. They walked down two flights of metal stairs, their shoes clanking on each step, it was like walking in a tin can. Once on solid ground, Derek looked around, fascinated by the expanse of solid steel, from the floor to the panelled walls and even the ceiling, it gleamed in the fluorescence of the inset spotlights.

"Come with me please." Wainwright strode past the impressive safe that towered over them. It matched perfectly with the walls, the only blemish being a keypad and monitor set in its face. They stopped at a small recess within one of the panels, it was the same size as the tablet Derek had in his hand.

"If I could ask you to place the reader into the compartment and place your hand as before." Wainwright requested, moving away to give his client access.

After an audible click, the tablet came to life. The slab of metal lost its silver sheen, fading into black then grey. Lines appeared rolling across the surface before disappearing into black. A red line scrawled across it, outlining a hand, it pulsed rhythmically.

Fingers spread, Derek placed his hand in position, moving it away as it bleeped. He was now looking at himself as if looking in a mirror. The tablet showed his handsome features, his name, age, height, weight and his passport number. It then displayed a multitude of other information scrolling over his image. The screen went blank for a few seconds before 'accepted' flashed rhythmically at him. The wall fell away, and the panel slid out of sight to reveal an ornate oak door, totally out of place in the room of steel.

"Wow, now that is cool." For a fleeting second, he felt like a secret agent.

"So, what now Moneybags?" He said, his voice deep with what he thought a perfect Scottish lilt. Wainwright, ignoring the attempt at humour, turned the brass handle pushing the door open.

"You will find a console at your disposal. Use your thumb where indicated and leave the key in the compartment when finished. Make your way back to the first floor, the door will open to allow you through." Derek entered the room.

"Oh, and one other thing Mr Gant… All the sensors in the vault are sensitive. I would advise against playing with the safe." It wasn't something he usually mentioned to his clients, but on this occasion, he felt it necessary.

"Sure thing buddy… leave the safe alone." He winked as Wainwright shut the door. 'Prick' he thought as he surveyed the room.

He could have been in the executive suite of a five star hotel. He stood on a Regency patterned carpet with leather Chesterfield armchairs in each corner. Dominating one wall was an impressive Victorian breakfront bookcase with three shelves containing several cognac and whiskey decanters. A notice encouraged guests to indulge, using the glasses provided. The burgundy criss-cross diamond design on beige wallpaper and the vintage wall lamps completed the scene.

In the centre of the room, completely out of place in such salubrious surroundings stood a rectangular desk of steel. A black executive chair sat before an opening just wide enough to fit his legs.

Settling into the plush leather, he pulled himself up to the desk.

The smooth surface was devoid of any accessories. A flat panel protruded a few millimetres above the surface, inset in the steel was a 20 mm square of black. He looked around for instructions mentioned by Wainwright but could see none. He shrugged, placing his thumb on the black square.

The panel opened and raised to reveal a monitor. It was covering a shallow recess housing a single key set in one of two slots. There was a design on one side of the head, but from its position, he couldn't quite make it out. It could have been lettering, the other side was blank. A red LED flashed below the key. The monitor came to life, he read as the words spread across the screen.

'Good morning Mr Gant… Please hold the key, ensuring the thumb rests on the plain side… turn clockwise. Do not release the thumb until the light turns green….'

He turned the key and holding it in position, the light changed to green.

The screen continued with instructions.

'… Remove the key… place it in the second slot… turn anti-clockwise. When the light turns green place the key in the housing provided… await further instructions…'

The LED under the second slot blinked red. Removing the key he inserted it in place as instructed, turning anti-clockwise. As the light turned green, a small drawer slid out alongside the LED, it was solid except for a key impression etched into its surface. He again looked at the monitor.

'Accepted' Flashed across the screen. The instructions continued…

'Place the key into the housing smooth side down… await further instructions.'

Pressing it into the slot until it clicked into place, he could see the inscription on the head now, KVP. The drawer slipped back into place leaving just two empty slots in view. The screen went blank before returning with only three words and a timer counting down from 20… 19…

'a MaileD pig'… Derek watched as the countdown moved into single figures. A mailed pig? What was that? It hit zero. The screen blackened and the monitor lowered over the recess locking into place.

He sat there for several minutes trying to work out what had just happened. What was a mailed pig supposed to mean? Did he need to post bacon to someone? Was it an invitation to a barbecue? What was all this about?

He left the room taking the stairs two at a time, leaving the vault to be met by Wainwright facing him at the green baize table.

"All done?" The bank manager smiled as his client sat down to join him.

"Sort of…" Derek said confusion etched across his face.

"What does a…"

"DON'T!…" Wainwright stopped him dead in his tracks.

"Please Mr Gant, don't repeat what you have seen. If you need to write it down, do it away from here and ensure you encrypt it. Only you can know what you have seen." Mr Wainwright pushed the mobile phone, wallet, car keys and loose change towards him.

"Yours I believe?" A smile crossed his face to show Gant his sudden curtness had now passed. Derek rose to return them to his pockets.

"What happens now?" He asked

Wainwright stood to meet his gaze.

"You will receive further instructions over the coming days." He extended his hand.

"Goodbye Mr Gant, we are glad to be of help. Please enjoy the rest of your day." He opened the door into the branch and swept his hands forward ushering Derek out.

Now what? Nothing of what had just happened made any sense. What had Colin got them involved in? The whole case was worth £200,000 to the firm which at 60% profit was not something he was willing to screw up. A simple proof of identity of all the beneficiaries, the validity of a second will was all it needed. After the issue of it allegedly prepared under duress had been sorted, it would be a doddle. He could handle this with his eyes shut, to be honest, the courts decided most.

It was an incredible fee for such a simple case, over twenty times it's worth. How Colin had negotiated this fee was anyone's guess. But that would save for another day, he had a cheque to cash. He decided to treat himself to a liquid lunch and a leisurely afternoon.

Walking past the queues waiting for service, he looked back at Wainwright who was watching him leave.

He nodded goodbye as he walked out.

High Street had come alive as shoppers, students and tourists took advantage of the warm weather. It would be another beautiful day. Derek Gant put on his shades as he strolled towards his car.

He pushed all thoughts of the weird meeting to the back of his mind as he became mesmerised by the number of gorgeous women dressed for the warm weather or better still, undressed. The skirt always got higher and the top lower when the sun came out, he loved it.

A group of girls passed laden with books, making their way to one of the many colleges dotted around the city. They all wore the shortest skirts, those who weren't wore crop tops or tied their shirts into a knot exposing their midriff. It was like a St Trinian's tribute, and they flaunted it, swaying their hips provocatively at every step, giving the come on to any guy who dared to look.

He was watching a girl cycle by, fully clad in lycra. It looked like she had sprayed it on. The contours of her body were in full view as she leant forward in the saddle. He had to admire her shapely rear moving rhythmically as she pedalled away from him.

He didn't notice the Ducati tailing him a few yards behind.

Turning into Turl Street he headed for Market Street and his Porsche. Turl Street was one of the city's original medieval roads. It was the heart of collegiate Oxford, providing the frontage for three prestigious colleges; Exeter, Jesus and Lincoln along its eastern side, a mixture of gothic and traditional architecture dating back to the fourteenth century. Built in most part from Bath stone it created a warm sandstone expanse which gleamed in the sunlight.

Along the western side, he admired the row of shops housed within medieval architecture. The multicoloured upper facade of pastel blue, pink and yellow overwhelmed the dark panelled storefronts at street level. It looked odd, but it worked.

Spotting a jewellery store amongst them reminded him of his expense cheque. Being a man partial to 'bling' this was an ideal place to start spending it. He owned several Rolex's, just as many Cartiers, two Tag Heuers and a Breitling. He had gold, silver and platinum bracelets and several eighteen carat rope necklaces. He still had room for a few more trinkets, so it was worth checking it out.

He watched the Ducati approach and waited for it to pass. Both rider and pillion dressed entirely in black with their opaque visors closed around gleaming helmets. The bike slowed to a stop before it reached him, its engine purring in the quiet street. Waving, he mouthed a 'thank you' as he crossed.

He walked one step, recoiling as something struck his shoulder. He stumbled back, instinctively placing his hand where it hurt. He felt wetness soaking through his jacket. Blood was seeping through his fingers.

He couldn't move his left arm but could feel a warmth running down it. His sleeve was soaked, drips of blood splattered to the floor. Searching for help, he focused on the motorbike ahead, as the pillion passenger climbed off and moved deliberately towards him.

He was carrying a gun. Before he could think of escape, his legs gave way, falling hard onto his backside. Sitting prone he watched the gunman approach before momentum forced him onto his back, his head bouncing off the tarmac.

His senses were all over the place. There was no pain as he couldn't feel his arm, he couldn't feel his legs either, and his head was full of stars from the impact with the road. He was aware of a weight on his stomach, but the biker's helmet blocked his vision. The visor flicked up, he was staring at grey eyes and a pale face, pinched into the foam of the helmet interior.

"What is the code?" The helmet said as he could see no mouth. He heard a European accent, but he couldn't tell from where. It could have been German, Austrian or even Russian but he was in no condition to fully concentrate on its origin.

"What is the code?" The helmet said again. This time the biker grasped Derek's lapels, holding him inches from the ground.

He stared at the alien and felt sick. A man came running from a charity shop having seen the guy collapse. He hurried towards them to assist the biker as it looked as if he was trying to help.

"Is he alright?" the samaritan asked as he crossed.

The helmet pointed the gun at him.

"Go!" He shouted waving him away.

The samaritan needed no further encouragement; he bolted back into the shop. Derek could hear his shouts of alarm in the distance. He then heard a heavy zip being drawn, the helmet looked down at whatever it was he removed from his leathers. It thrust a syringe full of a yellow liquid in front of his eyes.

"In around five minutes you will lose all feeling in your body..." It was an Eastern European accent.

"... And within a few more minutes your diaphragm will stop working, your lungs will stop functioning, and your heart will stop."

This wasn't happening Derek thought as he swallowed hard, gasping for breath. He kept his eyes on the grey retinas in front of him. What had they shot him with? It was a shoulder wound, it wouldn't paralyse him, would it? If he could get to a hospital, they would help surely. He should go, he needed help. But first, he needed to push off his attacker. One problem... his body wouldn't move.

"This is the antidote. You have around three minutes left, after which it will be too late to save you. Now I will ask once again, what is the code?"

Whether through his erratic breathing or the effects of the wound, he panicked. He didn't want to die. What code did he want? He tried to speak.

"W-W-ha-t-t... c-co-de?" He said, breathing heavily again.

"From the bank Mr Gant, I need to know the code from the bank." The helmet was now shouting. He didn't want to make the helmet angry as he wanted the antidote; he had too much to do. Money to spend, a business worth a fortune, women falling at his feet. Derek Gant had far too much to live for.

"Hurry Kurt!" A voice sounded from over the helmet's shoulder.

"You have one more chance to tell me the code or we will leave, and you will die." It was not beating around the bush.

He needed the antidote, he knew that, because he could not feel his body. His right arm had now died, he couldn't feel the weight of the helmet's body on his stomach anymore. Breathing was getting more difficult, he felt as if his lungs were shrinking at every breath. He was worried that he might not be able to speak... He tried.

"A mayed fig." He said, at only a whisper.

It was wrong, he knew it was, had he lost the coordination of his tongue? He could still feel it, which was good. But could he say the words? He braced himself for one last monumental effort.

"A mailed pig... A MAILED PIG!" He did it, and in his enthusiasm, he repeated it until he needed to take a much needed breath, coughing as he gulped air. From a distance Derek heard the growl of the motorbike increase until out of his right eye he could see the fat tyre of its front wheel. He could feel his body vibrate as the powerful engine idled near his chest.

"Let's get this over with." A voice sounded from above the wheel.

He could hear a siren. He was saved. The guy from the shop must have phoned the police. The helmet blocking his view suddenly disappeared, and he panicked again. Don't leave me.

To his relief the helmet, now accompanied by the body it was attached to, moved into view. They hadn't gone, he would get the antidote. The visor was closed, he watched it look down, hopefully, with the syringe he would use to give him back his life.

Derek Gant stared at the barrel of a silencer. The last thing he saw with living eyes was a flash.

CHAPTER SIXTEEN
Error Code

"Kurt! Why did you do that?" The rider of the Ducati stared at his pillion passenger. He then looked at the Englishman lying on the floor, a steady flow of blood spreading around his head like a halo.

Kurt rifled through the dead man's jacket removing a letter and a cheque before running back to his partner.

"You mentioned my name you dummkopf!" leaping behind, he slapped the rider on the back, they needed to get away fast.

Opening the throttle, kicking down into first gear, he dropped the clutch. With a screech of the rear wheel, the bike lurched forward and swerved left along Market Street.

With no consideration for the traffic, they swerved into Cornmarket Street. Hurtling through the lights at the George Street Junction at eighty miles an hour, they narrowly missed a Nissan Micra. The rider expertly pulled the bike straight before taking Magdalen Street at ninety five. By the time they hit the 4144, they were doing a ton.

Kurt Eichel punched the numbers into his mobile with his right hand as he clung onto the seat grip with his left. His Bluetooth headset bleeped twice syncing, after several rings, it connected.

"Speak!" The voice commanded.

"The code is a male pig" Kurt answered through the helmets built-in microphone.

There was a silence for several seconds before the response came. There was anger in the reply.

"How can that be the code? You idiot!"

"That's what we were told." It was all that he heard anyway.

"And Gant was in no position to lie."

"Then I suggest you revisit Mr Gant because he has lied to you.

The code is not words, but numbers. What the hell are we paying you people for?"

Kurt slapped the rider, signalling him to pull over. They were on a dual carriageway on the outskirts of Oxford, surrounded by fields. There were no buildings or turn offs anywhere in the distance which made it difficult. They spotted a lay by a short distance ahead and pulled in, killing the engine.

Kurt dismounted while his partner wheeled the Ducati behind a cluster of bushes to hide it from view.

Following behind, Kurt removed his helmet, hooking it onto his arm. He shook his blonde locks free and raked his hand through his hair to prevent flattening. He would have to wash and blow dry it every time if he didn't perform this ritual. Helmet hair was the bane of any rider who took pride in his appearance.

With the Bluetooth disconnected he put the mobile phone to his ear.

"We can't revisit Gant." Kurt continued

"We had to eliminate him." Silence greeted Kurt long enough for him to wonder if he had been cut off.

He strained to hear anything through the speaker, putting his finger in his other ear to block out the cars rushing by. Moving the handset a good six inches away until the profanities eventually died down, he put the phone back to his ear.

"We will look at the code you have given us to see if there is a way to decipher it." There was an audible sigh before the voice continued.

"For your own sakes let us hope that it brings us the answers we are looking for." Kurt gave a wry smile.

"But we have another problem." The voice controlled, albeit strained from the exertion of the last rant.

"The two people who could have given us the best chance of deciphering the code are now dead thanks to you two imbeciles!" He was not mincing words.

"You will now lie low until called. Stay in London, stay out of trouble and keep a check on Dolf; this is not a holiday." He understood the concerns regarding Dolf. When he wasn't breaking heads, he was usually drunk. It would take all his time to keep him occupied and away from the bottle.

"There has been a development. It involves a task force by the name of LARA, they are sending in an agent. They are a danger to our cause and must be eliminated. We will be in contact when he arrives, so you need to be ready. Do not fail us again Kurt. You have cost us enough already. I instructed you to keep them alive. This time is different. Leave the agent alive and you will pay with your own. You have been warned." The phone died.

Kurt looked at the mobile, his mouth curled to a snarl. They had been a good team for eight years, always completing their assignments. He thought back and couldn't see how they were responsible for any of this. Ok, Dolf had messed up the Thorn hit, he was supposed to shoot him in the shoulder to allow time to offer the antidote for the code. Unfortunately, after spending sixteen hours cooped up in the pool house, he had misjudged the trajectory. It was either through tiredness or an itchy finger, but he had assured Kurt he had not been drinking. He had better not have been.

Gant told them what they wanted to know. No one said they were looking for numbers, how was this their fault? He knew he'd heard a male pig several times. Had Dolf not shouted his name he may have let the Englishman live.

Dolf was the common denominator. But Dolf was the brawn, and he was the brains, which made them a great team whatever anyone said. What pissed him off more was that he and Dolf did all the work while they sat in their ivory towers barking instructions. Only one thing for it... they'll make them eat their words.

He placed the phone back into the shoulder pocket as he walked over to Dolf. His partner was sitting sideways on the Ducati, one foot on the footrest, the other on the ground. He had removed his helmet letting the sun burn his bald pate. Coming to the end of his second cigarette, he flicked it away as his partner approached.

"What did they say?" He said blowing the last intake of smoke from his lungs.

"We have a few day's holiday."

Dolf grinned, temporarily blinding his partner as the sun flashed over his gold teeth.

CHAPTER SEVENTEEN
Briefed

Jack Case stood next to a group of Yucca plants in the gardens of St Michael's Mount, looking over Mounts Bay to the picture postcard coast of Cornwall.

The warmth from the Gulf Stream soaked into the heat retentive granite walls, creating a subtropical environment. It was reminiscent of anywhere in the Mediterranean, on some occasions, far hotter. The garden was protected from the wind by pines and salt tolerant shrubs, enabling hundreds of exotic plants to grow unhindered. Scents from the fuchsia, tamarisk and other aromatic blooms filled the senses. It created a calm, soothing aroma that befitted the location. He spent as long on the island as he could when he had the chance to be at home. It was a place where he could forget his real life, providing the peace and tranquillity he needed to regenerate.

It was 3PM, Ed Ryker knew this was the best time to arrange a meeting with Jack. St Michael's Mount, connected by a four hundred metre causeway to the coast of mainland Marazion, at low tide providing a stunning six minute walk across the water, on a pathway built from granite setts.

As the low tide was between two pm and six pm during summer months, Jack had arrived at the mount after a casual ten minute stroll.

"I will never get used to this place." Ed Ryker stood by his shoulder. He had broken away from a group of tourists who wandered by to examine the rest of the garden.

"Hello Ed" Jack kept his eyes on the horizon.

"You are comfortable with the case?" Ed followed his gaze across the bay.

Ed was a matter of fact guy, no pleasantries, little in compassion just a single mindedness for the task ahead. He cared for his agents, but his first loyalty was to LARA. There was no man bigger than the organisation. However, Jack was his best agent, and if he had a chink in his armour at all, it was for his best man.

"You did a great job in Venezuela, Jack. Abu is full of admiration for LARA and has insisted on assigning you, should he ever need to use us again." He slipped it into the conversation knowing Jack was stimulated by praise. There are some who react best to either a big kick up the arse or to praise and criticism. Jack fell into the latter.

"It was an easy case, the kidnappers were amateurs." He appreciated the recognition, but any agent could have accomplished the rescue. It wasn't one of his most memorable assignments, apart from Rina perhaps.

"Well, let's hope this one proves a little more interesting for you." Ed offered, surprised at Jack's flippant manner.

Jack usually approached each assignment with professionalism and zeal. This approach not only helped in the performance of his duties, it also gave the client confidence that LARA would get the job done. He would always get his man. But, over the last few assignments he had been less enthusiastic, it had been down to Sara Moon to express her concerns. Ed needed to question Jack himself because in this arena complacency meant death.

Had it been any other agent, they would be reassigned or brought in for further conditioning. There would be three months of retraining and psycho-analysis, a full mental MOT. This tact would be pointless for Jack. He had designed most of the programs for the retraining regime, he could psycho-analyse the psycho-analysts. He would have them re-testing themselves before they had even begun. No, Jack needed more than that, a personal touch. The reason he was here.

"How are you, Jack?" No point in continuing with the small talk, Ed needed answers.

Jack turned, looking him the eye. Ed was pleased to see his steely gaze, still clear and sharp.

"Tired." He turned, looking across the bay.

Ed had seen this before. Ten years ago LARA's number one agent had gone to the top and asked to get out. He complained of being burnt out, felt his judgment was being affected, putting missions at risk. It was a hard life, and very few came out the other end. They were either killed or decommissioned, destined to be office bound for the rest of their lives. All agents knew there were no other options open to them, Jack would not suit an office. Ed Ryker was that very agent ten years ago, so he knew the score.

"Jack, I've been there." Jack nodded. It was no secret, the story was used as an example at the initial conditioning. They also learnt that after this request, Ed concluded a further eighteen missions before going upstairs.

"That is why this case is good for you right now. It may be routine, but in an environment which will allow you the time to re-evaluate and recharge. You will be part of a team over which you have total control. I've visited the place, it's like a home from home." Again he looked at Ed, this time he smiled.

"And close enough for you to keep an eye on me, check that I'm not losing it. You want me in a goldfish bowl." He knew he was right, and by his eye movement, Ed concurred. It was now Ed's turn to smile.

"You know me too well. So… what do you say?"

It was the right move. LARA could not afford to let him out on another seek and destroy or recovery mission until they were sure he was sound. They were worth millions, they needed to be sure there were more millions to come. One fatal error would put LARA back years, they could not allow that to happen.

Jack wasn't sure how he would cope with the scrutiny, but he needed this as much for himself as for LARA.

"One condition." Jack said, now he'd come to terms with it.

Ed narrowed his eyes. There was no negotiation here, it was do or die. He worried as he watched his former self from ten years ago. This was a guy on the edge and it was a toss-up which way he would go. He nodded waiting for the request.

"I want Sara to do it, my analyst. None of the scientists, psycho cops or quacks." Jack fixed him with a steely stare, challenging him. Ed knew what he was doing. By asking for Sara, he would bypass the system, going directly to the top, him. It was like looking in a mirror, and there was only one way to handle this. Ed had no choice, he needed this man.

"You've got it." No negotiation, no compromise. It was done.

Ed's PDA rang. He took the call, wandering away from Jack, settling under a Holm oak out of earshot.

Whether it was the influence of the Mount's garden or that negotiations had successfully concluded, he was feeling better. He hoped this latest mission might help him refocus. Mittand Burrow appeared to be a sleepy village with a secret and Ed was right, it sounded appealing. He'd had his fill of jungles and cities, car chases and gunfights, perhaps a cerebral challenge was just what he needed.

Ed returned in a matter of minutes, and by the look on his face, it wasn't good.

"We have another murder. The partner, Gant, gunned down in Oxford, same MO." He was reading the report from his PDA, updated by Sara in real time. Ed briefed Jack on the latest killing, of the bikers and witness statements.

"The poisoned shot was in the shoulder, so they intended to get information from him before blowing his head off. I guess they got what they needed. The force at Oxford is looking into it alongside the force from Lysbie, Gant's home town. You'll be assisting the Lysbie force, a DI. Walsh assigned as your partner. He is due to meet you at eleven tomorrow." They shook hands.

"Get some rest, Jack. We'll be in touch." Ed left, climbing the winding path to the castle before making his way back down to the north side of the island. The waiting shuttle would take him back to HQ.

Jack stayed for a while, enjoying a fish lunch at the Sail Loft Restaurant. He allowed himself the luxury of the surroundings while relaxing to the soothing music just within earshot. He sampled an exquisite bottle of wine before making the short journey across the causeway, back to the mainland.

He strolled through the streets of Marazion taking several deep breaths, making the most of the Cornish air. He didn't know when he would get to appreciate it again.

CHAPTER EIGHTEEN
Partners

Detective Inspector Mike Walsh leant against his car finishing his third cigarette; he wasn't happy. He had lost the case that had his name written all over it. He knew the patch, had narrowed down his suspects and would wager with anyone he would have his arrest in weeks. He wasn't used to being pulled from a case, it was the first time, and he wanted answers, which he wasn't getting. No one did that to Mike Walsh.

He was one of the youngest DI's in the force at thirty-three. It was all about how to play the system. He had flown through the ranks by getting himself partnered with the highest profile officers at the time. He made sure the chief knew his name, volunteering for all overtime, tackling everything they threw at him.

He became a national hero two years ago when credited with the arrest and conviction of the witness murderer Josh Levin. A clerk of the courts who was killing the witnesses of serious crimes for his own depraved gratification.

Walsh took a bullet in the neck for his trouble, losing the feeling to one side of his face through nerve damage. Having to suffer three months of rehabilitation, however, had all been worthwhile.

The publicity had given him an enviable reputation, not only in his own force but in every force in the country. They knew him as Scarface behind his back because of his injuries. It allowed him to feed off the notoriety when dealing with both the public and his peers. His superiors were quick to see the marketing potential of their hero cop, promoting him to DI soon after his return to full health. He ran a tight ship, his ratio of arrests to convictions was one of the highest in the country. The Thorn murder was another one with his name all over it.

The Commissioner was close to the case, and it would have done him no harm at all to be the cop who made the arrest. After all, Burrows was only keeping his seat warm. Unfortunately, it had all slipped away from him.

First, he had nothing from forensics to go on, then he was told they were to back off as a higher authority was handling it. It was something about national security or some such bureaucratic crap. Then to top it all, he was to partner with a government official or some special investigator. He liked to do his homework, but he could get nothing on this guy apart from he was ex-military. The Commissioner had met with Walsh personally, offering all the soft soap. He waxed lyrical about his fine record making sure he was malleable enough when asked to assist in the investigation, nothing else. A fucking assistant!

A case of 'my way or the highway' and he had no choice other than to accept. He hated being in the dark and hated partners. He worked alone these days, working with the only person he could trust to get the job done.

He was now staring towards the exit of Oxford station waiting for the Great Western train from Penzance to arrive. The last thing he wanted to do right now was nursemaid a civvy.

He lit another cigarette.

After five and a half long hours the train slowed as it prepared to complete its journey to Oxford. Jack stretched in his seat, rubbing the sleep from his eyes. He had spent the first few hours reviewing the Thorn case, now the Thorn/Gant case, bringing himself up to speed as far as he could. What he did have was sketchy, to say the least, which was why he was meeting the investigating officer. It also allowed him to get the feel of the place.

After a light lunch from the buffet car, he had managed two hours sleep which was always welcome, and he felt relaxed, ready to meet the DI from Lysbie CID.

He knew all about DI Walsh, known as Scarface, with a reputation as a go-getter, a bit of a maverick. He was a good guy to have on your side but a liability if he wasn't. He had to feel for him as they had stood him down, under the same circumstances he wouldn't be happy either. He would need to tread carefully to begin with as they were in this together and he would prefer a smooth ride.

He collected his kit bag from the overhead compartment before leaving the train, heading for the exit. Once through the barriers, strolling through the tiled station concourse he picked up a local paper. The headline caught his eye…

'OXFORD KILLING - NEW INFORMATION' - 'Police moving in on the killers'. The first column included a quote from his new partner. 'Detective Inspector Mike Walsh said earlier today. We are working on new information, uncovered over the last few days. We believe it will lead us to the killers of Derek Gant, and we are confident of making arrests imminently.'

Jack was delighted, he could be home in days. He folded the newspaper, slipping it in the side pocket of his kit bag for later.

He walked from the glass fronted concourse onto the street.

It wasn't hard to spot his ride. The driver of a black S type Jag opposite flicked his cigarette in the air, straightened from his leaning position and walked towards him.

He was wearing a worn suit with trousers used on many tours of duty, a shine glistened around the knee area. Those trousers had knelt under beds and chairs, crawled across many floors to find the tiniest scrap of evidence.

The baggy beige mac hanging from his shoulders would have suited a 1920s gumshoe. The large lapels were slightly curled from being slung over the shoulder far too often. His dark tie, loosely knotted around his unbuttoned grey shirt, was just enough to finish the image of a throwback to a seventies TV detective. This guy wasn't for real.

Facially the scar down his right cheek was clearly visible. The shot must have blown a lot of his face away; the surgery had left a prominent furrow giving the impression he was permanently sucking it in.

His sharp features, greased back hair and his gait reminded him more of a gangster from 30s Chicago than a small town plod.

Unsurprisingly as he approached, the detective took the lead.

'Mr Case … DI Walsh. Did you have a good trip?' He extended his hand and grasped Jack's with a firm, deliberate show of strength. Jack returned the grip which lasted several seconds, a psychological battle for domination.

"Hello detective, you can call me Jack." He released his grip, threw his bag onto the back seat and took his place in the passenger seat. DI Walsh walked around the front of the car, getting in behind the wheel.

"Don't tell me, your name is Case, Jack Case." The sarcasm was caustic as he swung the car out of the station.

"Yeah, something like that." Jack forced a smile.

Jesus, this would be one hell of a mission. He settled into his seat and buckled up.

CHAPTER NINETEEN
Arrival

Twenty minutes into the journey and hardly a word had passed between the two. Jack was okay with that; he sat back watching the countryside go by. Some villages they drove through had a quaintness he always thought showed England at its best. Thatched cottages, well farmed land, sheep grazing on the hillsides, stone bridges spanning trickling streams. Yes, he would enjoy this mission. Ed was right, this would give him a much needed rest.

They passed a sign, Lysbie 4 miles, as the road widened into a dual carriageway.

"We'll visit the station before the village. I guess you'd like to see how we are progressing with the investigation?" Walsh said, keeping his eyes on the road.

His irreverent tone implied he was going through the motions, following a plan not of his making. He would make it known at every turn that he had no choice, but he wasn't going to make it easy.

"That's fine." Is all Jack offered.

Again, silence reigned.

DI Walsh suddenly developed an itch. Not physically, but a sixth sense perfected over the years. He sensed they were being watched, it was just a feeling, an instinct, but one he'd had many times, and he was rarely wrong. He turned to Jack who was looking out of his window at the passing fields. He checked the rearview mirror at the road behind…. Empty. He looked through his window; the wing mirror found the itch.

A motorcycle was overtaking, both rider and pillion clad entirely in black… but… they weren't passing with any conviction. He saw the front wheel move into his peripheral vision, it stayed there hovering at the edge of his view, forcing him to glance over.

They were holding their speed to match the Jag's. Taking another look, he could see the pillion pointing. He was pointing at something inside the car.

"SHIT!" He slammed on the brakes just as his window exploded over him. He felt the air rush past him as a hail of bullets missed his head by millimetres. Fighting with the controls, Walsh brought the car to a halt. Jack had released his seat belt, trying to scramble into the back to get to his kit bag. It had wedged behind his seat, thrown there during the emergency stop.

It was too tight to move to the rear, so he leant over the headrest, pulling at his bag to yank it free. It had tipped upside down with the zip pressed into the floor.

"Drive!" He shouted back at Walsh as he tugged at the bag. They needed to give chase. The Jag pulled away.

The Ducati was a good distance ahead when its brake light flashed. Realising the hit had been unsuccessful the bike turned in an arc until it faced their vehicle. Smoke spewed from its rear tyre as it sped towards them. Walsh floored the accelerator, the car lurched forward picking up speed through the automatic gears. It was a joust to the death as the two machines raced towards each other.

"Come on, you bastards. Let's see what you've got." He was pissed off beyond belief.

Using all his strength Jack ripped the bag free, using both hands he grasped the Glock and a magazine. In one smooth movement, he loaded, released the safety and swung around, gun at the ready. He jabbed at the rest of the glass still hanging from the frame, preparing the way for a clear shot. Small shards flew all around them as the car picked up speed.

"Hold it steady!" Jack shouted over the turbulence as wind rushed into the car. Walsh held his course, aiming directly for the Ducati. In a fight, he felt confident the car would triumph, but he was a little unnerved they would even attempt to come back to finish the job.

Who were they?

The pillion passenger rose above the rider on the rear footrests, aiming an Uzi at the approaching target. The flashes from the barrel sent a volley of bullets into the ground in front of them. Chunks of tarmac smashed into the bumper and, as the range improved, punched violently into the metalwork. Walsh turned the wheel several times as he attempted to weave around it. Instinctively both occupants slid lower in their seats. One more volley and the range would put the bullets directly into the vehicle. Jack managed to get one shot in the rider's direction before the Jag's front tyre exploded.

The car spun in a full circle careering over the grass verge, flying inches off the ground headlong into a ditch. The front of the Jag collapsed in on itself as it hit the bank at an acute angle, the rear wheels spinning in fresh air as the boot pointed to the sky.

It threw Walsh through the windscreen leaving him prone in the furrow of a freshly ploughed field, his head buried in the earth, he was not moving. Jack lay halfway out of the windscreen, his arms spread across the bonnet. His right ankle trapped between the seat and centre console. He groaned at the pain in his hip.

Dazed and hurting, Jack shook the sparks and bubbles from the front of his eyes as he tried to focus on his predicament. He raised his head to look around, at the same time trying to tug his foot free. To his right, a short distance away, he could see the bike laying on its side, a boot protruding from underneath the engine casing. It looked like they had forced them off the road too, had he hit the rider? He saw nothing to his left. Ahead, a few yards away, stuck in a mound of earth, was his gun thrown clear in the crash.

He heard voices coming from somewhere behind the vehicle.

"Go und beenden den job. Case finden und ihn zu toten." They were alive.

'Go and finish the job. Find Case and kill him.' They were German, so he had a clue to their identities. But it wouldn't help if they ended up killing him.

A sound off to one side made him turn, the booted leather legs of a biker scrambled down the ditch only twenty yards away. He steadied himself, wiping grass from his knees, looking in Jack's direction.

Opaque visor still closed, the black clad rider walked towards him. He carefully stepped over the rocks and rubbish that had collected in the ditch's base over the years. Hanging down by his side was the Uzi. On seeing the trapped passenger still alive, he lifted the machine gun, cocked the weapon and raised it in his direction. It spurred Jack into action.

He frantically felt along the side of the passenger seat with his foot until he felt a protrusion in the smooth leather. Pressing hard against it until a motor sounded, the seat moved towards him. He tugged at his ankle at the same time, but it remained stuck, it felt even tighter.

The Uzi burst into life forcing Jack to push himself back into the car as far as he could. His head caught the frame of the windscreen as bullets demolished the wing. Moving his left foot behind the lever, he kicked forward, the motor whined again, this time moving the seat backwards. Tugging at his ankle to free himself, he felt his foot move. Another spray of gunfire forced him to take cover, the rear glass shattered and metal splintered as they peppered the door.

His weight managed to free his ankle. With nowhere else to go he dived headlong through the ruined windscreen, riding the bonnet.

Reaching the edge of the collapsed front end, he pushed his arms out to stop his slide. Grabbing the earth with both hands he rolled, tucking himself tightly as he tumbled along the ground.

Landing within a foot of his Glock he grabbed the butt and swivelled to face the gunman. He let off a shot just as the biker scrambled up the bank, he had seen his target reach his gun. The bullet caught the steel heel of his boot, bouncing harmlessly away. Jack scrambled to his feet just in time to see the two riders mount the Ducati. The other rider had got it started. The bike revved, heading towards him as he prepared to fire.

A cough from behind made him turn in time to see Walsh lift his head from the earth, he was spluttering and spitting dirt from his mouth.

The bike was getting closer. As it accelerated, there was a burst of gunfire. He grabbed the prone DI, dragging him towards the cover of the crashed car, just as clumps of earth flew all around them. Bullets rebounded off the metal undercarriage as they passed directly behind the Jag. They were aiming for the petrol tank. Grabbing Walsh by his lapels, he pulled the groggy DI away from the car, bracing himself for the explosion… It never came.

The Ducati was accelerating away from them as Jack jumped up and sent a volley of his own. They were just out of range. He watched them disappear into the distance, plumes of smoke in their wake as the damaged engine pushed them on. In less than a minute they were gone.

"The bastards! Look what they've done." Walsh was sitting up now, gesturing at his ruined car.

CHAPTER TWENTY
Lysbie

"I guess I owe you my life." Walsh said extending his hand.

They were travelling in the back of a squad car through the town of Lysbie.

"I'm sure you would have done the same." Jack returned the handshake. It wasn't the politest of thanks, and the handshake was weak.

Walsh still seemed to resent his presence, and it was even worse now he felt he owed him one. He always found it difficult to accept gratitude anyway so the fact it was grudgingly offered suited him fine. Too long in the job, he was used to the role of protector.

"Who were those guys?" Walsh asked.

"I have no idea, but they knew my name, and they knew my whereabouts. I can only assume that someone doesn't want me around." He was pointing out the obvious.

"So, an inside job?" Walsh smoothed back his hair, which by now was all over the place having been buried in earth. It wouldn't settle down until he had the chance to apply another application of gel. He continued to paw at the stubborn tufts before giving up and huffing, crossing his arms in frustration.

"Well, it could be someone on the inside, so unless you have any other ideas, I would suggest we look at anyone linked to both victims and start there."

"That's half of Mittand Burrow," Walsh added.

"And we have all the information you'll need."

He was quietly pleased and somewhat surprised that Walsh was prepared to open the case up to him as his resentment had been obvious.

Mind you, an ambush from an Uzi-wielding maniac can have that effect. Admittedly, Jack didn't know Walsh that well, what he did know was it wouldn't last.

Medics checked them at the scene, and apart from a few cuts and bruises mixed with dirt, dung and grass, they gave the all clear to allow them to continue with their schedule. Walsh's car was with forensics; he doubted he would ever see it again. There was no sign of the black Ducati despite all forces in the vicinity on alert. As with the Oxford killing, they had disappeared off the face of the earth.

The squad car pulled into Lysbie station, a two storey seventies built oblong, constructed of red brick and glass.

His PDA rang. He placed it to his ear.

"Jack, nothing on the bikers. I'm afraid." It was from Sara.

"We've run a check on the villagers, nothing really jumps out at us. The files are on your system for you to review. Oh, and you are staying at the Manor House, courtesy of the widow." He could sense that she was smiling.

Jack was no angel, but Sara had always looked out for him, which was useful if he needed to make a swift getaway.

They both also knew that under different circumstances there could have been something between them. They had been partners in the early days, and the camaraderie had developed into a mutual friendship. Unfortunately, they cared for each other first and foremost rather than themselves. The first rule of any assignment was self-preservation, it could mean the difference between success or failure. It had hurt when first reassigned, although looking back, they could see it had been for the best. They may get together again one day, neither could be sure, but for now, they had a professional relationship with mutual respect.

"Your station and supplies are waiting for you at your current base. Take particular notice of the medipack and ensure you keep it with you at all times. Take care, Jack, HQ out." Sara disappeared.

"Are you coming or what?" Walsh stared at him through the window, irritated at having to wait.

Retrieving his kit bag, he followed the DI CK into the station.

"Right you lot, gather round." Walsh barged his way into the office, throwing his muddied mac onto his chair.

Jack followed, settling himself at the back of the room. Four officers shuffled their chairs in front of the briefing board, watching as the chief positioned himself alongside it. He felt as if he was in an old episode of a seventies police TV series. All the rectangular desks were dark brown Formica monstrosities with drawers fixed to the undersides. Half the drawer fronts had disappeared, and papers poked out ready to fall to the floor. There were piles of brown folders and grey box files littered throughout the room. Across desks, on the floor, stacked on filing cabinets and filling every available space on the large terracotta window sills.

All the officers had their shirt sleeves rolled up, their ties hanging loosely from their unbuttoned collars. It was obviously the CID dress code. As soon as the DI had thrown his jacket on top of his mac, he rolled up his shirt sleeves, unbuttoned his collar and gave three tugs of his tie, shaking it loose.

DI Walsh stood by the portable whiteboard, one of the newest items in the room. There were numerous photographs set out to build a story of the case. At the top were the faces of two men. He recognised the first as Colin Thorn, and he assumed the other was that of Derek Gant. The storyboard continued with two photographs showing the corpse of each man with a small map underneath. A red ring pinpointing the position of the body in relation to the location they were found. Completing the story were the photographs of three women, two senior men and a business card. He assumed Major Paxton and Brigadier Thorn were the two men and he was confident the older woman was Linda Norwood. The other two women were both attractive, of a similar age, around 40. He knew he was looking at Annabel Paxton-Thorn and Eliza Winch, but he wasn't sure who was who. Walsh pulled the business card from the board holding it in front of him.

"George Wainwright, any joy, Jim?" He used the card as a pointer, directing it at one of the two officers sitting nearest to him.

"Yes, Guv. We know that Gant visited the Central Bank at 9.45 am on the 5th. He met with Wainwright who refused to give us any more information due to client confidentiality. So this morning we got a search warrant, we can now confirm that he was there to look at the contents of some security box." Jim Waite flicked through the rest of his notes.

"Wainwright is refusing to let us into the vault until he's had the chance to contact his client. Oh... he also said he would only talk to the man in charge. Over to you boss."

Walsh held the card in the air looking over to Jack.

"This is the business card of a George W. Wainwright." He read from the card. "The bank manager from the Central bank in Oxford. We found it in the top pocket of Gant's jacket."

He then pointed to the back of the room.

"Gentlemen, let me introduce Commander Jack Case from LARA. He's here to catch the killers for us." There was still an element of sarcasm in his tone, but less caustic.

"Just Jack will be fine." He made his way to the front, moving to the opposite side of the whiteboard from Walsh.

All eyes were on him, sizing up the man from the legendary task force. Two of the youngest, being aware of LARA only from glamorised internal press reports and rumour, looked on in awe.

One raised his eyes, faced his colleague silently mouthing "LARA" in wide eyed enthusiasm.

"Excuse me, sir." Vince Cardell, one of the old hands, looked over to him, his eyes firmly fixed on their guest. A typical psych test.

"Why would LARA be interested in this? I thought you were into high profile espionage and supervillains? Or are we dealing with Doctor Evil?" Sniggers and snorts of stifled laughter rippled through the group. Jack had experienced this many times before. He waited for the noise to die down before he answered.

It was DI Walsh who answered for him.

"Hang on boys. We were attacked this afternoon by some bloody lunatics with machine guns. Had it not been for this man, I might not be here now... And before you say anything, Cardell... You love having me as your boss, and you know it." The laughter was more jovial which helped bring attention back to the case.

"So before we judge the man, I would say we are dealing with someone here who we could all learn from. This case is unusual, and after this afternoon, I'm prepared to hear what he has to say." What was Walsh doing now? Jack found the game intriguing. He didn't need these guys, Walsh knew that, but to have them against him could make things awkward. He looked at the ramshackle bunch in front of him, hard pushed to see anyone he could rely on in a fight. Also, judging by the mountains of paperwork around the place, they were probably far more used to the pen rather than the sword. They were all he had to work with, for now, so he had better make the most of it.

"We believe that we are up against an Eastern European organisation. They are searching for something relating to the business of Thorn Paxton and Gant." He ran through the theories, the information they had obtained so far. He added their own opinions although slim, including it along with the current information already gathered. They added the two bikers to the whiteboard along with the curious use of the Curare laced Black Talons. It elicited gasps from the group and murmurs of concern from young and old.

"So, I would suggest that anyone assigned to the investigation should wear Kevlar vests when out and about, just as a safeguard. I will operate solo as often as I can, but there may be times when I could use some help." Jack was unsure how many would really be of use.

"Whoa… Whoa… Whoa! Hang on a minute!" It was Cardell again. "I'm not paid enough to do this. Kevlar vests? We're in Lysbie, not fucking Afghanistan; you can count me out."

Walsh focused on the older man, he had inherited him when he took over a few years ago, and he did nothing but moan. He was six years past standard police pensionable age, and he just couldn't get rid of him.

"Cardell, we will only use you if, and only if, we really have to, and when we do, we will use your literary skills instead of your brawn. You can run the reports for us, so you can leave your Kevlar at home."

Cardell looked at his boss. He had put him in his place, but Walsh could almost hear the cogs whirring in his brain. Here it comes, he thought as the old dog took a deep breath.

"Are you saying I'm not up to it, boss? Because I can tell you…"

"Cardell!" Walsh cut in. "Can we leave it now? We will all be utilised as and when, and when we are, we will all be ready. OK?"

Jack needed to conclude this as it wasn't getting them anywhere.

"We can't really add anything more today as we need to see what is in this box at the bank. I'll visit in the morning and report back anything I find." He looked at Walsh.

"Agreed?"

"Yep, sounds good." Walsh nodded.

"Right, I'd better get you up to the house. Jim, sort me out a car would you."

Fifteen minutes later Jack and Walsh left the station for the short trip to the Manor House. They left the four officers to bet on who would be the one to help LARA crack the case. Jack had concluded, however, apart from keeping Walsh up to speed, none of the others wanted to get involved, and they definitely weren't ready. He needed to tactfully bring this to the DI's attention before he got one of them killed.

"Don't mind them." Walsh explained as they descended the stairs on their way to the car park.

"They get little excitement around here, but when called upon they will do a good job." He must have read his mind, Walsh was trying to big up the team, either for the benefit of his unit or his own self esteem.

Jack thought it prudent to remain tight lipped and just nod. Once on the station forecourt, Walsh led them to his parking space.

"Oh, for fuck's sake!" He just stared at the gleaming Ford KA awaiting them in the bay.

CHAPTER TWENTY-ONE
Base camp

If Jack was to describe Mittand Burrow it would be picture postcard, an unspoilt village in the heart of the countryside.

The clear skies brightened by the soft glow of the afternoon sun brought the colours of the foliage alive. It exuded a sense of calm, a lazy way of life. Somewhere to rest, recharge or simply chill. It reminded him of home. It had the same effect on him, a place to relax and forget the rest of the world. He needed the solace and the solitude to recharge his engine. That was the life of Matt Collins, the nondescript IT specialist who liked to keep himself to himself. As Jack Case, he had work to do, but at the back of his mind, he wondered if he could mix business with pleasure. He would play it by ear.

They made their way through the narrow country lanes, passing small thatched cottages set back in their well kept grounds. Passing a farm, they slowed to allow the cows to cross the road on their way to pasture. A tractor weaved through the cornfields hugging the hillside behind, dust clouds caught by the sun's rays created a golden mist around it as it worked the field.

The lane opened onto the main thoroughfare surrounding the village green, the centre of Mittand Burrow. The main stores and amenities bordered the manicured lawn. The residential streets intersected through four narrow lanes.

The cricket pitch and pavilion took centre stage, with an unobstructed view for spectators. A small reeded pond bordered the southern edge to the west of an old style domed bandstand.

Two ducks floated blissfully in the waning sun, keeping out of the shade of the single oak tree watching over them from the bank.

They passed The Golden Fleece, a post office, the local butchers, next to the Grocers along the east of the green.

Looking across, he could make out another pub next to the village hall and a library set back from the village church, a sentinel keeping watch over its parishioners.

It was a fully self-contained community set within a square quarter mile.

Straight ahead to the south, the high walls and impressive gates of the Manor House came into view.

"Here's your new home." DI Walsh said as he drove up to the iron entrance. The gates automatically swung open letting the small car onto the grounds.

Jack gazed at the large Georgian House as they drove along the gravel drive, encircling the well manicured lawn. He couldn't see how something as large as this ten bedroomed palace would suit just two people. Eighteen sash windows, ten above and eight below dominated the front of the red brick 18th century property.

Steps led to a large panelled door surrounded by impressive Greek style pilasters. The entablature capping the structure was carved with the images of racing charioteers. The cornice seemed oddly out of place with the gargoyles looking down onto the driveway.

"I'll call you as soon as I leave the bank." He climbed out of the KA, prising his kit bag, slightly battered from the afternoon's exertions, from the tiny rear seats.

"Yes, you do that." Walsh pulled away stopping after only a few yards. Unwinding his window he leant out, looking back towards the house.

"Hey... Case..." Jack looked over to the car.

"... Thanks." Walsh faced front and drove towards the exit.

DI Walsh watched the man through his rearview mirror as he drove away. There was something about the LARA agent that scared him. He had studied him throughout the afternoon, the way he looked at people and thought long and hard before he spoke.

He seemed to observe everything within his surroundings before making his move. His whole demeanour fascinated him, but it also concerned him. He had seen these characteristics before, a few months ago at a seminar which analysed and theorised such behaviour.

Jack Case showed the traits of a killer.

The bell sounded with a traditional chime. He expected a butler resplendent in a morning suit with a plum firmly fixed in his mouth.

Instead of Jeeves, a pretty young girl greeted him in jeans and a plain yellow tee shirt. She had a cloth slung over her shoulder and a tool belt around her waist. The tools included a scouring brush and several squirt bottles suspended from the belt by their triggers.

"Mr Case?" She asked.

"Yes, that's right, and you are?" He stepped into the lavish hallway.

"I'm Bethany." She said, closing the door behind her.

"Mrs Paxton-Thorn is in the stables. She has asked for you to make yourself comfortable in the drawing room; she will be with you in a few minutes." She led him into an impressive room, decorated in white and gold, its high ceiling adorned with glimmering chandeliers of gold and crystal.

Bethany walked to a gilt and white marble cabinet, open to reveal a crystal glass housing full to the brim with alcohol of every denomination.

"Can I offer you a drink?" She asked pre-empting his choice by taking a tumbler from the shelf.

"Whisky and water, please." He said. "Anything will be fine." It helped Bethany as he could see several single malts alongside several mixed blends and sour mash. She correctly chose a single malt, adding water from a small tap fixed to the base of the shelving. She passed it to him.

"I have to go, I'm afraid, things to do." She pulled the cloth from her shoulder giving the cabinet a little wipe to emphasise her point.

"Mrs Paxton-Thorn will be with you in a few minutes. Please help yourself in the meantime."

She left the room, closing the door quietly behind her.

Bethany Claridge was the daughter of June and the sister of Lisa. They were the housekeepers for the Paxton-Thorns, Jack recollected from his notes. They were free from suspicion and after meeting Bethany he had to concur. June Claridge had been with the Paxtons for well over 10 years according to reports, more a part of the family than an employee. The daughters joined around five years ago, and now it seemed, with Lisa pregnant, the next generation of keepers were on their way.

He sat on one of the strategically placed gilt side chairs, its hard seat and back reminded him of his painful hip. Awkwardly positioning himself so that his good side took most of the weight he took a large draw from his glass. The comforting burn helped him to settle. He placed it back onto its gold coaster, taking in the lavish surroundings.

He knew that Annabel Paxton-Thorn had a significant influence in the decor of her home; her passion for Grecian neo-classical art was apparent. A walk-in fireplace dominated the room, housed within a pillared mantel of intricately carved marble ingrained with gold leaf swirls.

A gilt-framed mirror above the finely decorated mantle covered the rest of the wall, finishing just below the coving.

Grecian urns were dotted around the room on stands, on wall displays and two, big enough to hide a small child, stood underneath the large sash window.

Annabel Paxton-Thorn entered the room. She was a good looking woman, he could see from the photographs on file, but in the flesh, they did her no justice at all. She was stunning.

She dressed in beige jodhpurs pulled tight around her shapely legs, together with a green quilt riding jacket that curved around her defined hips. It pulled in around her tiny waist before fanning out to mould around her full breasts, a silk scarf covered her cleavage. Dark wavy hair fell to her shoulders, slightly tousled from her riding hat. Her emerald green eyes shone within her tired face, showing the strain of the last few weeks, but taking nothing away from her beauty. She appeared determined yet sensual, her smile was enchanting.

"Mr Case, sorry to keep you waiting, welcome to the Manor House." She extended her hand as she stepped towards him.

Trying to hide the pain in his hip, he rose to greet her, attempting to turn the grimace into a smile, he wasn't sure if he had carried it off.

"Jack please, Mrs Paxton Thorn. It's nice of you to invite me to your beautiful home." She took his proffered hand, impressed by his firm grip.

"I'm sorry for your loss, this must be a difficult time for you. You have the full support of my agency to bring the culprits to justice." It was the right thing to say, but he could see it was still raw.

Annabel remained silent, not releasing his hand as she fought to keep control. She had coped well over the past few weeks as she struggled with memories of Colin, the bad times a distant memory. She was at the stage where she could smile at the many happy memories. From their courtship, the fun times, their wedding, the early days at the manor, all things to cherish. But Derek's death only days ago had brought the dread, the fear and the sheer loneliness back to her.

She was determined to remain strong, she owed it to her husband and now Derek, to do what she could to help these people find the murderers. With a strength she had learnt to embrace since the funeral, she composed herself, releasing his grip. She smiled nodding in thanks.

"Well then, I would feel much more comfortable if you called me Annabel. Please make yourself at home while you are here. Your company have delivered equipment for you, they have taken it to your room." She walked to the cabinet and poured herself a vodka. She dropped in three ice cubes from the inbuilt dispenser, seating herself on an adjacent chair to study her guest.

She was grateful for his company, and she had struck gold; he was gorgeous. His tight black tee shirt and the leather jacket did nothing to hide his flat stomach, and she was sure the ripples in the fabric were all muscle. He had ice blue eyes and whether as a fashion statement or lack of facilities, his blue face and close shaved head enhanced his features even more. He had a ruggedness that screamed danger.

She was glad he was on her side, and although this was definitely the wrong time, she felt sensations which she hadn't felt for a while… Lust. She shuffled in her seat as she tried to force the feeling away, for now anyway.

"I have invited a few guests for dinner this evening, I do hope you will join us." She broke the spell. It was funny, but she sensed he might have the same thoughts. His eyes bore into hers, not threatening but warm, understanding. She wasn't sure, but she also thought she saw the attraction, but that could have been wishful thinking.

"Yes, thank you, but I could do with freshening up first. I should set the equipment up and check in, so if you'll excuse me." Jack rose, downing the contents of his glass.

Annabel showed him to his room, one of the larger guest rooms containing a four poster bed, in keeping with the grandeur of the house. A large space had been allocated as an office by the window. HQ had delivered a desk similar to the one he used at home, along with several attaché cases. A full wardrobe of clothes, already hung in all the right places, confirmed he would be here for a while. It was the same wherever he went; the agency preferred operatives to travel light, providing a base camp in all cases. This equipment could vary from a simple bag of equipment and supplies to the operation centre they had installed here.

He wandered into the en suite and smiled as he looked at the sunken bath full of steaming water, scented with fragrant oils. He undressed... first things first.

CHAPTER TWENTY-TWO
Cluedo

He dressed casually for dinner, light trousers, white shirt and black sports jacket. He checked in through the sat system, reported contact and location, before logging off. Feeling refreshed he left his room to meet the others.

"Good evening, Mr Case. If you would like to follow me." Bethany met him in the hallway, leading him towards the dining room.

She had changed into formal attire, black skirt with a crisp white blouse, just a show for the dinner party, a way of Annabel Paxton-Thorn keeping up appearances. He couldn't imagine this formality being an everyday thing. He was glad he hadn't, but Jack felt that perhaps he should have worn his dinner jacket. Bethany held the two large oak handles, pushing the doors inwards.

"Mr Jack Case." She announced to the waiting guests.

As heads turned to look, his heart sank when he saw all the men in formal attire.

"Jack, how nice to see you." Annabel Paxton-Thorn came towards him. Taking two full champagne flutes from a tray on a side table she placed one in his hand. She had changed into a daring full length dress that hugged every contour of her trim figure. There was no scarf to cover her cleavage this time, a stunning ruby necklace replaced it instead. He made sure he didn't admire it for too long.

"Thank you, Mrs Pa... Annabel." He corrected himself before she did it for him. He took a small sip, looking over the glass at his surroundings.

The white walls and decor gave the room a continental feel, it was the artwork, the Apotheosis of Napoleon and the Apotheosis of Homer by Jean Auguste Dominique Ingres that made it, presenting an altogether Mediterranean flavour. The dining table, the centrepiece of the room, was lavish in its decoration. Two gold candelabras were positioned at each end burning four candles. They covered the table with a warm glow, flickering over fruit bowls and crystal decanters of red and white wine, lending a shimmer to the gilt edged dinner service, set for eight.

"Come, let me introduce you to my guests." She put her arm in his leading him towards the group gathered around the Steinway grand piano. One of the female guests was playing a gentle sonata from Beethoven's repertoire. The music stopped at their approach as the pianist swivelled around in her seat. She stood as Annabel made the introduction.

"This is Linda Norwood. That was so beautifully played Linda, can I introduce you to Jack Case?" Annabel released her arm so that Linda could shake his hand.

"Pleased to meet you, Mr Case. I hope you can help this marvellous woman, she has been through so much." Annabel squeezed Linda's arm in thanks as Jack released himself from her vigorous handshake.

He knew of the long standing feud and could see it was now at an end, although he couldn't help noticing that one guest had kept his distance. Annabel introduced the rest of the company as Jack shook hands with each in turn.

"In no particular order..." She began, "This is Colin's father Brigadier Thorn, Eliza Winch, Father Gerald Richards, Commissioner Harry Burrows and finally my father Major Reginald Paxton."

He couldn't quite believe his eyes. He was standing in front of the initial suspects from the Thorn murder, and he couldn't get the mystery board game out of his head. In front of him were Miss Scarlett, Professor Plum, Colonel Mustard, Reverend Green and a host of new characters. Agatha Christie would have a field day with this cast.

"Shall we be seated?" Annabel gestured to the table, directing him towards the chair on her right.

June Claridge had done Annabel proud. The meal was magnificent, the meats succulent and perfectly cooked, the desserts varied and sweet. They served the food with professionalism reserved for the highest class of restaurants. The Claridges beavered around the table, ensuring all the guests had a full glass, serving each course with military precision. Conversations were littered with compliments for the whole experience.

Full and satisfied, the ladies retired to the drawing room while the men remained at the table sampling port, along with a fine selection of Columbian cigars. It was a tradition that existed amongst the gentry, something Jack would never understand or want to. But, on this occasion it did give the men a chance to learn more about Annabel's guest and for him to build profiles.

"So, Case..." The Commissioner started the ball rolling, "... I understand you nearly got my DI killed this afternoon." He didn't know what to expect after the less than warm welcome from DI Walsh, but it seemed the Commissioner was just as abrasive.

"I don't think I was directly to blame Commissioner. Something is going on in the village that is creating a lot of interest. It appears to be directed towards Thorn Paxton and Gant or their clients, I cannot tell which yet."

"Well, there's only one partner left now... my daughter." Major Paxton said from the end of the table.

He had been seated well away from Linda Norwood during the meal as their relationship was still less than cordial, even though Annabel was trying her best to bring an end to hostilities. From his place at the far end of the table, he had raised his voice more than he should have, probably due to the alcohol. He realised as soon as he uttered the words, he could have been a little more tactful.

"Sorry Warren, I didn't mean anything by that." Paxton had done it again, mouth in gear before brain.

"No, you never do Reggie." Brigadier Thorn sighed.

"Never mind, what's done is done. Whatever is said won't bring back my son." Jack could sense a tension in the group which he knew was partly due to his presence, Ed had briefed him on that, but there was something else. An overriding sense that something wasn't quite right between them, but he couldn't put his finger on it.

"So where do we go from here?" It was the Commissioner again.

"Well, first we need to see what is in the safe deposit box. It will give us something to go on as I understand the instructions were to leave everything there."

"The contents were not to be removed, only viewed for some reason. So it makes sense that whatever Derek Gant had seen before he was killed should still be there when we open it."

"Well, let us pray that it is the name of the murderer." Father Richards joined in with the conversation.

He seemed a quiet man and leaving his collar on indicated that he was still on duty. He could be worth talking to away from the others, he might be very useful indeed. Jack made a mental note to arrange a meeting.

"Whatever you find, I'm just glad you are here, Case. I know you will take care of my daughter." The Major raised his glass.

"To LARA." He toasted… on his own.

There was an awkward silence as Major Paxton downed his port in one gulp. He gasped loudly with relief as the bittersweet liquid finished its journey down his throat.

Jack could see that Paxton seemed to be on the periphery, although the Major had known the present company for years. Also, the priest seemed uncomfortable, he noticed a change in him when the toast was proposed. He couldn't be sure, but he could have sworn he saw him scowl.

The rest of the conversation tended towards general chit chat. Talk around the military, a little background information on Jack, the little he was cleared to give them, followed by a brief history of the village. Nothing more regarding the case. The drink was flowing but only succeeded in killing the conversation, after a while, they were drinking in silence.

"Well …" Father Richards checked his watch,

"… It appears that I should be going, I have some work to do in the morning." He got up from his seat, collecting his jacket from the coat stand.

"Nice to meet you, Mr Case, good luck tomorrow. I hope you find what you are looking for." He shook his hand warmly as he left the room.

Leaving the table to be cleared, the guests went back to the piano to listen to Linda as she demonstrated more of her skills on the ivory.

Jack went to pour himself another scotch from the bar when Eliza Winch joined him. Again, the photograph at the station did not do her justice. She was a pretty blonde, slightly younger than Annabel, but equally trim and her black lace dress showed that she was just as blessed. Was it something to do with the country air around Mittand Burrow? The village certainly had its fair share of beautiful women.

"Mr Case, I'm sorry I haven't had a chance to talk to you tonight." Her smile was infectious, and her hazel eyes sparkled, lighting up her face.

"Call me Jack, please... this evening has been quite an introduction. It has been difficult to get to speak to everyone, but I hope to meet you all individually during my stay." He would need to get around to that eventually although he was very much a private man, a loner who found even one to ones were one person too many. He wasn't very good in crowds unless he had someone under surveillance. But for now he was acting, he was doing his job. In this role, he could be as sociable as anyone.

"That would be lovely." Eliza cooed, very keen to have that one to one. She lowered her tone, leaning in towards him, making sure no one was in earshot.

Annabel had left to commend the Claridges on their hard work while the remaining guests were lost in Linda's performance as she played on. The conversation had died, Major Paxton, in particular, seemed to be in a dream state, swaying slightly like a tree in the breeze.

"I need to see you as soon as possible." Softening her voice to a mere whisper.

"I think I have an idea of what's going on here, but I must see you alone." He kept his head down, pouring water into his glass as he listened to her.

"There was a file in the office that Derek was very interested in. He kept saying that he was about to become a very rich man. While he was away I took a glimpse at a letter that he had tucked in the front. I can't quite believe what it said..."

"What's all this then, Eliza..." It was Annabel, "Are you trying to keep our guest to yourself?" She had returned from the kitchen and was standing behind her. How long had she been there, Jack didn't know. But it spooked Eliza enough to put her in a flap.

"No…I..he..it was…I mean …" She couldn't get her words out.

"Ellie, I'm joking." Annabel leaned forward hugging her, laughing.

"Silly girl…" She playfully chastised her, kissing her gently on the cheek.

"Come on; let's give Linda some support." Grabbing both Jack and Eliza by the hand she pulled them towards the piano.

The party lasted a few hours more, and Linda proved to be quite the performer.

She successfully lightened the mood with some old classics before getting them all involved in a singalong to some Beatles hits. It wasn't long before the Major had to be escorted to a cab, definitely the worse for wear, as the others drifted off one by one. Linda was the last to leave, hugging Annabel with genuine affection, the years of conflict now well and truly behind them. She left to walk back to the rectory, her new home.

The Claridges had finished for the evening, which left Jack and Annabel to tidy up the remaining glasses. They left them in the kitchen to be dealt with in the morning, returning to the drawing room.

Annabel poured a vodka, offering him a whiskey, one last nightcap before bed.

"Thank you for a lovely evening," Jack chose the same chair he had used on his arrival.

"Oh, that's my pleasure, I'm glad you enjoyed it. They're not a bad bunch, my father can be a little tactless and Eliza is doom and gloom. I apologise for abandoning you earlier, I hope she didn't bore you." He wasn't about to tell her of their conversation, but after his visit to the bank, Eliza was definitely his first call on his return.

"No, they were all fine… lovely people." Was all he would offer in reply.

Annabel put her drink on a side table, walking to the bureau at the back of the room. She took a letter from the top drawer, handed it to him and returned to her chair.

"This arrived this morning." She took a drink, watching him as he opened the envelope and read.

Dear Mrs Paxton-Thorn,

I would first like to offer my condolences for the untimely death of your husband, Mr Thorn. He was a unique man who had been a great help to our family over the years. We will miss him.

I realise things have been very difficult for you which is why I have waited a respectful length of time before sending this request. I am writing to you to ask for your help in continuing the investigation relating to the Barth Probate case that your husband had been handling for many months.

All paperwork has been prepared, and I have issued representation by proxy to allow you full access on the family's behalf. It is imperative you take adequate identification to assist with this when you arrive.

Mr Thorn notified me he has left information at the location on the business card which will allow you to continue with the investigation. I must stress that the intelligence gathered will have a major bearing on the case for the good of our family name and will prove extremely rewarding to you and your business for many years to come.

I have enclosed a cheque for you personally to cover your expenses in this matter and trust I can rely on your discretion at all times.

I will contact you in two weeks to arrange a meeting to discuss your findings and will provide you with further details which will help to progress the case towards its conclusion.

Yours

Jayne Langfield (Mrs)

Jack checked the postmark, Vienna, the envelope had been typed along with the letter. A coincidence or something else? He wasn't sure, but this seemed like a setup. The business card was the same one found on Derek Gant, and it belonged to George Wainwright at the Central Bank. The cheque was for fifteen grand, one hell of an expense account. He wondered if they had lured Gant to the bank with the same offer.

"Mrs Langfield?" He enquired looking at Annabel, who was watching him intently.

"A client of my husbands. She wanted him to look into the validity of a second will in the probate of her mother's estate. I'm not sure about the details of the case, Derek was handling it after Colin was killed. The police have the file now." He hadn't noticed the file when he was at the station, but then again he wasn't looking for it, another mental note to add to the rest.

"Well, the safe deposit box is the key to this case, or at least a good starting point." He stood as he drained the glass.

"I think I will need to sleep on it." He said excusing, himself. "goodnight."

He took the letter and the business card with him, leaving Annabel toying with the cheque as he left her and went to his room.

He fed all the notes gathered from the dinner party into the sat system. Father Richards, Eliza Winch and Jayne Langfield were of particular interest. He would check the data in the morning before leaving for Oxford.

The amount of alcohol consumed throughout the evening provided an excellent sleeping draft. He was comatose in minutes.

CHAPTER TWENTY-THREE
Infiltrate

The mobile rang for the eighth time. He knew he had to answer it, but didn't fancy the flack he was bound to get.

"If you don't answer they will send someone else, you know that." Dolf finished yet another beer, slamming his empty glass onto the bar.

The barman should have been home an hour ago, but hotel policy meant that as long as paying guests continued to drink, the bar stayed open. The overtime was always welcome, but Kings Cross station in the early hours was not a nice place to get home from. Even though the hotel was only across the road, he hated walking through the area late at night, let alone tackling the tube. When the nutters weren't on the train, they were harassing people on the platform, and there were never any guards around late at night to stop them.

Refilling the pint glass, he realised he would be here a while yet. This guy was a sponge, he had counted fourteen pints since the start of his shift at six. Now, seven hours later, he hadn't slowed at all, he didn't appear to have a stop button.

The other one, the blonde, preferred wine and was still only part way through a bottle of Pinot. He seemed agitated, he'd been pacing the bar for the last hour. He kept staring at the mobile on the table every time it rang, every half an hour to start with but now, every ten minutes.

"I'll get it soon." Kurt continued to pace out the floor. This call was not going to end well.

Two jobs and both had failed. The first was to get a code. He had done that, and he knew he had heard a male pig. But it should have been a set of six numbers, so after some lateral thinking they came up with the word BOAR. Using the alphabet in number form gave them the numbers 2,15,1 and 18, six digits, 215118. But it was wrong. They still needed the code.

The second job should have been easy. The car was travelling at a steady fifty, an easy shot and enough rounds to annihilate it. But that pig detective had noticed them, braking before he had steadied himself. The bastards had been lucky twice because the car had left the road giving them cover. A fluke shot from the LARA agent had thrown them from the bike, wrecking the engine. Dolf had his leg trapped, he could have helped him, but he needed to finish the job. It caused a problem as their escape was paramount for the sake of the Zukunft Reich. So while Dolf was struggling to get free, he was left to tackle them alone.

Jack Case was one of LARA's elite agents, his reputation as a ruthless assassin had spooked him. As he watched him roll out of the car grabbing his gun, he panicked and ran. They agreed that Dolf would have done the same, but they needed to cover their backs. They had to find a convincing story for the failure. Unfortunately, they could not make any excuses sound plausible. He'd gone through several in his head. Gun jam, thrown off and injured, forced back in a gun battle. None would persuade the boss as he knew the agent they were dealing with would have taken advantage, they would be dead by now. But if Kurt told him the truth, they would be dead anyway as failure was not an option. His mobile rang again.

This time he picked it up, watching the screen pulsate in time with the chime. Bracing himself, he pressed receive.

"Ja." He tried to sound strong although his heart was fluttering.

"There had better be a good reason it has taken me FOUR hours to get hold of you." The scream made him jump, he nearly dropped the phone.

"Yes, sir, a very good reason." He was now thinking on his feet.

"I would suggest that I make it easy for you." The voice was calm again. "I suspect that since you have yet again failed to bring us the results we require, you have ignored my calls for fear of your life." The voice went silent, letting the words sink in. Kurt needed to think fast, or he was a dead man.

"No sir it…"

"QUIET!" This time he did drop the phone, it span out of his hand. He caught it, juggling it between both hands, catching it again before it hit the floor. He thrust it back to his ear, hoping he hadn't been disconnected. The silence was frightening, he could hear a connection, hear breathing then finally a sigh of exasperation. He braced himself for what was to come.

"Plans have changed." The voice was calm again.

"You are booked into the Golden Fleece at Mittand Burrow. The code will be brought there and you will retrieve it. This is where your university education will finally be of use to us. You are registered as Kevin Johnson, we have prepared your papers, and you will use your English accent at all times."

"Case is in the village so there will be an opportunity for you to eliminate him. We need Dolf back here. You will find plane tickets at the reception desk tomorrow morning, along with your rail tickets. A car will be outside at 9am to drive Dolf to the airport and provide you with the equipment for your mission." Relief surged through Kurt's body. This time he would not screw up, he had a lot to prove after recent events. He didn't want to admit it, but perhaps without Dolf, he would have a better chance of succeeding.

"I would suggest that you both leave the bar to get some sleep. You will not fail us this time." The call ended.

Kurt walked over to his comrade, signalling to the barman.

"Give me that bottle of Jack Daniels, we are celebrating." He turned to Dolf, placing a hand on his shoulder

"Let's make ourselves comfortable, I have our new instructions."

The barman placed the sour mash onto the bar with an empty glass. As he filled the bucket with fresh ice, he couldn't help thinking he might just be home for breakfast. He watched the two men huddle together in the corner by the window. Settling down for the night he sat back on his stool to reread the paper.

He'll remember to bring a book next time.

CHAPTER TWENTY-FOUR
Revelation

They served breakfast on the sprawling patio. Jack had chosen omelette, two slices of toast and orange juice.

It was a beautiful morning, clear blue skies with brilliant sunshine.

The garden was a sun trap bathing the ground in warmth. The vibrant colours and aroma of the flora filled the senses with long summer days and warm summer nights. Bethany looked comfortable in her jeans and tee shirt. She poured more coffee as she cleared away his plate.

"Mrs Paxton-Thorn will be with you in a moment. She is changing after her ride."

He had watched Annabel trot past the house from his window this morning, a daily ritual to keep her sane throughout the trauma of the past few weeks. Studying her as part of his research, he found her to have a natural affinity with both humans and equines. Apart from a few blots on her copybook, he could find no real evidence that she had instigated a hit on her husband.

There were a few things he needed to clear up still, but murder was not one of them. The data sent back from the sat system had the background on the others he'd asked for.

Father Richards, born in Warwickshire, gained a theology degree at Oxford University. He became curate at St Andrews Church in Lysbie. Six years ago he became the priest of St Matthews in Mittand Burrow as a result of the death of Father Driscoll, a natural death, age had overcome him. Not much here, no skeletons so far.

Eliza Winch, born to Martha and George in Lysbie, moved to Mittand Burrow five years ago. Library clerk for two years before joining

Thorn Paxton and Gant. No relationships to speak of although it was common knowledge she had a thing for her employer.

Colin hadn't reciprocated, many said that he had been oblivious to it all being too focused on his practice. Would that be a motive to kill him? He didn't think so, but he resolved to find out more when he returned from Oxford.

Jayne Langfield provided more questions than answers. The several pages of data so far dealt with her mother, Gloria Barth.

Mrs Langfield had proven elusive. No location, no contact number, seen only once in Mittand Burrow. A shadowy figure whose actions had cost two lives already, with people out there willing to kill more. It all pointed to the Barth case, in particular, Langfield. She was the key to unravelling this whole affair.

"Good morning Jack, how was breakfast?" Annabel had changed into jeans and a white tee shirt. Sipping her orange juice as she approached, she looked the perfect advert for summer. She pulled a chair from the table, sitting down opposite him.

"Yet again my compliments to the chef, perfect omelette." He poured fresh coffee into his cup and taking a sip, placed it back on the saucer.

"Tell me about Derek Gant." He wasn't surprised when he saw a furtive glance to the right. It was a question straight from left field, meant to confuse, her eye movement showed he had hit a nerve.

"That's a strange question. Why would you ask?" Delay tactics, she was trying to figure out the reason for the question. She had to provide an answer without exposing herself. Her expression had hardened, she narrowed her eyes, tilting her head slightly; a show of mistrust. He needed to pull her back.

"Nothing of any consequence…" He lied

"You would know him better than most as you were partners. I wanted to learn a little more about him. There aren't many people around here who particularly cared for him. From what I've heard he was brash, loud and altogether a nasty piece of work. He was also lazy, had little ability and seemed to hang on to Colin's coattails, his ticket to riches. Why was he allowed to stay around for so long?"

"You know about the affair don't you?" Annabel lowered her head.

"Was it an affair?" He asked as she looked him in the eye, no deviation, more resignation.

"Not an affair, he was available, good looking and paid me attention. It was a fling, nothing more, and it only lasted a month." She sighed, her eyes welled, her bottom lip quivered.

"Try to be with a man married to his work. The only affection I get is from the stables, from my babies. He was never there when I needed him." She sniffed, sipping juice to lubricate her dry mouth.

"So, when it was over you wanted him out of the business, your friendship wrecked. Was he the one to finish it?" By softening his voice he knew he could get more.

"I wished Colin dead." She stared at him, knowing what he wanted to hear. Jack kept his eyes on her, raising one eyebrow as she continued.

"Derek informed the police of my rash statement. All I was trying to get across was that I wanted a life. I wanted someone to love me, need me, someone to share things with. It was a stupid throwaway remark born out of frustration, I didn't mean I wanted to kill him!" She held his gaze, seeking reassurance.

He watched her dab her eyes with a serviette. He could tell this was hard for her, but there was a resolve there, a determination to see it through. She was no murderer.

"Now he is gone I miss him. It's so hard to explain, but I finally realise that he did everything he could to make me happy. He didn't question the stabling, the vet bills, the running costs. I had the house exactly as I wanted it, he didn't complain, not once. All he wanted was his own space, and somewhere he could relax. He asked for nothing more than that. All the hours he worked, all the trips, all the stress. It was all for me."

She lowered her head again, her shoulders rocked as she sobbed in silence. He could only watch until her crying subsided.

He poured coffee from the silver pot, sliding it across the table. As she raised her head, she managed a smile.

"Typical man. If a woman cries offer her a hot drink, that'll do the trick." She poured cream into the blackness and stirred.

"I didn't have a handkerchief." Placing her cup on the saucer, she smiled at him.

"Sorry, I know you have to ask these questions. It's still a little raw." She straightened in her chair. She'd given him what he wanted, now it was her turn, time to move on.

"So, where do we go from here?"

"Well, I'm going to Oxford to have a chat with a certain Mr Wainwright. I need to get to the bottom of this safe deposit box." He checked his watch. His car should be here in twenty minutes.

"We're going to Oxford you mean." She expressed a determination that surprised him.

"I don't think so; it's far too dangerous. Look what happened to Derek, and those guys are still out there. Definitely out of the question. Spend time with your horses, I'll update you when I get back." There was no way she was coming along; he would need his wits about him.

"They killed my husband, and you believe that letter led Derek to his death. I'm going, either with you or I'll meet you at the bank." She crossed her arms. "And don't patronise me, the horses will be fine."

She was fascinating. The steely determination she was showing was not worth challenging. Jack could not stop her from going, but it was a risk. She would be too exposed on the drive into Oxford, even more so on the way back unless he was with her. He realised he had no choice.

"One condition. You do what I tell you to do, no questions, no compromise. It could save your life."

"Deal." She extended her hand across the table. As he accepted the handshake, they both laughed, the tension from the last few minutes disappearing into the morning sunshine.

Jack drove the Range Rover onto the dual carriageway towards Oxford. It was Colin Thorn's car, lent to him by Annabel for the duration of his stay.

They cancelled the car arranged by the Lysbie force, he was thankful as he didn't think the KA had air conditioning.

"So what do we know about Jayne Langfield?" Annabel said,

rereading the letter.

"From the information, I received this morning it has more to do with the mother, Gloria Barth. She appears to have changed the original will during the last two years of her life. She named the main beneficiary as Claudia Robertson, Mrs Langfield's sister. That was the reason for your husband's appointment months ago after it was contested."

He decided there was no harm in sharing this information with Annabel; she may even help fill in some gaps.

"It's a simple probate, so why the drama? Unless you are sole survivor, there is always someone in the family who thinks they deserve more."

"Yes, but in this case, Mrs Langfield has two very good reasons to contest. First, the validity of the will, Gloria Barth had a history of mental illness. Second, she claims that Claudia Robertson is an imposter."

"Hang on a minute. She wants to contest the validity of her own sister?"

"It's a little more complicated than that. They haven't seen each other for fifty years, Mrs Robertson didn't show until two years ago. That is a good enough reason to question her motives." He knew it would help if he let her know a little of the history, checkered as it was.

"To understand it, we need to go back to 1941. Gloria Barth married her first husband, David Gordon at St Andrews in Lysbie. It was during wartime, and they settled in Mittand Burrow in a small cottage off the green."

"Gordon was working in communications, he was posted to France towards the end of the war on a maintenance mission. He was killed just east of Lyon, not long before he was due to return home. Gloria Gordon, as she was then, went into total meltdown and was sectioned in a hospital in Oxford. She spent five years in and out of institutions before transferring to Broadmoor in 1950."

"Poor woman..." Annabel couldn't imagine what she must have gone through.

"What about her family, there must have been someone to help?"

"All dead…" Jack explained.

"Parents killed during the blitz, Gordon was a foster child. His parents died when he was very young. So it was up to the authorities to look after Gloria as best they could." He continued with the second half of the story.

"During her incarceration, she befriended a nurse, Henry Barth. He made it his mission to care for her. The change in Gloria was remarkable, she soon showed signs of improvement. The relationship blossomed to such an extent, Barth obtained a care order. In 1954 Gloria Gordon was signed off the register to set up home with Barth in Debervale, twenty miles from Mittand Burrow. They married in the summer of 55." Annabel, enthralled by the story, rolled the letter into a tube, unrolling it and rolling it again, as he finished the account.

"In 1961, Gloria gave birth to twins, Jayne and Claudia. They moved to Mittand Burrow, partly for Gloria. Henry worked as an orderly at Wishwell House Care home in nearby Mittand Parva. In 1962, he was a carer on a Papal visit to Rome with some Parva residents. The coach was involved in an accident which injured several, killing five, one of whom was Henry Barth."

Annabel thought of Linda Norwood as the story unfolded, of her struggle when her husband had died.

They had met many times over the last few weeks. A new friendship born from tragedy, she also knew how it felt to lose a loved one. A feeling of total loss which could take you to the edge if there is no one there to help, to have it happen twice was incomprehensible to her.

"Don't tell me, once again there was no one to help Gloria." She could predict the outcome.

"Yep, you've got it. Henry had no family, losing his parents in his teens. He had a sister but she was severely disabled, she died when he was in his early twenties. She was the catalyst that drove him to dedicate his working life to the care of others."

"Gloria Barth was sectioned again in 1962. She was self harming, and for the safety of the children, they were taken away. After the assessment, doctors recommended that Gloria should spend the rest of her life under mental care."

They passed a sign - Oxford 2 miles.

"The children were put up for adoption, and at 18 months old they were separated. Jayne remained with her foster family in Hertfordshire, while a family in Lancashire adopted Claudia. You couldn't blame the adoptive parents, but neither daughter was told of their true parentage until they were 21."

"By this time Gloria had been diagnosed with dementia and was placed in a psychiatric care home in Oxfordshire. Jayne Langfield tracked her down in 1989, and they were reunited in the spring of 1990. Although dementia is a degenerative disease, Gloria seemed to react positively to the reunion, and the disease notably slowed during her later years. Ten years on, as Gloria reached the age of 80, Jayne got her mother admitted into Wishwell House in Mittand Parva. The reports were good, it would seem she did well within a normal environment. Mrs Langfield often took her mother to Mittand Burrow, which we should be able to verify later."

She thought of something.

"Well, if anyone could verify that, it would be Linda Norwood. Her husband Roland would have known them, and Linda would know anyone who Roland knew." Annabel now felt she could play her part in the investigation, even though she didn't know them. She felt as if she needed to help, if only in memory of Gloria.

"Good point." He admitted. He was now getting to the real reasons for the contesting of the will.

"Jayne Langfield was employed as a PA in a London law firm, married to John Langfield one of the investors. So the cost of the care home for her mother was no problem. Once she looked into all the estates and insurances in Gloria's name, she instructed the law firm to put all the investments and dues in order."

"Papers were drawn up and under the supervision of medical advisors, solicitors and the health authority, a will was prepared. The proceeds were to split between Jayne and Claudia, even though Claudia had not yet been traced. This was when the safe deposit box was discovered. Under legal supervision and with power of attorney,

Jayne was given access to the vault. The contents were verified, but never disclosed."

The spires of the city centre came into view in the distance as they entered the ring road.

"This is where it gets interesting. Jayne Langfield visited her mother as often as work would allow. Sometimes her role dictated overseas travel, the law firm has offices abroad. According to the staff at the care home, she was the only visitor Gloria had during the ten years of her residency. Shortly after her death at the age of 90, a new will revealed Claudia as her sole beneficiary."

"It was all above board, signed by Gloria, witnessed by a top flight practice. It caused Jayne to begin searching for a solicitor local to Mittand Parva. She came across Thorn Paxton and Gant which is where we stand today, but with a few loose ends to tie up. Where is Claudia? How involved was Colin in the case? What is in the safe deposit box? And why has Jayne Langfield disappeared?"

"We can answer one of those questions today, with any luck." It was all Annabel could think to say.

There were a lot of things to digest. How much had Colin known about the history of this case? She knew him well enough to know that he would have been thorough in his investigations. He would be in Jayne Langfield's corner with the ruthlessness of a Rottweiler. Had he uncovered something that had led to his death? Something important enough to make Colin leave the house on Friday 13th. What was it that had caused him to ignore his fear and take that fateful trip?

The Range Rover pulled into a vacant space on the High Street, a few yards from Central Bank.

He turned to Annabel, who seemed deep in thought.

"Ready?"

CHAPTER TWENTY-FIVE
Oxford

Before leaving the car, he took a small case from the glove box. It contained a syringe and two vials of Neostigmine, an antidote to Curare poisoning, reversing the paralysing effects of the drug. He hoped he wouldn't have to use it, but better to be safe than sorry. He left the car and went to the passenger door, opening it for Annabel.

"Stay close and head for the entrance." She waited until Jack placed a hand in her back, nudging her forward.

They rushed towards the bank, his gun sandwiched between his stomach and Annabel's back, ready for use in an instant. His head moved from left to right searching every face, watching for any sudden movement. As they reached the glass double doors, Jack tucked the gun into his belt behind his back, covering it with his sports jacket. They walked inside.

The girl on information led them into a sparsely furnished office. A thin, balding man in a three piece suit rose from a green baize table to greet his guests.

"Mr Wainwright, Mrs Annabel Paxton-Thorn and associate, here for their appointment." The young girl announced as Jack and Annabel entered.

"Thank you, Karen." He met them at the door, extending his hand in greeting.

"Ah, Mrs Paxton-Thorn, a pleasure to meet you. I am George Wainwright, manager." He offered a firm handshake.

"Please take a seat." He pulled a chair away before pushing it gently forward, following Annabel's movement.

As he took his own seat, he ignored Jack completely, leaving him to find his own way.

"First, please accept my sincere condolences on the tragic death of your husband; it must be very difficult for you." Annabel just smiled, nodding slightly in thanks.

"And I must say how shocked I am to hear of the same tragedy befalling Mr Gant, frightful business." He clasped his hands together staring into Annabel's eyes, the sympathy clear in his woeful expression. An expression perfected from years of condolences; after all, he was the distributor of many a financial inheritance.

Annabel stared at the metal plate in front of her. She remembered this from the meeting about Colin's new security measures, but she had no idea why it was here.

"What are you doing with this?" She didn't take her eyes from the smooth surface as a rush of emotion coursed through her. She could feel her bottom lip quiver.

"Your husband left it with us for your client, Mrs Langfield." He was surprised that she was unaware of its origin.

"This is all for the Barth case, a Probate?" What had Colin done?

"I would suggest it might be more involved than that, Mrs Paxton-Thorn. They chose us as the first bank to use this system at the behest of the client. Our whole security protocol was changed, our vaults reworked with funding from Mrs Langfield and her sponsors." Wainwright waited for the question. It was Jack who obliged.

"Sponsors? Do you have information on them? That's a hell of an investment just to protect some old lady's estate." Wainwright turned to look at the man opposite.

Who was this man with the audacity to attend such an important meeting without even shaving?

"… And you are?" His look of disdain remained, however hard he tried to quell it.

"Oh, I must apologise Mr Wainwright…" Annabel offered, suddenly realising that no introduction had been made. "This is…"

"Jack Case…" He cut in. "I am here on behalf of Lysbie police and head of the protection unit for Mrs Paxton-Thorn." The man's searing eyes made Wainwright uncomfortable. For a second he felt as if he should apologise, but only a second. It was his bank after all. How dare he!

"I would like to remind you both that the letter clearly states we can discuss the matter with the addressee only. In this case Mrs Paxton-Thorn." He felt in control once again.

"And this letter…" Jack passed a folded sheet of A4 across the table.

"… Is a search warrant, which gives me the right to turn this place inside out if I'm not given the information I need." Wainwright studied the warrant. The Crown Court magistrate's office had signed it, giving authority to the Lysbie Police, naming Jack Case as the lead investigator. He was tasked with gathering all necessary information in connection with the deaths of Mr Thorn and Mr Gant. He folded the sheet, placing it into his inside pocket. He tried desperately to hide his disappointment as he faced Jack.

"I cannot help you, Mr Case. We were told that we were having a renovation funded by a third party. Mrs Langfield was the only name given."

"But as I said earlier, one hell of an investment?" It made little sense.

"Oh, this is not just for one client." Wainwright could see their scepticism.

"Since the alterations, the vaults now house some of the worlds most valuable possessions. Our new clients are some of the worlds richest, most influential people, our major investors even more so." He felt an element of pride as he delivered such a prestigious overview.

There is more to this than meets the eye. Jack was trying to piece things together, but not a lot was adding up. He hoped the safe deposit box would shed some light.

"Shall we get this over with?" He needed answers, and obviously, they were not in this room.

Wainwright outlined the procedure as Annabel's hand activated the reader. She held onto it as they moved to a second door.

"I must relieve you of your possessions before we enter the vault I'm afraid."

The door from the branch opened, and a man mountain walked towards the table. His suit bulged at his biceps, and his shirt was at least two buttons short at the collar, forcing the lapels back towards his ears to accommodate his tree trunk neck. His tie was there to keep them from receding any further.

"Charles here will look after them for you. Mobile phone, any valuables in your pockets, anything that could prove a security risk." He looked at Jack as he finished the last requirement. Annabel dutifully placed her handbag on the table, emptying her coat pockets of her mobile, a little loose change and a lipstick.

"Mr Case?" They all looked at him. He could have sworn the muscle had grown a couple more inches taller and broader as he expanded his chest.

"Not gonna happen." Jack looked at Charles rather than Wainwright.

"I am assigned to protect Mrs Paxton-Thorn. I have all I need to provide backup should I need it and I have far more confidence in my own resources than I have in those of a high street bank."

Wainwright was surprised that Charles had not taken control of the situation, relieving this thug of his possessions. But his guard just stood there, dumb, eyes flicking between the two men.

He had never seen this before, and it unnerved him. Was his uncertainty fear? It looked to him that his head of security was stuck to the floor.

"Mr Wainwright…" Annabel just wanted this over. "I can vouch for Mr Case. After everything that's happened, I would prefer he remained by my side."

It was true that some of the clients were allowed one bodyguard to accompany them. But the decision was sanctioned well in advance, from a lot higher up. He, for the first time, was unsure of what to do. Should he let it pass on this one occasion? Should he involve higher up, exposing a weakness? He felt all eyes on him, his decision needed to be in the best interests of the bank.

The exposure regarding the Thorn murder had already filtered through to investors. It was no surprise as Thorn was instrumental in the vault reconstruction, he was one of the exclusive clientele. Now with the Gant business, it would raise more concerns. Given the circumstances, the murders, the search warrant and his ineffective head of security, he made an executive decision.

Holding his card over the keypad he pushed the door open, gesturing to his two guests.

"Shall we go?"

Jack inspected the whisky on the breakfront bookcase, an impressive collection. The vault uncovered more questions than answers. The technology was state of the art, even revolutionary, it made no sense. This was a murder with an agenda, a death connected to a mysterious letter that had brought them here. German bikers with a mission, Jayne Langfield, whose only connection to all of this killed at his home, add to that the hi-tech security room, more suited to a palace than a high street bank, all because of a contested will.

Annabel was staring at the steel desk, her hand resting on the back of the leather chair. She was gently rocking it from side to side as she thought of the two men who had sat there before her.

"Why didn't Colin tell me about all this?" She expected no answers, and none came. "I could have been there for him, helped him, supported him."

Her shoulders began to shake, she looked for a tissue in her handbag, then realised she had no handbag. She checked her pockets, desperately searching for something to wipe her nose. Defeated, she rested her arms on the back of the chair, burying her head. She burst into tears.

Both partners, her husband and former lover, the bad memories gradually fading as the days passed, were now gone. She loved them both, and they had left her to deal with this on her own. Colin would have been there for her, calming her down, assuring her that everything would be fine. Derek would persuade her to trust him as he would sort it. What should she do? Who would be there for her now?

Jack placed an arm on her shoulder.

"Come on Annabel, let's do what we came here for." As simple as that, no emotion, he had a job to do.

He was there to protect her; he was there to sort it. He would make sure everything would be fine. She wheeled around, falling into him, feeling his muscular arms wrap around her. She felt safe, protected, comforted. Jack let her exhaust the tears, allowing the grief to come to the surface. She needed this, it would strengthen her. He held her tight, absorbing the tremors, gently stroking her back. He would keep her safe.

….'Place the key into the housing smooth side down… await further instructions.'

He studied the markings, running his finger over the raised inscription. KVP.

"Who is KVP?" Annabel watched him examine the key head, she could tell he was as confused as she was.

"I'm not sure, I'll get it checked out. But it has to open something, and it's programmed with your prints."

He placed it into the drawer, watching it slip from view. The screen went blank before returning with just three words and a timer counting down from 20… 19…

'a MaileD pig.' Jack captured the image on his PDA, watching the counter 12..11.

"What does that mean?" Annabel watched the screen 8… 7.

"No idea, but we need that key." As the counter reached zero, the monitor blanked out and descended, closing over the recess.

"No, you don't." He grabbed the top of the screen, stopping the descent, pushing it back. As he let go, it closed again. An alarm sounded, a cacophonous squeal, piercing, angry.

"Shit!" He had to think fast.

"Annabel, get in the corner, behind the chair". He pointed to the armchair shouting at the top of his voice. She looked at him quizzically. What was he going to do?

He didn't have a lot of time, he was sure the muscle along with backup would soon appear.

"Go!" He barked at her. Even over the alarm, his shout made her jump. She ran to the corner and turning the chair around, dropped behind it.

With his left hand still holding the protesting monitor, he brought the Glock from behind his back pointing it at the thin lines of the closed drawer. Here goes nothing, he fired.

The bullet struck the metal enclosure, ricochetted past his ear, embedding into the oak door behind. He surveyed the dent in the steel; it was substantial, but the drawer remained closed. The screen was still fighting with his left arm, he felt the pressure as it was winning. With little time to spare he changed tack. Using both hands, he pushed with all his might. Once it was as far back as it could go he pushed more, he could feel the steel give, creaking in protest. The screen cracked, he pushed again. He could feel the monitor bend as he forced it on. There was an electrical short, sparks erupted from beneath the screen. Acrid smoke from the fried electronics began to fill his nostrils.

An explosion knocked him away as data, power and processors came together erupting in protest. The console warped and buckled as the heat found its own way to escape its confinement. The drawer shot open. It was a lot easier than he thought.

He grabbed the key, thrusting it into his pocket. He called over to Annabel, time to go…

Air rushed from his lungs as muscular arms squeezed around his waist. Jack flew through the air, coming to rest against the decorated, but unforgiving concrete wall. Any breath he had managed to draw in while airborne quickly escaped again.

Shaking his head to clear the mist from his eyes, he got to his knees, pressed his hand against the wall for support and slowly got to his feet. The boot caught him just below his diaphragm. Jack fell backwards, landing in a heap. He caught a glimpse of Annabel cowering behind the Chesterfield, a look of terror in her eyes. He could do nothing more than wink at her. They'll get through this… somehow.

Charles was towering over him, satisfaction spreading across his face. He bent forward to lift him to his feet, large hands heading for his shoulders. He had only one course of action. His boot scored a direct hit, straight between the legs. Eyes wide, testicle ruptured, the security guard fell towards him. He rolled away just as Charles collapsed head first onto the carpet.

Jack knelt beside the writhing figure, raised both hands above his head and linked his fingers together ready to bring them down on the guard's neck.

"Stop all this!" The alarm now quiet, allowed the voice of George Wainwright to carry clearly across the room.

He stood in the doorway surveying the mess. The console was a wreck, small plumes of smoke rose from its centre. Part of the wallpaper hung from the wall, and two of the crystal decanters lay shattered on the floor. Wine, whiskey and cognacs continued to spread their stain into the plush regency carpet.

"What have you done?… What have you done?"

The board will be furious.

Everyone sat in silence at the baize table, Jack held his hands in his lap occasionally rubbing his ribs, happier now the pain was subsiding. He'd had no time to tense before the boot came, but no harm done.

He traded stares with the guard positioned by the door. He wasn't as big as Muscles, but he looked fit, he was sure he could handle himself. He couldn't see the man directly behind him, present on the insistence of Wainwright, but he could feel his stare too.

Annabel didn't know what to think, her head was full of questions. She had never experienced such violence before, and it scared her, Jack scared her. If Wainwright had not put a stop to it when he did, she was sure he would have killed that man. What had Colin got them into? She had never felt so alone, so scared, so vulnerable in her life.

Wainwright looked from the woman to her bodyguard, to the paperwork in front of him. He was wearing his bifocals, only used when he needed to exert authority. They enabled him to glare over the lenses and fix his eyes on his victim. He felt menacing, in control. Having spent the last hour trying to sort this mess, he had only managed so far to anger the board and frustrate the security forces, who had raced to the bank as soon as the alarm sounded.

To top it all, he was told from on high, higher than he'd ever been, to assist Mr Case with whatever he needed. He would help as much as he could, but his courtesy would only extend so far. He was grateful for his bifocals.

"It appears that I am to let you leave and be on your way." Peering over his glasses he addressed Jack first before sweeping his glare over Annabel. The woman was more malleable, lowering her eyes to avoid contact.

"But before you leave, I must insist Mr Case that you hand back the key you took from the room."

"Evidence…" He was having none of it. "… I'll sign for it and return it when we have concluded our investigation."

"What… no, you can't… totally out of the question." Wainwright was incredulous, he looked towards the door, then back at Jack.

"Otis, would you relieve Mr Case of our property please." Two hands gripped his shoulders, holding him in position as Otis moved away from the door towards him.

"Mr Wainwright, I will remind you that you are still under a search warrant. I have evidence I believe is directly apportioned to the death of Derek Gant and connected to the death of Colin Thorn. I am here on behalf of the local magistrates to assist the police on a consultancy basis, but used by a much higher authority." That was his official line out of the way.

"Finally, I carry a Glock 17 semi-automatic pistol which holds 33 rounds of ammunition, lethal up to 55 yards. I have a license to protect my client at all times using maximum force. I have 24 rounds left, I intend to still have 24 rounds by the time I reach my car." The hands disappeared from his shoulders as Otis froze for a second, before backing away to his original position by the door.

"Are you threatening me, Mr Case?" He tugged at his waistcoat, pushing his glasses up to the bridge of his nose, covering his eyes. He was confident that you don't hit a man in specs.

"Yes." Jack was in no mood to spend his time arguing with this man. He had things to do, loose ends to be tied. He wasn't going to shoot anyone, but he was getting pissed off with this guy's rules and regulations.

Wainwright hesitated, either to reflect on his options or to control his nerves. But he knew he had no choice. He stood, straightening his shoulders to emphasise his six foot four, he had two inches on Jack. Keeping his eyes fixed on the man he sighed, pointing to the exit.

"Get out of my bank… go on go… and I hope I never see you again." He waved both hands as he ushered them into the banking hall. Holding the door for them, Otis bowed as Annabel passed by. Jack winked at him, following close behind. Otis gave him a wry smile.

"Where would you like me to sign for the key I'm taking?" He was trying to do the right thing.

"I don't …out..out!" He continued to shoo them to the exit, putting his hands on his hips as he watched his unwelcome visitors leave.

Several customers in the banking hall turned to watch him as he ushered his clients out. Wainwright, realising he had an audience, dusted himself down and smiled, tipping his head in greeting. Many of them averted their gaze for fear of attracting his attention. He looked over to a young girl standing at the information desk.

"Karen, can you get the Pargetter file, please? We need to get the account back in order to help these people." He hoped he was loud enough for the audience to hear, as he passed her shaking his head.

"I don't know, millionaires… what to do… what to do." He entered his office, slamming the door.

Karen followed him, who were the Pargetters?

They stood in the entryway while Jack checked the surrounding area. He pressed the remote, unlocking the Range Rover.

There were several people on the street, some walking to and from lectures, shoppers and tourists. A group walked by following a tour guide presenting the history of the artists and architects responsible for the main designs of Oxford. He pulled Annabel by the arm, joining the back of the group, peeling off as they passed their car.

They entered without incident.

"I have a feeling that Mr Wainwright still has a part to play in this." He put the car in gear, before pulling out into the mid-morning traffic.

He dialled into the PDA, the ring tone filled the car.

"Hi Jack, how are things?" Sara was relieved that he was away from the bank. She mentioned nothing of the trouble in the vault, and she assumed Ed Ryker would have calmed down by the time he saw Jack again.

"Fine…" Jack wouldn't mention it either.

"Sara, can you run a check on the initials KVP, I have a key for some sophisticated lock. Check corporates, military, banks, agencies, the normal. Someone has gone to a lot of trouble to bring these people into this. I need to know who. I've also sent an image from the bank… see if you can decipher it for us."

"Got that, a mailed pig…. I'll check it out, won't be long… Caio!" The line went dead.

Annabel was surprised at the informality of the conversation. For an agency portrayed as the best of the best, she would have expected the communication to be more official, even military in its dialogue. It had been more like a chat amongst friends. Were they involved? Call it woman's intuition, but there was something there.

Away from the bank, she relaxed. So many things still played on her mind, Colin and Derek, the strange machine in a ridiculously opulent room just for a key, and the violence.

It was the violence which troubled her most. She hadn't led what you would call a sheltered life, but the most she had ever witnessed so far was nothing more than pub brawls. Alcohol playing a significant part as it always did, usually late on when most people were too drunk to notice. Invariably, after the scuffle, the drunks would either walk home arm in arm laughing or forget it ever happened. They would be back again after a few days drinking happily together.

She doubted whether Jack and Charles would be seen doing the same thing. And murder, something she never imagined would come into her life, particularly in a village like Mittand Burrow.

She would now be the focus of her neighbours, the main topic of conversation. Her face plastered all over the news, the local papers, the nationals.

Under any other circumstances, she would thrive on the exposure. But not like this. She felt for the village and the people who lived there. It was a place to relax, to enjoy the good things, to live out your days.

Most of the residents and ancestors before them had built this idyllic life, her family had changed all that. For how long she couldn't imagine, but notoriety often brings with it a certain fascination to those who thrive on scandal, gossip and the macabre. They would become a focal point for the curious, a spectacle for the tourist and a cash cow for the press. She owed them so much, she would not let it happen if she could help it.

Annabel looked over at Jack as he concentrated on the road ahead.

The fear she felt earlier had waned, replaced with a strange sense of calm. He showed a strength she had never seen before in a man. The way he walked, his stance, his mannerisms and the way he spoke, all showed a man in control, carefully calculated to cope with any situation. He stood out in a crowd, even at her dinner party and not because of his physique, his good looks or his mysterious organisation. He had an aura that exuded a powerful tenacity, giving her every confidence he would get the job done.

"What can I do, Jack?" She was a part of this whether she liked it or not.

"I'm involved in this and need to help as much as I can."

He stayed silent for a few seconds as he tried to piece things together. He was missing something, but nothing was jumping out at him.

"I think we need to get you home, out of harm's way for now. The connection between Langfield and your practice is too closely linked, and as you are the last remaining partner, there could be more to come. It may be nothing, but I'm not prepared to take the chance." He didn't believe that he knew she was in danger. He didn't know why.

"But I have resources, I know the village. They will trust me more than the police and meaning no disrespect, an outsider." She was determined to help with this, she wasn't happy at being portrayed as the poor little victim, the mourning wife, the weak woman.

She had a point, she could help with Mittand Burrow. He had experience of a close knit community himself in Marizian, his home. If things couldn't be sorted by themselves in their own backyard, then no amount of police would help. They would rather just bury it and move on.

"I know what you can do. Have a chat with Linda Norwood, see if she knows anything about Langfield or her mother, there might be something we could use. I need to see a few people when we get back, we can swap notes then." It was a good idea. Her neighbours would open up to her, in particular, Linda, the village oracle. She would glean more information than he ever could, and in the meantime, he would take down the killers before they could cause any more damage.

They rode in silence, both wondering what would happen next.

Opening his briefcase, carefully placed on the leather inlay of his desk, he took out a small tupperware box, prised open the lid and removed a neatly cling filmed sandwich with a slice of madeira cake. He poured a cup of tea from the china teapot and dialled the numbers from the card that arrived this morning. It connected after three rings.

"Hello, Wainwright here. Just to let you know that they have taken the contents … Yes, Mr Case and Mrs Paxton-Thorn …Yes, it went exactly as planned … Of course … Should they call again, I will let you know immediately … Thank you … Oh and Mrs Langfield … are we to expect any more guests?… No? Oh good, that's fine, I will await your instructions … Thank you, you are so kind … Goodbye."

Replacing the receiver, he took a bite from his cheese and cucumber sandwich and smiled.

CHAPTER TWENTY-SIX
Tell Tale

Eliza Winch had been feeling better for days now. The sun was shining, the birds were singing, and her house was looking immaculate. She polished the glass coffee table for the third time. She had been checking the shine from different angles, she kept finding new smears. Newspaper had done the trick, working the printed pages into the glass in a circular motion cleared any marks and blemishes instantly.

Her mother had given her the tip. It worked on mirrors, windows and glass furniture. She had spent a fortune over the years as she built her glass collection, thanks to mum the house glimmered when the sun shone through the windows.

She had bought a new freshener 'golden summer'. It smelt of newly cut grass with a hint of spring flowers, as if the walls had disappeared and her cottage was open to the elements. She occasionally stopped to take a deep breath, fresh and clean, altogether uplifting. Today would be the best day of her new life without Colin.

She had the dishy LARA agent coming over today, and she wanted to impress. The house was spotless, her new outfit was hanging on the wardrobe door ready to slip on, and she had her hair appointment in half an hour. She had some vital information to give him. Perhaps if she held back some facts, it would make a great excuse to keep popping by to add more snippets as they came to her.

Coping with the death of Colin had been hard at first. She was inconsolable for well over a week, sleeping mostly with the help of pills. Had it not been for Linda Norwood she would probably be dead by now. She had checked on her every day, forcing her to leave the house, sometimes just to walk around the village, avoiding the green at first.

After a while, they tackled the green, and on that first trip, Linda had arranged for Annabel to be standing by the Manor House gates as they passed by. Annabel and Eliza worked through their grief together, over coffee, lunch and the odd night of heavy social drinking. It helped all three, with Linda relishing taking control, enjoying her role amongst her new close friends. Together they had come through it; slowly things were getting back to normal.

This week had been the first one on her own. It had done her a world of good, as she now possessed a confidence that had been hidden away forever. She felt alive.

The thought of being the talk of the village was exhilarating but, unlike Derek, she would never contemplate blackmail. Just the recognition for uncovering this incredible secret would be enough to boost her self esteem, something she had been missing for far too long. For the last three days, she had been putting her notes together, making sure all facts were in place.

Annabel had given her the week off while the office was being refurbished in readiness for the new partner, Brett Simonsen. She had sold half the practice to him and like her husband years before; he decided to go it alone. The deal included keeping Eliza as a legal secretary and in honour of Colin, keeping his name. At the end of the refurbishment, they were planning a launch evening to celebrate the opening of Simonsen Paxton and Thorn. That was next week, so Eliza planned to use the rest of this week to persuade Mr Case to attend the evening as her plus one. She gave the house a quick once over, checking everything was in its place before taking a cardigan and leaving for the salon.

She lived on the Copse Road in one of four terraced cottages positioned on the edge of Mittand Burrow. It was the last sign of habitation before the road changed into two miles of open country. It was peaceful most of the time as it was the old road to Lysbie and mostly ignored in favour of the new dual carriageway.

It was now only used by a handful of the older generation who preferred the traditional country roads to reach their destination.

She got into her car, putting the key in the ignition. The radio came to life with a talk program which was clearly inappropriate for such a beautiful day.

She pressed auto search until she hit her favourite music station which was halfway through 'Here Comes The Sun'. Singing along, she pressed the switch for the sunroof, watching the blue sky come into view as the rays flooded the interior. It felt great to be alive. She turned the ignition and started the engine.

An explosion ripped through the Peugeot. The force shattered the windows of all four cottages into a thousand pieces, flying into the air like a deadly mist. Eliza had no time to scream as the inferno stripped away her skin, the intense heat gnawing at the remaining skeleton.

Thick black smoke spiralled skywards as two of the thatched roofs smouldered before bursting into flames. Shards of glass, timber and metal rained from the sky, crashing into the gardens, along the pavement and across tarmac hundreds of feet from the epicentre.

Within minutes, all that could be heard was the crackling of straw as the cottages continued to burn.

CHAPTER TWENTY-SEVEN
Wheat from the Chaff

The black cab pulled into the side street opposite Kings Cross Station. Kurt and Dolf climbed inside, Kurt just shutting the door before the car took off, joining the havoc that was the traffic on the Euston Road.

"Are we in a rush?" Kurt asked as he fell back into his seat.

The driver ignored him as he weaved his way through, using the bus lane wherever he could. He was trying to get them to their destination as soon as possible. Kurt surveyed the equipment waiting for them on the cab floor. An easel folded for easy transportation, a portfolio case large enough to carry canvasses of all sizes and a rucksack full of artist equipment, watercolours, oils, stencils and lead. The perfect disguise for the former art student from Queens College, Cambridge. He had been a residential student for four years. It allowed him to satisfy his love of art and to study the English way of life. It would also help in preparation for his role as the pathfinder for the Zukunft Reich. He now had a chance to blend into the village, see where it all began.

If he could prove himself, he might even be granted an audience with the Director. He was a man of legend, a man to be revered, also worshipped. Part of the training and conditioning included the story of the Director's role in the development and growth of the Reich. He was a God amongst men.

But things had not gone to plan lately. The first target had died, the USB from the safe contained nothing, just an encryptor. Their second just gave useless information, and then the LARA agent eluded them. He could not fail again and he wouldn't.

This task was a solo mission, no Dolf. He couldn't blame Dolf for everything, but had he been on his own he would have played things differently. This time he would please them, earn the right to be praised. Gain the recognition that would elevate him in the eyes of the all powerful. He would not fail.

They had issued them a media cab fitted with a TV screen for passengers to view a range of adverts, events in London as well as some selected programs. He flicked through the menu, pressed comedy and found a selection of old BBC sitcoms. He chose a classic episode of 'Only Fools and Horses,' the one with the chandelier scene which Kurt had seen many times but was a favourite. Dolf having limited English, would find the visual comedy an ideal way to pass the time to Paddington. Dolf had other ideas, he closed his eyes to shield them from the light, having overdone the whiskey a little too much last night. He began to snore.

Kurt nudged Dolf awake as they arrived at Paddington Station.

"Energie und ruhm fur die neue welt." Kurt shouted to Dolf as the cab pulled away. His comrade acknowledged with a wave before resting his head back, closing his eyes.

As the cab turned the corner heading for Heathrow, he dozed off with his partner's final words drifting him away. 'Power and Glory for the new world.'

Entering the old station, Kurt searched for the departure board. There were trains to Oxford every forty-five minutes. He was in no rush, and he had missed breakfast, so he took the escalator to the mezzanine. Sitting outside the coffee bar on a rattan sofa surrounded by plastic trees, he drank his latte, planning for the most important mission of his life.

After nearly an hour, the cab entered the lane for terminal 4. Dolf had watched all the channels available on the TV, of which he had understood less than half. He closed his eyes again.

He was pleased to be going back to Berlin as he missed the food. The English liked their grease; they had no idea how to cook meat. The beer was no better, cold and tasteless. His first stop this evening would be the Hackescher Markt where he would eat his fill and drink into the night. Yes, it would be good to be home.

As they passed the terminal entrance heading towards cargo, Dolf sat up, tapping the glass partition.

"Sir, you are missing my terminal." He said in broken English. He received no answer from the driver.

They passed a DHL container warehouse, where the road continued on through the rear of the airport. Tall fences, electrified at the highest point, ran both sides of the small dual carriageway. There were cargo planes in and around large hangers, some taxiing in for maintenance, some towards the runways. Again Dolf tapped on the window to attract the driver's attention, harder this time. The cab turned into a security gate blocked by red and white striped barriers. A guard left the glass booth to meet them. He opened the passenger door and leaning in asked Dolf for his passport. Checking against the information on his clipboard he gave the passport back. The barrier rose as he signalled to the booth.

They headed towards a hangar where a Cessna faced the exit. The twin propellers sparked into life as the car approached. Dolf was impressed; they had arranged a private plane to get him home. After pulling into the hangar, the driver left his cab and opened the passenger door. Dolf grabbed his bag, stepping out into the dimly lit building. He headed towards the Cessna.

"Hello, Dolf." He turned back towards the cab. Standing beside the passenger door was Leon Ubermann, he had been the driver all along.

Dolf dropped his bag. There was no use running; it was over.

"Hello Leon, long time no see." It was all he could think to say. What does someone say when they know they are about to die?

"Yes, it has been a while. Pity we have to meet after so long in such a formal way." He walked towards Dolf, drew his silenced pistol and without breaking stride fired one shot. Dolf stood perfectly still as a hole appeared in the centre of his forehead, a trickle of blood escaped, dribbling to the bridge of his nose. His legs gave way, as he slumped to the floor, dead.

From out of the shadows two men approached. The one dressed as Leon, same height, same build, same blonde crew cut, took the keys from the assassin and walked to the cab. The other man helped Leon carry Dolf into the Cessna. They zipped the corpse into a body bag filled with lead weights, securing it in the rear with restraints usually reserved for skis. Once in the cockpit, the second man took a seat and buckled up. Leon joined the pilot as he put on his headset.

"Let's move." He ordered.

The Cessna taxied out of the hangar. Leon watched from the cockpit as the cab approached security, smiling as the barriers lifted automatically to let it through.

"Heathrow Tower, Cessna Mike Bravo Oscar 4411 ready for takeoff, runway four." The pilot awaited instructions from the tower.

"Mike Bravo Tango Oscar 4411, Heathrow Tower, you are cleared for takeoff, runway four." Confirmation came back immediately.

"Mike Bravo Tango Oscar." The pilot returned heading for the runway.

Leon checked his passport. He would be Dolf Schneider until clear of security at Kidlington Airport, Oxford, a short twelve minute flight. He would pick up the car from long stay and be in the village by early afternoon. The Cessna was scheduled to make a quick fuel stop before returning to Berlin. Once over the sea they would dispose of Dolf and return to base. His weighted body would not be found.

Leon Ubermann was their best man. A member of the Elitetruppe, he was known as the Caretaker. His role was to clean up any mess, bring order to operations, and eradicate any problems.

He had cleaned up one mess for now, but Kurt Eichel was on borrowed time. He was a bright student, and there were still hopes he would be an asset to them. What hadn't helped was being partnered with that idiot Dolf, but Leon was yet to be convinced. Kurt had some significant backing from above, which also caused Leon a problem.

For now, he would just watch and bide his time. But first… There was Jack Case. He was a challenge to be relished.

CHAPTER TWENTY-EIGHT
Clue

The Range Rover turned onto the dual carriageway out of Oxford when Jack's PDA rang.

"Jack, KVP has come up with some options that might relate to a key." Sara was good, this had taken less than an hour.

"If you are looking for railways, then we have Kiveton Station in Sheffield, England and Kavaraippettai in Tamil Nadu, India. Nothing on airlines except for the Kilovolt Peak that measures x-ray energy in airport scanners."

"Ok, what about banks?" He had an inkling for a bank.

"I was just getting there." Sara didn't take kindly to being interrupted.

"So far we have uncovered Karur Vysya Bank, or the Kisan Vikas Patra KVP, which are investments similar to bonds, again all point to India." Jack thought for a moment. Asia made little sense. There was no evidence of anyone associated with the Barth family having connections in India. So far everything seemed to point to Europe. Hopefully, more would turn up soon.

"And the image?"

"Ah yes… The mailed pig, an interesting one. There have been several reports recently of pigs' heads and feet posted to American politicians. Also, Islamic and Jewish leaders, either as a protest or racially motivated, throughout the years, sent pig parts to each other as a way of insult. We also looked at it in the literal sense, and we found a council in the south of England who sent a vote registration letter to a pig called Blossom in 2010. Other than that we are still…" Sara stopped in mid-sentence.

"Jack hang on… we have something." The line went silent.

"Well, it doesn't seem to have given us anything." Annabel was trying to understand why Colin would reference a letter to a pig. She had definitely never heard him mention a Blossom before, could he mean a flower, perhaps?

"Early days, we'll find it." He had every confidence Sara would come through.

"Jack…" Sara's tone had altered. "There has been an explosion in Mittand Burrow."

They both turned to look at each other.

Flooring the accelerator, the turbo kicked in, shooting the car forward, pressing them into their seats. He weaved through the traffic at breakneck speed.

"It was in the Copse Road, outside a row of terraces. There's not a lot left."

"Ellie!" Annabel shouted. "Oh my god, they've killed Ellie."

"We know nothing yet." He tried to reassure her.

"She may not have been there." He knew she had been. They were due to meet at her home once he returned from Oxford.

"Sara, I will get back to you once we've checked the scene." He disconnected the call.

Jack poured a second vodka for Annabel and placed it on the island counter of her kitchen. She was sitting on a high stool with her head in her hands, having not spoken for the last fifteen minutes. Placing the glass in front of her, he rested a hand on her shoulder.

"Why don't you lay down for a while? It might help?" She looked up at him through reddened eyes.

She wouldn't let him take her home first, insisting they get to Eliza's house as fast as possible. She was hoping they would be in time to save her. The devastation was total.

What had once been four quaint thatched cottages were now the badly burnt remains of one linked to three piles of charred rubble. All that was left of the car outside was a chassis with front wheels and a partially covered engine. It was still smoking when they arrived. Roughly fifteen pounds of C4 had been connected to the ignition, which explained the devastation.

One pound was all that was needed to kill several people, just over a pound would destroy a truck. It had been a particularly brutal attack ensuring nothing was left after the explosion.

Forensics had found residual evidence of one occupant in the vehicle and a gold ring embedded into the engine casing. He was sure it would be identified as Eliza's. She'd had a hairdressing appointment that morning, the timing of the explosion coincided with the time she would have left.

He needed to remove Annabel from the scene forcibly. She became hysterical as she learnt how the explosion had disintegrated the body, made worse when described in graphic detail by Detective Inspector Walsh.

He was matter of fact, with no emotion and no consideration for the widow. He would need to have a quiet word with him one day soon.

"They are killing us all." She said, tears running down her cheeks.

"We're still here." He said encouragingly.

"And we will get them."

"How!" She raised her voice.

"You don't know who they are, what they want or who is next… Well, we do know who's next, don't we …ME!" She started to cry uncontrollably, turning to him she buried her head into his chest. As he held her tight, he looked over to Walsh, he would definitely have a word.

The DI noticing his displeasure shrugged in resignation and returned to the investigating team.

Jack had called June Claridge, telling her to take time off. It didn't go down well as she was concerned about the upkeep of the house. But after reassuring her it would only be for a few days, she reluctantly agreed. He could not be sure how long it would take, but at least he could safeguard the Claridges by keeping them away from this. It was precautionary as Annabel was probably right. All the deaths so far had been directly linked to Thorn Paxton and Gant. In particular, anyone with knowledge of the Barth Case. It was unlikely that the murderers would target home helps, but he didn't want to take the risk.

The doorbell rang.

The Lysbie force had assigned two officers to provide twenty-four hour protection for Annabel.

Their timing couldn't have been better as he had to be elsewhere. Walsh was taking this seriously as he'd organised a pair of heavies for the job.

PC Morris was at least six foot six with large square shoulders. You could tell Rugby was his game by his broken nose and cauliflower ears.

Finch was one of Walsh's men, again built for protection. Shaved head and square jaw, with the kevlar emphasising his already prominent chest, these two will do.

"I need the place scoured every half an hour." He laid down his instructions.

"One of you is to know where Mrs Paxton-Thorn is at all times. Stay close by, the other needs to check the perimeter, the pool house, the summerhouse and stables. Don't be a hero, anything suspicious call it in."

The problem was, the UK didn't arm their force. Each officer had a baton, handcuffs and a can of CS gas, only effective at close range. These guys didn't look stupid, he just hoped that neither wanted to make a name for themselves.

The decision not to assign armed response had been the Brigadiers. He saw no reason to upset village life any further with gun toting police, as the increase in numbers of the Lysbie force had already caused enough. The commissioner agreed to position armed officers to monitor incoming roads from the outskirts.

Both men nodded at Jack, but the look in their eyes showed the same disdain he had seen from Walsh and the commissioner. Resentment of LARA appeared to have infected the whole Lysbie force. Thankfully, PC Morris didn't let his personal feelings sully the job he had been tasked with.

"Don't worry Mr Case, we'll look after her. She'll be perfectly safe with us." He seemed convincing enough although he did get a side glance from Finch, clearly unhappy having someone speak for him.

Annabel moved from her stool.

"I'll show you to your rooms." She said heading for the hallway.

"It's alright love, I'll bed down in the kitchen and Doris can take one of the front rooms." Finch walked to the island planting himself on one of the stools.

All three looked at him, Morris for the Doris reference, Jack for his cocky attitude, and Annabel who had never been called 'love' in her life.

Jack walked up behind him, casually drawing his Glock from his jacket. He grabbed Finch by the back of the neck and slammed his head onto the counter, pressing the gun hard into his temple. He clicked off the safety, the sound in the shocked silence made the CID man flinch.

"This is a serious operation DS Finch, and I suggest you rethink the attitude. Three innocent people have been killed, and I am trying to prevent a fourth. I will nail these bastards, either with or without the so called professionals you guys seem to think you are. So, is this the job for you or do I request that they send me someone from CID with brains?" The question required a yes and no answer which confused Finch, as he started to shake and nod his head in the hope, one must be right.

He released him, put the gun away and walked back to Annabel, purposely keeping his back to the CID officer.

"Here is my number." He took her mobile from the counter, programmed the number into her phone and handed it back to her.

"It's on speed dial one. Should you need me for any reason, call me. I won't be more than a few hours."

"Where are you going?" She didn't want him to leave.

"I need to go back to where this all started, and I think on this occasion you would be safer here. Isn't that right guys?" He looked at Finch.

"Yes, Mr Case and… I apologise Mrs Paxton-Thorn, it was insensitive of me." Finch visibly shaken, his face red with embarrassment, kept his eyes on them as if waiting for approval. Jack barely nodded, Annabel felt a little sorry for the big lug.

"Oh, forget it… and call me Annabel." She smiled her winning smile, a smile confirming that she had enjoyed seeing him ridiculed but was prepared to forgive him this once.

"I would suggest you get some rest while you have the chance

Annabel when I get back I will fix dinner." He had a feeling she wouldn't sleep much tonight but a rest for an hour or two would do her good.

Annabel looked at him.

"You can cook?" She sounded genuinely surprised.

"Well, I do eat. So yes, I can cook, probably not as good as Mrs Claridge, but passable."

"I'll look forward to it." She smiled at him.

He finished by briefing the officers again; they were much more attentive this time around.

He checked his gun, felt for the two spare clips in his jacket and grabbing the keys to the Range Rover, he left the house.

He had an appointment at a rest home.

It was late afternoon, the sun was still bathing the green with warmth, and it was busy. It was full of kids, some playing football, some playing cricket, some just running aimlessly around, their parents trying to calm them down.

An ice cream van, parked alongside the solitary oak tree, struggled to serve the queue that was growing by the minute. There were several sunbathers and picnickers spread out on a kaleidoscope of towels. Even the workmen refurbishing Linda Norwood's old cottage, had stripped overalls from their shoulders, enjoying the weather and taking another of many impromptu breaks. It was a warming sight, one that in normal circumstances would lift any spirit.

A solitary artist was painting the church on the hill. He looked typically arty, his easel positioned at a right angle, oval paint pallet hooked in his left hand, mixing paint with his right. His blonde hair rippled in the gentle breeze as he worked with deliberate strokes reminiscent of a classical conductor. The village green was a perfect canvas for the creative mind.

Jack left the green and followed the signs for Mittand Parva.

CHAPTER TWENTY-NINE
Wishwell House

Wishwell House was set in sixteen acres of gardens and woodland walks. A large fountain sprayed water twenty feet in the air from the mouth of a granite dolphin breaking through the surface. Baroque statues bordered the 300 yard gravel drive, depicting angels and deities. The surrounding circular floodlights ensured that they were displayed day and night. This wasn't cheap he thought as he parked in front of the building.

The rest home was a purpose-built seventy-seven room grand house built in 18th century style to mirror the architecture of Mittand Parva. It was modelled on a chapter house with four tall chimneys running across an angled roof, towering bay windows with an arched central doorway opening into a clinical tiled reception area. He couldn't help thinking, as he walked up to the stone steps, of a Victorian mental asylum. The only thing missing was wails and moans emanating from its walls, perhaps that was to come. It surprised him to see the brightly lit modern reception as he stepped through the archway. Automatic glass doors swept silently aside to allow him in. There were garish coloured sofas on a plush beige carpet in an area surrounded by flat screen TVs. Half were showing virtual tours of the home while others tuned into news and sports channels.

Sitting at an aluminium and glass desk was the receptionist. She wore a headset, a tiny earpiece with a thin wire microphone stopping at her cheek, she smiled perfect white teeth at him as he approached.

"Good afternoon sir, you must be Commander Jack Case." She pre-empted the production of his id, very thorough.

"Hi, just call me Jack. Yes, I'm here to see…"

"Martha Joyce yes, I have already called her, she's on her way.

Would you like to take a seat? She'll be with you in a moment."

Impressed by the greeting and thorough professionalism, he took a seat and watched the virtual walk through. This was one hell of an operation.

The interior of Wishwell was a glimpse into the future, in stark contrast to the 18th century facade portrayed on arrival.

Martha Joyce's office, glass fronted, opened into a modern showroom for the twenty-first century. Her desk had a thin topped walnut surface on slender chromed legs. It supported a large touchscreen 'all in one' PC and a tablet she used when on the move. The storage was also glass fronted, with files neatly arranged in order. Behind her head were several diplomas and awards giving credit for the home's condition and patient wellbeing. She ran a tight ship.

Martha was an attractive woman in her late forties. She was wearing a formal navy business suit which complimented her slightly large but well formed figure. She flicked through the information, turning to Jack as she found what she was looking for.

"So, you need information on Gloria Barth and any relationships she had at Wishwell?" She swiped her fingers over her tablet, making notes.

"Well, I wanted to find out a little more about her one visitor, Jayne Langfield, but yes, her relationships would also give me more of a picture about her stay here." He wasn't sure what he expected to find.

"Ah yes, Mrs Langfield, lovely lady, doted on her mother. Such a sad story, they never really had the time together they would have liked. Gloria was so happy; she looked forward to the visits so much."

"How often did she visit?"

"Let me see." Martha checked her screen. "Yes, here we are, every weekend for the last seven months and at least twice a week for several hours at a time. Oh, and Gloria had the odd week away, staying with Jayne and her husband."

"Did you say Mrs Barth stayed with the Langfield's during the last seven months, or the ten years of her stay?" He might be on to something.

Again Martha checked her notes, swiping several screens, cross sectioning.

"Yes, she stayed with them a couple of times in the beginning, but it was more regular during the last year."

He was missing something, but he wasn't sure how it all fitted. How could Jayne, being power of attorney allow the change of beneficiary? Where had Claudia been and why show up all of a sudden? Now Jayne Langfield had gone AWOL, none of this added up.

"And it was Jayne Langfield who came to pick up her mother?" He asked, already knowing the answer.

"Oh yes, although she came as often as she could, she was Gloria's only visitor. All the staff knew her. It was definitely Mrs Langfield, we have stringent procedures to protect our residents." Martha held his gaze. What was he after?

"What about at Wishwell, did she make friends here?" Someone must have seen the other visitor.

"Very few, her condition meant that she would often go into her shell. Most of the residents like to chat, so they tended to give up when the conversation became one sided." She paused for a moment to think.

"There is Albert. Yes, Albert was probably her closest friend here. He spent a lot of time with her, helping her, listening to her, persuading her to take part in the activities, I can remember him coaxing Gloria onto the croquet green once. It was a great triumph. He was also her dinner partner." She continued to take notes, making a record of the meeting.

"Is Albert still here?" This could be the lead he was looking for.

"Albert?" She smiled. "Albert is part of the furniture, he's ninety-three with the constitution of a fifty year old. He will be our first centurion resident." It would be a proud moment for Wishwell and Martha was determined to get all the PR she could.

"Is there any chance I could have a word with him while I am here?"

"Yes, of course. He should be in his room by now getting ready for dinner. Follow me." She put the tablet away; the drawer bleeped as it locked.

Everything was set up to ensure the residents led as normal a life as possible. They passed a games room where some were deep in concentration over a chessboard, a cinema room with a large screen projector, and a library full of books for all tastes. At the end at the hall, a hairdresser and small shop providing daily papers, cigarettes and supplies ranging from mints to whisky.

As they mounted the stairs to the first floor accommodation suites, Jack had to wonder how Gloria could afford such luxury. She would have had insurance from her husbands' deaths, along with proceeds from house sales, but not enough to cover her record of regular confinement in institutions.

If Jayne Langfield had financed her mother's care, she was obviously a very wealthy woman. This begged the question, what was it all about if it wasn't for the money?

Gloria alone would have struggled to fund her care, let alone in style like this.

They entered a wide corridor with rooms on either side. Each door was individually styled to represent the front door of many modern houses. Some were wood panelled with arched windows above, some were plain with square panes of glass in the upper portion, and some had an antique feel. Each had its own postbox fixed on the wall with the number identifying each room. The lights were daylight tubes giving the whole area the brightness of a summer's day.

"Here we are." Martha indicated door 48 and knocked. "Hello Albert, you have a visitor." There was no answer, so she knocked louder. The door came ajar.

"That's strange?" She looked at him. "He would have locked his door if he wasn't in… perhaps he's in the bathroom. Albert!" She called again as she pushed the door open a little more, poking her head through as she did so.

"Albert!" She screamed as she ran into the room.

Jack followed as Martha rushed to the bed. The old man lay there fully clothed, his head was back with his mouth and eyes wide open as if in a frightened scream. He could see the abrasions and bruising around his neck. A scarf, possibly the murder weapon, lay crumpled on the floor beside the bed, cast down by the killer.

"Oh, my god… Albert… I need to get security." Martha hurried to the alarm by the door.

The silenced bullet slammed into her chest, she dropped like a stone, dying instantly. Jack wheeled around, his hand reaching for his Glock.

"Don't Jack." He froze at the voice from behind the door, a voice he recognised.

CHAPTER THIRTY
Family

The man was tall. Jack stared at the barrel of the silencer pointing at his face, a tiny plume of smoke drifted into the air from the tip… He raised his hands in surrender.

"Hello, Brigadier." He couldn't feign his surprise.

"Where is the key, Jack?" The old man waved the gun to his left, prompting him to sit on one of the visitor chairs.

"Please sit on your hands. I don't want any surprises." He did as he was told, turning the chair to face the gunman, keeping his eyes fixed on him. He sat on his hands.

"The key is at the house." Untrue but he needed time.

"Then we'll find it there. Let us hope Annabel is accommodating." A smile crossed his face. This wasn't good.

"You killed your own son." He needed to keep him talking while he thought of a way out.

"NO!" The Brigadier spat. "I killed my father." He looked towards the old man.

Jack's head was whirling. What the hell was going on? The Brigadier moved across from him, sitting on the edge of the bed.

"You should never have come, Jack. I tried to warn Ed off at the start, he has only succeeded in signing your death warrant." The Brigadier looked tired, Jack could see the gun shaking in his hand as the weight told on his tired muscles.

Seeing the agent staring at the gun the Brigadier crossed his leg and rested it on his knee to keep the barrel steady. It would prove to be his undoing.

"Don't I deserve an explanation as I seem to have arrived at the end?" He had to work fast as he was eager to get back to Annabel. But he needed to know what he was up against. The Brigadier thought for a moment.

"As you will not be here to see the glorious day, I agree you should at least know that you were beaten by the New World Order." The Brigadier began as Jack took it all in, trying to make sense of what he was hearing.

"My father, the man you see here," there was no emotion in his voice, "is Gerd Haas, the director of the Zukunft Reich."

"Zuki what?" Never heard of them.

"The Future Empire or as it will be known once we start our administration, the Fourth Reich." Nazis? So that was it, he was dealing with a neo-nazi cell?

"And before you think you are dealing with a fanatical neo-nazi cell, you would be wrong. We will soon have the financial resources and already have the manpower to create a New World Order. A perfect new world, begun by our one true visionary Adolf Hitler and to be completed by his many disciples."

"So your father was a member of the Hitler youth I presume." He knew of the history. They were formed in 1922 in Munich, Bavaria, coming into prominence in the early thirties. They recruited boys from the age of 11, and by age 14 they were indoctrinated.

"Father was a prominent member of the Hitler youth, praised for his intelligence and strength by none other than the Fuhrer himself." A pride came over the Brigadier, Jack saw it more as madness.

"In 1935 father arrived in England, at an orphanage in Hammersmith. The real Albert Thorn and his parents were killed on orders from the then Director Alberic Heuller, the young Thorn's body was disposed of. It was simple to make the switch because at fourteen my father was the same build and so similar in looks, only his mother would know the difference. He was then sent to live with a distant relative. She believed that young Albert was the sole survivor of the tragic accident which had claimed his family."

He could see the Brigadier's concentration lapse as he recalled the history, the gun beginning to lower. He still needed to know the full extent of this madness, and he also hoped his lack of concentration would continue, allowing Jack to make his move. The Brigadier continued.

"Heuller was given the role of conditioning the new recruits sent to England, inserting them into normal society. He was also instructed to develop my father as his successor, which happened by the time he was 22. Two other recruits whose names I know you will recognise from your research on Gloria Barth and her family, were Eric Ahlers aka David Gordon and Erwin Shierling aka Gerald Barth. The real Gordons were a family who made plans to move to Mittand Burrow from Warwickshire. Rose, George and their son David were replaced in transit by our own Gordons, who began a normal life in the village. There was no bloodline, so it was simple."

He watched the old man, occasionally glancing at the gun which was now pointing at the floor. Jack added his own assumptions.

"And David Gordon's role was to find a wife to continue the normal life he needed. But I have a question. How did you arrange so many infiltrations with no one noticing? Presumably you had to ensure there was no trace, while having the correct papers for all of them? Quite a task."

The Brigadier smiled, taking pleasure in recounting the ingenuity of the organisation.

"That part was the easiest. The last Census in the United Kingdom was taken in 1931. It was in standard paper form, whole dossiers of files were collated and stored in a complex in Hayes, Middlesex. We had people on the inside who had full lineage records for every family throughout the United Kingdom and Wales. Replacing existing residents with no bloodline was a simple record check; we were one hundred percent successful. Orphans in those days were simply numbers, cared for by the state."

"One boy was much like any other, checks were sadly inadequate which made it easy. We were to be in position with a task force on the inside once Germany invaded. In 1939 this country was in chaos, what with the immobilisation of most of the men and mass evacuations, so they issued national identity cards. Simple cards easily copied, with our people on the inside updating the records, they issued many at the time of our transfers, which made it foolproof."

"It was the year prior to the Fuhrer's invasion of Poland, and hundreds of our youths were posted to England. There was no census in 1941 due to the outbreak of the war, and luckily the warehouse in Hayes was completely destroyed by fire on the 19th December 1942."

"It wiped out all family records of England and Wales. With reliance on identity cards only, we could send in hundreds more. So... Mr Case, your country is already primed for occupation."

This was frightening. Jack was desperate to get out of there, but he needed to know more.

"So where does the key come in? Do you have to start the Fourth Reich like an engine?"

The Brigadier chuckled. "Your humour is honourable, but I see no reason for you not to know the full extent of our plans before you die. I can assure you there will be nothing to smile about." His face hardened as he continued.

"Eric Ahlers or David Gordon as you know him, married Gloria in 1941. To cut a long story short, he became a senior member of an SS task force along with Gerd Brandt, a childhood friend. Our links to get in and out of the country were foolproof. You would not believe the lapse in security for 'nationals'. In 1944 the friends were tasked with the transportation of 500 gold bars across the border. They were to take it from the refinery near Berlin to a bank in Switzerland." He was in full flow now. He seemed to grow in confidence as the tale invigorated him.

"As the Reich weakened, it became clear they were in danger of losing the war. The New World Order needed to step away, to regroup, to view from afar the aftermath until the time came to rise again. Part of the contingency was to double cross the Fuhrer. He was after all their puppet, a pawn, their voice to mesmerise the people to do their bidding. He had failed them. It was the time to remove the resources, cut the funding and take the gold back for themselves." Hitler was a puppet? Now that was hard to believe. Where was this going?

"Ahlers headed the convoy of eight trucks into Switzerland under armed guard, a force on the payroll of Ahlers and Brandt. They deposited one truckload at the bank as instructed by the Reich to avoid suspicion. The other seven vehicles were to deposit the gold in a location as yet unknown. Now, it transpires that Ahlers betrayed us all, he wanted out, taking it all for himself. He was power hungry, greedy and deluded enough to think he could take over the Order to make it his own. This meant he would have to betray Brandt, his childhood friend. He disposed of his crew before they could report back to Germany and returning to the Swiss bank, deposited information on the whereabouts of the main consignment in a safe deposit box, along with one gold bar for the manager as payment for his silence."

He made a mental note of the names. The Brigadier was beginning to relish this.

"Ahlers arrived in England with a present of a brooch for his new bride, Gloria. Inside was the key to the box, we know that now. Brandt had his suspicions, even though his friend was the closest he had to a brother, his allegiance was to the Order. Suspecting a double cross, he intended to confront him once their mission was complete. But Ahlers got there first, leaving him to die on the street in Zurich."

"Brandt's death should have been the perfect opportunity for Ahlers to escape with the gold. However, the Reich became aware of the betrayal, ordering Ahlers to Berlin under the guise of another mission."

"Unfortunately, Ahlers was killed by Allied forces on his way there. One can only surmise he intended to frame Brandt for the betrayal once they confronted him. It would have been easy to convince them as his friend was dead." Jack could see the whole thing forming in front of him, but still a little hard to believe. He continued to listen as the story took a turn.

"However, unbeknown to Ahlers, Brandt survived... for a while. He was rushed to a Swiss hospital after being discovered, close to death, on the street. He was kept alive for three days, during which time he managed to give an account of the plot against the Fuhrer. He was delirious by then, omitting details including the existence of the Order, but the SS could still gather enough information on Ahlers to try him as a traitor. They would ensure they extracted the whereabouts of the missing gold before his execution. Of course, the meeting didn't happen and the location of the gold died with him."

Fixing his eyes on Jack, the Brigadier seemed to struggle to finish his story. His mouth moved as if to speak before pursing his lips, contemplating his decision to give further information. He straightened his shoulder and continued, it would die with the agent anyway.

"His wife and young son, Fabian, survived Brandt. A visionary, a man of immense power and …now our glorious leader."

He was seeing the whole picture now as it was racing towards present day.

"So I assume this is where Henry Barth came in." He knew he could take him now.

The madman was too engrossed to notice that he had turned the gun away from his captive. Jack needed the final pieces of the puzzle.

"Yes … We knew the key was in the possession of Gloria Gordon. But with her incarceration in the hospital we had to have a plan, so we assigned our man Shierling or as you know him, Henry Barth to bring it to us. Unfortunately, Barth was an idiot and fell in love with the deranged cow. He was supposed to gain her trust, marry her if necessary and find the key, but they had children, built a life he treasured and he decided he wanted out. He must have been delusional to think he could resign and walk away. Through our own sources we discovered he had moved everything to a new Swiss bank. A bank that had just developed an electronic coding mechanism, revolutionary technology for the day. He left all the records in a vault in Oxford. We were due to bring him in when the fool got himself killed, but we now know you have the code and key we need."

"So loyalty doesn't appear to be a prerequisite in your New World Order, they all wanted out." He stared at the old man, watching the anger build in his eyes.

Jack slid his hands out from under his legs, gradually moving them onto his knees. The Brigadier hadn't noticed. He asked him another question to keep him focused.

"So the gold is to fund an operation to take over the world?" He had to know the full extent of their plot. The Brigadier regained his composure as he described the master plan, looking forward to seeing this man die at his feet.

"Partly yes, but more so to fund the New World as we will hold the world's currency after operation zero." The Brigadier saw Jack raise his eyes questioningly and held his hand up to stop him before he could ask.

"We have selected five locations around the globe. When the funds are in our possession, we will fly to the major financial centres, London, New York, Frankfurt, Tokyo and Shanghai. Our nuclear warheads will devastate each and every city, creating a wasteland that will take years before it is safe enough to redevelop after the fallout. Meanwhile, we will be ready to create the New World Order capitals of the world."

He was taken aback. This was far bigger than they could have imagined.

"Wow, you have it all planned, don't you? I can see why you need the gold. Your operation would be useless without it. You were so fixated on taking over the world you even had your son killed. What I don't understand is why wasn't Colin in on it? Surely you would have been grooming him for greater things?" It was a low blow, but he needed the time to think.

The Brigadier lowered his head, his anger edging to the surface.

"My son was a fool, but I didn't kill him, I loved him. But he got involved in something I was unaware of until it was too late. I realised from a young age he was weak, he got it from his mother. He would not have understood, so I tried to protect him. The Order agreed that his analytical mind and legal skills would be vital in the new world to establish and maintain the new laws of the land. My role was to support him until we had taken control, by then he would have no choice but to work with us. I would not have harmed my son."

"So you killed your father instead." He was taking a risk by baiting the Brigadier but felt as if he needed more of an explanation before dealing with the old man.

"This whole mess came about when my son took on the Barth case. Father was providing information to the Order but failed to inform me that Colin had become involved. That bitch Langfield had assigned him to take the case. Six months ago they travelled to Switzerland, moving everything to a new, almost impenetrable location with a highly sophisticated security protocol. He had no idea he was doing anything other than following his client's instructions. But it threw all our plans into disarray. We needed to know the new code, so the Order sent agents to get it. The idiots assigned were supposed to wound, gather the information and report back. They killed him instead." He sighed, remorse clearly showing on his face.

"Once the report came in of Colin's death, and the pathologist identified the poison, I knew the Order was responsible."

"So why kill your father, surely you should be looking for the man who killed your son?" So a Swiss Bank, that must be it.

"That has already been taken care of. No, my father kept it from me. He wouldn't allow me the opportunity to get the code in my own way. The bastard wanted to prove that he was still the ruthless director of legend even though he was close to death. He was ultimately responsible for the death of my son." His anger returned, this time he knew it wasn't aimed at him.

"When I knew that you were on your way here I couldn't risk a meeting, he was frail, his mind was all but gone. Also, I wanted to be the one to end his life, in exchange for my own sons. I planned to be long gone by the time you arrived, but the bastard took longer to die than I thought."

"So they killed Gant for the same reason, you needed the code. But why Eliza Winch?"

"Gant was the same, he was only supposed to be wounded, but again the idiots screwed up. Eliza had the file with the list of names of all personnel stationed in the UK. Colin had uncovered the names from records placed in the Oxford security box by Shierling in the sixties. It was a foolish attempt to use it as a bargaining tool to gain his freedom so he could spend his life with Gloria the mental case and their two brats. We had to ensure we destroyed the files and the girl along with it." Anger coursed through Jack's veins as he thought of the timid, pretty girl who had innocently uncovered information that ended her life. She probably discovered the file when clearing the office for the refurbishment. One or two names must have jumped out at her, leading her to investigate further.

Just then the Brigadier noticed that he had moved his hands from under his legs and he stood up sharply.

"Get up." The Brigadier ordered. "We have spoken enough, I am sorry Jack, but I can't allow you to leave this room. Now give me the code, and I will make it quick and painless. Delay, and it will be excruciating. Get out of that chair and kneel before me."

Jack used the arms of his chair to raise himself from the seat.

When he was halfway to standing, he spun to his left, hefting the chair with his right hand, throwing it with all his might.

The gun went off, the bullet harmlessly embedding into the wooden frame, before the flying seat smashed into the Brigadier. It gave him enough time to grab his gun and shoot Thorn in the shoulder, sending the weapon from his weakened hand clattering to the floor.

Taking advantage of the old man's shock, Jack launched at him, smashing him in the temple. Brigadier Thorn collapsed in a heap.

Collecting the gun from the floor and taking the scarf from beside the bed, Jack tied the Brigadier securely to one of its legs. The old man was still out cold and he was sure the police would arrive before he woke. He checked on Martha but the bullet had gone through her heart, there was nothing more he could do. He left the room slamming the door shut. Racing down the corridor, he called Walsh.

Sprinting from the building, he jumped into the Range Rover, filling the DI in on the information about the local killings, leaving the details of The Order to himself. That was a need to know. He floored the accelerator sending gravel flying in all directions as he left Wishwell, heading back to the Manor House. He briefed Sara on the way.

"… And Sara, get me information on the KVP Swiss bank. That's where we are looking, concentrate on the security system, who developed it and how we can get past it. Also, get a file on Fabian Brandt, he seems to be prominent in this. I'll call again once I get to the house… out."

The gates to the Manor were open when he arrived. Screeching to a halt, he could see the front door ajar, lights from the hall bathed the porch in an orange glow.

He rushed the steps, drawing his gun as he entered the house.

215

Once in the hallway, the bloodied face of PC Morris greeted him. The officer was sprawled on his back. A blood trail leading from his boots showed they had blasted him with such force that his body had slammed back along the hallway for several feet.

Gun in hand he edged along, checking every room as he passed by. Each one had been totalled. All the furniture was either turned over or destroyed, the contents of every cupboard, scattered across the floor.

He reached the kitchen to find DS Finch resting on the countertop of the central island. He had a hole in his back that should have contained the heart and lungs. Whatever had shot him had blown him half away. The kitchen had a red hue where blood had spattered in all directions.

A phone rang on the counter. Annabel's mobile was vibrating on the marble. Grabbing it, he checked caller ID; it was blocked. He put it to his ear, pressed receive and waited. He didn't have to wait long.

"We have the bitch. You have until noon tomorrow to give us the key along with the code or she will die." Jack recognised a German lilt to the English accent.

"Where shall we meet?" He asked

The phone went dead.

CHAPTER THIRTY-ONE
Missing

He found an unbroken bottle of single malt amongst the rubble of the drawing room. He picked up a chair and setting it straight, sat down, pulled the stopper, taking several gulps. He winced as the burn hit his throat.

"What a mess!" Walsh appeared, he was not talking about the ransacked rooms.

"Finch was a good guy, and he was getting married in a month… SHIT!" He kicked a broken vase. It shattered into pieces against the wall.

"What the fuck is going on? Let me have it as you see it, Case." Walsh picked up a chair and brought it over to Jack, sitting a few feet from him. He opened his notebook and licked the end of his pencil.

"Ask the Brigadier." Jack took another swig.

"I can't, he's dead."

He looked at Detective Inspector Walsh.

"Don't tell me, cyanide."

"How did you know that?" Walsh regarded the LARA agent suspiciously.

"Lucky guess and history repeating itself." He remembered it was a Nazi favourite, an easy way out when they were caught.

The Brigadier wasn't going to be interrogated. He had lost his son, killed his father and failed in his mission. Altogether, it amounted to a man who had nothing left. He'd have known, had he remained alive, the New World Order would have taken the necessary measures to prevent him from talking, he was dead in days anyway. What riled Jack was that it would be seen as an honourable death amongst his group of fanatical maniacs, a martyr for the cause.

In reality, he was a deluded old fool, responsible for the death of innocent people, including his own son.

Walsh was growing more frustrated as he watched the agent casually read the label of the whisky bottle, taking another mouthful. The DI was a man down, still in the dark, with three murders and one suicide on his watch. He'd had enough.

"You know more than you're letting on, you'd better start talking Case. I've lost one of my best men, and I'm not providing any more support until I know the facts." He leant forward to emphasise the point. He was fed up with messing about with this. He was either involved or LARA were on their own.

"SUPPORT!..." Walsh sat back in alarm.

"You call that support? Did you take a good look at the position of your 'good' man when he was blasted in the kitchen.... He was sitting on his arse reading the fucking paper, his radio was found in here. Morris died running to investigate, and the person they were assigned to protect has gone. So forgive me if I don't lose any sleep because of your threat to remove the support of Lysbie's finest." Walsh stood, kicking the chair out of the way. Jack rose to meet him throwing the bottle aside; it shattered against the wall.

"And you think fighting amongst ourselves will solve this, do you?" Commissioner Burrows entered the room followed by Major Paxton. He casually walked between the two men pushing them apart before facing them.

He looked at each man in turn. His DI was angry and knowing Walsh as he did, he was about to get himself seriously hurt. He knew he would have taken the LARA agent on but looking at the veins pulsing in Jack's neck and his stance favouring his back foot; he was ready for him. There would only be one winner, and he couldn't afford to have his DI out of action with all that needed to be done.

"Stand down gentlemen." He ordered. "We are all in this together." He walked over to Jack, extending his hand.

"Agent Case, I would like to apologise for the way you have been treated since your arrival. It's due to the possessive nature of our patch, not a personal thing. We like to keep everything in-house as much as we can, very parochial you might say, typical of a small community." Jack looked at him in disbelief.

How can the man in charge of such a ramshackle bunch offer any excuses for clear ineptitude? Burrows raised a hand to stop any interruptions as he finished what he had to say.

"Ed told me everything, and I'd like to offer any assistance I can." The Commissioner ignored the stifled objections coughed by Walsh.

"I will assign DI Walsh to provide all you need, and you will have full access to our systems. Just let me know if there's anything else and I'll organise it."

DI Walsh just looked at the floor, shaking his head.

"Well, the first thing is to find my daughter." Major Paxton walked over to Jack.

"Have you any idea where they've taken her… is she hurt… what did they… oh god…" The Commissioner put his arm around Paxton's shoulders as the Major fell to pieces.

"Come on Reggie, we'll find her." He led him over to a chair and sat him down.

"Find her Jack, she's my life." Paxton looked up at him, eyes pleading through his reddening gaze.

In the last few hours, the Major's life had turned upside down. His friend of many years had turned out to be a murderous traitor. It left his own reputation, in particular, his acceptance within society's hierarchy in the balance. But worse, far worse, his daughter had been kidnapped, and he was devastated.

The Commissioner briefed the men on his conversation with Ed Ryker after which Jack, now comfortable with it, filled in the gaps.

"Hang on a minute. Are you telling me we've got a load of Nazis running around threatening to take over the world? How can this happen? I thought we only had the Jihads to cope with these days." Walsh was finding it hard to come to terms with what he had just heard. The three locals looked to him for answers.

"All I can say is that there are many factions around the world with underground cells of all different allegiances and beliefs. Some we know and some we don't. This one is a major operation, funded worldwide. It's a global sleeper cell, letting the Neo-Nazi movements deflect from what they were doing. While they were creating headlines, in their own small way, they acted as a perfect cover for the Future Reich or New World Order as they are calling themselves. They are trying to create the Fourth Reich." He watched as the three men took it all in.

"The Fourth Reich?" Walsh again "What, like another Hitler thing?" This was surreal, and it sounded as scary as hell.

"Well, the Hitler thing as you call it was the third attempt at creating a superior race..." He provided a quick history lesson courtesy of Sara.

"The First Reich was the Holy Roman Empire. It included Germany, Austria, the Czech Lands and Northern Italy from around 962AD to the early 1800s. The Second Reich was Imperial Germany from 1919 to 1933 and the Third Reich as you already know was 1933 to 1945. I cannot imagine there is any connection between the unified Germany of today and the New World Order. But you can bet your life that there is an insurgent seam running right through it. We all have them. It is something our people are looking into now."

He briefed Walsh on what he needed from the local CID. To his surprise, the DI was more than eager to comply. It looked like he had finally come to terms with the fact they needed to work this together, either that or he had realised this was way out of his league, and he didn't want to lose face with the Commissioner.

"We need to organise a house to house throughout the village and surrounding areas as fast as we can just in case Mrs Paxton-Thorn is here. Check all outbuildings, farmsteads and warehouses. Also look for any new faces, anyone who has recently arrived."

"Right, I'm on it." Walsh left the room barking orders into his radio as he headed down the hallway towards his squad car.

Case wasn't his cup of tea, but he would not let those German bastards get away with murder on his patch. They had also taken a pop at him, so it was personal. He would do what he could to help get the Paxton bird back, that would do his kudos no harm at all. The chief had also assigned him to the LARA agent to keep an eye on him, that much was obvious.

He could see himself as a secret agent, he quite fancied a break from the mundane paperwork of petty thefts and arson. As he got into his car and fired the engine, he prepared for his mission. He checked himself in the rear view mirror, giving himself a ruthless glare.

"The name's Walsh... Mike Walsh." Tyres screeched along the drive, away from the house.

Commissioner Burrows paced the drawing room outlining his part in the investigation.

"I have the support of our neighbouring forces, and we've managed to set up cordons along the A roads as well as two motorways covering around a ten mile radius. We have traffic checking all goods vehicles and transporters, who have records of passing through or around this village over the past few hours." Jack nodded in thanks before turning to Paxton.

"Major, you should get back to the house just in case they communicate with you. They want to use Annabel to get to me, but they might try through you." The Major was in no fit state to help at this moment in time; it would be better to get him out of the way.

"I have three officers assigned to you Reggie, please stay put, and I will be over when I've finished here." Burrows needed to get to work, and like Jack, he felt the Major would be better back at Paxton Hall.

Reluctantly Major Paxton left the house with his escort, leaving the Commissioner and Jack alone. He wanted to stay, wanted to be involved in the search for his daughter, but he knew deep down he would be more of a hindrance. At times like these, it was best to leave it to the professionals. Once he was out of earshot, Burrows turned to him.

"Will we find her?" He wanted LARA to convince him that they would. It took the onus away from him, and his force, who he suspected were way out of their comfort zone.

"We have to." Jack replied. "Because once they get the information they need, she is of no use to them." He wished he hadn't said it, but he knew he was right. He was also convinced she was nowhere near the village and he only had nineteen hours to find her.

As the Commissioner left the room, Jack headed for the stairs. He needed answers.

CHAPTER THIRTY-TWO
Bad Reception

The devastation downstairs was repeated throughout the upper levels of the Manor House. He passed a Monet that had been smashed to the floor exposing a safe, blown apart. It was empty. All the rooms on the way to his own were ransacked, clothes scattered everywhere. When he reached his room, he wasn't surprised to see his workstation overturned along with attaché cases broken open and thrown around. But he was more concerned about his clothes being touched. Now that was a personal violation.

He strained to lift the desk back onto its legs, he needed to contact HQ. The sat system was bomb proof, holding technology and data deep within its enclosed body. It was secure against everything save for a nuclear attack. He used the fingerprint scanner and waited for the workstation to come into view. While it was ascending, he pushed the leg support accessing the panel containing spare ammunition. He selected one of his favourite Kabar knives and clipped the sheath to his belt. He took four spare clips and three HG85 pearl grenades, no larger than two table tennis balls, slipping them into the lining of his trusty leather jacket.

The monitor clicked into place and powered up. He logged on, waiting for the connection. Within seconds Sara's image greeted him, her warm smile reminded him of better times.

"How are things over there?" He could tell from her tone she had come up with some information.

"Well, we have the force mobilised locally, but I'm not hopeful. What have you got for me?" The powerful graphics card powering the screen further enhanced her blonde hair and sultry hazel eyes. He would have loved to have spent a few minutes catching up, something they hadn't done for a while, but now was not the time.

"We're building a dossier on the move, so I'll feed information as I get it. First, Fabian Brandt, sixty-eight year old billionaire with bases in Paris, Munich, New York, Dubai and a development plant in India." A picture of the billionaire popped into the corner of the screen.

The full head of silver hair gave him the look of someone younger while the dark eyes topped with thin black eyebrows appeared menacing. His gnarled face and heavy crow's feet were the only giveaways to his true age. Even in 2D, the image portrayed the determination and ruthlessness of either a high ranking executive or that of a maniac; he could see Stalin, Hitler, Manson and others like them, a look of control, hiding the real terror of the mind.

"Development plant? Development of what?" He was thinking nuclear

"Electronics, an area that made his fortune." Sara explained.

"He was an electronics engineer by trade and then stumbled into the dot coms where he made his initial fortune. He sold two resource sites for close to one billion dollars in the late nineties. He used the funds to start several businesses around the world, mainly computing and microchip research. He was close to developing a self-cooling CPU chip which would have given him the world market. It was shelved, which shocked the IT world; we are yet to discover why. We haven't enough intelligence yet to check whether it is all a cover. It's proving more difficult as he has close associations with several world leaders. It's making it awkward to gather all the information we need without jeopardising the whole operation."

So he was moving in all the right circles, no doubt providing donations to various ruling parties. This would allow him to build his reputation, becoming an ideal vehicle to recruit from within. Money talked even among the rich.

"Where is he now?"

"We're not sure…" Sara checked the information in front of her.

"… He was last seen three weeks ago at the Museum of Modern Art in New York, a charity function held by the Mayor. And get this, he was the guest of honour, apparently in recognition of his support for the New York art foundation."

"Wow, he's a real upstanding citizen, isn't he? What about the family? Wife? Kids?" Two more faces popped into the lower corners of the screen, a female, mid to late thirties, sharp features, green eyes and styled red hair. Also a male, blonde crew cut, blue eyes, tanned rugged features with an almost square jaw.

"Klara Brandt. His daughter born in 1982. Degree in physics and head of research and development for BEE, Brandt Electronic Enterprises. The male is her fiancé Leon Ubermann, 39, head of security for BEE Global. Again we don't know their whereabouts."

"We do know that Fabian Brandt is due to attend a high profile fashion show in Milan in three weeks. Klara is also on the guest list, and wherever Fabian goes, Leon Ubermann is never too far away."

"Well, before we get to Milan, we have a missing woman and a code to crack. Any luck on either?" They were running out of time with nothing to go on so far. If they didn't get a break soon, they would not only have another dead body, they could be looking at millions more.

The screen changed and in Sara's place was a building. A large white turreted construction complete with drawbridge and portcullis. It looked like a medieval fort. Her disembodied voice provided the information he had been waiting for.

"This is your KVP, Jack. It is the Klauss Van Privatbank situated in the hills to the northeast of St Gallen, Switzerland. Built in 1896 by Bernhard Klauss and Dietrich Van. Two financiers who during the start of car production in Switzerland, created an investment bank for the specific use of the car workers. Using other investors plus lucrative investments of their own, they financed most of the manufacturing plants. In the early 1900s as the bank grew, they sold off the plants and changed their model to a private bank funded by some of the worlds richest investors. They were one of the first banks in the world to develop a digital lock mechanism. It was crude and mainly mechanical with electronic push rods but revolutionary for the time. It now has the most up to date security systems, it even has its own army patrolling the area like a fortress. Today it is one of the most secure independent holding banks in the world with a gold reserve that could fund several countries."

"And I would imagine a high proportion of that is Nazi gold." He added, thinking of Eric Ahler.

"Never proven I'm afraid…" Sara continued.

"… The Swiss Banking Association has powers of non-disclosure. It's watertight, impossible to get enough proof to make any Swiss bank accountable to anybody but their investors."

Just then Jack's PDA sprang into life. He listened to the excitable voice of Detective Inspector Walsh.

"Bingo! We know where they've taken Mrs Paxton-Thorn, but if you want to catch them, I suggest you grow wings."

CHAPTER THIRTY-THREE
The Chase

"Paris!" It had taken him twelve minutes to get to Lysbie CID where DI Walsh had been lounging, feet on his desk, as Jack entered the room.

He shot up and dropped his mug onto his files; coffee seeped into the cardboard folders.

"That's what she said." Walsh nodded behind him. "She was the one who booked the Eurotunnel tickets." He opened the door to the interview room.

He sat opposite a woman from the care home, she had her head bowed as she scrunched a handkerchief in her clenched hands.

"This is Bridgette Simpson, a receptionist at the Wishwell Rest home for the past five years, on the payroll of the Brigadier for the last four." Walsh made the introductions as he sat alongside him.

"Don't say that!…" Bridgette wailed "… It wasn't like that at all!"

"It wasn't like that?" Walsh's shout made the girl jump, her hands began to shake.

"They paid you three grand a time to set up Gloria Barth with an imposter, convincing her the visitor was Jayne Langfield." There's your starter for one.

"You kept it from administrators, and you forged visitation papers. Two."

"You informed the Brigadier of Mr Case's meeting with Martha Joyce and you arranged tickets for the kidnappers to escape to Europe. Three."

"We have you for extortion, deception, accessory to kidnapping and accessory to murder. So how would you like to describe it, Miss Simpson?"

"No!" Bridgette screamed. She covered her face with her

handkerchief, sobbing into the cotton. She started rocking in her chair.

"Tell us how you see it, Bridgette. What were you doing?" Jack placed a hand gently on her wrist pulling her hands away from her face. She looked at him as she dabbed both eyes, he tried to put on his best reassuring smile.

"Brigadier Thorn was a regular visitor to see his father. He would stay behind sometimes, and we would have coffee and chat. One day he told me that Albert had a soft spot for Gloria. He wanted to ensure that she was given the best possible treatment while she was a resident in the home. A few months before, her daughter Jayne stopped visiting for some reason and it upset Gloria terribly. The Brigadier told me they had hired an actress from a local agency to play the part of Jayne Langfield. All they wanted me to do was to keep it to myself and help them to make sure Gloria was convinced. The actress did look very much like her and when Gloria returned from trips away with her she was so happy, I assumed it was doing her a world of good. To be honest, the money was too good to turn down, and it was doing so much for the old lady I didn't think I was doing any harm at all."

"What about warning Brigadier Thorn when Mr Case arrived?" Walsh wasn't buying any of it.

"It wasn't a warning! Brigadier Thorn asked me to tell him as soon as Mr Case arrived as he needed to see him about an urgent matter." She answered quickly and lucidly. She could be telling the truth he thought.

"Ok, what about the Euro tunnel booking?" She was good, Walsh thought. She had an answer for everything.

"Brigadier Thorn told me he was taking his father to Paris for a few days. He was in his father's room helping him pack when he called down and asked me to book in his vehicle for that evening. The calls are logged on the system and recorded, you can check it if you want." She was praying they believed her.

He had heard enough.

"Thank you for your help, Miss Simpson. I'm sure Detective Inspector Walsh will check out all the facts and make the right decision." He left the room closely followed by Walsh.

"You don't actually believe her?" Walsh asked as he watched the agent dial into his PDA.

"She's not clever enough to make it up and if you think about it, it all makes sense. If they can manipulate an innocent to do their bidding, it becomes even more difficult to cut through what is real and what isn't. This whole case is based on deceit and misdirection, with plenty of cash to oil the wheels. No Walsh, the most you'll get her on is deception and tax evasion." He was sure she was telling the truth.

"Thorn would have used her somehow to give him an alibi as soon as I arrived. He intended to leave us with the dead body, but he screwed up. Killing his own father took him longer than he thought, he couldn't risk the old man talking. The intention was to take Mrs Paxton-Thorn as soon as I left the Manor House, leaving a dead body at the care home to add to the confusion." His call connected.

"Sara, I need a lift. Can you get me to Brandt's Paris location as soon as possible?" He updated her on the conversation with the receptionist, before cutting the call. If they were heading for Paris, there was only one place they were likely to take her, and there was no reason for them to suspect anything yet.

"Here are the car details." Walsh handed Jack the vehicle registration that Bridgette had registered. He screwed it up, giving the ball of paper back to the bemused DI.

"It will do no good. There is no way they will leave the shuttle in the same vehicle, and you can forget the plate, that's long gone."

Walsh's mobile phone rang, he moved away from Jack to take the call.

The death of the Brigadier and his father would mean the UK operation had taken a knock. But if any of the Brigadier's claims were true, more cells were operating throughout the country which also needed to be stopped.

Ed Ryker was in talks with NATO, with task forces ready to deploy as soon as the locations of the aircraft had been identified. Agents worldwide were activated to shut down rogue cells with known Neo-Nazi links. All military eyes were on LARA to pinpoint the aggressors, and Jack Case was at the centre of operations.

The PDA rang again. Sara had been working fast.

"We've scrambled a police chopper to be with you in thirty minutes. There's a field at Hodges Farm, half a mile away from your location, it will touchdown there. The Brandt estate is northwest of Chanteau in the Loriet region, an hour from the city. We are dropping you in Paris to meet with the Judiciaire. Antoine sends his regards by the way and can't wait to meet with you again." He could tell Sara found this humorous. He winced when told he was to join with the Judiciaire.

Antoine Valois, his old friend, was the craziest Frenchman since Clouseau. When he wasn't drunk, he was just plain odd. He had never progressed past Lieutenant for a very good reason, the heads of the Judiciaire would never allow it. But on the plus side he had a one hundred percent record, he had never lost a case. He usually left chaos in his wake, the cases shorter to complete than the time it took to clean up the mess. But his success rate was worth the pain. It also gave them kudos with the PM, who proudly waxed lyrical about the qualities of the French version of the CID.

Walsh rushed over to Jack interrupting his call, he put Sara on hold.

"I've just had a call from my unit. Now I'm not sure if it's anything, but the Carrington's have a missing punter at the Golden Fleece. He checked in just after midday, did a bit of painting on the green and hasn't been seen since. His room was empty when we checked it out, but his art equipment is still on the grass. Paints, easel, bag, the lot." Walsh watched as realisation registered on Jack's face.

"Who was he?" He asked putting two and two together.

"A guy called Kevin Johnson." Walsh studied his notes.

"Blonde by any chance?"

"Yes, how did you know that?" The LARA agent no longer surprised him.

"I saw him painting on the green before I left. He had long blonde hair, nearly white." He put the PDA back to his ear, Sara was still waiting at the other end. He gave her a rundown on the mysterious blonde, it would be a good idea to get Judiciaire support at Calais.

"Get the guys to check the passengers in the vehicles, just routine, don't challenge them. If he is there, put a car on him and keep us informed."

"Will do Jack. I've got one last thing for you. We have found more information on Jayne Langfield, but you won't like it."

"She doesn't appear to exist."

Jack was sick and tired of bombshells going off every five minutes, he was getting lost.

"Tell me…" He sighed into the PDA. Sara relayed the new information, frustration sounding in her voice as she was struggling with lack of Intel.

"We tracked back through all the records from the care home. We investigated common knowledge, new intel from the Commissioner and cross-referenced all the known data on the daughters of Gloria Barth. There are no records past 1989 relating to Jayne Langfield, so we don't know if she is really Jayne Barth, the natural daughter, or another imposter. The cost of the care home was paid from a central London bank slush fund under the name J. Langfield in an auto-fund account. No addresses, no contact information. It runs concurrently as long as the funds exist."

He wasn't surprised that all trails were leading to dead ends, this was all part of the New World Order strategy. But why would this Jayne Langfield, or whoever she was, go to all the trouble to involve Colin Thorn and Derek Gant to change codes and gather information? Who was she? Friend or Foe? It didn't make sense.

"Well, I can't see it making much difference now as we have moved on to world domination and mad billionaires. So apart from cracking the code, changed by Colin Thorn, what more has she got to offer?" He knew he was right. There was nothing this mysterious woman could offer apart from her reasons for leading two men to their deaths.

"Maybe so Jack, but there has to be a reason why she needed the help of Paxton, Thorn and Gant. Until we know for sure, whoever she is, she's important to all this." He left Sara to find more questions with no answers.

CHAPTER THIRTY-FOUR
Paris

The Eurocopter 355 dropped onto the impromptu landing pad of a lush green field north of Avenue Gabriel.

Once again the Judiciaire would have to account for the actions of their Lieutenant.

"You should jump out now before I'm impounded." The pilot prepared to take off again.

Jack grabbed his kit bag and left the helicopter, running away from the downdraft of the propellers as they rotated to full power, lifting back into the air.

In the distance a man strode purposefully towards him, his knee length leather overcoat wafted behind him like a cape. As he came into view, his greased back black hair glimmered in the glow from the street lamps, the light emphasising his roman nose. Lieutenant Antoine Valois smiled brilliant white teeth that sparkled as he continued to stride forward until he slammed into Jack, wrapping his arms tightly around him.

"My friend, how is it we take so long to meet again." His English had improved little he realised as he dropped his bag, returning the hug, patting the Frenchman's back in submission as he was finding it difficult to breathe.

"Hi, Antoine, great to see you again." He wrestled free from his friend and held him by the shoulders, pushing him away to take a good look at him. The years of constant alcohol had taken their toll. He had greyed above the ears, his stubble was nearly white. Black circles hung below his eyes and crow's feet stretched their toes towards his sideburns. Three years his junior he looked ten years older than Jack. But he hadn't lost his boyish enthusiasm, he could feel the adrenalin pumping through his arms as he held him tight.

"So, we are here to save the world, no?" He liked Antoine, straight to the point.

"We're gonna try." He replied.

A dull whine of sirens filled the air, growing louder, drawing closer.

Several marked Peugeots screeched to a halt around the edge of the turf along Avenue Gabriel. The sirens drowned any conversation into a cacophony of wee's and wah's. Gendarmes leapt from their vehicles, training their guns on the two acquaintances. A senior officer of the Police Nationale illuminated the pair in a white circle of light from the floodlight held above his head. He barked inanely into the microphone linked to his car's PA. It was a distorted mess of French words, sirens and shouts from other officers running from their vehicles.

Jack instinctively raised his hands in surrender, but Antoine pushed them down again.

"Don't worry my friend; I have this." He left Jack illuminated in the fluorescent circle, heading towards the cars with his warrant card held in the air. He waved his arms as he shouted into the face of the man with the floodlight. The light extinguished as he put it down to gesticulate in an argument of arms with Antoine. In the lamplight, they looked like two tic-tacs competing for the best odds in the next race. After several minutes the officers returned to their cars and drove away. Their lights remained flashing until they disappeared into the traffic of the Avenue des Champs-Élysées.

Antoine returned and handed him a piece of paper.

"Parking ticket… Apparently, you can't park a helicopter here." Antoine remained deadpan for a few seconds before the absurdity of the situation got the better of him, and he started to laugh. As they walked towards the car, Jack screwed the document into a tight ball and threw it over his shoulder.

Before climbing into the Peugeot, Antoine ripped a page from his notepad and passed it to his friend. It read "littering of a public parkway. 320 euros."

CHAPTER THIRTY-FIVE
The Road to Chanteau

Paris came alive as darkness fell, the warm evening bringing people onto the streets. The Avenue Des Champs-Elysee pushed away the night with brightly lit canopies lining the street. They were packed with diners who preferred the balmy evening to the air-conditioned restaurants and bars. The well tended horse chestnut trees stood sentry along the length of the avenue creating a green canopy of leaves, richly illuminated by the ornate street lights poking through the foliage. Jack briefed Antoine on the latest developments as he weaved in and out of the traffic. He pressed an imaginary brake pedal in the footwell as they nearly hit yet another Citroen.

"Damn French cars. So ugly, they have the big backsides of your English women, no?" He dodged another vehicle bringing the blare of several horns as he slipped into another gap.

"I'll ask you to repeat that to Mrs Paxton-Thorn when we get her out." He retorted.

"And another thing … At least our women wash … and shave!"

As they approached the Arc De Triumph, the Peugeot took its place in the demolition derby also known as the Place Charles De Gaulle, a roundabout full of maniacs. There were no rules, no speed limit and full of drivers with a death wish. Antoine took it in his stride, tackling the arena with the skill of a rally driver, his hand flicking through the gears as he spun the wheel, avoiding cars by millimetres. A full rotation later they hurtled down Avenue Marceau towards the river.

Antoine was proud of his city, and he loved to play the tour guide. Jack knew there was a quicker way out but wherever they went Antoine would insist on taking the scenic route. As they reduced their speed to a more leisurely pace, he popped a cigarette into his mouth, unwinding the window an inch to allow the smoke to escape. He took a long draw and turned to his passenger, a large puff of smoke shrouded Jacks face as the Frenchman began to speak.

"We have RAID officers on the outskirts of Chanteau to support us up to the chateau. You will like Captain Renard, he is a good man, as mad as a man with a hat, but a good man."

"You mean a mad hatter." He coughed a laugh through the haze of smoke. He was forever correcting his English as Antoine liked to attempt colloquialisms he neither understood, nor when translated made any sense.

Their friendship had begun seven years ago when his career as a wraith was in its infancy. His assignments included kidnapping, national security missions and governmental embezzlement. It was during the latter when he first met Antoine and was introduced to his unique style of law enforcement.

A French dignitary was thought to be filtering government funds to a South American drugs cartel in return for several properties worldwide. It was his way of elevating within government through intimidation and brutality. Antoine had posed as a member of the cartel to gather information, unbeknown to his unit. He soon found himself with the cartel, the government and the Judiciaire all after him, with orders to shoot on sight.

LARA was assigned to prove his innocence. Several deaths, six resignations and a charge of grand larceny later, Antoine was cleared of all charges and decorated by the Prime Minister for bravery above and beyond the call of duty.

But the Judiciaire were less than charitable, and they had the excuse they needed to remove the maverick from their ranks. Through manipulation, skullduggery and evidence tampering they stripped him of his badge, kicking him out of the force. This caused a public outcry, and again the Prime Minister intervened.

He was reinstated and promoted to the rank of Lieutenant. He had only one supporter who was, luckily for Antoine, the Director of the Judiciaire himself, Gerard Piquant. Piquant could see himself in the younger man and although unorthodox, Valois always came through. But he had been powerless to overrule the decision at the time, with the evidence presented to him.   But now it made him near on bulletproof. Since then he had faced numerous charges; each time they had been dismissed. He was up on three charges now, but Antoine would never change, and as long as the Director was still in control and taking all the credit, he didn't need to.

They crossed the Seine via Pont De L'ama driving south along Quai Branly, heading toward the A10, the route to Chanteau. Even though he had seen it many times, the Eiffel Tower still held a magical aura for him. It illuminated the night with the orange glow of thousands of lights, exuding a power stretching well into the sky, a beacon of France, forever to stand guard. As they passed within yards of the monumental base, he watched as hundreds of tourists milled around. Flashes from cameras burst into the night as they captured the monstrous crisscross structure. Some were happy to just stare in awe at the enormity of the tower.

Antoine started singing La Marseillaise at the top of his voice, occasionally pausing to draw on another cigarette. He watched a tear roll down the Frenchman's cheek as he hit the second verse.

Eventually, they reached the outskirts of the city taking the N118 towards the motorway to Orleans. They were at least an hour ahead of the Chrysler Voyager, the kidnappers' vehicle of choice. Thankfully, he had guessed right, the blonde man had been spotted in the passenger seat as they disembarked at Coquelles. Information had been sent to Jack's PDA, along with images from the Chrysler as it passed security, heading for the motorways. The blonde man had been confirmed as the artist seen on the green at Mittand Burrow. The driver was even more interesting, he recognised the blonde crew cut and square jawed features of Leon Ubermann, head of security for BEE.

Music blared from the speakers as Antoine added entertainment to their two hour journey. He had chosen a French music station playing classic rock twenty-four hours a day. Antoine knew Jack's musical preference, programming the radio especially for this evening.

"We are doing good time my friend. Will you join me in a drink?" Antoine was thinking of his favourite addiction to pass the time. They would definitely lose the hour advantage if they stopped for a drink, as the wine would last long into the night. On three occasions Jack had lost at least one day after a night out with him.

"Antoine, we don't have time to stop for a drink, we'll miss the bus. Just keep driving." He would not compromise Annabel's safety.

"Never mind my friend, we can stay right here." Antoine chuckled as he leaned across Jack's lap and opened the glove compartment, pulling out a large chrome flask. He unscrewed the top, taking a long swig and gasped in pleasure as he swallowed. He wiped the lip of the flask on his sleeve, passing it to Jack. The strong smell of the oaky Cabernet filled his nostrils, giving him enough of a hit to persuade him to pass. The Lieutenant shrugged, taking another measured swig. This was going to be a long drive. Just as the melodic introduction to a Guns and Roses' classic escaped from the speakers, the PDA rang. It was a restricted number.

"Case." He answered, turning Slash down mid solo.

"Mr Case? This is Jayne Langfield. I need to meet with you before you go to the chateau." She was well spoken with a deep husky tone that in normal circumstances would be appealing. Now it was just plain sinister.

"Mrs Langfield, nice to finally get to speak to you." How did she know his intended destination?

"I can't speak for long. Just listen." She was forthright.

"There is a small farmhouse west of Route De La Pervenche just 1 kilometre from your destination. I will send you the co-ordinates. I will light the top right bedroom as you approach to show you I am there." She had thought this through, but how had she got his number and more importantly how could she track his movements?

"This is all fascinating Mrs Langfield, but how do I know I can trust you?" Knowing there was a good chance this woman did not exist, it was an obvious question.

"Because if you don't Agent Case, you will never see Mrs Paxton-Thorn again." The phone went dead.

"Problems?" Antoine could see the concern on his friend's face.

"Nope, we have a slight detour." Jack took the flask from between Antoine's legs and took a swig.

CHAPTER THIRTY-SIX
Scared

Annabel was terrified and she was finding it impossible to stop from crying every few minutes. She was entombed in the floor of a car, in a space just long enough to allow her to stretch and wide enough to flex her restrained arms. They had covered her with a duvet which by the smell of it could have been her own. She had no recollection of how she had got here, she only remembered the attack on her home.

She had been in the drawing room pouring another vodka while she listened to the haunting melodies of Enya. She was trying to distract herself from thoughts of poor Eliza.

There was an almighty bang from the kitchen prompting PC Morris to run out of the room to investigate. She watched in horror as another bang, closer this time, sent him flying past the door on his back, coming to rest just past the doorway, leaving only his boots in view. They were twitching horribly. She was staring at the boots in shock when a young man with long blonde hair strode purposely up to her, so fast she had no time to react. He stabbed her in the arm with a weapon which she now assumed was a syringe. That was the last thing she remembered until she awoke, seemingly hours ago, to the rhythmic movement and clatter of a train.

Disorientated, trapped in total darkness she panicked and struggled. But her hands were tied behind her back, her ankles bound and a gag fixed tightly around her mouth. Her struggles soon ended as she realised her exertions were pointless. She could only breathe through her nose, making it difficult to inhale and the more she struggled, the worse it got.

The announcements from the channel tunnel PA told her she was on her way to France. Listening to her captors, she could make out a few words of German; although she was by no means fluent, she could work out they were on their way to a chateau to wait for Jack Case to bring them the code. She also heard something that sent a chill through her body. One of them wanted her dead whatever happened.

An argument broke out, in language so fast she could not make out many words, all she knew was that one wanted her dead and one didn't. She began to shake, using all her self control to stop from sobbing, allowing silent tears to run along her face and into her ears. The car bounced and jostled her as it moved off the train, she felt the vehicle smooth out as it hit tarmac. After a few minutes of stops and starts, it began to drive smoothly, accelerating until constant. They must have taken a motorway.

Suddenly, Annabel was bathed in dull light as the hatch to her enclosure was lifted. They hauled her out by the tops of her arms, dumping her unceremoniously in the aisle of the large people carrier. Disorientated she looked around to see the blonde man place the hatchback into the enclosure, purposely modified to transport a body. The driver was also blonde, his hair close cropped, military style.

"Get her up." He said, in English so she could understand.

The long haired man lifted her, placing her in one of the seats. He untied her hands, allowing her to sit comfortably. Instinctively she rubbed her wrists and arms feeling the blood return, pins and needles prickling at the tips of every finger. He ripped the tape from her mouth causing her to yelp, tears stung her eyes again.

"Good evening Mrs Paxton-Thorn, I apologise for the uncomfortable start to your journey. Please relax and enjoy the view, we will pass some lovely scenery." The driver kept his eyes on the road as he spoke. He was controlled, and in charge, she could tell in an instant he was the one who wanted her dead. Despite acting like a tour guide, his voice carried a sinister edge. The accented English helped it, delivered softly and deliberately.

"Who are you?" She asked, almost at a croak.

"Kurt, give the lady something for her dry throat."

The long haired man moved to the rear of the vehicle, returning with a small bottle of water. He removed the top as he passed it over. She drank gratefully, sighing inwardly as the water refreshed her.

"This helpful young man is Kurt Eichel, and I am Leon Übermann, at your service." He turned to face her and nodded. She felt herself move back slightly as his eyes seemed to burn into hers. It was only for a few seconds, but it was enough to scare her.

"You will be our guest this evening Mrs Paxton-Thorn, and hopefully, if your friend Mr Case comes through, you will be home by tomorrow night. I would suggest you make yourself comfortable for the time being as we have a few hours of our journey yet to complete." Again he turned to look at her briefly, to emphasise his next point.

"Please don't be foolish and think of escape because I will have to get Kurt to kill you."

She looked over to the long haired man who moved his jacket slightly to reveal a gun. He looked her straight in the eyes, hoping to see fear. She would not give him the satisfaction, merely nodding in acceptance before looking out of the window.

She tried desperately to control her shaking legs. Jack, where are you? She hoped he was on her trail because she feared that if her rescue wasn't imminent, she would never see her home again.

The motorway was sparsely populated as the people carrier cruised steadily on its way to the chateau.

CHAPTER THIRTY-SEVEN
Farm House

As the Route De La Pervenche ended, Antoine swung into a dirt road between two large hedgerows. The headlights of the Peugeot danced wildly ahead as the wheels bucked and bounced along the rutted track.

"She could have chosen somewhere better for the suspension." Antoine moaned, his wrists were wrenched yet again as the car hit another divot.

"Well, she wants us to work for our information. I for one, can't wait to meet her, she has got a lot to answer for." He instinctively drew his Glock, pulling out the magazine to check for bullets, sliding back the barrel to engage the first one. He clicked on the safety before placing it back into his jacket.

After a couple of bends, they passed a wooden gate, propped open by a milk churn. The road smoothed out a little allowing the now steady gleam of the headlights to pinpoint the small farmhouse a few yards ahead. A light appeared in the upper right window almost immediately.

"Well, at least we know she's in." Jack said as he surveyed the surrounding darkness for movement. Driving past the house they parked beside a pigpen, domed shaped arks stood silent in rows on the back fence as the swine inside bedded down for the night.

He approached the front of the sandstone building while Antoine, armed with his SIG, took to the rear. Crawling past the first window, shutters closed tight, he chanced a look through the second where they had been clipped open. With only the light of the moon to aid him, he could see no movement in what he could just make out to be a kitchen.

Crouching below the paned glass section of the door he twisted the handle, it clicked free from the latch and swung open. Keeping hold of the handle, he entered gingerly, careful to be as quiet as the hinges would allow. When the gap was large enough for him to squeeze through, he moved forward flicking his head from side to side, alert to the slightest movement. The moon shone through the window filling the room with shadows. He could make out the shape of a dresser full of plates on stands, some of the detail glimmering in the pale light. He also noted eight tall chairs surrounding a table. The chair furthest from him was a different shape to the rest. Someone was sitting on it.

Light flooded the room, the suddenness of the glare made him squint, but he remained focused, aiming at the shape.

"Put that down, Jack and take a seat." Ed Ryker pulled a chair away from the table, gesturing for him to sit.

"Ed! What are you doing here?" Jack was startled to see the director of LARA.

"Come and sit down while I explain."

He stood where he was, lowering his gun to his side but leaving it cocked just in case. Ed looked up at his agent for a few seconds, knowing it wouldn't get any better until he was fully briefed. The director looked towards the door leading to the rest of the house.

"Gerard, come and join us will you." He called.

As the door opened Jack stiffened, positioning himself in front of his boss, gun at the ready. He had no idea what was going on. He braced himself, prepared for action.

A man in his early sixties, smartly dressed, walked into the room followed closely by Antoine. The Frenchman raised his eyes, shrugging at him as he went to the chair furthest from the LARA chief and sat down.

"Jack let me introduce you to Gerard Piquant, Director of the Judiciaire." Ed Ryker pulled out the chair next to him which Piquant accepted. He looked at Antoine's boss and then at his friend. Once again he shrugged, as much in the dark himself. Jack clicked the safety back on his Glock, putting it away he sat down next to Antoine, facing their chiefs.

"We should introduce someone else to you both before we continue." Ed said, facing the two wary operatives.

"Come in my dear." Ryker called across the kitchen.

She was aware of all eyes on her as she entered the room, walking around the table she took a seat next to Ed Ryker. Wearing a roll neck sweater covered by a cardigan, her soft features topped with long red hair pulled into a bun. Jack could have been looking at a schoolteacher.

"Gentlemen, let me introduce Jayne Langfield or to give you her real name; Jayne Brandt."

Both men looked at the woman, emotions in check, before returning back to their chiefs. It was Jack who spoke first.

"You knew didn't you?" He aimed the question at Ryker, who looked down at the tabletop. He had expected this from him.

"We had our suspicions but only knew for certain a few days ago, when Mrs Brandt contacted us for help."

He looked over to the woman, she was picking at her fingers as they rested on the table.

"So you lure two men to their deaths, try to lure the widow, then wait for another innocent woman to die and leave it until the widow is kidnapped before asking for help. Nothing like shutting the gate after all hell has bolted." He would not apologise for the venom in his voice.

"It wasn't like that…" Ryker explained.

"Oh no? It certainly looks like it from where I'm sitting." This was going nowhere.

"Well, until you know the whole story, you shouldn't…"

"Shouldn't what? Jump to conclusions, get angry, shoot her right now…" Jack shoved his chair away from the table and got to his feet. Antoine rested a hand on his arm to calm him, but he swept it away as he walked around the table to face the woman. She leaned back in her chair as Jack leant forward with both hands pressed against the table's edge.

"Why don't you tell me why we should help you, Mrs Brandt?" He held her gaze, challenging her to come up with something that would change his mind. Ryker had had enough.

"Case! Sit down now! This is solving…"

"Gentlemen, gentlemen… can we please stop this? Have you forgotten that you have a woman to save and once you have succeeded, you need to stop my husband." Jayne Brandt kneaded each temple with her forefingers, gently easing the headache that had been with her all day.

Closer now, he studied the woman. Her complexion was fair and unblemished, no lines to speak of and her makeup had been perfectly applied. Her emerald green eyes contrasted with her red hair giving her a timeless beauty. But there was a weariness hidden behind the makeup, but not from Jack. As he watched her further, he could see her shoulders sag as the weight of her burden pushed at her.

Ed Ryker had already taken his seat, Jack walked back to Antoine, taking the seat next to him. He would decide on his next move once he had heard what she had to say.

"Go on." He prompted. All eyes turned to Jayne Brandt.

"My mother was Gloria Barth." She began, clear and concise. She wanted to get this out, and her shoulders lifted as she spoke. Her burden was about to be shared.

"I met Fabian at a company where I was temping as a legal secretary, the law firm Langfield Latter. He introduced himself as John Langfield, a major investor. I was flattered by his charm, and with the attention he paid me, he was also very kind and after a short while we became a couple. He whisked me away to the chateau after a few weeks, he explained everything, including his real name; Fabian Brandt."

"So he told you he was a megalomaniac who planned to take over the world?" Jack cut in.

Jayne smiled at him.

"No, he told me all about his electronics empire. He also said he had invested in the law firm because he believed in his friend Keiran Latter. To add credibility to the business, he used the pseudonym John Langfield to anglicise the practice. I had no reason to disbelieve him, perhaps due to my naivety or the lifestyle on offer, I was swept away with the glamour of it all. As far as I was concerned, he wasn't harming anyone. We married as Brandt in 96, but I used Langfield as my married name to all but the staff. Again, I could see no harm in it."

"What changed your mind?" This could be plausible. Jack relaxed a little as she continued.

"Well, at first it was like a dream come true. Fabian was charming and treated me like a princess, he couldn't do enough for me. I became his PA, spending most of my time in our villa in Spain, or on the yacht in the Caribbean or condo in Florida, a lifestyle any woman would die for. He spent a lot of time away, so I had personal bodyguards who became my friends, none more so than Hugo." She bowed her head, her voice softening as she mentioned his name.

"And Hugo became more than just a bodyguard?" He could guess the obvious. Jayne's eyes misted as she prepared for the next part. She dabbed her eyes with a hanky and continued.

"They told me about my mother when I was 21 and I spent years in turmoil wondering if I should trace her or leave well alone for the sake of my parents. I had a wonderful family upbringing, and Carol and Bob were the best parents a girl could ever have hoped for. Carol was so worried about telling me that it put a strain on their marriage. It was Bob who told me one night over dinner." She looked at the handkerchief and refolded it, turning it to a dry spot.

"After days of tears, fights and general unrest, I decided to leave well alone. I was 25 when I left for London. With good education and a degree in law, I wanted to start a career as a legal secretary. Before I left, Carol sat me down and told me to find my mother. Whether it was the realisation of me leaving home or the turmoil she had been putting herself through, she felt it was time." She could tell by the faces of the men around the table that her life story was probably irrelevant and should be saved for another time. So condensing most of the detail, she moved on.

"I found my mother in Chelsea, and we were reunited in 1990. I visited as regularly as I could, I was working long hours to finance the high cost of London living. It was hard at first as she was not responding at all, but then as time went by, she asked for me when I wasn't there. She showed general improvement year on year as I visited more after my marriage. Then one year, out of the blue, Fabian gave me a birthday gift of Wishwell House. He had arranged permanent residence for my mother at the home, something I will always be grateful for, as she was happy there for the rest of her life." Mist now turned to tears, and she took a few minutes to compose herself, regularly wiping at her wet cheeks.

"Madame, can I ask? When did you find out about your husband's other life?" Antoine was getting bored and wanted to get on with it. His throat was dry, he had left his flask in the car. Jayne regarded the Frenchman through wet eyes, nodding to acknowledge the question.

"Hugo told me all he knew, then tried to help me escape... but Fabian killed him." Her story only lasted a few seconds before she broke down again.

"Gentlemen, I think I can take over from here." Ed Ryker patted Jayne on the hand to calm her as he continued.

"Mrs Langfield had an affair with Hugo Dahl, an ex-government security specialist. He had joined Fabian's security team with a specific role, to look after his wife."

"Her marriage was a sham, it was Brandt's way of getting closer to the prize, the KVB stronghold, without drawing attention to himself until the time was right."

Jack didn't like this, too many loose ends with more added every day. Why the trust in her all of a sudden? He listened some more as Ryker continued.

"Hugo was not an extremist, he was just doing the job he was paid for. But he became suspicious, reading between the lines of some operations undertaken by the other members of Brandt's crew. Using his government contacts, he uncovered the true extent of Brandt's plans."

"He felt a loyalty to Mrs Langfield for obvious reasons and tried to get her away. With the help of Hugo's old colleagues, they arranged for a safe house in Freiburg but were ambushed en route and Hugo was killed. Ever since then, Mrs Langfield has been on the run so to speak, with the help of a small group of Hugo's friends."

"A small group of friends?"

"Three German ex-security police officers who served with Hugo are employed by Mrs Langfield to help protect her and expose Brandt and his operation. We are in contact with them, and they check out."

"Right, so we have a snapshot of the situation. Now tell me about the Colin Thorn involvement. It is one hell of a coincidence you managed to employ a direct descendant of the Fourth Reich's UK main man." Jack could see the story unfolding, but Colin Thorn just didn't add up.

Jayne, now composed, continued with the story.

"It was Albert from Wishwell House. He seemed such a nice old man and helped mother settle in during her first few weeks in residence. Whenever I arrived to see her, I would always find them together. I know what he is now and I hate him for it, but he would never have harmed her, he looked after her. I am somewhat torn in my feelings towards his motives as she didn't suspect a thing. Anyway, I was putting mother's estates and insurances in order when Albert suggested speaking to his grandson who owned a law practice. The association with Mittand Burrow seemed a natural route to take, and it was like bringing her home."

"So Colin had access to all the accounts, knew the existence of the bank vaults, including the contents in the Swiss bank?" He still wanted more.

"Yes, that's correct, he proved to be as good as his grandfather had said he was. But I don't think he realised how serious his grandson took his ethical code of conduct. He insisted on non-disclosure of all items and travelled with me to Switzerland to ensure the vault was secure, making sure all of our interests were best served." She could tell the two operatives were still finding this hard to fathom. She needed them on her side, or it wouldn't just be Mrs Paxton-Thorn who was in danger.

"Colin was a good man, an honest man. He knew nothing of the existence of Fabian, and we even gave him lasting power of attorney to give him sole responsibility for my mother's welfare, along with the finances. He was meticulous in his approach, he left nothing out. Colin and I knew the combination to the box at KVP until I had him change it and keep it to himself once I knew they were after me. My only concern was for my mother, I needed to ensure her welfare and Colin was the only person I could trust. I had no idea they would target him."

"A mailed pig." Jack said out loud. All looked at him.

"I beg your pardon?" Jayne asked, bemused.

"A mailed pig. The code left in the safe deposit box at the bank in Oxford. Does it mean anything to you?" He could tell it didn't, but he began to get agitated as there were too many holes.

"No, not at all. Colin insisted I be left in the dark for my own safety." Jayne replied. She could tell he hadn't finished.

"Right, so tell me, Mrs Brandt…" He emphasised the Brandt a little too sternly, spitting the name rather than saying it.

"… I can understand the reason for your husband's need to silence you. But I can't quite see why you would contact us to help, other than for your own protection. What use are you to us now? You have no idea what the code is, and we know of the whole operation apart from the location of the gold. Unless you have a map with x marks the spot in your handbag."

He wanted answers that would help them with the current problem. The whole story, sad as it was, wasn't the priority. Why had he been sidetracked from the mission just to hear an update of something they would find out in the end anyway? Nothing so far had any bearing on the rescue.

"It's my eyes." Jayne said lowering her face instinctively as everyone turned to look.

"Iris scan." Ed Ryker explained.

"The KVP security systems are the most advanced in operation today. Part of the access protocol includes biometric technology, in this case, iris scanners. Colin and Jayne are registered, but as Colin Thorn has since been cremated there is only one person who has access." He looked over to Jayne as he finished.

"I approached LARA to help end this. My husband has to be stopped."

Jack looked at Ryker, wanting to wring his neck. 'Take this job Jack, it will do you good to have a rest from bombs and bullets'. He could remember his words in the gardens of Mounts Bay and had believed him.

"So I can assume the letters sent to Derek Gant and Annabel Paxton-Thorn inviting them to Central Bank weren't from you." His instincts were now in overdrive. Surely he wasn't the only one to see this?

"No, I sent no letters." Her gaze was unwavering.

"And the key I assume is fingerprint activated?" This was going the way he expected. Pulling her handbag from the floor and rummaging through it on her lap, Jayne pulled out a key, sliding it across the table towards Jack. He stopped it at the table's edge and examined it. He traced his fingers over the KVP logo, it was the same.

"They are unique to the holder, and with the iris scanner and code, along with the military security assigned to protect the bank's contents, it makes access near on impossible." Again, he knew she would confirm this.

"Then we have a problem." He leaned forward, stating the obvious, surprised nobody in the room had picked it up during the conversation.

"Derek Gant and Mrs Paxton-Thorn received the letter." He rummaged in his pocket and pulled out the key discovered in Oxford with KVP emblazoned on the grip. He showed it to Jayne.

"That is the key from the bank in Oxford, unique to Annabel Paxton-Thorn. Derek Gant would have produced a key when he was there, where is it? More importantly, what use is the key… unless they have the same access as you?" The room went quiet. Jack needed more.

Ed Ryker broke the silence as they processed what had just been outlined.

"So both Paxton-Thorn and Gant had their eyes registered." Studying her he noticed Langfield's eyes show a slight change, they widened, only for a second, but enough to show that she hadn't realised. Could she be the real Jayne Langfield?

"So it all makes sense, with you out of the picture they needed another set of eyes. We need to get Annabel before it's too late." He also wanted Annabel to answer the question now screaming at him. Why hadn't she told him about her eyes? Jayne looked into her bag again, producing a small bunch of keys and two swipe cards.

"I think these might help you in the chateau. The keys are for the ground floor, and swipe cards give access to the lower levels, the wine cellars and the storerooms." He pocketed the keys and studied the cards marked with W01 and S01.

"Let's hope your husband hasn't changed the locks." He slid the cards into his top pocket.

"Oh, he won't change the locks. He has an army patrolling the whole area; he would expect no one to break in."

Ryker checked his watch. The kidnappers would arrive in twenty minutes. He needed to let his agent go.

"Jack, we will take Mrs Brandt into protective custody and escort her to Klaus Van Privatbank. We will rendezvous with you once you clear up here." Director Piquant, who had been quietly observing, addressed Antoine.

"Lieutenant Valois, you will accompany Mr Case to the conclusion of this mission on behalf of the French government. We will offer all the support necessary within the French borders, and we are awaiting NATO clearance for you to cover the rest of the assignment. We are expecting confirmation in a few hours. I remind you that you have the support of myself and the Prime Minister. Do not let us down." Jack noted the pleading in his eyes, he didn't blame him.

He looked over at Antoine, watching as a tear rolled down his cheek. Jack shook his head, he knew that this would go straight to the Frenchman's head. Antoine was a patriot with a capital P, and to be the French representative of the task force assigned to save the world was too much for him. He cried when France won the World Cup in the '90s, weeps when he recounts the heroics of the French resistance in the war and mists up every time he hears La Marseillaise.

Antoine stood and facing his chief, made a speech. A simple yes sir would have sufficed, but this was Antoine.

"Director Piquant, I am most honoured to be given this task on behalf of my country…"

He began to choke as he continued, taking a seat as he felt the emotion overwhelm him.

"… I will not let you down sir…it…" The Director cleared his throat and bowed his head, hiding a grimace as he listened to the blithering of his emotional Lieutenant.

He had made the right choice to pick Valois to head the operation as he was without a doubt their best man. He broke the rules but got the job done. He reasoned that had there been no rules, the havoc that would ensue would ruin the reputation of the force irrevocably. It was just a matter of managing the amount broken and to be on hand when it was too many. But, he was also dispensable, as apart from the Prime Minister and himself, Antoine Valois had no supporters, so for them it was a win, win. He would either return a national hero or die in the attempt. Either way, his two advocates would walk away unscathed.

Jack looked over to Ed and raised his eyes as if to say, 'Really boss, I've got to nursemaid this lunatic?' Ed could only offer an expression that said, 'don't look at me'.

"Is he OK?" Jayne Brandt asked as she watched the drama unfold.

"He'll be fine." He grabbed Antoine under the arms, hauling him from his chair. He led his friend towards the door.

"We'll call when we've finished here." Telling no one in particular.

He closed the door and followed the Lieutenant to the car.

CHAPTER THIRTY-EIGHT
Rendezvous

"Antoine, will you keep your eyes on the road!" He grabbed at the wheel again to stop them from driving into a hedge as the French Lieutenant tipped his head back and shook the flask into his mouth to catch the last few drops of wine.

"Merde!" He swore as he threw the empty into the back of the car. He stared straight ahead, with a steely determination that added pressure to the accelerator.

Jack was worried. Antoine was a friend, he had a lot of time for him, and he found his strange quirks amusing, but he wasn't keen on tolerating his idiosyncrasies during a mission. They needed to focus on avoiding being killed, and he couldn't recall Antoine ever being that single minded!

He checked his watch, the kidnappers should arrive in around twenty minutes. The pursuing Judiciaire had indicated three passengers travelling in the MPV, one more than when they left Coquelles at the Channel tunnel exit. It meant they had taken Annabel from her hiding place, allowing her to ride in full view, confirming they hadn't noticed the tail.

The decision not to intercept was to minimise the risk to the hostage. They needed to get Annabel clear of the vehicle and hope to grab her when they transferred her to the house.

In truth, Jack decided to let the operation move to the chateau. Annabel could become collateral damage if the extraction took place while she was still in the vehicle. He had already made a mistake when he had put the two numb-nuts in charge of her protection, it was his decision to keep her at the Manor House.

He owed it to her to ensure her safety, and he owed it to himself and LARA to get back on his game. The only positive to take from the latest information was proof she was more valuable to both sides alive. The odds were on her side.

Rescuing her would also cause a significant dent in the plans of Fabian Brandt. It would sever or slow down his influence in France, similar to the problems now facing him in the UK. As long as he could keep casualties to a minimum, his judgement may just prove beneficial to the operation.

Antoine pulled into a lay-by behind two unmarked trucks and was out of the car before Jack had time to react. He was met by a RAID agent in full riot gear, minus black balaclava. The two Frenchmen embraced, patting each other on the back like old friends. The RAID officer then opened the cab door of the leading truck and producing a bottle took a long draft before passing it to Antoine.

'Jesus, these bloody French and their wine.' Jack shook his head as he approached the two men.

"Don't you think you have had enough?" He voiced his concerns to Antoine as he stood watching him take two more deep swallows.

"It is good for the blood Jack, and mine is now perfect." He winked at the LARA agent and smiled his cheeky smile. Even though he was trying desperately not to, he couldn't help but smile back.

"Jack, let me present to you Captain Renee Renard, a good friend and head of the Black Panthers." Renee Renard? Poor guy, his parents obviously had a sense of humour he thought as he shook the Captain's hand.

To have the support of the French Tactical force had been a good move, they were disciplined and well trained. This could very well work.

"Commander Case, it is a pleasure to assist you in this mission." The young Captain said as he stood to attention after releasing his hand.

"Just call me Jack."

"Ah, yes I forgot..." Antoine added.

"Jack likes everything informal. Stand at ease, Captain."

"What have you got so far?" He was keen to get this moving.

"The vehicle has just pulled onto Route d'Orleans. They should be with us in 15 to 20 minutes. I have officers stationed around the perimeter awaiting instructions."

He produced a map from his jacket sending the beam of his torch over the unfolded diagram. He had marked twelve red crosses showing his officers spread evenly around the dark lines outlining the boundary walls of the grounds.

Jack spoke into the PDA.

"Sara, can you send me details of the building and surrounding area. Show us what we're up against." He knew the sat image would show heat sources within the grounds, and he should be able to pinpoint where the guards were stationed.

"Sending them now, be careful Jack they are not only within the grounds, there are also hostiles patrolling the perimeter."

"Thanks, Sara, out." The signal dropped. He switched the PDA to full screen, an image of the chateau appeared as a solid box of green, a thin line surrounding it highlighted the perimeter wall, the forest showed up as a transparent green fog all around. Red dots were moving in every sector, like ants around an anthill. There was no way to distinguish RAID from guards which would prove to be a problem. He counted 18 dots within the forest which meant there were six hostiles amongst the RAID units.

"Captain Renard, can you order your guys to dig in. They've got goons on their tails." The Captain radioed through the instructions to lie low and hold their positions.

After a few minutes, there were four moving dots and fourteen stationary.

"We have immobilised two of them." The Captain announced.

"That's two down at least. Don't kill them, we may need some of our questions answered once we get inside." He was impressed with the way RAID had gone about their task. He would need them as there were red pulses all over the place inside the complex. Captain Renard turned to Jack.

"Commander Case, we are not killers. We neutralise and gather intelligence. We use only the force necessary to complete our tasks." This guy was easily offended.

"That's perfect Captain, but you do know, once inside the walls your men will come up against considerable firepower. Let's hope your neutralising tactics are enough to safeguard your officers and the hostage." He checked his watch, they would need to make their move.

"I can assure you, Commander, that should we be subject to lethal force we will respond in kind. Death is also not alien to us. Now if you will excuse me, we need to get into position for the assault." The Captain left them and headed for the trucks, barking orders into his radio.

"That told you." Antoine remarked as he scuttled after Jack who was striding towards their car.

The time for talking was over.

CHAPTER THIRTY-NINE
Stake Out

The chateau could only be reached by a fifty yard driveway leading off a narrow country road north of Route de la Pervenche. The road was used as an artery linking all the villages in the area to the main A-roads. Cars travelled along unnoticed making it perfect for the Peugeot, parked 100 yards from the illuminated approach road. They had made it to their vantage point with five minutes to spare. Jack, hidden deep in the undergrowth, communicated with Antoine via his earpiece as he watched the guards patrolling the gates. He had a good view of the front entrance through his binoculars.

"Three at the front with one in the box and it's lit up like a Christmas tree." He reported back to Antoine who was keeping the car ticking over under cover of a small copse.

"Great, then we'll be able to see what we are doing. The last thing I would want to do is shoot you by mistake in the dark my friend." Antoine was being serious as his aim wasn't the greatest at the best of times.

"With the amount of alcohol you've consumed Frenchy, I'll be behind you whether its light or dark." He was serious too.

"Hey, I told you, it is good for the blood, and I intend to keep my blood in my body. Don't worry; we make a good team." Jack smiled to himself. One thing they definitely were not, was a team, more like two mavericks working together.

Suddenly light swept the tarmac in front of him, flooding across the road and leaking into the undergrowth as the headlights drew closer. He sank back into the brush and watched as the black Voyager turned into the entranceway. The floodlights burned down from both sides of the driveway, illuminating the silhouettes of two long haired passengers as the MPV drove through the gates. He assumed one was the artist from the village green, the other was Annabel, but he couldn't tell which side she was sitting. Another good reason to wait until they had removed her from the vehicle.

"Let's go, Frenchy." He gave the signal to Antoine.

Within seconds the Peugeot screeched to a halt in front of him. Antoine popped the boot, and Jack climbed inside, pulling it shut.

"Captain, wait for the signal then come in over the walls. We will already be there." Antoine radioed the head of RAID as he made for the drive.

"Lieutenant, we are in position. We have neutralised all exterior threats. We will mobilise once the CCTV lights extinguish." The signal had been agreed.

"Affirmative Captain… and when you hear the bang." Antoine replied.

"What bang?" The Captain queried, but Antoine had switched the radio off and thrown it into the glove compartment. He took a final swig from his refilled flask before locking it away for later.

CHAPTER FORTY
Illegal Entry

The tall street lights illuminated the road from either side. Antoine noticed CCTV cameras following the movement of the vehicle, activating in sequence as he drove steadily past each lamp post. He resisted the urge to wave regally as he headed towards the security gate.

"I think they know we're coming." Antoine spoke into his earpiece.

"Just stick to the plan, and we'll be fine." Just stick to the plan, this was Antoine he was speaking to.

"There's two in front of the gate now, one behind, and it looks like one in the box." Antoine described what he could see.

"Aim for the hatch in the window, that's your first pitch. You need to get out of the car and throw underhand; otherwise, it might drop short. If that happens get back to the car as fast as you can. The other one will take care of itself."

"Oh, do not worry my friend, I won't be hanging around for the fireworks." Antoine stopped the car a few yards from the entrance and watched the two guards advance, M16 assault rifles aimed at his head.

Massive iron gates blocked the approach road. The initials FB surrounded by a flaming phoenix dominated the centre, they were definitely in the right place.

The guardhouse stood to the left of the entrance. Two men patrolled the gates while one remained inside at a bank of monitors, flicking through different sectors of the grounds. The counter positioned below the reinforced glass had been designed to accept ID without the driver leaving the vehicle, but at night the shutter was down.

"The slot is closed, Jack." Antoine was getting nervous now.

"Then get it open!" Jack whispered a shout, not risking any sound echoing from the boot.

Improvisation was one of the key traits Antoine used to get the job done, but this one was on the fly. He had two pearl grenades under a clipboard on the passenger seat. He was to toss one in the hatch and roll the other under the gate, getting far enough away if they both hit their target. But if he couldn't get the first one in they would be in trouble.

The guards, wearing grey military uniforms, looked better suited to an army base than a country house. The guns pointing at him showed they meant business. Antoine needed to think fast. As they split up to approach from both sides, Antoine grabbed the clipboard, with the grenades spooned in each palm. He swiftly got out and stood next to the car.

"Halt." The guard on the driver's side commanded, startled by the speed at which Antoine appeared in front of him.

"What is your business here?" He was a stocky man and distinctly German. The fact he was speaking English was an advantage as he knew Jack was rusty in other languages and he needed him to hear the conversation.

"Put that gun away soldier before I report your employer to the Gendarmes for threatening behaviour to a government official."

"I am Albert Moreau, inspection officer for OzonAction and the United Nations Environment Program. I am here to approve the extension to the pool."

As it came out of his mouth, Antoine had no idea where it was going. Perhaps Jack was right, he might have to curb his drinking a little. The man lowered his gun to waist level, looking the Frenchman up and down.

"The owner is not in residence and anyway, why are you here at this hour?" The man had a point Antoine thought.

"Ah, well…" Think man, what am I doing here this late? Antoine's mind was in overdrive.

"… Before I could approve the extension, I needed to be sure there is no noise throughout the night, disturbing the wildlife living in the surrounding area. I have been monitoring for the past month, and I am pleased to say that I see no reason to delay the approval any longer." You are good Antoine, he thought to himself, ignoring the groan from Jack in his ear.

"Well, you can't come in. As I have already said, the owner is not here, and he is not due for another few weeks." While the guard was speaking, the other one was circling the vehicle, stooping to look inside. He needed to work fast.

"I don't need to see the owner, I just need a signature here …" He flicked the cover open on his clipboard using both hands while holding tight to the pearls.

"… And I'll be on my way." The form was one of his expense claims. It was in French, he was hoping there were no linguists amongst them.

"Give it to me, and I'll sign it." The man lowered his rifle, holding out his hand to take the clipboard. Antoine turned in time to see the other guard walk around to the back of the vehicle, he was sure to push the release.

"Alas, I appear to have lost my pen this evening. If I could borrow yours?" Antoine was pushing it now, but he hoped he had guessed correctly. The man patted the pocket of his tunic and shouted to his colleague. It drew the other guard away from the car as he too patted himself down. Thankfully, he had got it right.

"We have no pen, go to the window. Grant will have one." The shutter opened, ready to accept the clipboard. Here we go.

"Can you open the trunk?" The guard checking the vehicle had returned to his search. Antoine turned just as he was about to post the pearl.

"What … Oh yes … Sure. I will be with you once I have my signature." It was now or never Antoine knew as he placed the clipboard onto the sill, pushing it halfway into the slot. The guard looked down at the boot of the Peugeot.

"Don't worry, I can do it from here." He pressed the release button.

All hell broke loose in a matter of seconds.

As the boot rose, Jack kicked with all his might. The guard, still stooping, caught it on the chin shattering his jaw as the bullet from the Glock finished him for good measure. At the same time, Antoine rolled the pearl grenade through the slot while rolling the other underneath the gate. He ran back to the car drawing his SIG, sending a bullet into the head of the man with all the questions.

The explosion ripped through the sentry station blowing a hole in the wall behind. Bricks flew in all directions, three smashed through the windscreen of the Peugeot. The gates lifted into the air and clattered onto the bonnet, flipping the car on its roof.

Jack and Antoine flew backwards just missing the rear axle, landing on their backs yards away. The floodlights extinguished, plunging the drive into darkness, lit only by the orange glow of the fire from the demolished guardhouse.

"I hope you're fully comprehensive." Jack shouted to Antoine as he sat up and looked at the devastation.

As the dust settled, he could see the driveway, now unobstructed by wrought iron, leading directly into the grounds. Antoine lay next to him in the same position. He leaned over to his friend.

"I think my career as an environmentalist was very short lived." He said, watching the smoke billowing into the air.

As the barrage of noise calmed, they could hear gunfire. Captain Renard and his team had entered the grounds.

"Come on, let's get Annabel." He got to his feet, running past the remaining gate pillar to look into the courtyard.

The chateau stood regally in the background, a brilliant white renaissance castle with two towers standing above the battlements. It was illuminated on all sides, obliterating the darkness of the night. Lights shone from numerous arched windows, and at its centre, a large pillared staircase led to the grand archway entrance. In the middle of the grounds, a large fountain stood on a large circular lawn surrounded by globes of light on decorative pillars. Some were occupied by guards, using them for cover while they shot at the RAID officers. One fell as Jack watched the French special forces advance on them.

Antoine joined him a few minutes later, stuffing his flask into his coat pocket.

"At least the door still worked." He said showing Jack the radio retrieved from the glove box. It was broadcasting a babble of orders and instructions in French as Captain Renard drove his team further into the grounds.

Through the spray of the fountain, Jack could see the Voyager. He watched as three people left the vehicle, making their way up the steps. The long haired artist, dragging a struggling Annabel, took the lead. Following behind, gun raised and taking potshots at RAID, was Leon Ubermann.

"Come on, let's go!" He left Antoine behind as he darted towards a pillar which a guard was using for cover. He didn't notice the LARA agent approach from the south as he concentrated on the east wall. The bullet caught him below the temple.

"That's my space." He said shoving the dead body away. Crouching down he waited for Antoine to join him.

The kidnappers had reached the top of the stairs as Antoine arrived, staying close.

"I've got to get up there." He turned to Antoine. "Cover me."

Before he could answer Jack leapt into the open and went after them. Antoine immediately broke cover, shooting indiscriminately towards the guards closest to the building. He saw two of them drop before his foot caught on the dead man that Jack had removed earlier. Falling headlong into the grass his gun slipped from his grasp, landing yards away from him.

Lifting his head searching for his weapon, he locked onto the eyes of a gunman who appeared from his hiding place behind the fountain.

He was smiling as he knelt, raising the sights of his M16, aiming at the head of the Lieutenant. Antoine's mouth went dry, but he doubted that he would have time to take a drink. He closed his eyes, waiting for the crack of the rifle.

He had been told that the crack came after the bullet hit, meaning he would not hear the gunshot, which was surprising as it actually made him jump. He had heard it and felt no pain; nothing at all. Slowly he opened one eye and looked straight into the eyes of the guard. Dead eyes stared through him, blood flowing from the gunman's head, dripping down his chin. Like a falling statue, he tipped forward, landing head first onto the lawn.

A hand appeared in his peripheral vision. He looked up at Captain

Renard.

"You really need to go easy on the wine Antoine." He said as he helped the Lieutenant to his feet.

"Tomorrow." Antoine answered, pulling the flask from his pocket and swallowing deeply. Captain Renard retrieved the fallen SIG and handed it back to him.

"I saw Commander Case enter the house. I think he could use our help." He said, watching the Lieutenant dust himself down.

Antoine looked at him ready to agree when a movement over the Captain's shoulder changed his mind.

"I think we have unfinished business." Renard turned back to see more guards streaming around the side of the house.

"Looks like back up." Antoine shouted as he took cover behind a pillar just as the light above shattered all over him.

CHAPTER FORTY-ONE
Chateau

Jack burst through the oak doors and skidded across the marble floor, just stopping short of slamming into the wall opposite. He was alert for sound, hearing footsteps to his left he ran headlong through the wide corridor full of priceless paintings and embellished side tables. Nearing the end, there were only four doors left, two on either side. He held his breath, listening. Creeping forward he could hear movement from his right. Moving his head nearer he could hear furniture being moved and a whimper from a female. It had to be Annabel. Taking hold of the handle he held his Glock at the ready. He flung the door open and rushed in, ready to put a bullet into his first target. The room was empty.

He was in the library, books adorned every space of the floor to ceiling oak shelving, meticulously arranged and worth a fortune. There was nothing else in the room apart from an oak circular table and one high backed winged armchair, not a kidnapper in sight. He could have sworn he had heard movement from this room. The only other access was through the double glass doors leading to the gardens. He tested them; locked with the key on the inside, so they couldn't have gone that way. He unlocked them, pushing them open. He could hear gunfire from the front of the house, but the gardens to the rear were empty.

As he closed them, he caught a movement from behind, reflected in the glass. He ducked instinctively just as the door shattered above his head. Turbulence from the second shot whistled past his ear as he dived for cover behind the winged chair.

In the doorway was the blonde artist, gun in hand and raised ready to take another shot. Seeing the trajectory of the barrel, Jack dived the other way as the bullet exploded through the aged padding of the chair, thumping into the books behind. He let off a shot as he rolled away from his hiding place; he was encouraged to hear a yell as his bullet hit home.

As the door slammed shut, he could hear footsteps running away from the library as the blonde assassin fled along the corridor. Jack rushed after him, but he was fast. He saw his attacker disappear around a corner at the far end of the hall. He was holding his shoulder, and by the looks of the blood trail, he would be easy to find. He heard a door slam behind him, unmistakable this time. It came from the library.

He left the shooter alone for now and eased back into the room, closing the door with care. He froze, straining his ears for the slightest sound. He heard it again, movement of furniture or a sliding door, or something scraping across the floor. He headed to a row of books, throwing them to the floor. He tapped the back of the shelf, solid. He repeated it on the next row along, again solid. Pulling more books from the next column, littering the floor with priceless collections, he tapped the back of the shelf and found what he was looking for; it was hollow.

Emptying the shelves he pulled each one, but nothing moved. Frustrated he kicked the plinth, there was a click as the whole column slid forward. Grasping the unit he pulled, it swung open easily to reveal a steel door. He released the magazine from his Glock, replacing it with a full clip, sliding the barrel to engage the first bullet.

The door opened to reveal a set of stairs leading down to a narrow corridor. Lights shone from domes fixed to the wall. He crept down trying to keep the noise to a minimum, although the creak of steel as he took each step echoed in the narrow space. The corridor was fifteen yards of grey concrete as if cut from a block of stone. It reminded him more of a bunker than a basement.

The first few doors opened easily with a simple handle, but they were just empty grey cubes. As he moved along, he found one room containing a table and three chairs, a private meeting room of sorts, and two more with cardboard boxes full of supplies, toilet rolls, paper and cleaning aids.

At the end, either side of the corridor, were two doors made of reinforced steel, one marked W01 and the other S01, the wine cellar and the storeroom. Each door had an electronic locking system. He pulled out the two cards given to him by Jayne Brandt. He chose the S01 card to the storeroom as he expected the wine cellar to be out of bounds to hostages.

He put the card in the slot and swiped. The indicator light turned green as the door unlocked. The clunk, louder in the confined space, made it impossible to conceal his presence.

Gun at the ready he opened the door.

CHAPTER FORTY-TWO
S01

Jack had found Annabel Paxton-Thorn. Her eyes were wide and pleading, tears were streaming down her face, and she was choking. She was hanging from a steel support in the ceiling. A thick nylon rope wrapped around her neck, balancing precariously on a chair, her toes barely touching the seat. Her hands tied securely behind her caused her body to rotate as she struggled. Occasionally her feet missed the chair, strangling her. The gag already restricted her breathing; she would not last much longer.

The rope ran along the joists, tied off at a lever attached to a large steel box at the back of the room. Lights red, green and amber flickered on the bevelled front edge. Six barrels surrounded the box. He could see from the wires on top that they were attached to several blocks of C4 explosives.

He ran towards her, placing his gun on the chair as he grabbed her feet, ready to pull her free. As he released the pressure from her throat, Annabel breathed frantically through her nose.

"Stop exactly where you are Agent Case. I wouldn't lift Mrs Paxton-Thorn any higher if I were you." Leon Ubermann walked out from between two shelves of racking, where he had been waiting patiently.

He froze as he watched the man approach, gun raised, pointing at his head.

"You will have noticed that I have tied the rope to the lever over there." He pointed to the steel box.

"It is, shall we say, an insurance policy. Should the lever fall it will complete the circuit, and the building will disappear along with you and the lovely Mrs Paxton-Thorn, so I would think carefully about lifting her too high." Ubermann's grin spread across his face, his eyes portraying a fascination, a pleasure almost erotic as he watched the agent hold the woman in the air.

"So, now we are all comfortable; it is time we had a little chat." Ubermann pulled the chair from under Annabel, relieved Jack of his gun and placed them six feet away, leaving the weapon on the seat.

"You may need this shortly." He held their eyes as he sat on the chair.

"What is the code, Agent Case?" He sat cross legged, comfortably resting the gun on his knee. Jack was stuck. He could take Ubermann, he had no doubt, but Annabel would hang. He could go for the gun and shoot him, but he was sure Ubermann would shoot Annabel before he reached it. Should the German decide to kill him, she would hang anyway. He would need to bide his time.

"It's just a phrase; A Mailed Pig, we have no code." He had no choice but to offer the information, he hoped it was just as spurious to him.

Ubermann thought for a moment. A mailed pig improved on a male pig, given by Kurt and Dolf before, but still no numbers.

"We need numbers, not words, what is the code?" He could wait a little longer.

"I've told you, that's all we have. There were no numbers." He was struggling to hold Annabel up, as although she was not heavy, his grip around her legs was awkward, it was putting a strain on his muscles. He tried to shift position, but a muffled scream from Annabel forced him to stop.

"Ok, let's say I believe you. What about the key?" He would send the phrase back to headquarters to decipher there, but he also needed the key.

"It's in my kitbag, in the back of the car at the entrance." He lied.

"And you expect me to believe that do you?" Ubermann stood and walked towards the bomb. He read the display above the flashing lights. Satisfied he returned, circling them both, looking them up and down.

He punched Jack in the stomach. He doubled over releasing Annabel who squealed as the rope bit into her throat, cutting off her cries. He was still in pain as he reached for her, holding her until the rope slackened a little. It allowed her to breathe once again, frantic laboured breaths through her nose.

"WHERE IS THE KEY!" Ubermann shouted into Jack's ear. He aimed the gun at Annabel's face, looking at the agent who was still grimacing from the pain in his stomach. With one hand he searched Jack's pockets, throwing the contents onto the ground. Coins, Euro notes and bits of paper bounced along the storeroom floor, but no key. He checked his jacket finding only the key card for the winery which he tossed away, followed by the PDA. Searching with one hand, the German had missed the pearl grenade and key, tucked into a concealed pocket of the lining. Patting his way down Jack's leg he discovered the knife, pulling it free from the ankle holster.

"Nice, a Kabar, you have a good eye for weaponry." He turned it around in his hand, hefting it as if ready to throw.

"It would look better cutting a slice across your throat." He kept his eyes burning into the German.

Ubermann held the knife to Jack's throat instead, pushing just enough to feel the keen edge, ready to break the skin.

"You are either brave or stupid Agent Case. Or is it just bravado in front of your lady friend, huh?" Locking eyes, he moved closer until he could feel the German's breath warm the inside of his nostrils.

"But … no matter." He backed away, pleased with himself for controlling his temper.

He could have finished them, but it would have been too easy. No, he would leave now and get his enjoyment from the torment they would go through in the few minutes they had to live, it excited him. He walked to the door pulling it open to leave.

"I will allow you to say your goodbyes. Oh, and should the tension and fear get too much, and you can't face being blown into tiny pieces, feel free to use the gun." He pointed to the bomb.

"The explosive is on a timer, there are twelve minutes left before 'boom'!" Ubermann raised his arms to emphasise the explosion.

"I am sure you will work out how to free Mrs Paxton-Thorn and as I am not a monster, you will have time to say your goodbyes. I will retrieve your kit bag along with the key and be at a safe distance to wave adieu. It's a pity Agent Case, I wish we had met under different circumstances. You might have proven to be an interesting adversary." Ubermann turned to leave the room.

"You don't want to do this." Jack wondered, why would they want Annabel dead?

Ubermann looked back from the doorway.

"Oh, but I do Mr Case, I do." The door slammed behind him.

He heard the gunshot before the door double locked and held firm. Ubermann had shot out the electronics activating the secondary security system, sealing the door permanently. He looked up at Annabel.

"Don't worry, we'll get out of here." He wished he could believe half of what he said, as he had no idea how he would manage it.

He loosened his belt and felt around the oversized buckle until he came across the hilt of the small pen knife hidden within the design. Pulling it free of the metallic sheath and with one hand still holding onto Annabel's legs, he felt around to her bound wrists. A few slicing actions later and the bindings fell to the floor. As Annabel ripped off the gag, she gasped at the air as she sucked it in.

"I'm so sorry, this is all my fault." She was crying now, which wasn't good as he needed her to concentrate.

"Annabel! Listen!" They didn't have time for personal guilt. They had to get out of there.

"Grab the rope above your head and pull, keeping the pressure on. Then try to unhook the noose from around your neck. Can you do that?" He hoped it was a slip knot.

Thankfully, it was. Weak from the trauma Annabel tried several times to wiggle the noose over her head. After several attempts she switched hands while Jack still supported her, struggling to keep the power in his muscles. After two attempts she pulled free.

"Now, I will let go for a few seconds. I need you to put the noose around your wrist and tighten it while you hold on to the rope with your other hand. You need to keep your hand around the rope at all times. Got it?" Annabel nodded, fear still etched on her face. Seeing a solution, he prepared to move.

"Right, you will take the weight until it suspends you and then I'll be back before you know it. Ready?" She nodded.

He lowered her gently until he could feel the pressure move away from his arms and prepared to let go, sizing up the best route as he did so. Annabel held on, grimacing as the noose cut into her wrist, she began to rotate.

Positioning the chair, pulling two directories from a shelf, he placed them onto the seat, sliding it underneath her. He grabbed her ankles and guided her feet onto the volumes. Thankfully she had remembered to keep the pressure on the rope as she was lifted. She held it at her waist as if ready to ring a church bell.

He ran to the shelving and grabbing one more directory, he approached the bomb. The lever, held up by the rope, had a copper connector at its tip. Looking at the device, a small curved plate protruded from its housing with a similar connector, the contact point. Preventing the connection would be simple.

Resting the directory onto the plate and lining it up with the lever, he cut the rope. Using both hands, he eased the lever onto the directory. The spring was strong enough to hold the volume in place. He looked at the digital readout on the bomb casing in front of him, ten minutes and counting. Apart from the flashing lights which were now all blinking amber, there was nothing else, just an enclosed steel box. There was no way to defuse it.

Nine minutes thirty-seconds and counting. Annabel banged and pulled at the door. He left her shouting at nobody as he collected his PDA and Glock, searching the shelves for something to use. There was no signal on the phone, so he couldn't even call Antoine for help.

Antoine, where was he? He had hoped he would have seen the secret door from the library and found the corridor unless something had happened to him.

Eight minutes thirty-seconds and counting. Jack moved Annabel aside and tested the door himself. It was solid. He thought of the grenade but remembered the C4, he could try the gun but couldn't chance the ricochet. He wasn't about to give up, but time was running out.

Seven minutes thirty-seconds and counting.

The ceiling exploded, debris crashed to the floor and contents spilled from several shelves, shattering across the floor. Piles of paper, once neatly stacked, filled the room floating down like rectangular leaves.

Annabel screamed as Jack pulled her to the ground, bracing himself for the aftershock.

Raising his head, he scanned the area of the explosion. Dust was billowing in the air, filling the room in a dense fog. He could see silhouettes of the shelves coming into view, ducking down several times as he coughed.

As it thinned out, a large square hole had formed in the ceiling. A head appeared, its eyes blinking from the dust. And it was coughing.

"Need any help?" Antoine sneezed as the dust billowed around him. The resourceful Frenchman had made his way through the air conditioning ducts and had kicked the grill free to get access into the room. Still upside down, his eyes fell on the C4 strapped to the barrels.

"Zut Alors!" He shouted, as the full extent of what he was seeing registered.

Six minutes and counting. Without speaking, Jack grabbed the chair and positioned it under the opening. Grabbing Annabel, he pushed her through the gap. He could hear the aluminium clang as Antoine and Annabel scuttled along the duct. Pulling himself up he saw her disappear a few yards ahead. Antoine must have gained entry to the grill from the corridor outside the room.

He slid along for a few seconds before he dropped, landing just below the metal stairs leading to the library. Both were already running up the stairs, he sprinted to catch up.

"This way, we have a car waiting." Antoine shouted back as he left the library via the main hallway.

They ran down the broad marble floor, barging through the entrance. All three were now side by side as they negotiated the stairway to the courtyard.

Annabel was holding on to both men, her legs were moving, but she wasn't sure if she was actually touching the stairs. A black RAID truck waited at the bottom, its side doors open, engine running. All three dived in as it accelerated, tyres squealing on the tarmac before circling the lawn towards the exit. Antoine leaned out to shut the doors before collapsing onto one of the bench seats, gasping for breath.

Bullets rattled against the truck walls as the remaining guards tried to prevent escape. The armoured truck continued unscathed. Captain Renard was the last RAID representative within the walls. He had ordered his team to withdraw once he realised the severity of the situation. They had suffered only two light casualties which were more than could be said for the chateau's security detail. They had also taken six prisoners from an estimated count of thirty and from what he could see there were less than a handful left.

"Everyone Ok?" Captain Renard asked as he skilfully steered a path through the debris and the dead. They passed the ruined guardhouse accelerating beyond the devastated front gates and Antoine's wrecked Peugeot, hitting top speed along the driveway. They held on tight as the Captain turned into the narrow country lane at breakneck speed.

No one spoke as they waited for the explosion, bracing themselves against a buffeting, or any aftershocks that were sure to come. The truck swung onto Route de la Pervenche heading towards the town of Chanteau.

Within a few yards, they saw a flash of light followed by an explosion so powerful the side of the truck boomed like the skin of a drum. Everyone looked behind them to see a mushroom of white cloud, dust and fire rise into the night sky. Several trees crashed onto the road behind as part of the perimeter walls collapsed onto them.

"Well, it was a pretentious, ugly building, anyway." Antoine said as he watched the warm glow in the distance pulse orange to the beat of a silent song.

He raised his flask and toasted the beginnings of the demise of the New World Order.

CHAPTER FORTY-THREE
Rested

The rope cut into her throat as the chair disappeared. She kicked her feet trying to find purchase on something, anything.

"Don't worry Annabel, I'm here." Through tearful eyes she could see Jack Case standing by the door, arms crossed, resting against the frame. He was smiling. Why isn't he helping me? She tried to cry out, but the rope had closed her airways, her mouth moved, but no sound came.

"Come on Annabel, we have to go now." Lieutenant Valois poked his head through the door to check on her and tutted when he saw her still hanging.

"Jack, do something will you, the car is waiting." Valois was getting impatient. Jack pulled his gun from his jacket and pointed it at her head.

"Hold still Annabel, I'll get you free." He aimed at the rope and fired...

She screamed as she hit the ground. The floor was soft and pliable, not the hard concrete she was expecting. She sat up sharply.

Jack was beside her, placing a hand on her arm.

"Annabel you're ok, it was just a dream, you're safe now." His words were soft, comforting. The storeroom had disappeared, replaced by golden Art Deco panelling, the room illuminated by the sun as it shone through silk nets.

It took only moments for her to realise that she was in a bedroom of the Prince de Galles Hotel. Her throat was sore on the inside and out. Rubbing her neck, she winced as her hands brushed the welts under her jaw where the rope had chafed her skin. She found it painful to swallow, but it had eased a little after the fitful sleep.

"What time is it?" She looked at him as he checked his watch. He was fully dressed, alert and refreshed. Over his shoulder, she could see the discarded quilt and crumpled pillow on the small chaise longue. He must have used it as a makeshift bed while he watched over her.

"Just past midday, how do you feel?" He looked into her eyes, scrutinising her as he spoke.

"Apart from my sore throat, I'm fine. How long have I been asleep?" She recalled the aftermath of their escape.

"Well, we checked in at around three this morning. The doctor examined you, giving you a sedative which knocked you out by about four. A nightmare disturbed you, but apart from that you slept right through." He was so precise she could tell he had been with her all night. She looked straight at him. His eyes like blue crystals and his face strong, protective, giving her all the reassurance she needed. He made her feel reliant and helpless. She felt emotional as he returned her gaze with an air of compassion. Leaning towards him she placed her arms around his neck, feeling his shoulders tense, the muscles as taut as steel.

"Thank you, Jack. I wasn't sure if you would come, those men wanted to kill you. It was awful." She felt the tears roll down her cheeks. He pulled away from her.

"Hey, you are safe now; they are long gone. For the time being, we have them on the run. Their UK operation is in tatters and so now is the French. It won't be long before we find the other locations and stop them altogether." That was the plan anyway.

"Tea?" Jack walked across to the regency bureau. He poured hot water into the silver teapot before carrying the tray, complete with milk and sugar over to the bed.

Once she made herself comfortable, he placed it across her lap. She took a sip, wincing at the pain as she swallowed but soothed by the refreshing brew.

"I have ordered a light brunch for you, it should be here soon. In the meantime, just relax and enjoy your tea." He smiled at her as he returned to the chaise longue to concentrate on his PDA.

He dialled and waited for the connection.

"Sara, what have you got for me." He spoke as soon as she answered.

"And good morning to you too!" Sara was relieved to hear his voice.

"Sorry Sairs, you know how it is." He replied, trying to apologise but underlining the importance of the request.

"Well, I'm just glad you're ok." She let the pause linger for a moment to emphasise her feelings and to protest his lack of concern.

"This is what we've got so far." She gave Jack an update on the operation.

"We've uncovered several sleeper cells in the UK. We also uncovered multiple armament caches through the documents found at Brigadier Thorn's house. We are confident of uncovering more in the next few days. The French authorities are hoping to gather similar intel from the guards captured last night at Brandt's chateau. Two of them are looking at a deal, so again we should be able to make more inroads there. As yet we have nothing on the aircraft locations, although we are homing in on a couple of sites in North America and Africa where we have intel of unusual activities." Things were coming together he was pleased to hear.

"Anything on that bastard Ubermann?" Even speaking the name made him want to hit something.

"Well, he got away. I can tell you that. The chateau is now a hole in the ground, completely obliterated, there are still fires being extinguished within the grounds. Ubermann and Eichel made their escape in the MPV minutes before you got out. Two RAID officers attempted to stop them, but they had the firepower to drive them back."

"And they stopped at the entrance to retrieve my kit bag?" He was hoping they had.

"Yes, they did. It blew out the back end of the MPV just outside La Buissenniere, a few miles away. Two men, matching the description of Ubermann and Eichel, were reported stealing a Mercedes from a house in town. So I guess apart from a headache, they escaped."

The kitbags were rigged to detonate remotely should they fall into the wrong hands. He had detonated his from his PDA once they were well clear of the grounds. Unfortunately, it had missed the target.

"Ubermann will be pissed off." He could just imagine the arrogant German's reaction to being duped, he had to smile.

"And he will be after you Jack, he knows you escaped." Sara's concern was palpable.

"One guard reported in just before they captured him. We traced the call to a mobile phone registered to BEE at a location near the wrecked MPV. It has to be Ubermann."

"Then he will definitely be pissed off." The wry smile remained. Let's see how good an adversary he really is. But he must have known he might escape. This really did not make sense. Why try to kill Annabel and why leave her behind? They needed her to get in the vault, all that was missing was the real code. Was there another agenda?

"One other thing Jack, the bomb that totalled the chateau was built into the basement during its construction. They were careful to ensure there would be nothing left if the site was compromised. All of Fabian Brandt's sites are constructed specifically for BEE, so it is highly likely that they all have the same contingency."

"We have warned agents worldwide that Brandt knows of the threat to his operation, he may look at countermeasures. Watch out for booby traps, we can't be sure he hasn't rigged some sites in readiness. I'll report further intel as soon as I have it. Tread carefully, Jack." Sara cut the call without waiting for a reply as she knew nothing he could say would stop her from worrying.

There was a knock on the door. He walked over to check the spy hole.

"I'll leave you to freshen up Annabel." He said as he let the maid into the room. She carried a tray with covered plates which Jack lifted to reveal fluffy egg, crispy bacon, sausage and tomato, a selection of pastries and a cafetiere filled to the brim with steaming coffee. He smelt the heady combination of cocoa and hazelnut, the same blend he used at home. It reminded him of the Cornish coast and his other life, a life a million miles away.

"Shall I clean the room now, madam?" The maid asked as she placed the tray on the bureau next to the tea. Annabel moved to the bathroom with a fresh towel.

"Yes, that will be fine, I'll be finished in here in five minutes. Where shall I meet you, Jack?"

"I'll be out on the patio, Antoine should be there already, testing the local brew." He left the room. Leaving the maid pulling the sheets from the bed, Annabel went to the bathroom and turned on the shower.

As the warm water soaked her shoulders, she was lost in thought, going over the past few days. Her emotions ran through fear, terror, excitement, tears, comfort and back again.

Her musings all led back to Jack. Fears, she felt he was there to allay them for her. Terror and he would make it go away. She felt excitement when she was with him. Tears, Jack was there to wipe them away and comfort. His strong arms and reassuring words enveloped her like a quilt, warm, safe and secure.

Jack, Jack, Jack, she could not get him out of her head. Was it love? She couldn't tell, as she had never felt like this, so if it was love, then she had never truly loved before. She trusted him with her life, as had already been proven.

But then again, this was his job. Perhaps he was playing a role, the role of the protector reassuring the target, a target he was assigned to safeguard. She didn't want to believe it, wanting instead to believe that there was something between them, that he protected her because he wanted her. She would gladly give herself to him.

She lathered herself, imagining his hands gliding over her body, picturing him walking into the bathroom, pulling back the curtain and climbing in beside her, wrapping his arms around her. She kept her eyes closed as the thought aroused her.

The bathroom door opened.

CHAPTER FORTY-FOUR
Lapse of Concentration

Jack walked along the opulent corridor towards the lifts. The art déco styling had been mixed skilfully with 21st century technology. The blue, black and white design of the carpet and walls, along with the intricate decals on the ceiling, brought the twenties alive. The pictures above the stylish dado rails depicted the angular style of the era. Eccentric furniture designs, buildings with porthole windows with ladies and gents in all their elegant finery.

They flickered, transforming along the walls propelled by wafer thin LCD screens. They were programmed with a delay to give enough time to appreciate the beauty of each image before fading to show another. They were housed in authentic picture frames creating an impressive visage.

The only blot on the landscape were the modern day trollies of hotel housekeeping. Filled with discarded breakfasts, dirty linen and cleaning utensils, the maids, darted from room to room with military precision.

As he waited for the lift, his thoughts drifted to Annabel. The plan was to get her back home as soon as Eurostar would allow. She would be under armed guard until this was over, although he doubted they would need her as bait any longer. But he wasn't taking any chances, he cared for her in a way that perhaps he shouldn't and furthermore she intrigued him. Her strong character along with a stern exterior had been replaced with the vulnerability of a little girl lost, he would try harder to keep her safe from now on.

A young couple joined him, dressed for the gym in the basement. They clung onto each other as if afraid of falling if they let go. He smiled politely as they looked over at him; the guy had a pleased grin on his face, the girl a coy smile. He averted his gaze praying for the lift to hurry. He noticed a maid's trolley parked outside a room with the door wide open. He could hear water running as the maid cleaned the bathroom. It looked like she was working around the occupants who must have had a heavy night. He could just see the end of the bed where a pair of legs lay still, feet hanging over the edge. She must have had a good night he thought as it looked as if she slept where she fell, one of her white sandals had fallen off and was lying on the floor. Those were the days, out all night, sleep through the day and out all night again. He couldn't remember three out of the ten days leave he took in Ibiza in the late nineties. Ku was the club, it opened at ten closed at seven, cage dancing, house and garage on the decks and enough alcohol to float an island. The lift doors finally opened and as he entered, he recalled the painful hangovers and gut wrenching after effects. It reminded him of why he now preferred his cocoa and hazelnut caffeine fix.

They had travelled one floor when the lift slowed to take in further passengers. The doors swept open, and a trolley trundled in, pushed by a maid. It split Jack and the young couple to either side of the car, everyone breathing in to make room. The maid moved to the rear, barging past him to get into position ready to push the cart out once they had travelled to the next floor.

She said nothing, staring straight ahead deep in thought. He couldn't help but be impressed. Housekeeping was conducted with methodical precision at the Prince de Galles, reinforced by the cleanliness of the trolley's neatly arranged contents. The towels were expertly folded and plumped to a softness that caressed the skin. Bedsheets were stacked into sharp edged squares in unblemished pastel colours. All the tools of the trade, brushes, mops and dusters were organised in purpose built compartments. Even the clothing had a military feel. Gold epaulettes attached to the shoulders of purple and white tunics finished with gold buttons. White pork pie style hat and white sandals completed the look.

Jack noticed something which made his blood run cold.

Too late, the lift doors had closed tight as the car descended. He looked at the number slowly moving from three to two as if deliberately delaying him. Come on!

His senses screamed, he needed to get back to Annabel. Impatiently waiting for the lift to reach the next floor, he removed his Glock from his jacket to check the magazine. Both women screamed, and the guy babbled in what could have been Polish as he stared at the man with the gun. He held his hand up to calm them using his best smile.

"Gendarme!" He shouted, pointing up to the fourth floor. But the three terrified passengers were oblivious to his gesture and raised their arms above their heads. He then realised French was probably not their first language.

"Policja … Policia … Polizia …" He tried his best to find the right word. The doors finally opened on the next floor.

"Oh … Forget it."

He vaulted the trolley, leaping clear of the lift leaving the occupants screaming in multilingual cries of help as he searched for the stairwell. He raced the stairs, two sometimes three at a time, sliding around each turn as he bounced off the walls before attacking the next flight. How long had he been away? Five minutes… ten? He hoped he wasn't too late. As he climbed, he plucked his PDA from his pocket and pressed speed dial.

"Antoine, we've got trouble. Meet me in Annabel's room. Bring everything!" He cut the phone without waiting for a reply. He was hoping he was wrong, but knew he wasn't. He had taken his eye off the ball and yet again had put her life in danger. How had he been so stupid?

The shoes, he should have noticed the shoes. There was no drunk guest in the room across from the lift. The white sandal laying on the floor belonged to a maid, an unconscious maid. He had no reason to question the fact that the maid had entered their room wearing jeans under her tunic. An observation he knew now would never have been allowed, she was no maid.

He bolted through the doors on the fourth floor and sprinted along the corridor. He allowed himself only a cursory glance into the room where the legs remained still. Was the maid dead? Fear gripped him as he realised Annabel may also be by now. Reaching the room he swiped the keycard, it glowed red.

He crashed into the door with his shoulder, but it held fast. He shot at the lock, blowing it to smithereens, leaping through before it hit the floor.

Annabel lay naked on the bed, her hair still soaked and the droplets on her skin showing that she had been pulled from the shower by the maid. The maid who was now straddling her, holding a scalpel close to her head.

"Freeze!" Jack took aim as she looked up at him. He recognised her immediately from the data sent by Sara; Klara Brandt.

Instinctively, the assassin threw the blade towards his face. He ducked away letting it clatter to the floor, bouncing off the wall behind him. Before he had time to straighten, Klara leapt from the bed and with martial art precision kicked him in the head. He was propelled into the bathroom. His Glock flew across the tiled floor coming to rest by the sink. He left it there as the woman stooped to retrieve the knife. Getting to his feet, Jack launched at her, but she was quick. As he was almost on top of her, she sliced at him. He moved back just missing the blade intent on carving him from hip to hip. As he fell, he slid his left leg forward and kicked out, catching her shins and bringing her crashing to the ground. Her weapon flew across the room, landing out of harm's way. Klara turned and tried to scramble away. He grabbed her by the ankle, attempting to pull her back. She thrust her free heel into his face smashing his head against the wall, allowing her to escape.

Grasping both handles of the floor to ceiling windows, she pulled them open and ran onto the small balcony. They were four floors above Avenue George V. The room filled with the roar of vehicles as they fought for space on the streets below. Jack shook his head clear, licking at the blood escaping from the corner of his mouth. He watched the woman straddle the balcony rail and without hesitation disappear over the top.

Getting up slowly, stopping a second to allow the bubbles and stars to clear from his eyes, he stumbled towards Annabel. Grabbing a towel from the floor, he covered her, concerned that she had not moved since he arrived. One of her eyes stared wildly, pinned open by a wire speculum stretching her eyelids unnaturally, prepared for an operation. Thankfully her eyes were moving, flitting from side to side fixing on nothing in particular. She was alive but she wasn't speaking, her arms were by her side; unmoving.

"Annabel, can you hear me?" Her eyes flickered but her response was a gurgle as if she was trying to speak but she couldn't. He knew why; Curare. Paralysis had coursed through her body, affecting her breathing.

He carefully closed the speculum, lifting it from under her eyelids. Throwing it across the room, he cupped her head in his hands wiping her damp hair from her face. He stroked her hand as he spoke, trying to act as calm as possible, knowing he had to move fast.

"Annabel, listen carefully. She has poisoned you, and I need to get the antidote. Antoine has it in my kit bag; he is on his way up now."

"I'm going to meet him so I will be away for only a minute." She whimpered to object, but the words wouldn't form. He pulled over a pillow and rested her head, so she faced towards the door.

"I'll be back before you know it." He looked at her one more time before he left the room, he had seen this terror in her eyes before and he hated it. She did not have a lot of time left as the paralysis was affecting her vital organs.

If it reached her heart, she would die. He had to assume the Brandt bitch had escaped as he had no time to waste.

CHAPTER FORTY-FIVE
Breakdown

He bolted along the corridor in search of Antoine, he should have been here by now, but there was no sign of him.

Heading for the stairs, he stopped short just as he was about to leave the floor. The lift lights were out. He sighed with frustration, this can't be happening. Calling Antoine's number again it came back unobtainable, it could mean only one thing; he was stuck in the lift.

"Antoine!" He called his name in frustration, berating him for not using the stairs. Why the hell hadn't he used the stairs? Because he hadn't told him, he answered his own question and again chastised himself. He was getting sloppy. Frantically looking around for something to help, his eyes locked on the trolley discarded by the incapacitated maid. He threw it on its side, sending the contents sprawling across the carpet. Gripping the side wall closest to him, he pulled at the rail using his foot to hold the cart steady. The metal protested with creaks and squeals as the momentum weakened the bar. Four almighty tugs later and it snapped off. He had a three foot steel bar flattened at one end in his hand. It was exactly what he needed.

He jammed the flat edge in between the lift doors and levered the bar...

"Monsieur arreter!" A young gendarme appeared in the corridor from the open room and faced Jack, his gun raised. He had been checking the condition of the maid and heard the commotion from the hall. Seeing him destroy the trolley and try to prise the lift doors open had alarmed him, he thought Jack was responsible for the maid's condition.

"No! Hang on, you have this all wrong." He went to his pocket for his ID.

"Please Monsieur, place your hands on your head, or I will shoot." His English was polished, and he was not about to take any risks with this man.

"Look, there is a woman who will die if I don't act quickly." He pleaded, taking his hands from his head as he moved forward towards the gendarme, arms outstretched.

"It's too late Monsieur, she is already dead." The young officer nodded back to the room. "Now put your hands back onto your head, or I promise I will shoot you." His gun shook as he faced the Englishman who was only a few feet away from him. He knew if he moved again the gun would probably go off. He tried a different approach.

"Look, officer, I am working on a case with Lieutenant Antoine Valois, a case sanctioned by the Prime Minister and the Director of the Judiciaire. Please call in and check. My name is Jack Case, and Lieutenant Valois is in the hotel somewhere on his way to meet me. Look, check in this pocket, you will see my ID. Hurry, the woman I am concerned about is down the hall." He risked turning side on to the officer thrusting his hip towards him allowing him access to retrieve his papers. The officer looked at the pocket, looked back at his face and looked back to the pocket again.

"Come on!" Jack shouted. "Just check my jacket and take my ID for Christ's sake!" He edged ever closer until he was only an arm's length away.

In one move he grabbed the officer's wrist, bent it back and released the gun. Within seconds he was pointing the gun at the terrified man, who raised his hands instinctively.

During the momentary standoff, he heard a noise from behind. A thump repeated every so often, and a voice, distant, muffled. He wanted to risk a look, but he wasn't confident that the young gendarme wouldn't try anything stupid. He backed up, taking his ID from his pocket he threw it at the officer.

"Catch!" He said before turning back towards the lift, hoping to gain a few seconds while the officer caught the wallet.

The noise came again as he neared the lift doors. It was coming from behind them, someone was banging from the other side, and Jack knew who it was.

"Antoine?" He shouted at the door.

"Jack?" came the muffled reply.

He grabbed the bar from the floor and jammed it into the gap. He levered at the join turning towards the gendarme.

"Come over here and give me a hand will you?" He shouted as the doors gave way an inch.

"Antoine, can you explain to this job's worth who you are and get him to shift his arse!"

The young officer listened to Antoine's explanation, a lot clearer now the doors had opened slightly, and he ran to join them. He grasped one side, pulling the door further apart, Jack released the bar, grabbing the other door. They slid back after a little effort and held in place.

Antoine's head peered over the ledge by their feet, black from oil and dust. He had climbed from the lift's roof hatch and ascended the maintenance ladder between the first and second floor. With careful negotiation he had managed, using the lift cables and footholds, to clamber up to the fourth floor with Jack's kit back slung over his back.

He grabbed it and ran.

"Meet me in the room." He shouted as he headed back to Annabel. He left the gendarme behind to help his friend. The lift failing was too much of a coincidence. Someone in the hotel was watching them. He had to leave that thought for now though, Annabel needed him.

The hoarse rasp for breath welcoming him as he hurried into the room was a good sign, she was still alive. The bad news was she was fading fast. He rifled through his kit bag, grabbing the plastic case he needed. Pulling out one syringe and vial, he filled to the level required and inserted it into Annabel's arm. Resting a pillow below her neck he pushed her head back to help open the airways. The impact the drug was having on her respiratory system affected her, and even though she couldn't move, panic was written all over her face.

"Hold on Annabel, it will take a while for the antidote to take effect, but your breathing should ease in a few moments." He held her hand although he knew she couldn't feel it, there was no grip, it was limp and cold.

"I'm not going anywhere, we'll get through this and in an hour or two we'll get you some food. You must be starving." He tried to calm her as she began to shake. Leaving her side for a second, he collected the sheets from the chaise longue, pulling away the wet towel as he draped them over her.

Antoine joined them, breathless from the climb.

"What has happened?" He gasped.

"Klara Brandt is what happened. She knew where we were and came after Annabel. Send for a doctor, someone you can trust."

Antoine called from his mobile, speaking fast as he relayed instructions.

"Doctor Ansel will be with us in around ten minutes. He's one of ours, we can trust him."

"Good, check the balcony can you? She escaped through the window. See what you can find." He was still holding Annabel's hand, staying nearby to reassure her.

A whistle came from outside. Antoine returned with a purple uniform in his hands.

"That girl was athletic." Antoine said with respect. "She must be like some kind of spider woman. That is a sheer drop, and she was barefoot." He showed the uniform to Jack along with the regulation white sandals.

"Something bothers me." The Frenchman said as he threw the tunic onto a chair. "Why have they come back for Mrs Paxton-Thorn? They must have realised she is of no use to them? They tried to blow her up!" He thought for a minute, remembering the way Klara Brandt had prepared Annabel for the knife. Still holding her hand, he looked up at Antoine.

"They know that Annabel is of more use to them than they first thought, but we are missing something, and I don't know what it is. It was messy, not what you would expect from an organisation who think they can rule the world." It made no sense, and something else troubled him, but until he was sure he would give her the benefit of the doubt

"I am also certain that Annabel has no idea how important she has become to us all."

He hoped he was right, but he needed to find out for sure.

CHAPTER FORTY-SIX
Clarity

"Let her rest and she should be fine." Doctor Ansel advised as he packed away his equipment.

"You got to her in time. All of her vital signs are normal, blood pressure is slightly raised but it will reduce once the drugs leave her system. She may complain of a headache but it is to be expected from neostigmine."

"Thank you doc, we'll look after her." Jack shook his hand as he showed him to the door. Antoine and the doctor passed each other in the hallway, the Lieutenant having completed his investigations with the gendarme. Once pleasantries had been exchanged and Antoine returned to the room, Jack pushed a chair under the handle of the damaged door locking them in. They could not risk moving Annabel to another room so they would need to be resourceful until she recovered.

"Well, it appears the barman was in on it. He cut the elevator from the basement before escaping with the Brandt girl." Antoine read from his notepad. "They drove away in a Saab stolen from a guest. I would not expect them to travel too far in it, but I'm afraid we have no news on their whereabouts."

"It looks like we still have an active cell in France then. What do we know about him?"

"Not much of any use I'm afraid…" Antoine concluded

"Christophe Frank. Twenty-three, a backpacker on a gap year from UBIS University in Geneva. Studying Media and Communications, no police record, an exemplary student." He closed his notebook.

"He doesn't sound like a villain, but then again neither did the Brigadier." He thought aloud.

"Did you get any more on Klara Brandt, our spider woman?"

Antoine asked as he pulled a new flask from his pocket. He poured the wine into two clean glasses from the bathroom, handing Jack a healthy measure. He took a long swallow.

"The intel so far tells us she has been based in France for three years. She moved away from Daddies R&D department in favour of orchestrating the preparation for the glorious day, prompted by a lust for power and money, like father like daughter obviously." He was piecing things together.

"I have a feeling we have also found the actress who posed as Jayne Langfield at the rest home to get Claudia added to the will. Claudia I can guarantee is dead, and Klara becomes Claudia. It all seems to fit together nicely. They con the old girl, grab the information legally, unlock the treasure, blow up the world. I guess they didn't count on Jayne Langfield and Colin Thorn, related to one of their own, being as thorough as he was and together screwing it up for them with the code at KVP." He sipped the heady wine, staring at Antoine deep in thought, something was on his mind.

"Ok, if that is the way you see it, tell me. Why don't they simply take their army, blast a hole in the vault, grab the gold and blow up the world anyway?" finishing his wine Antoine refilled his glass, Jack put a hand over his own before he answered.

"The missing gold …Without it, he can't build the master plan. He's gambling the world bodies won't combine to stop him before he gets what he needs. He has the ear of many, and all they see is a billionaire businessman with deep pockets. He already funds a large chunk of their economy, either through employment in his many plants or through relief efforts, charitable funds or state sponsorship. To be honest, he probably rules half the world already. It's the superpowers and financial centres who can stop him taking it to the next level. He knows they can't leak it, broadcast it to the world. At least a third of all nations will rebel in favour of their benefactor. We'd have riots, reaction groups and supporters wreaking havoc. It also wouldn't help him much either, but it would be a disaster for the major leaders. It would create an anarchy neither could control. No, for both sides it's a black op where the winner takes all."

Antoine gave a low whistle.

"Well, my friend, I am ready for the fight, but I would like to leave

France soon. Too many explosions and murders will ruin my reputation." He toasted the air and finished his glass.

"I would suggest we get some rest and wait until Annabel recovers before we plan the next move. We have decisions to make and I need to confirm my suspicions regarding the Brandt girl." He looked over to Annabel who was in a deep sleep. Her breathing had returned to normal and for the first time in days, she looked peaceful.

CHAPTER FORTY-SEVEN
Who, Where and Why

The patio of the Prince de Galles Hotel doubled as an atrium, positioned in the centre of the complex. It was an oasis of tropical plants, varying in colour and fragrance, with exotic trees rising as high as the second floor, creating a natural shade within the tranquil setting. A mosaic of red tiles cut into the neat lawn supported circular tables, neatly decorated with red gingham cloth and white overlays, each table finished with a pure white parasol.

Annabel was thankful for the parasol, keeping the glare of the lamps from her face. Her headache had improved, but the dull throb buried deep behind her eyes reminded her of the recent horror. She could remember everything, it kept coming back like a recurring nightmare. The strength of the woman who pulled her from the shower was frightening. But it was nothing compared to the fear of paralysis, feeling every muscle give up the ghost and stop working. She could see herself trying to breathe, feeling her chest fail to expand. Worse still, she kept seeing the woman on top of her, watching as the scalpel moved closer to her eye, helpless to prevent it.

Jack returned from the bar and sat opposite, distracting her from her torment. He placed sparkling water in front of her and added one lump of sugar to his coffee.

"How's the head?" He had noticed her pinching the top of her nose as he approached.

"Throbbing, but a lot better than a few hours ago." Was all she would say.

She owed him her life, and she would never forget it. He stayed with her throughout her recovery and had been close by ever since. But there was something wrong, she could tell. He had been charming since she had known him, from Mittand Burrow to the horrors of Chanteau. She had felt close to him, whether as her protector or as a friend.

But now he seemed cold, thinking of other things which was understandable, but the distance she felt made her believe there was something else.

"Where's Antoine?" She wanted to ask him what was wrong but couldn't face it just yet.

"Called out on a job, he shouldn't be long." He had been stirring his coffee since he sat down, his thoughts turning over in his mind. There was an uncomfortable silence for a while as he put the spoon down and sipped his drink.

Annabel watched a young couple at the next table enjoying a romantic meal together. She ran her fingers around the rim of her glass as she watched the man spoon ice cream into his partner's mouth. They were totally wrapped in each other, making the most of the warm Parisian evening. She felt a pang for Colin as she watched them collapse into fits of giggles as a blob of ice cream fell into the girl's lap.

In the early days, their relationship had been full of laughter and romance, often taking long weekends away in Europe just for the hell of it. Paris had been one of their favourites.

"Annabel, I need to ask you something, and I need the truth." He knew she was still suffering from the drugs, but he had to know.

Nudged out of her trance she turned to him. He moved his coffee to one side, resting his arms on the table as he leaned towards her, keeping his voice low.

"What do you know about KVP and the contents of the vault?" His tone implied more than a question, it seemed accusatory.

"Nothing at all, only what you have told me about the key we found in Oxford. Why?" It was a strange question, after all, they'd been through.

"You're lying Annabel, you know more than you are letting on and before any more people die, you need to come clean. They want you for a reason and it wasn't just to get me to give them information. So I'll ask you again; What do you know about KVP?" He kept his eyes locked on hers with a look of mistrust, it could have even been contempt.

"How dare you!"

She thrust her chair back sending it clattering behind her as she jumped to her feet. The canoodling couple jumped, all eyes on the woman shouting at the next table. They looked on in astonishment.

"I have been drugged, kidnapped, hung, nearly blown to smithereens, drugged again, and paralysed. Now you think I am all part of this… You…You…BASTARD!" Her headache was now pounding as she wheeled around and stormed back into the hotel.

Antoine Valois entered the atrium as Annabel stormed towards him.

"Ah, hello my dear, how are you feeling?" He smiled.

"Fuck you too!" Annabel pushed past him, heading for the lift. Jack followed close behind without acknowledging him, he just stood watching them storm away.

"Jack, what have you done? Our English rose has grown thorns." He turned around and followed them.

Jack caught up with her at the lift as she stood thumping at the button.

"Annabel, wait! Calm down; let's talk." He stood a safe distance. She ignored him, continuing to pump at the controls.

"Sorry Mrs Paxton-Thorn, the elevator is still broken." Antoine had caught up with them, standing behind Jack for cover. She shrieked in frustration, looked left, looked right then headed for the stairs.

"Wait!" He grabbed her by the wrist stopping her before she could make her way to the room. Annabel swung around and slapped him in the face.

"Let me go!" She screamed, everyone in the lobby turned towards them. The concierge moved from behind the desk and approached, ready to assist.

"Excuse me Madam. Is everything alright?" He looked at Jack's hand holding tight to the woman's wrist.

"Please unhand her sir, or I will call the police." He was a big man and no doubt the police would be called. But not until he had administered his own form of assistance to this damsel in distress.

"Good idea young man." Antoine said, pulling his warrant card to prevent a nasty incident.

"Police! Unhand that woman at once!" He shouted with an air of authority.

Jack looked at Antoine quizzically, noticing his friend's eyes straining to make himself understood 'Let her go, Jack, let's not cause a scene' he was trying to make his face say.

He got the gist and let her go, watching as she stormed up the stairs towards the room.

"I'll take over from here." He said, pulling Jack by the arm towards the Regency bar. The concierge watched them leave, disappointed he hadn't delivered at least one punch.

"Antoine, what are you doing? We can't leave Annabel on her own." He ignored the protests, sitting him down on one of the stools facing the ornate mahogany bar. He signalled for the barman to serve wine.

"It's fine Jack, we have a gendarme posted on the floor until we leave and the Brandt girl is far away from here, I can guarantee that." He placed two glasses of red in front of them, and Antoine wasted no time to test the vintage.

"You've found the car then?" He looked at his wine, leaving it where it was.

"Oui, just outside Orleans, over one hundred kilometres away. The keys were still in the car along with a body." He turned to Antoine.

"The barman I assume?" He took the glass, trying a small sip.

"Oui, as dead as a nail in a door, asphyxiation according to the forensic reports at the scene."

"As dead as a doornail." One day he would get it right.

"I guarantee forensics will find traces of curare on the corpse, it looks like he outlived his usefulness."

"We have every force looking for her, but I am not hopeful." He took another sip placing the glass back on the bar.

"We need to get a move on Antoine. The sooner we get to Switzerland the sooner we can put an end to this. Come on, let's go to the room." Antoine finished his glass and so as not to be wasteful, finished Jack's for good measure. He downed it in one and followed him to the stairs.

CHAPTER FORTY-EIGHT
The Legacy

"Please, Mrs Paxton-Thorn, we have to talk." Antoine knocked again for the third time and waited. At least he didn't get the 'go away' he had received last time, perhaps they were making progress. Jack leant on the wall opposite, keeping out of it. If they hadn't changed rooms, they could have just barged in and resolved it in seconds. Perhaps he did owe her an apology, he probably could have been a little more tactful. He had never trod on eggshells during questioning though, he usually held a knife to the throat!

"Jack, can you please apologise, I have a head that hurts from banging the wall." He looked exasperated.

"You mean banging your head against a brick wall. If you will use these terms can you please get them right?" He pushed himself up and walked to the door, he didn't bother to knock.

"Annabel … Listen, I'm sorry for the way it came out, but we have to know all the facts; otherwise, we are at a disadvantage. She is after you whether you like it or not and unless we know why I can't protect you. Too many innocents are dead, and many more will follow if we don't pull together. Look, if not for Antoine or me, then for Colin and Eliza." The lock clicked, and the door inched open. Both men entered, Antoine staying a few steps behind.

Annabel walked to the bureau, turning to face them as they came into the room. She had her arms crossed and glared at Jack as he approached. She didn't look happy.

"So what is it exactly I am supposed to have done?" Her glare remained as she took a seat, waiting for his response.

"I'm not accusing you of anything Annabel, but I need to know if you have ever visited Switzerland, perhaps with Colin, and visited KVP bank. Or have you registered for an iris scan for passport control or ID purposes over the past few years?" Annabel narrowed her eyes for a moment or two as she thought back.

"Don't you think I would remember something like that?" She was curious but had settled down a little.

After all, Jack had far more to worry about than a widow from Mittand Burrow. Perhaps she should be a little more understanding of the pressure he was under. She still did owe him her life. Thinking a little more, trying to remember anything that could help, realisation dawned, it might be nothing but then again...

"We had an eye test together last summer if that makes any difference? I remember it was a strange one." She recalled thinking how odd the whole day had been.

"Colin had to have an eye test and got a two for one deal, so he asked me to go along. He was like that; he liked a bargain. So we went to an eye clinic in Gloucester, and I remember commenting on how the tests had changed since my last one around six years before. They didn't even give me the results there and then." She was about to explain when Jack chimed in.

"You stood a couple of feet away from a camera and was asked to look at a symbol on an LED screen while they took several pictures?" He suggested.

"Oh, you've had one too?" She was impressed.

"No, Annabel, you were giving a biometric reading for an iris scan. They would have used a special CCD camera which would have taken readings of the cilia, contraction furrows, crypts from your iris, to provide a unique signature of your eyes. Colin was providing an insurance policy in case anything happened to him, and that insurance policy was you." He knew he was right and confirming Annabel knew nothing of this, came as a relief.

He also knew Colin had used the same tactic on Derek. Colin Thorn thought he was protecting his client the best way he could and had provided a lucrative contract for the business, the partners and his family.

Unbeknown to him, his insurance policy had assigned a death warrant to all those connected to him, without their knowledge.

"Your information would have either been issued as an iris code token or sent as data to the KVP database. Either way, you have the passport to get us into the vault, and Klara Brandt came to retrieve it. She was after your eyes, Annabel."

It sent a shiver along her spine. Not only had she been set up by her husband, but that woman had come to mutilate her.

"Oh, my God! She would cut out my eyes?" She didn't mean to squeal, but the thought was so horrific.

"I'm not going to lie to you, it was her likely intention. Even away from the subject, the eye signature would still provide the biometric information to gain access." He could see the fear grow on her face and moved closer to reassure her. Crouching down in front of her he rested a hand on her knee.

"Don't worry, we won't let that happen. But you will need to come with us tonight as I can't risk another attempt on your life. We need to end this tomorrow." He lifted his kit bag onto the bed checking its contents.

"Tonight? Where are we going?" Annabel watched him rummage through his pack, laying his Glock and several magazines across the duvet. He was taking plenty of firepower with him, which made her worry even more. What had Colin done to her?

"KVP … We're going to Switzerland to open that damn vault." He zipped his bag and slung it onto his shoulder.

CHAPTER FORTY-NINE
Heart or Head

Sara strode through the glass corridor, a tube 60ft above ground level linking strategical to executive at LARA HQ. She was oblivious of the lake and mountain vista surrounding her. It was a walk that generally took twice as long as the breathtaking panorama slowed the pace, captivating anyone who saw it.

This time she focused on the blue tiled floor ahead, her steps echoing in the chamber, a metronome of determination. Entering the glass elevator to the top floor, she ignored the clear blue sky rising above the snow capped mountains in front of her. She was concentrating on what she had to say. The scenery that had captivated her every day for the past five years was nothing more than a blur.

Lindsay was watering one of the Chinese evergreens covering the sill of the south facing full length window. She was proud of her collection. The colours were vibrant this year, and the aroma had a sweetness that transformed her beige and mahogany office into a country garden.

The ping from the elevator caused her to turn, and she smiled as she saw Sara at the entrance.

"Hello, Sara. What brings you up to the gods on this fine day?" Sara smiled as she moved into the office and continued to walk towards the double doors behind Lindsay's large mahogany desk.

"Is he in?" She asked as she watched Ryker's PA move from her plants in an attempt to reach the desk before her.

"Yes, but you can't…" Too late, before she could reach her, Sara had pushed her way through the doors and let them shut gently with a soft click.

Exasperated for a few moments, Lindsay looked down at her spray bottle and shrugged. She turned back to her plants and her misting.

Ed Ryker was looking through his main window, devoid of any brickwork. He was standing, hands behind his back, taking in the panoramic mountain view. It was a moment of contemplation to help his thought processes, clearing one situation to prepare for the next.

Seeing the reflection of his next problem as the door to his office closed, he turned to greet his visitor.

"Hello, Sara, what's so urgent that I don't get notice?" He wasn't annoyed, but it had to be said, or she wouldn't be the last. Lyndsay must have been tending her plants; otherwise, this would never have happened.

"Sorry sir, but we have a situation. Jack's taking that woman with him." She stood just inside the door presuming she would not be invited to sit.

Ryker surprised her by pointing to the leather sofas as he sat down himself, gesturing for her to take her place opposite. He stared at her as she took her seat on the slim square black and chrome chair, knowing this was going to be one of those conversations.

"Yes, I know Sara, do you have a problem with that?" He knew she did.

"Yes, sir. She's a civilian, and we cannot guarantee her safety in Switzerland. They are heading straight into conflict, with assassins on their tail. It would be madness to allow her to go; it will compromise our agents." The last part was a reminder to Ryker of why she had been pulled from the field. It was felt her partnership with Jack was being compromised, albeit for a different reason. Ryker continued to look into her eyes digesting what she had said. He identified the derogatory description of the Paxton Thorn woman, and it didn't come as a surprise.

"Sara, it was Jack's decision and one that I have sanctioned. Mrs Paxton-Thorn is our passport into the vault at KVP. She will be safer once we have her inside than she would be if we tried to protect her in a safe house. They are after her and will not stop until she is either captured or killed. A day from now, once we enter the vault, she will no longer be of any use to them. It is the right decision, Sara."

He watched as his mission commander struggled with the situation. He knew of her feelings for Jack, but also aware of the commitment she had to LARA, as well as the other nine agents she and her team were assigned to assist. She was not a complicated woman; she was a damned good agent, internally and in the field, but her relationship with him had affected her thinking.

"Sara, you have to let him go. He will be back when he is ready, that I can guarantee, but now is not the right time. You're letting your heart rule your head, and that is dangerous, particularly to those out there who rely on your judgement." He didn't want to pull her from this, as she was the best operative for the job. But now, particularly as it involved a civilian, he could not afford to take any risks.

"Are you trying to tell me that you think my concerns are fuelled by jealousy?" The stern expression was mirrored in her voice.

"Aren't they?" Ryker challenged, she had yet to convince him otherwise.

"Absolutely not, sir. Of course, I am worried for Jack, I would be lying if I said anything else. But my first concern is for the success of the mission if we fail the future of the whole world is in jeopardy. I think we are taking an unnecessary risk with Mrs Paxton-Thorn when we have Jayne Langfield in protective custody." Her fixed eye contact was meant to express to Ryker that she had a point. Perhaps in part, she did.

"Langfield is still a risk Sara. We have enough intel to seemingly find her on our side, but not enough to make us certain of her motives. Remember, she is Brandt's wife and her emotional state at this moment is suspect. I need to gather further information before a final decision can be made. The discovery of the Paxton-Thorn biometric registration means we can move now, and that is what we are going to do."

Sara looked on impassively, trying to suppress her emotions. She had put her case forward and lost; she expected as much but had to try.

Determined to keep her composure she tapped on her tablet PC bringing up further information. The wall to the rear of Ryker's desk immediately flickered into life. The floor to ceiling screen relayed the information from Sara's tablet in sharp clarity.

"We still have no word on Ubermann, Eichel or Klara Brandt which means they are lying low. We are scanning every second for cellular activity, and we have all eyes on the street searching. When they make a move, we will find them." She was telling Ryker what he wanted to hear rather than believing it herself. They couldn't have just disappeared, she suspected they had cloaking devices of some sort, jamming devices more likely. But until she could work out what it was, or create a workaround, they were invisible to her.

"Sara, find them!" He didn't want excuses.

"How in God's name can we lose all three of them, damn it! LARA doesn't lose people, most of the time we find them! Get everyone in your team on it Sara, and I need to know where they are twenty-four seven! Jesus!" Ryker tried to control his anger, but he was ex-Navy Seal. One of the key rules was the protection of the team at all times, it was the difference between mission success and failure.

He had one of his men in the field escorting a civilian, with assassins closing in. They had to watch his back, and Jack needed to know he could rely on them, Sara knew this. Had she let her feelings compromise the mission? He would need to keep an eye on this.

"What else have you got?" He knew she had got the message, and he wanted her back at her station as soon as possible.

Sara was taken aback by the verbal assault. It was accusatory, which angered her. He was intimating that she was letting her feelings for Jack cloud her judgement, causing her to miss things. She wasn't sure if the anger she felt was because of the criticism or because of the guilt she was feeling. Was it her fault?

Composing herself, she pressed another field on her tablet and the plasma changed image.

"Fabian Brandt spotted three days ago in Saint Petersburg meeting with Anatoly Duranichev, one of the senior physicists during the cold war. They were together for four hours before Brandt flew back to New York. Duranichev left for Bangalore yesterday, collecting a prearranged first class ticket from the Aerosvit desk." The screen showed a picture of Brandt shaking hands with a thin man who wore an ankle length overcoat covering his wiry frame. His balding head and pale skin made him look unwell, even his smile as he greeted the billionaire couldn't disguise a disease that was taking its toll. Ryker raised his eyes.

"Duranichev? Wasn't he involved with the nuclear weapons program in the old days?"

"Yes, he was based out of Zarechny at the Penza-19 research centre. After its dissolution, the staff were replaced with a new regime. Most of the research was either destroyed or conveniently lost. Apart from his employment registers, all of Duranichev's research notes were missing. We are still exploring avenues to gather more intel, and we expect a report in the next few days. All we know for sure is that he is on his way to the Brandt plant in Bangalore."

Ryker studied the picture of the scientist, thoughts coming together in his mind.

"So he is off to Brandt's plant for what reason? It's an electronics site full of microchips and silicon. What do they need a nuclear physicist for?" It might be the breakthrough they needed. It would confirm Brandt's involvement in nuclear armament and in turn forces his investors to turn their backs on him.

"Could be completely innocent sir. The plant is powered by a light water reactor using mox fuel, a reactor grade fuel passed by the IAEA." She was now in the zone.

"It is inspected twice a year under the Nuclear Non-Proliferation Treaty and has always come back clean."

"Apparently, orders are up by thirty percent and production is being increased by forty percent." Looking at Ryker, she knew she'd managed to pull it back.

"The theory is Duranichev is being employed to ensure the reactor can cope with the increase. That's the assumption among several governments anyway and as yet he has done nothing to raise suspicion."

"Well, let's keep an eye on this and notify me if you get anything. Who have we got on it?"

"Bennett sir, he's on the flight and meeting with Indian intelligence when he arrives." Ryker was satisfied. Bennett was a good man, one of the least gung-ho of the team.

"Great!" Ryker used the remote to blank out the video wall.

"Anything else Sara?" She was tempted to bring up her concerns again. She had a feeling in her gut, one of trepidation, worry and more than anything else, frustration. She couldn't win, and she knew it, but she would take no pleasure in proving Ryker wrong.

On occasions like this, she wished she was still in the field, in control and more importantly teamed with Jack. Ryker looked at her to continue. She would leave it for now.

"No sir, that's all. I'll report back as soon as we get anything." She stood up and walked to the door.

"Sara ..." She turned to face Ryker.

"Use the comms system next time, huh." His expression told her it was an order rather than a request, he had no time for sentiment. He would not look kindly upon further intrusion unless it was case critical, even then he would prefer it over the comms rather than face to face. At this moment in time, she needed to get a fix on the three assassins, had to prove to him she was on top of her game, and she would. Sara acknowledged him and left.

Without a word she crossed Lyndsay's office, aware of the stare from the PA boring into her back. The elevator door was still open, and as she pressed corridor level, she locked eyes with her as Lyndsay stared back in disgust.

Sara had a feeling she wouldn't be on her Christmas card list this year.

CHAPTER FIFTY
Sleeper

Annabel was captivated by the beauty of the main entrance of Gard de l'est. The columned archways and nineteenth century statues adorned the carefully crafted angular roof. It made her feel as if she had entered a palace rather than a train station. The entrance foyer did nothing to dispel the feeling. The magnificent glass ceiling arched serenely across its whole length, illuminated against the night sky. Along each wall, more archways created entrances to shops, booking offices and information desks.

She walked over to one of the electronic boards and checked the platform number for the sleeper to Zurich. She felt much better now after freshening up. A little retail therapy also helped. For the sleeper, she had chosen a pair of black designer jeans along with a cream sleeveless top. A stylish black and cream jacket with a black leather clutch bag completed the look. She felt very cosmopolitan. Jack joined her, his kitbag slung over his shoulder, keeping his hands free to carry her vanity case and two shopping bags.

"Platform eighteen. 22:45 departure." She said as she felt his presence at her shoulder.

"Great, we have half an hour, let's get settled in." They turned to look for Antoine, spotting him as he barged through a small group of tourists. He was laden down with five large shopping bags and his rucksack. He stumbled, knocking against a young couple, sending one of the bags sliding across the floor. A pair of black panties propelled themselves from the spiralling contents, landing at the feet of a woman with her young child. Noticing the racy item she gasped and covered her daughter's eyes before sending a tirade at the lieutenant. He ran over and swept them up, hiding them in his pocket. He backed away apologising profusely. He collected his baggage and scurried away to join his companions.

"Mrs Paxton Thorn, are all of these items necessary?" He was out of breath and slightly red from the embarrassment of his last altercation. He held the bags out to demonstrate.

"I only had an hour before the shops closed. There was no time to choose, so I had to cover every option!" She walked towards platform eighteen, happy with her explanation. Jack smiled as he watched Antoine struggle. In his own inimitable French style, he insisted Annabel should carry no luggage. A suggestion she found utterly charming and accepted gracefully.

He walked just behind him, ready to catch anything else he might drop and was just in earshot to hear the Frenchman mutter to himself as he soldiered on.

His French wasn't great, but from the tone, he guessed Antoine was far from happy.

They booked into grand class cabins, compact but fully equipped with bunks, WC and shower. Jack and Antoine would take turns to guard Annabel, allowing the other to get some sleep in the adjoining cabin. Jack was not going to let her out of his sight until they were inside the vault, far better to be safe as the saying goes.

"Hungry?" He asked as he watched her hang three new tops in the small wardrobe.

"I could certainly eat something." Realising she hadn't eaten properly in two days.

"The restaurant is open until one. It's excellent by all accounts."

He watched Annabel stop herself from putting her last top away; instead, she held it up to herself as she checked her look in the small mirror, tilting her head both ways to confirm suitability. He took the hint and left the cabin.

"I'll be outside." He closed the door behind him. Antoine was in the corridor, wafting the last remnants of the cigarette smoke out through the upper vents.

"That's a two hundred euro fine you know." He said, staring through the window as France passed by.

"Then I will not get caught." Antoine said as he pinched the end of the butt, stamping out the glowing embers that sparked from the tip before putting it into his pocket.

Annabel joined them minutes later. She had changed into a white low cut sweater.

The Frenchman whistled.

"Vous regardez magnifique Madam Paxton Thorn." Jack raised his eyes at the lieutenant's smarm, although he had to admit she did look stunning.

Annabel just smiled coyly; she liked it.

"Are you coming?" She set off towards the restaurant car.

"Nearly!" Antoine mumbled as he watched her hips sway provocatively in her figure hugging designer jeans.

Jack slapped his friend around the back of the head as they followed her.

The limited menu of chicken or salmon, accompanied by rich sauces and pasta, did nothing to spoil their appetites, they were famished.

Antoine managed two servings of salmon, while Annabel demolished the chicken followed by the apricot dessert, all washed down with a bottle of Bordeaux.

Jack picked at his meal, preferring to use the downtime to go over the operation and the odds against success and failure. He had two problems which he had brought on himself, and he was struggling with both of them.

The first was Annabel. Once they were inside the vault she would be safe, but as soon as they tried to leave he suspected, they would have the whole of the New World Order on their tails. Short of locking her in the vault, he couldn't guarantee she would get out of there alive. His back up was Antoine, and that was his other problem. Working alone had always been his preferred method of operation. If he was forced to team up, his preference would be an operative from special forces whether it be MI5 or CIA, SAS or Navy Seal. Antoine was none of these. He was a good officer albeit a little unorthodox, and he was keen. But Jack had reservations when it came to covert missions. Antoine's eccentricities and his drinking would one day be his downfall.

He didn't want to be responsible for narrowing those odds. He struggled to prioritise his primary concern. The innocent civilian pulled into a world of guns and bombs or his close friend who would lay down his life for him? It was an impossible conundrum and one he couldn't solve. He needed Antoine to escort Annabel back to England once they had breached the vault. Only then could he be assured of their safety

"You're quiet?" Annabel noticed that Jack had hardly touched his food.

"Just going over a few things." He continued to swirl his chicken through the cream sauce.

"That's concentration, my dear…" Antoine offered.

"Jack likes to have all of his geese in a line."

"Ducks in a row!" Annabel and Jack corrected in unison. They looked at each other and burst into laughter.

A waiter arrived to clear their table.

"Come on guys, I think we need some shuteye." He slid out of the booth, waiting for the others to join him before leaving the car and heading back to the cabin.

Kurt Eichel stopped clearing away the plates, pleased with himself. His new dyed buzz cut, together with his fake tan, had allowed him to go unnoticed in the face of the enemy. The nerves he'd felt as he approached the table replaced with an exhilaration that made him feel indestructible. He put his receiver to his mouth.

"They are leaving now." He told the watch.

"Good. You know what to do." Leon Ubermann's voice echoed in his ear.

"I'm on my way." Kurt pulled his gun from his waistband and checked the full clip, tucking it away as he left the restaurant car.

"Take this, and I'll wake you at three." He gave Antoine an earpiece as he arranged the watch. He would take the first shift as he doubted that sleep would come to him quickly tonight, too many things to work out.

Antoine placed the tiny transmitter into his ear as he walked away.

"Just going to get some air. Goodnight Mrs Paxton-Thorn." He bowed as he backed away from them before turning and making his way towards the end of the carriage.

"Cigarette." He answered Annabel's questioning look as she placed the keycard into the door, pushing it open.

"His smoking habit is second only to his addiction to wine." He closed the door behind them. Manoeuvring around Annabel he leapt onto the top bunk, using his kit bag as a pillow. Switching on his PDA, he flicked through his emails.

Only one had any relevance, from Sara.

It outlined Brandt's appointment of Anatoly Duranichev at the plant in Bangalore, the nuclear connection and the increased activity at the facility. There was nothing he could do, for now, so he returned a 'keep me posted' mail and awaited further information. It was her sign out that made him smile, just one word… Mexico.

Mexico was a three day R&R that they decided to take after a difficult mission in Nicaragua. They had infiltrated, eventually bringing down a drugs cartel who had threatened to ruin the government, plunging the country into anarchy. It was a mission that nearly killed them both. Against LARA protocol they went off the grid for three days, mingling amongst the tourists in Cancun. A mixture of the revelry and copious amounts of Tequila pushed their relationship further than either of them expected. They spent the night together, a night full of passion so ferocious they collapsed into pained exhaustion. It was at this moment when they were at their most vulnerable, Sara moved close and whispered into his ear.

"I will always be there for you."

In the cold light of the next morning, there was an awkwardness between them stemming from their LARA training. Gender became secondary to their role as agents. Agent first, gender second, human third, a life they had all signed up to and understood. Their relationship had changed overnight, a bond which would eventually split them as a team. There were no expectations, only an understanding that would stay with them for the rest of their lives. He missed her.

A few minutes later Annabel left the bathroom. She had changed her revealing top to something more appropriate but decided to stick with the jeans. She placed the white top into her small case and climbed into the lower bunk. It had been an exhausting day, and although she had spent most of it asleep, she still felt a weariness in her body and behind her eyes. Feeling comforted by the presence of her bodyguard above, she immediately sank into her mattress, drifting, floating ever deeper, until natural sleep carried her away.

Antoine stood by the carriage door with the window pulled down an inch, to suck away the thick smoke from his Gauloises. He hated the no smoking laws sweeping through Europe. No smoking in restaurants, in hotels, in public places and even in his own office. He now had three ashtrays at work with plants stuck in them, a gesture from the chief at the time of the transition. He threw the butt out of the window, sliding it closed and blocking the harsh roar of the train as it cut through the countryside. The carriage returned to the dull rat-a-tat-tat as the wheels traversed the rails. They had dimmed the lights for the passengers benefit leaving only a soft glow. Occasional luminescence flickered along the carriage as the train sped past street lamps and provincial stations.

A passenger walked towards him hugging the window side of the corridor. Antoine moved to the left to allow him to pass. He instinctively touched his forehead in a casual salute of greeting. The passenger returned the gesture with a punch to his stomach so powerful it doubled him over. Shocked, Antoine straightened, grabbing the shoulder of his attacker. He couldn't see his face even though he was moving closer, stopping an inch away from his ear. He spoke softly and clearly.

"This belongs to your friend I believe. I thought I would return it." The stranger moved away from him and looked down. Antoine followed his gaze, stopping when he reached the hilt of the knife protruding from his stomach. The pain was excruciating as his body reacted to the trauma, his legs buckled and the floor came racing up towards him as he collapsed onto his side. He couldn't move, only stare at his attacker. He could hear a gurgle as he tried to call out. He moaned as the pain from a cough coursed through his body, tasting the metallic tang of blood as it filled his mouth making him cough again. The carriage slowly disappeared, ebbing away until darkness took hold and the world went quiet.

Leon Ubermann strolled away from the fallen Frenchman, satisfied he had reduced the threat by half. Now he only needed to finish off Case and take the woman. Kurt Eichel stood by door 234, holding up the keycard confirming he had obtained the master from security. Ubermann stood a yard to the right of him, just far enough away to block the view from the cabin until the occupant moved into the carriage. When in position he nodded and stood firm, his gun trained on the door. He slid the card into the slot, being careful to minimise the sound as plastic scraped into metal. Nodding at Ubermann, he pushed it home and grabbed the handle, gun at the ready.

The light turned green and bleeped in acceptance. Kurt braced himself to rush the cabin.

He was thrown backwards as four bullets punched into his chest and stomach. As he fell, two more blew away the left side of his head. Ubermann was stunned for a few seconds as he saw his comrade collapse against the far wall. He became instantly alert as the nozzle of a Glock 17 appeared from the doorway pointing in his direction. He ran towards the restaurant car, stooping and dodging as shots flew all around him. He reached the end of the carriage and leapt into the door recess, just as three shots slammed into the wall where his head would have been.

Risking a look along the corridor Jack swept the Maglite both ways. The beam stopped as it fell on the leather coat of Antoine's crumpled body, his heart sank.

A bullet ricocheted off the frame behind him forcing him back inside. He sent a volley back as he ran into the carriage, just in time to see the adjoining door to the restaurant swing shut.

"Annabel, check on Antoine NOW!" He shouted back as he ran towards the restaurant car, placing a new clip into his Glock. Annabel came out from the shower compartment hauling aside the mattresses that he had placed in front after he shoved her in. She gingerly stepped past the grisly remains of the lifeless body in front of her. She could taste the sauce from dinner as she gagged at the mess. Moving away from the sight, being careful to watch where she trod, she looked along the carriage and saw Antoine slumped against the wall. He was not moving.

"Oh, Antoine no!" She ran towards him and knelt by his face. Relieved, she smiled at him as his eyes flickered open. His face was damp with sweat, and his mouth dribbled a small stream of blood that ran down his neck. He swallowed several times as he struggled to speak.

"I am afraid that I have been skewered, Mrs Pa..." He coughed sending agonised tremors through his body.

"Shh! Try not to speak." She stroked his head as she looked him over. She stopped herself from calling out when she saw the knife protruding from his stomach, she needed to keep calm.

"We need to get you some help, Antoine. Hold on, you'll be fine." She hoped she was right. She ran to the emergency stop and pulled the chain, yanking it three times.

"Stop damn you!" She screamed at it.

Almost at once she felt the carriage jolt as the train slowed.

Jack huddled behind the first booth in the restaurant car. He flashed the torch around, bracing himself for gunfire, nothing happened. Rolling across the car to the corresponding booth, took him a yard closer to the far exit, shining his torch again showed nothing. Edging closer to the door he stooped in front of the small bar, the last available place to hide. If Ubermann was in the restaurant, he was behind it. He thrust his hand over the counter and unleashed three shots in an arc, wide enough to cover the cramped space. Jumping up he leant over to check the result. Apart from broken bottles leaking everywhere, the area was clear.

He heard a slam from the next carriage, those shots had prompted his assailant to move. Opening the adjoining doors, he found himself in a standard coach with three rows of seats along each side of the central aisle. Three young couples sat in the first few rows, two of the girls were crying.

"Where did he go?" He whispered loud enough for his voice to sound more like a rasp. A long haired youth still wearing his saucer shaped headphones pointed to the back of the car towards the far exit.

"Did he leave?" He rasped again. Two of the young men nodded in unison, pointing behind them, keeping their heads toward him, afraid to move.

"Stay in your seats until I get back. Don't leave the train." The sleeper had slowed to a walking pace and would stop at any minute, he couldn't risk innocents milling around in the line of fire.

Approaching the next car cautiously, he waited for the air brakes to cease hissing as the sleeper rocked to a halt. Pulling the handle, he opened the first intersecting door and looked through the glass at another standard carriage. This one was occupied, some passengers were checking through the windows to see why the train had stopped. Others were reading or dozing, carrying on as usual. Strange, it was as if Ubermann had not been here.

He was about to enter when he heard something that made him stop and concentrate on the sound, a rhythmic thud coming from somewhere above his head. Then it hit him, he was running along the roof... back to Annabel and Antoine. Leaping through the exit, he steadied himself between the two carriages.

Grabbing the rungs of the service ladder, he climbed to the roof. The breeze was light as he shone his Maglite at his assailant who was running away from him with surprising speed. He fired one round. Ubermann had reached the end of the carriage, jumping in between the standard and restaurant car just as the bullet shot past, missing him by inches. Jack gave chase, pausing as he came to the roof's edge, ready to shoot on sight. He risked a glance, nothing. Jumping down onto the intersection he peered through the window of the restaurant car. Ubermann shot behind him as he ran, shattering the window and covering Jack in tiny crystals of safety glass. A quick look through the open window showed Ubermann disappear into their sleeper carriage. Moving through the restaurant car, his eyes locked on the door, he was ready to take evasive action if Ubermann turned back. He was halfway across the car when he heard a gunshot. Throwing caution to the wind, he yanked the handle and entered the sleeper carriage. Another shot came, and he dived into the recess as a bullet smashed into the ceiling a few feet ahead of him. The slam door was wide open. Cold air rushed into the cabin. Twenty yards away he could see a dark figure scramble up a shallow bank at rail side and disappear over the top.

He was too late to take a shot, but as far as he could tell, it looked like Ubermann. He was running awkwardly, dangling one arm uselessly by his side.

Had he caught him? Or was someone else shooting? If this was Ubermann, who had just shot at him?

Jack shone his torch along the carriage, ducking back in time to avoid another bullet as it ricocheted along, well away from his hiding place.

"Annabel! It's me, Jack. Hold your fire!" He shouted.

"Jack?" a tiny voice replied, fear obvious in her tone.

"Yes, it's me. Don't shoot, I'm coming out." He moved the beam of the torch onto his face at arm's length to show her it was him and carefully moved into view. He braced himself, ready to duck out of the way just in case, but nothing happened. Thankfully, the lights came back on as the train operators realised there was a severe problem.

Annabel was sitting in front of Antoine, her outstretched arms resting on her bent legs, pointing his SIG in both hands directly at him. She was staring through him, her shoulders shaking as tears streamed down her face.

"I'll take that, Annabel." He leaned down to switch on the safety before attempting to remove the gun. She was holding on tight, he had to prise her fingers apart before he could bring it free. He tucked it into his belt before kneeling alongside Antoine to check him over. Anger overcame him as he saw the hilt of his own Kabar sticking out of his stomach. He snatched up his PDA and dialled.

"Sara, get emergency services here as soon as you can. Antoine's down he's badly hurt."

"What are his injuries, Jack? I'm directing services to you, just awaiting an ETA." Sara had pinpointed Jack's PDA and attending to his request as she spoke.

"Knife wound with the weapon still present, get them to hurry would you." He knew she was working as fast as she could, but emotion made him state the obvious.

"You are near Troyes, the good news is you are less than ten miles from Central hospital, but it would be quicker to get the train to pull into the station. We are onto the rail service to notify them of the situation. The ambulance will meet you there." The PDA went dead as Sara got to work. He looked over to Annabel who seemed to have cleared her mind and was kneeling alongside Antoine, smoothing his hair.

"You Ok?" He asked as he tried to gauge her mood.

"I'll be better when that bastard is dead. I think I got him, but he got away." She looked at him with anger etched on her face.

"We'll get him, Annabel. Believe me, I owe him for this." He looked down at the sad figure of his friend, his breathing had reverted to shallow gasps, and he could feel just the faintest pulse. He removed Antione's earpiece. If the lieutenant survives this, the little bud could have just saved all their lives.

They were joined by train security, the restaurant manager and the inspector, all in various states of dress, having been woken from their sleep. Jack organised security at each end of the carriage to prevent pass through, the inspector woke the rest of the carriage to tell them of the impromptu stop, advising them to remain in their cabins. It was easier to leave them sleeping but protocol was protocol insisted the inspector. The restaurant manager busied himself clearing out the two cabins. Annabel told him to leave everything behind except for her small vanity case. Her wardrobe was the last thing on her mind.

"Will he be Ok?" Annabel asked as she continued to stroke Antoine's hair. Apart from placing a pillow under his head, she felt helpless.

"I don't know." The five inch blade had been pushed all the way in. The damage caused was anyone's guess, he couldn't predict the outcome.

"But he's a tough son of a bitch, he'll fight this." He said that for his own benefit as well as Annabel's and he hoped he was right.

"I may be doing an impression of a kebab, but I can still hear you know." Antoine sounded hoarse and increasingly weak. He coughed twice which sent two splatters of blood onto the pillow.

"Antoine, for once in your life, keep your mouth shut!" He could see that the Frenchman was struggling to reassure them he would pull through. Jack hoped he was right.

He looked down at the bloodstained shirt wrapped around his ruined wrist, bound loosely to prevent it from snagging the ulna bone, poking through the skin. A lucky shot had wrecked his hand, and it hurt like hell.

"Don't worry baby. We'll have you fixed in no time, then we can finish the job." Klara threw the SLK around the bends further into the mountains towards Chaumont.

A private hospital was on standby to await Leon Ubermann, the future son-in-law of the famous billionaire Fabian Brandt. He had been involved in an accident cleaning his weapons, in preparation for a shoot in the Loire Valley.

The hospital was on a total press blackout and all staff carefully handpicked to ensure anonymity.

"That bitch will suffer. I will make sure she takes three days to die." He thought of the instruments he would use.

The scalpel, the drill and the hacksaw were his favourites, his record was thirty-seven hours. He could recall the screams of the man as he sawed through his achilles tendon and the gurgles of protest as he drilled through his larynx. Oh yes, she would suffer.

Klara screamed, pushing her foot hard onto the accelerator as they came away from the last bend, hurtling along the straight towards Chaumont.

"I'll fucking kill her!" She continued screaming as she floored the car forward, drifting in and out of the white lines as they sucked under the chassis.

"Well, let's hope we stay alive long enough to fulfil our dream darling" Ubermann placed his good hand onto her thigh, squeezing gently. Relaxing her foot she slowed down. Turning to her fiancé, she smiled a tender smile. The madness in her eyes aroused him; if he had all of his limbs, he would take her now.

"We have time on our side." He said as he ran his finger along her lips. She drew it into her mouth and sucked, writhing in her seat as her desire grew inside her.

"They will be with that French pig until he dies, which could take a while. Gerald will tell us when they leave and when they do, we will be waiting."

CHAPTER FIFTY-ONE
Unscheduled Stop

As the siren cleared the path for the ambulance, the medic worked feverishly on Antoine. He was lying on the gurney with a gauze mountain taped securely around the hilt of the knife, to provide enough pressure to stem the bleeding. They raised his knees to release the stress on his stomach while oxygen was pumped regularly to help with his breathing. The electrocardiogram beeped to the rhythm of his heart, 58 BPM stabilised by the medic as he worked the drips like a sound engineer on a mixing desk, a little more tempo here, fine tune this, ramp it up there, all the time checking the ECG. He ignored the two additional passengers as they looked on in concern.

"Will he be alright?" Annabel asked as he moved away to fill out the information on his clipboard, his eyes never leaving the ECG.

"Too early to tell." He replied, his broken English far more polished than expected.

"He has a serious wound, but there is no way of telling how much damage it has caused until we get him into theater." He adjusted one of the drips before placing a stethoscope to Antoine's chest.

"He'll be fine." Jack patted Annabel's hand. She had gripped his arm for comfort.

Jack had been involved in many scrapes and had come away mainly unscathed, however, his worst fears were now becoming a reality. This was not the place for inexperience or complacency and Antoine had bucket loads of the latter. He ran his cases with the finesse of a politician with an expense account, he would get the job done but would leave a costly mess behind him. Looking at the patient he felt a sense of responsibility, it ate away at him like a septic sore. This had to stop happening. He grabbed the PDA.

"Sara, can you patch me through to Ryker?" If he didn't get it off his chest now, it would only fester.

"Sorry Jack, he's in a conference with India, the executive suite is in lockdown. Is there anything I can do?" He wanted to share his thoughts but he couldn't yet.

"No, it's fine. Get Ryker to call me…" He stopped as the noises within the ambulance had changed, the metronomic beep of the ECG was racing at an alarming rate.

"Sara gotta go." He cut the call and looked at the machine. 98BPM… 110… 140… 165… 0. The continuous tone screamed from the ECG, alarms sounded, shouting to be heard.

The thin green line cut across the screen, pushing away the signs of life that had once been there.

Antoine had flatlined… he was dead.

CHAPTER FIFTY-TWO
Arrivals

It had been a long flight and Natalia Lozinski was looking forward to her two days off in Bangalore. Nineteen hours wasn't one of her longest flights with Aerostat, but with the four meal runs and regular top-ups, her feet were killing her.

She had cleared first class, leaving only a few passengers from premium, to smile at on their way out. She was only an hour away from freedom and a hot bath to soak herself in until the chill forced her out. She had arranged with Julia to visit the Bull Temple this time around as the rest of the crew had told her how beautiful it was. It would make a change from the nightclubs and bars she usually ended up in. She had learnt the hard way on the return flights, performing duties with a killer hangover. On this trip she was determined to relax, catch the sun and arrive back in three days, refreshed and alert.

As the last passenger disembarked, she walked the aisles, checking the seats for any forgotten items. On occasions she had done very well, winning three iPods, a digital camera and an ebook reader, still unclaimed for a month. Checking each seat pocket, beneath every seat and each overhead compartment, she moved methodically from row to row.

She smiled when she saw a lone passenger fast asleep in the last section of premium class, a regular occurrence on long haul flights, consuming too much alcohol to pass the time. She leant over to wake him, giving him a gentle nudge, which she then followed up with a push on getting no response. This guy was out for the count. She recognised him as the good looking Englishman, very polite with a lovely smile. She hadn't remembered serving him a lot of alcohol though, he must have started on his duty free.

"Hello sir, you need to leave now." She set her best hostess smile so that he would wake to a friendly face, as she shook him a little harder. He flopped to his right banging his head on the window, one eyelid popped open, staring straight ahead, sightless, dead.

It annoyed her, as her short two day break would be even shorter now that she had to wait for the police to arrive to take a statement. She took his bag from the overhead compartment and laid it on the seat next to him. His travel documents were poking out of the side pocket, she would need to check them against the manifest to identify him in her report to the captain.

He had an English passport as she expected. His name was Roger Bennett.

Klara Brandt waited in the visitor suite of the Laroursel private hospital, staring out of the window at the beautifully illuminated gardens. She focused her attention on the lighting, ornate globes positioned on top of decorative lamp posts. They brought out the colours of the Azalea and Rhododendron bushes as they flourished around curved wooden benches. She became fixated on the moths as they fought tirelessly to enter the glowing bulbs, incessantly throwing themselves headlong into the glass repeatedly.

The door opened, but she remained where she stood, the surgeon would come to her and tell her the operation had gone well, she knew that. They were paid enough; they dare not fail.

"Any news?" The voice was unmistakable, she wheeled around in an instant to face the man who owned it.

"Papa!" She squealed as she ran into the arms of her father. Fabian Brandt held his daughter, running his fingers through her hair as she rested her head against his neck. He moved her away kissing her gently on each cheek. She looked into his eyes, smiling sweetly.

He smashed his palm across her face so hard she stumbled sideways, coming to rest at the back of a fortunately placed armchair.

"You fools!" He roared. "We are on the brink of the birth of a New

World, everything our ancestors and our beloved Fuhrer had dreamed of, and you and that idiot boyfriend of yours can't report in when I call. The woman is to remain alive at all costs, do you understand? You do not harm her in any way… her eyes are needed yes, but in a living body. You would have known this had you returned my calls. We cannot guarantee the eyes of the dead will work. She… has… to… stay… alive." He laboured the point and glared at his daughter as she cowered in the armchair holding her face. As he walked towards her Klara pushed back into the seat, thrashing her legs as she tried to clamber onto it. The chair legs scraped along the wooden floor as it was forced backwards.

"Jack Case is one man against the two of you! I expect to hear from you that he is no more, sooner rather than later. We will have the world at our feet in less than thirty days, and you expect to be on the throne alongside me. Well, from what I have seen so far, I will have you both cleaning my palaces for the rest of your lives… do you understand!" Brandt was furious, everything he had worked for was about to be realised, his destiny was at hand. The New World Order, a perfect world, ruled by perfect people. His armies were in place, his government prepped, his aircraft were in position awaiting the warheads, being processed, almost complete. He would not fail.

The Fourth Reich would prevail, fulfilling the dream of the Fuhrer, avenging his father's death and more importantly, promoting the birth of a new empire, the Fabian Brandt empire. He would go down in history as the man who changed the world forever. He relished the thought of inviting the current world leaders to join his cabinet and the retribution that would befall them if they rejected his offer. Klara ran her fingers gently over the reddening weal covering the left side of her face. She stood with her mouth open, tears streaming, part from shock and part pain. She stared at her father. His eyes burnt through her, unblinking and reddened with anger. His black eyebrows pointing inwards to add to the malevolence of the man. Klara tearfully ran to Brandt and fell to her knees, wrapping her arms around his lower legs.

"Oh father, please forgive me, I have failed you." She wailed. She knew her father would expect this, and she hoped it would work. She had everything to lose, the power she so craved, the money she so needed and the legacy her father's death would leave behind.

It took only a short time. Fabian Brandt, pleased to see his daughter in such distress, leant down and grabbed her gently by the arms, pulling her up to face him. He stood for a moment looking into her face, studying the tears before moving his hand towards her red cheek. Klara flinched away, the matador evading the bull. His hand rested on her face as he stroked the blemish so gently she hardly felt his touch.

"You are a good girl, Klara." His grizzled features smoothed.

"But I need you to do better. It is imperative you follow orders. I need to be proud of my family. My people need to be proud of my family. LARA has to be stopped, we need the map, and I need the gold. You will not return until all these objectives are achieved. Is this understood?" He softened his gaze, almost appealing.

"Yes, father. I promise you, we will not fail in our objectives." She had won him over.

"I know." Brandt's face had reverted to the menacing glare, a glare which shouted 'or else'.

"I am going to the island to make the final preparations. You will call me when you have the gold. Goodbye, Klara." He turned and left the suite.

Hoffman leaned into the room taking hold of the handle to close the door behind his boss. The hulking bodyguard looked at Klara with an undisguised look of disgust. Fucking spoilt brat, she was going to be trouble.

She returned the gaze and gave him the finger. When she was in charge, she would put a bullet through his head.

CHAPTER FIFTY-THREE
Road Trip

"28,29,30…" The medic counted the compressions as Jack squeezed twice on the bag valve mask covering Antoine's face when instructed.

"1,2,3,4…" He continued to compress his chest as Annabel looked on in horror.

"Why can't you shock him? It's over there." She pointed to the defibrillator.

"You can't." It was Jack who answered. "He still has the knife in his stomach, it would act as a conductor and fry his insides." He gave two more bursts of air at the end of the thirty count.

"Administering epinephrine, one milligram." The medic announced to the driver through the comms.

He injected into the vein and began compression again. Jack held Antoine's head still as his body was being pumped. The ECG continued to sing a single note. It wasn't working.

"Come on, buddy." He watched his face, waiting for a flicker, a blink, anything.

Annabel felt helpless, hugging a blanket around her she swayed as her anxiety increased. She had not known Antoine for long, but she had grown fond of him with his weird sense of humour and his infectious enthusiasm. She also worried about Jack, he felt responsible for his friend, and it was hitting him hard. She watched as he squeezed out two more bursts of air.

"Administering atropine, one milligram." The driver was informed again.

Again, with the second drug injected, he continued to compress, counting to thirty before nodding to Jack to squeeze the BVM. He complied with two more bursts. Every emotion ran through him as he recalled his first encounter with Antoine.

At the beginning they had taken a dislike to each other, the renegade cop and the mercenary, partnered together to bust a terrorist ring. Antoine's stubborn attempts at destroying the English language on every occasion making him impossible to understand. They had fought halfway through the assignment, arguing jurisdiction. After the bust, however, they got absolutely hammered in a strip joint. He smiled as he remembered the debrief, nursing the monster of all hangovers. Come on Antoine, breathe! He squeezed two more blasts of air.

The medic began again "1,2,3…" The ECG bleeped. Everything stopped as all eyes watched the machine. It bleeped again; the spikes moved along filling the screen. Bleep, bleep…

"Go Antoine." The medic laughed, a mixture of nervous pride, knowing his efforts had worked, to blessed relief that he had saved the man. Placing a hand on his patient's chest, he looked at the ECG as it moved up to 58 BPM flickering between 56 and 60 with regularity.

"Your friend is a tough cookie." He was still smiling as he reached for his stethoscope.

The clinical corridors of the hospital smelt of overused disinfectant, sweat and illness. Forty-five minutes had passed as he threw his third cup of bitter vended hot water passing itself off as coffee, into the steel swing bin. The clang echoed in the empty corridors. Annabel, still holding her first cup of tea, barely warm, put it to her mouth and sipped.

"I hope we were in time." She said, just to break the silence. She recalled too many frightening memories as she only had her own thoughts to keep her company.

"He'll be fine." Jack fished in his pockets for two euros for another coffee. "He's more resilient than he looks." His PDA rang and looking at the caller ID, he excused himself before moving along the corridor to find privacy. He chose the men's bathroom at the end of the hall, leaning against a sink, he took the call.

"Jack, how are things? How's Valoire?" Although he remained official, there was a hint of concern in Ed Ryker's voice.

"Nothing yet boss, he's been in there for nearly an hour. It's a bad wound, but I'm counting on him coming through." There was a short silence as he knew what he was about to say would likely blow up in his face, but he had to try. This couldn't go on.

Ryker took the lead.

"The fact you've called me boss leads me to think there is something on your mind Jack?"

"I need Sara, Ed." He went straight to the point.

"But Sara said you wanted to speak to me?"

"Not to speak to, I need her in the field, here with me Ed. We are up against it with the Brandt girl and Ubermann. I need a LARA agent with me, not police or army. We need to get to Switzerland, and I'm staying away from public transport, so I need a vehicle. But I also need backup, I need Sara, we know each other. I trust her, she has my back, and she's a woman Ed. I think she could serve as Mrs Paxton-Thorn's escort, she could be by her side 24/7." He knew he was right. He had to get to KVB, and he needed to keep Annabel safe. But keeping an eye on her as well as neutralising the threat to a woman with no tactical nous made him nervous.

"Not going to happen Jack. She stays right here where she can head operations. She's your eye in the sky, and she has your back, front and sides where she is. She is as important to this mission as any of our field agents, no Jack, it's not happening." King takes pawn.

"Ed, we can stop this before it starts once we get to the vault and find the location of the gold. We grab it, and it's all but over. Brandt won't have the financial clout to carry out his threat."

"I have an agent on route to meet you in Zurich. He is accompanying Jayne Langfield." Ed was pushing the operation forward, his request had been noted and rejected.

"Whoa … Hang on Ed. You're bringing Langfield? I thought Intel was still being gathered. You were taking her straight to KVP?" It was not going well.

"We are looking at a contingency to help guarantee our mission objective. We have two alternative ways of getting into the vault. With Jayne Langfield and Mrs Paxton-Thorn, and with two LARA agents as escorts, we can double team. Two chances to get through the vault and two targets for Brandt to try to stop. We are putting together two routes to Zurich where you will meet Captain Benzli Oberlin of ARD

10 who will give you support the rest of the way." He had to agree it was a good call, although it was getting less covert the further they went.

"So why Swiss special forces? I thought they would steer away from anything involved with the banks. That's a disaster waiting to happen, I can't imagine it will be a straight withdrawal."

"Exactly why ARD 10 are involved. We had to involve Congress as there is a stash of Nazi gold somewhere in their country and they decided ARD 10 would be the best group to take care of it. All world leaders have backed the decision, and Congress have given rights of passage against the Brandt master plan. We really had no choice." Ryker was at his best when it came to diplomacy and many world leaders admired his negotiation skills. He mulled everything over and concluded that Ryker was probably right. Sara had made a name for herself in Ops, and it was true, she had his back from the air.

"Ok Ed, who is my contact in Zurich?" He would have thought it would be Robson or Brett, ex SAS, good men and experienced covert specialists. The silence on the line made him wary, he had a distinct feeling he would not like the answer. He was right.

"You'll be meeting Anthony Riggs with Mrs Langfield at a location sent to your sat once you enter the city." Ryker smiled as he could imagine Jack's face at this moment.

"What! Riggs, why Riggs? The guy is a loose cannon, Ed. Are you mad?" From all the agents they could have chosen, Riggs would have been the last on his list.

Anthony Riggs, ex CIA and a pretty boy who used it to his advantage. One for the ladies, forever checking himself in the mirror to ensure he was at his best when he schmoozed them. He was quick with a gun and a brawler, a good man to have by your side in a fight. But a covert op?

"Riggs spent three years escorting the President of the United States. He prevented two assassinations and the kidnapping of the First Lady single handed. The guy knows safe passage, Jack." It was an easy decision for Ryker, and he was rarely wrong.

"He's a bloody liability Ed, and he's a Yank..." He closed his eyes when he realised who he was speaking to.

"Sorry Ed, no offence intended, I meant to say, as an American, he will be out of his comfort zone." It was not quite what he meant to say but for a backtrack, not bad.

"Believe it or not we Americans do sometimes leave our trailer parks, you know."

"Yeah, yeah, I know. Sorry boss, Riggs it is." He took defeat gracefully and cut the call.

As Jack turned the corridor, he saw the surgeon standing over Annabel. He was speaking to her while she sat with her head in her hands. He wasn't sure whether to speed up or slow down, unsure whether he wanted to get it over with or take his time. He wanted a few more seconds of a world where Antoine still existed.

Annabel saw him walking towards her. She stood and ran to him wrapping her arms around his neck. He wasn't sure if he could be any comfort for her, but he held her close anyway.

"He will be alright." She whispered into his ear.

He opened his eyes and pulled her away from him.

"What?"

"He's going to be alright." She said again, as a beaming smile spread across her face. Grasping Annabel by the arm, he strode towards the surgeon who hadn't moved since Annabel had run from him. He extended his hand.

"Hi, Jack Case, I understand Antoine has come through?" He shook the surgeon's hand warmly.

"Yes, Mr Case, the operation was a success. He was a very lucky man; no vital organs were hit. He has lost a lot of blood and has a lot of sutures both inside and out, but we are confident he will make a full recovery in a few weeks."

He hadn't had a lot to smile about over the past month, and this felt good.

"Can we see him?" Annabel asked, squeezing Jack's hand continuously like a stress reliever.

"I'm sorry Miss, he is still in recovery. We won't transfer him to a room for another hour or so. You are welcome to wait."

"Try and stop us." Jack smiled as he popped two euros into the vending machine.

Antoine was hooked up to wires and drips, but he looked peaceful. The ECG bleeped encouragingly next to him at a steady 67BPM. Annabel sat beside the bed, stroking the back of his hand.

"Do you think he knows we're here?" She turned to Jack who stood by the end of the bed staring at the steady rise and fall of his chest

"I think he is likely to be out for a while yet."

He pictured him in recovery. He would give the nurses hell, they would be chasing him around the grounds as he tried to find a secluded spot for his Gauloises. How he would survive without a drink was anyone's guess. If he knew Antoine, he would be checking out as soon as he could walk.

The Captain of RAID entered the room.

"Mr Case, I apologise for the intrusion, but I have brought your car for the journey."

Jack shook Captain Renard's hand.

"Thank you, Captain. What brings RAID here outside of your jurisdiction?"

"Orders, sir. Command has tasked us with guarding Antoine until they discharge him." He noticed two RAID officers take a position either side of the glass door.

"Great news Captain, that makes it a lot easier for us to leave." Annabel looked up at him.

"We're leaving?"

"We need to I'm afraid. It will take us four hours to get to Zurich and we have a rendezvous at 8 AM. Antoine is in good hands, with any luck, we will be back in a few days to see him when he's awake." He checked his watch. 3.30 am.

She leaned over and kissed Antoine's cheek.

"Get well soon."

As the Land Rover pulled away from the hospital, Jack checked the satnav pre-programmed for Zurich. Drive time was three hours forty minutes.

"Why don't you relax and try to get some sleep? We have a long day ahead." He looked over to Annabel who had already worked out the controls to recline her seat.

"That's a good idea." She leant into the headrest and looked out of the window, feeling her eyes go heavy. It wouldn't be long. He turned on the radio, picking a soft rock music channel at a low volume to entertain him on the journey.

The black Jaguar moved away from the kerb as soon as the rear lights of the Land Rover disappeared.

"They have just left the hospital, Miss Brandt. I will notify you when Case is dead." The driver threw his phone onto the passenger seat, heading for Zurich.

CHAPTER FIFTY-FOUR
Zurich

As the sun moved across Platzspitz Park, Annabel breathed in the fresh morning air of Zurich. Sitting on a bench opposite an ornate bandstand, she became transfixed by a small bird as it skipped along the carousel roof. It was chasing a butterfly fluttering inches from its beak, baiting it. She sipped her tea, purchased from an early morning cafe bar along the Sihlquai and sighed.

"This is beautiful." She turned to Jack who sat alongside her, his head down, deep in thought. He looked up and followed the line of trees along the gravel path to the square cut bushes surrounding the impressive Landesmuseum. The Swiss National Museum, the location of their rendezvous.

"Better than it used to be." He said taking a sip of his coffee.

"In the eighties it was known as Needle Park, a well intentioned attempt by the Zurich officials to control the drug problem, designating this park as a legalised area for the purchase and sale of drugs."

"As you can see, it's surrounded by the Sihl and Limmat rivers, making it a virtual island and an ideal location to police. But in the early nineties, it was raided, having developed into a haven for addicts Europe wide. By the end, there were twenty-thousand users here, and the rubbish they left behind included thousands of discarded syringes. The risk of HIV and public pressure gave the police no choice but to close it down."

"Really? How could they let that happen?" She looked around at the clean benches, tended lawns and ornamental statues, the bandstand set amongst healthy trees and the impressive architecture of the Museum bordering the rear of the strange island park. It was hard to believe such a thing.

"We are in the Altstadt or Old Town, and it was an attempt to move all drug issues away from the corporate, the media and the financial centres of modern Zurich. At first, everyone was comfortable with the arrangement, but eventually, it got out of control. It's taken years to get it back to this." He had seen the images of hundreds of addicts huddled together amongst mounds of waste, Woodstock on speed as it was reported locally. He had to admit, it was quite a transformation.

They sat in silence, wrapped in their own thoughts as they finished their liquid breakfasts.

The Landesmuseum built in 1898 in the form of a French Renaissance chateau, had a castle like appearance. Several high circular towers, complete with conical spires created a sense of the medieval. It was embellished by the supporting high brick frontages, filled with stained glass windows. Entering the grounds from the park brought them to the expansive entrance, leading to an impressive courtyard, used regularly for shows and tourneys.

They made their way through the centre of an oval garden area bordered by neatly trimmed square hedges. It contained a multitude of brightly coloured blooms housed in low brick surround flower beds. In any other circumstances, Annabel couldn't think of a more romantic setting, in fact it took all her resolve to stop her from linking arms.

"I think our welcome party has arrived." Annabel followed his gaze to an arched door as it opened to reveal two men in the courtyard, twenty yards ahead.

"I don't believe it." Jack sighed as he recognised one of them.

"One thing to remember, Annabel. Should you ever think you might be under investigation by CIA or FBI, look out for the black suit, black tie and dark glasses. If you see that combination behind you, then you are."

She studied the two men walking towards them. One was distinctly military, shoulders back, purposeful steps, eyes locked on his target. He was dressed in black fatigues, which contrasted with his cropped blonde hair, gleaming in the early morning sun. The other man, dressed in a black suit, black tie and white shirt, was hiding behind small square shades. He walked with a confident swagger, playing with his cuffs to ensure they were only just protruding from his jacket sleeve. He smoothed back his hair when he spotted Annabel.

"He's FBI, CIA?" She asked taking note of Jack's descriptive.

"Used to be." He said incredulously. "Meet Anthony Riggs, former CIA, now a LARA agent, here to team up with us en route to the bank. He's here to escort Jayne Langfield." God help her, he thought to himself.

"Jayne Langfield is here?" It was news to her.

"She should be. I guess she is inside."

Annabel wasn't sure how she felt about meeting the woman who had involved her husband in a case which cost him his life. She also thought of Derek Gant and Eliza Winch, both involved but ignorant as to why they had become a statistic. She needed to know, but was this the right time to get the answers? Her stomach churned, filled with trepidation for the meeting ahead.

Suddenly, the ex CIA man pulled a gun from inside his jacket and fired at them. Annabel screamed as Jack fell into her, knocking her off her feet. They landed behind one of the walled flower beds, providing cover from further shots. Jack took no heed, rising with gun drawn to face his attacker.

"Drop your gun, Riggs!" He had his sights firmly set on the American's head.

"Whoa buddy, chill. I'm friend, not foe. You had a tail you dufus!" Riggs holstered his .45 and pointed to Jack's right. Following Rigg's direction, he turned to see the body of a man sprawled across the lawn beside a tree, his rifle a few feet away from his outstretched arms.

"Boy! Do you need a hand." Riggs patted him on the shoulder as he walked past to inspect the body. "Never fear, Riggs is here!"

Jack shook his head as he bent down to help Annabel up. The American crouched by the dead man, rifling through his pockets he found nothing of any use apart from a few Swiss Francs, which he kept.

"Deadeye Riggs strikes again!" He said inspecting his work. "Right between the eyes. Now that's what you call shooting." He dusted himself off, scooping up the rifle as he got to his feet. He walked back inspecting the weapon.

"Damn! This AK47 is locked and loaded. He was after all of us." He pulled out the magazine and emptied the chamber, pocketing the ammunition.

"You're losing your touch old buddy. Had I not been here you'd be splattered on the floor by now." He passed them on his way back to the military man who was looking on impassively. Quick as lightening Jack grabbed Riggs by the forearm, wrenching it behind his back, causing the rifle to clatter to the floor. Using his other hand, he whipped out his knife and held it to the American's throat, forcing back his head. He peered over his captive's shoulder from behind and looked into his face.

"Uh … Ok, perhaps not." He held his free arm up in surrender. Jack released him and sheathing his knife, held his hand out.

"Good to see you, Tony." He smiled as his handshake was returned.

"Always a pleasure, Jack." Riggs began straightening his jacket, tugging at his cuff to ensure it lined up with his other arm. Grooming his hair to ensure his side parting was back in place he removed his sunglasses and approached Annabel. She watched him sidle towards her, dazzled by his perfect white teeth as he drew closer. He was certainly a pretty boy. Good skin, deep blue eyes and the most infectious of smiles. She couldn't help but grin to herself as he lifted her hand and kissed it.

"You must be Annabel Paxton-Thorn. Anthony Riggs at your service." Annabel's head was a whirl. It was just too much to take in all at once.

Only a month ago she had been a lady of leisure, tending her horses and enjoying a normal life in a tranquil village, taking every day as it came. In less than thirty days she had been kidnapped, nearly blown up, poisoned and shot at. Now, faced with this overconfident

American, she didn't know whether to laugh or cry. It was surreal.

"Pleased to meet you." She regretted saying it even before it was out of her mouth, the fact it came out as a squeak made it even worse. She wished she could turn around, find the nearest airport and fly home.

"I think we should get inside before we attract any more attention." Jack could see he needed to move this on.

"Great, have you met my new buddy, Benny?" Riggs looked over to the military man, who was standing practically to attention in the same position as he had left him when he'd shot the gunman. 'Although his social skills take a lot to be desired.' He whispered. As they approached him, the soldier visibly relaxed his guard and moved to meet them.

"Guys, can I introduce Captain Oberlin, Benny to his friends." He stepped aside. As the man approached he glanced at Riggs, a look of disdain in his eyes. Turning back to Jack and Annabel his face softened, he nearly smiled.

"My name is Captain Benzli Oberlin of ARD 10 at your service Commander Case." He shook his hand assertively.

"Just call me Jack." The Captain ignored him as he faced Annabel.

"Mrs Paxton-Thorn, welcome to Zurich." He took her hand, bowing his head in greeting.

"If you would like to follow me." He turned and headed towards the museum.

"Don't let him fool you. Get him in lederhosen, put an alphorn in his hand and you can't stop him, he does a great rendition of California Girls." Riggs started to whistle the tune as they followed. He shut up instantly as the ARD officer stopped in his tracks keeping his back to them. They all waited for him to turn and confront the American.

Seconds passed before he thought better of it and marched on until he disappeared through the door.

They walked along in silence through the halls of the museum, taking in the unusual design where nineteenth century and modern day collided in a kaleidoscope of shapes and colours. The first hallway they walked through, introduced as the history of Switzerland, was a narrow room bordered by clustered columns, supporting the ogival arched ceilings. It gave the place the feel of a cathedral. The floor and cabinets made from highly polished maple housed exhibits in glass enclosures of vivid blue. The centrepiece looked like a twelve foot high film reel with circles of different sizes cut into its body, each containing tools and images from a bygone era.

The next hall labelled the new exhibition gallery, housed modern art of all descriptions from statues and sculptures to photographs and paintings, some suspended from the ceiling.

The marble floor echoed with their footsteps as they passed through. Captain Oberlin then took a turn at a sign pointing in the direction of Swiss homes and furnishings, pushing through a door labelled 'useable living room with contemporary furniture'.

"Welcome to IKEA." Riggs announced as they all entered the room. The Captain once again showed Riggs disdain, and the American once again ignored it. Jack knew he would need to keep an eye on that.

The walnut floor and high beamed ceiling contrasted with the dull grey walls of the small room. Furnished with a three seater wood framed sofa in grey, dark oak contemporary wall units, two wood framed armchairs and to the rear, a walnut table surrounded by six dining chairs of different shapes and colours, Jack tended to agree with Rigg's initial comments. Seated on one of the dining chairs was Jayne Langfield.

"I need to get my crew to collect the body in the park. If you will excuse me for a moment." The Captain left the room, talking into his radio.

Annabel couldn't tear her eyes from the woman at the table. She was attractive, only slightly older than herself. Her clear complexion and green eyes portrayed a soft elegance which contrasted with the thick glossy red hair falling to her shoulders, giving the overall look of a sultry femme fatale. No wonder Colin had spent so much time on the case. She was transfixed, unable to move even as she watched the woman walk around the table towards her. What was she going to do, what was she going to say to her?

"You must be Annabel?" The woman had a soft voice, pleasant, friendly. Before she could reply, Jayne put her arms around her and held her in a warm embrace.

"I'm so sorry about Colin, he was a wonderful man. He loved you very much."

Annabel, taken by surprise failed to move away. As the words began to register she returned the hug, feeling emotion flood through her. She suddenly felt weak as the warmth of their embrace brought a comfort she hadn't felt for a long time. Feeling tears gather she closed her eyes trying to keep them at bay.

Riggs gave Jack a questioning look which he returned with a shake of his head. He felt it best to leave them for a while and took his seat at the table. Riggs followed suit, sitting opposite.

"So, I hear we have a new Hitler in town?" Riggs was never one for subtlety, using every opportunity to wisecrack. He was a good agent, but with a style which conflicted with his own. The positives overcame the negatives, however. Riggs was handy with a gun and as brave as a lion, under these circumstances he ticked all the boxes.

"He's a dangerous man with a ruthless team doing his bidding." Jack ran through the trip so far, emphasising the dangers and in particular the part Klara Brandt, and Leon Ubermann played.

"I can't imagine they will let us leave KVP without a fight. They need what's in the vault, and we hold the tickets for admission." He looked over at the two women who were in deep conversation in the corner.

"Keep your eyes open Tony and don't underestimate them, they appear to know our every move." It worried him as it was something he had yet to work out. Somehow they had stayed with them all the way.

"Hey, they don't call me eagle eyed Riggs for nothing, in fact, there are eagles out there who envy my eyes, in fact, mice run a mile when they see me because they know that I saw them way before they knew I was there…" He jumped as Jayne sat down beside him.

"Jeez, sneak up on someone won't you!" He rechecked his hair, in case a strand might have moved out of place.

Captain Oberlin entered the room and joined them at the table, sitting at the head so he could address everyone.

"My men have disposed of the body. Now I would like to arrange our route to KVP." He admired the Swiss Captain's matter of fact manner. He had a job to do, and he would carry it out with precision. Oberlin unfurled a map of Switzerland and indicated two routes marked with a red and black marker.

"We will travel thirty minutes apart. A colleague and I will escort Commander Case and Mrs Paxton-Thorn directly to St Gallen where we will approach KVP from the south. You, Mr Riggs, will travel with Mrs Langfield, escorted by two of my men and will approach from the north. We will rendezvous with the rest of my men near Buel." He then took another sheet of paper from his pocket and laid it over the map. It was a plan of the KVP complex and grounds.

"Klauss Van Privatbank is built in its own grounds, modelled on a Bavarian castle, the drawbridge across the moat is the only way in and out. The bank has its own security force guarding the grounds twenty-four hours a day. It would be madness to launch an attack on the castle, so we assume it is likely to occur once you have learnt the location of the gold. My men will provide protection when we leave for our next destination."

"Looks like you have everything covered, Captain." He was impressed; it would certainly be a challenge for the New World Order to attempt anything before they were well away from the bank. This was encouraging as he had a feeling the stakes would raise once they had the information. He was confident that as soon as they had it all, they would have the advantage. He hated being in the dark for even the smallest detail, it made him nervous.

"May I ask?" It was Jayne Langfield. "Have you managed to decipher the code for the combination?" She was referring to the code left by Colin 'A mailed pig'.

"You mean the flying pig thingy?" Riggs added his valuable input.

"A mailed pig." It was Jack who took the lead. "No, we haven't got there completely although we have a few ideas." He would leave it, mainly because they hadn't solved it yet, but also he would feel more comfortable waiting until they were inside the vault.

"Well, I'm sure between us all we should be able to work it out." Jayne looked over to Annabel and smiled.

Annabel smiled back. She liked Jayne, she seemed genuine and having suffered a similar heartbreak with the death of her mother, they had a common bond. As they packed away and prepared to leave, Annabel could feel a new found determination.

She had a partner in grief with a commitment to see this through to the end. Not just for the sake of Colin, Eliza and Derek, but the world.

CHAPTER FIFTY-FIVE
Klaus

Entering the clearing, the convoy was transported back seven hundred years as they drove towards a magnificent castle. The moat full of reeds emanating from the green filled water surrounded its entirety, broken only by the drawbridge, opened to accept it's guests. The backdrop of the evergreen forest curved around the structure like a green mist, the only thing missing was Robin Hood and his Merry Men.

"Oh, how beautiful!" Annabel gasped as they drove towards the entrance. Jack had noticed a change in her on the drive to KVP.

She was more talkative than before, pleased to have met Jayne Langfield as they had so much in common. It was as if a cloud had blown away to be replaced by clear skies. She talked about Colin, the early years together, the rebellious years when as a young couple in love the world just revolved around them. A world where nothing was as important as the time they had spent together. She had shown her commitment to see this through, to avenge the death of her husband, an hour long trip of constant chatter. It was good to see her in such high spirits, the first time he had seen her like this since they met. He hoped her positivity would continue after the announcement. He would be leaving her behind once they discovered the location of the gold. They followed the lead car driven by Captain Oberlin onto the drawbridge and waited as the portcullis rose to give them access through the gatehouse.

The castle was an authentic reproduction of a 13th century Bavarian original. The sandstone structure comprised of high cylindrical towers with a Swiss flag fluttering on each conical spire, the curtain walls including arrow slits cut into the upper quarter. Along the parapets Jack noticed armed guards patrolling the ramparts, their bows and arrows replaced by high powered assault rifles. The whole complex seemed impregnable.

Once the last of the four car convoy entered the gatehouse, the portcullis descended, locking them in. A second portcullis remained closed in front of them, a security measure to allow ID checks before granting them access. A wall of blue light shot across the enclosure ahead of them, filling the space from floor to ceiling, sweeping across the bonnet of the first car. The sensors monitoring for explosives, chemical residues and radiation, like a laser fed car wash. The beam enveloped all four vehicles bathing them in neon. Once it extinguished completing its cycle, the portcullis rose to allow them to move into the main grounds of the castle. A mixture of disappointment and wonderment greeted them as they drove through the gatehouse into the courtyard.

The Keep, a tower constructed in line with the castle structure, dominated the rear of the grounds. Built in sandstone and rising higher than the battlements, it presented a stronghold seen in most castles throughout the world.

What was unexpected was the glass frontage covering the rest of the interior, the heart of KVP. Built within the walls, a state of the art facility of aluminium and opaque glass with sloping solar glazed roofs surrounding the courtyard. The castle ramparts and battlements completed the facade twenty-five feet above, accessed by stone steps constructed either side of the Keep. There were at least a dozen armed guards patrolling from above, all studying the convoy as it came into view.

Each car was assigned its own guard who pointed to a parking slot next to the tower. As Jack brought his vehicle to a stop, he couldn't help notice the line of eight Bentley's, two Ferraris and four Porsches already in the bays. KVP obviously paid well. Their driver's door was blocked by one of the guards, he was wearing a Kevlar vest; were they expecting trouble?

After Captain Oberlin had provided the paperwork, they were free to leave. They assembled in the centre of the courtyard.

"Wow, I'd hate to see the bank charges for going overdrawn in this place." Riggs shouted as he turned full circle, taking in the entire complex. He wandered over to Jack, still feigning interest by looking skywards and whispered in his direction.

"One exit with a maintenance shaft to the moat in the gatehouse. Twenty guards all with Kalashnikovs, three entrances to the main building and one into that big fucking brick thingy in the corner."

"The Keep." Jack assisted.

"Right, one entrance in that big fucking Keep thingy in the corner."

Annabel and Jayne stood together, continuing to develop the relationship they had started at the museum.

"And Colin has been here?" Annabel asked as she too circled the complex, taking in the impressive sight.

"Yes, he has. Once we travelled together, and he made several trips on his own. He wanted to make sure personally that he fulfilled the wishes of the family to the best of his ability. He was a good man, Annabel." Jayne squeezed her arm tenderly.

"Yes, he was a thorough man." She agreed. "… And extremely popular. It wasn't until the funeral I realised how many friends he had, not just through business but also at home. Most of the village attended the church; it was incredible." Annabel was still annoyed with herself for not realising this at the time, rather than following her own selfish pursuits.

"Ah yes, Mittand Burrow, Colin would often talk about his life at home and of your Manor House. He was proud of his village. Perhaps, when this is all over, I could come and visit?"

"That would be lovely." She genuinely felt Jayne could become a good friend. Call it women's intuition or a sense of familiarity, she hoped they would stay in touch.

They all turned as one of the glazed panels slid apart with a hiss of air, an authoritative looking gentleman strolled towards them, immaculately dressed in a sharp suit and bronzed silk tie. He was mid to late fifties, cleanly shaven with carefully styled silver hair. The laughter lines sprung from his face as he saw Jayne Langfield, and rushed towards her, his arms outstretched.

"Mrs Langfield, what an absolute pleasure and my, don't you look beautiful." He held both of her hands as he gave her the customary European kiss.

"Hello Johannes, and you look as dapper as ever." He bowed in appreciation and took a step back to look at the rest of the group.

"Everyone, I'd like to introduce you to Johannes Klauss, Director of Klauss Van Privatbank." Jayne made the formal introductions. When she reached Annabel, the Director's expression changed to one of sadness and walking up to her, he took her hand and kissed it.

"Ah, Mrs Paxton-Thorn, may I offer my condolences. Mr Thorn was a fine man, it was a terrible business, terrible." His expression showed one of genuine regret which Annabel noted. Another person to whom Colin had made an impression.

"Thank you, Mr Klauss, you are very kind. Everyone has been very kind." She looked over to Jayne. "Colin certainly made many friends."

She was hoping she sounded sincere, although she couldn't help thinking that Colin had been leading a double life which excluded her to a degree. It hurt a little or maybe it was jealousy, as both Jayne and Johannes were more her type of people than Colin's. But then again, he may have been protecting those he loved from the dangers surrounding his association with them. Annabel preferred to think it was the latter.

"Please, if you would care to follow me." The Director led them from the courtyard and through the entrance into the bank.

The opulence of the Director's office befitted the man responsible for the safekeeping of vast fortunes. Similar to the castle, the room was a mixture of classic, regency and current vogue separated into two halves.

Johannes Klaus's work area consisting of a Dickens burr walnut desk topped with a turned gallery flanked by four small drawers, the surreal element of a laptop sat in the centre of the black leather writing insert. Behind the desk was a mahogany Carver chair stylised with JK etched into its back. Standing on four splayed legs with lion claw feet, a Regency mahogany sofa with elegant swan carvings and scrolled arms dominated the soft seating area. The floral fabric and matching bolster added a hint of colour to match the antique rug. Regency side tables, a chaise longue and a magnificent mahogany chiffonier sideboard decorated with filled crystal decanters and glasses on a polished silver tray completed the decor.

Annabel was impressed by the paintings on the walls. She recognised two by Picasso, a Rembrant and a Whistler, but she wasn't expert enough to know whether they were prints or an original. Johannes noticing, read her thoughts.

"Only one is real." He smiled, not about to tell them which one it was.

"Shall we?" He gestured to the modern half of the room, the group took their seats around a meeting table finished in black glass and aluminium. The table presented a selection of canapes, pastries and fruit, accompanied by a compliment of champagne, tea and coffee.

Riggs tried one of the canapés and nearly choked as raw meat slithered down his throat, what he wouldn't give for a burger right now. He settled for a croissant washed down with coffee. He was feeling on edge as he concentrated on a strategy for their escape. LARA was sure KVP was genuine and not a threat, but there was no way of knowing how far Brandt's influence had reached.

The gold was the key, hopefully, they were about to find the location. Unfortunately, the knowledge would bring the whole of the New World Order down on them. It was about to get hairy out there.

Jack could see his concern, and it pleased him. As the youngest member of the team at thirty-two, Tony Riggs had created the flamboyant piss taking Yank as a way of getting noticed. He also used it as a cover for any inadequacies he might feel, surrounded by a squad of ex-military elites. Unbeknown to him, he was rated highly throughout LARA. His tactical know how and fast reactions had elevated him to 'the' man to be alongside in a fight. No one told him because it would go straight to his head, and to feed his ego even more would be unacceptable. No, hard as it was to admit, he was better off as he was.

After a short break where everyone took advantage of the refreshments, Johannes pointed a control at the sixty inch plasma screen hanging on the wall at the head of the table. The screen came to life with an image of the Keep.

"This, Ladies and Gentlemen, houses the subterranean vaults of KVP. We have five of them, each with five hundred safe deposit boxes. We also have twelve deposit rooms housing three retina accessed sub vaults in each. Room six is where you will find the Langfield vault. Our normal procedure would be only one client and chaperone per visit. But after discussions with Congress and Mr Ryker of LARA, we understand in this case there are extenuating circumstances. The seriousness of the situation has caused us to allow a dispensation. Therefore, Mrs Langfield and Mrs Paxton-Thorn, along with Mr Case and Mr Riggs will have access to the vault. We will provide one guard for protection, and by agreement with Congress, ARD 10 will secure the Keep." He gazed at each in turn, looking to Captain Oberlin for confirmation of acceptance of the plan. He received a nod in agreement.

"Fine, shall we make our way to the vault?" He switched off the screen, watching as they all rose from their seats.

Jack could feel the adrenalin flow through his body as they left the office. Things were about to get interesting.

CHAPTER FIFTY-SIX
Numbers

The fortified oak door of the Keep had opened with a traditional iron key, the size of a rifle. Once pushed aside it revealed a steel security door.

The director punched the code into the keypad, as the steel panel slid aside he led them into a sparse room of stone. The guard pushed the button closing the door behind them. It hissed as air displaced; hermetically sealing them in.

"This is the anteroom where we prepare our guests before our descent to the vaults." Johannes explained as the group circled him, his voice echoed off the high ceiling.

The anteroom was built traditionally in stone, right down to the authentic worn flagstones covering the chamber floor. Four heavy oak doors within their arched housings prevented any further access to the building. The only item of furniture in the room was a marble altar, strangely out of place amongst the sandstone and brick.

Johannes positioned himself behind it, placing both hands on the surface. He leant forward looking at each in turn before speaking. Jack, amused, thought it looked like he was about to deliver a sermon.

"I am going to have to ask you to leave your weapons and electronic equipment, along with any bags. They will be perfectly safe, but I'm afraid, not allowed within the vault." The altar bleeped as Johannes keyed numbers into a pad concealed under the plinth. Two hidden drawers appeared at its base, velvet lined and empty.

"Sorry, Mr Klauss no can do." Riggs was the first to react. "We are here to protect these two ladies. We need to be ready for any threat, and if I don't have Marilyn with me, I miss her." Jack shook his head in a 'never mind' gesture when Johannes queried Marilyn.

The director addressed the young American. It wasn't the first time he had received an objection at this point.

"I can assure you, once within the Keep you and your clients are completely safe. The whole structure is titanium lined, as are the security doors and the vault rooms. Except for a direct hit by a nuclear missile, the whole tower is impregnable. You will be escorted by Erich here who, as are all our team, protection experts. And finally, Captain Oberlin and his men will be here in the anteroom until we return. So your weapons will be completely safe." Riggs looked at Jack, seeking back up. He couldn't offer it as he had expected this.

"Before we comply, we would like a confirmation of the security systems. May we see what is behind the four doors?" It was a reasonable request and one the director was happy to oblige. Behind the doors to the east and west were stairs leading up to the battlements. Secured by steel doors like the main entrance, protected by codes known only to the director and security staff. The codes changed at the end of each shift.

Out of the two doors behind the altar, only one provided access to the rest of the Keep. The other was a lift to the vaults below. The rest of the ground floor consisted of the security force living quarters. Fourteen dormitories sparsely decorated with bunks, storage facilities and a plasma TV.

Along the passage, a recreation room complete with a pool table, dart board, video games consoles and a cinema surround system connected to a fifty inch screen. The room fully occupied with off duty security staff enjoying their R&R.

The last two rooms consisted of the mess hall complete with a kitchen and a chapel. Jack could see no exit, other than through the anteroom.

"All the security staff have been with us for the last five years as a residential force. Each man has been carefully vetted before recruited." The director was more than happy to answer their concerns as he escorted them back to the others.

"They are all paid well and trained by our head of security, Wilhelm Sadel, who prepared the security detail for today's visit. Trust me, gentlemen, I can't think of a more secure location at this moment in time."

"I have a feeling this is one electronic item you will want us to take along." He took the key from his pocket and handed it to the director.

"Ah, this must be Mrs Paxton-Thorn's. I heard about the misfortune in Oxford." He looked at him and wondered if he was aware of the cost of the damage. Jack returned his gaze, he didn't care.

They agreed to the conditions, placing their weapons along with their PDAs onto the altar, the ladies gave up their handbags. The mobiles would be useless in the underground vaults, and Jack was confident, if they needed a weapon, they could overpower the guard and relieve him of his Kalashnikov anyway. He did, however, print one document from the PDA before relinquishing it. He also forgot to include his Kabar, just in case.

"Keep safe baby, I'll be back before you know it." Riggs placed his gun in the drawer alongside his PDA.

The ride in the elevator was a short one, within minutes they were walking along the steel corridor of the vault.

"Wow, I expect Ripley to run around the corner any minute with a fricking alien in tow." Riggs exclaimed, feeling like he was walking the corridors of the Nostromo.

"It certainly is eerie." Annabel agreed, unnerved by the echoes of their footsteps clattering along the barren tunnel.

"It is utilitarian." The Director explained. "Most of our clients would prefer that we don't waste money on decoration where it is not required."

As they reached room 6, the Director touched his hand to the palm sensor. The door opened with a resounding click and he led them through. Although not as luxurious as the main offices of the complex, room 6 was comfortably decorated. Walls were wood panelled in burr elm, matching the table and four comfortable meeting chairs. A storage unit provided refreshments, a well-stocked optics selection, a varied choice of cheeses accompanied by grapes and celery with crackers.

They were faced with three plain steel drawers devoid of any markings, locks or handles. A circular opaque glass disc positioned at head height beside each one, the only means of access; The retina scanner.

"If you would like to open the door, Mrs Langfield." The Director gestured for her to proceed. Jayne Langfield positioned herself in front of the disc next to the middle door. Then she hesitated as if contemplating her next move, before moving away.

"No, Annabel, you should do it." She looked over to her new acquaintance and held her hand out for her to join her.

"Colin lost his life arranging this for us. He also made sure you could carry on his good work should anything happen to him. He would want you to open it. You have come this far, have been through so much and all for the sake of our family. Annabel, I would be honoured if you would open the vault."

Annabel didn't know what to say. It was true; she had the means to open the door, and yes, she had been through a lot over the past few days. But she felt out of her depth, and the thought of the retina scan terrified her. She looked around at the group, and all eyes were on her as she stood rooted to the spot, not knowing what to do. She looked over to Jack, the one she had known longest, the man who had saved her life on more than one occasion. He indicated with a slight nod and a gentle shrug, it would be fine. His reassurance also confirmed he was there for her whatever decision she made. Swallowing back her hesitation, she took hold of Jayne's hand, letting her guide her to the scanner.

"Now, lean forward, close one of your eyes and with the other look into the disc." Jayne spoke softly holding her hand for support. Bracing herself, Annabel closed her left eye, staring into the disc with her right. Her knees started to shake as she waited for something to happen.

A thin horizontal strip of neon appeared at the top of the disc and descended until it disappeared. A vertical light from the right appeared moving slowly to the left. There was an audible click followed by a release of air as the door began to move. The vault door was open.

It reminded Jack of the Matryoshka Russian nesting doll. A smaller toy when parted, until all the dolls opened to reveal the tiny figurine at its centre. They entered yet another room, again made of steel, containing a small table and two chairs.

On the far wall was their prize.

Twenty small safety deposit lockers, ten on either side, surrounded a black iron door. Two keyholes positioned beside a digital panel and keypad, the only discernible markings. The Director moved to the door and took a key from his jacket pocket. It was a key like their own, apart from the initials KVP, etched on both sides of the grip. Johannes placed it into the lock and looked back to Jayne to follow suit. She looked over to Annabel.

"This is your right Mrs Paxton-Thorn. Your husband would want you to do this." The Director handed Annabel her personalised key. This is it, she was about to uncover the secret that started it all. That had caused so much death and destruction. Perhaps Jayne was right, it was her destiny.

Approaching the door, she placed her key into the vacant keyhole. She turned the key a quarter turn clockwise as instructed, the Director turned his key a quarter turn anti-clockwise. There was an audible clunk as bolts disengaged. The digital panel sprung to life showing six square panels, five of them empty. The first square blazed green with the number six.

"Six?" Jack questioned. "Is that the first number of the combination or a test digit?"

"No, this is the first number." The Director looked at the group.

"I assume you have the combination?"

"Sort of." He admitted, trying his best to sound confident.

"Oh dear, I hope you haven't had a wasted trip, for without the combination there is no way the door will open."

Jack explained they needed a few minutes to work out the cryptic clue left by Colin and all would be fine. He hoped he was right; he was banking on the fact he had Annabel and Jayne to help, plus added input from Riggs. With the four of them, they should be able to crack it, knowing the first number might make it a little clearer.

The Director looked at them, bemused to find they had travelled so far without the combination. But it was of no concern to him, he merely shrugged.

"I will leave you now, allowing you some privacy. When you have concluded your business, press the release button beside the door to open it. Erich will stand guard in the reception room outside and will alert me when you are ready to return to the anteroom." They left the vault, closing the door behind them. It clicked several times, sealing the four of them inside.

He took the print taken from his PDA and placed it onto the table. It was the photo of the code he had taken in Oxford. A four inch by three inch image of 'a MaileD pig' from the console display.

"Well, here it is." He announced as he flattened it out.

"Colin's clue to the combination of the safe. Any ideas?" He looked at Annabel and Jayne for answers. As they stooped over it to study the words, he could see they were as much in the dark as he was.

"I left that to Colin." Jayne confessed. "I had no reason to believe he would not be here to open it." She looked over to Annabel as if to apologise, but Annabel was too busy studying the slip to take any notice.

"I have no idea where he would have got this from. We have never kept pigs, only horses. And I can't think what it could mean." Annabel was trying to concentrate, but nothing came; it didn't make any sense.

"Do the capital letters mean anything?" Riggs was seeing the note for the first time, and Jack looked at him for a moment, annoyed he hadn't noticed it himself.

"That's a good shout." He agreed. "So if we take the M and the D away from this we end up with a aile pig. It now looks like it could be an anagram." He stopped and stood away from the table.

"Annabel tell me about Colin, anything you can think of, his hobbies, interests, likes and dislikes, anything that is Colin." They were getting close

Annabel thought for a moment, it wasn't that difficult.

"Well, he had no real hobbies. When he wasn't working, he watched sport on TV, or played computer games on his console. His interests were fairly standard. His practice was paramount, and he enjoyed the occasional pint in the local pub. I suppose his dislikes centred around his paranoia. Superstitions like black cats, umbrellas, magpies, ladders, the number thirteen. That type of thing."

"Magpie fits?" Riggs had been listening to the conversation without taking his eyes off the paper. Annabel could see it now. Colin had a fixation with magpies during the last months of his life. He always commented on how beautiful they were but at the same time they terrified him.

"Take the M and add the letter a,g,p,i and e. Take the D and you're left with the letters i,a and l. And if the D is the start of the next word, could be Dial, and I make that Magpie Dial or Dial Magpie." Riggs walked away and began circling the room as he started to think of numbers to coincide with the words.

"So, we have six letters in Magpie if that's what Colin meant. Dial the number that coincides with Magpie. But where does the six come from?" Annabel was still looking at the paper, trying to think like her husband. How did he arrive at the numbers?

"Wait! Hang on… I've got it!" Riggs ran to the table and using his car keys he scratched a 3x4 grid into the metal surface. In the top row of three boxes, he scratched 1,2 and 3. In the next row 4,5 and 6, in the next 7,8 and 9 and a 0 in the centre of the last row. Inside the 2 box he scratched ABC, in the 3 box DEF, continuing to fill each numbered box with letters, finishing with WXYZ in the 9 box.

Jack could see it now.

"Of course, Colin literally meant Dial Magpie into the key panel using the numbers from a telephone." He studied the grid.

"So we know the first number is 6 which coincides with the letter M on a telephone keypad. So it would give us … 6-2-4-7-4-3." So simple, yet everyone missed it. The retina scan was the real code, Colin may have just been having some fun, it was an aide memoir purely for himself. He chuckled when he thought of the millions of pounds of computer equipment HQ had used to try to crack the code. In the end, it just required four people scratching the solution on a metal table.

"Hey, don't mention it! Quizzes are my thing."

Riggs sat on one of the chairs and leaning back placed his hands behind his head.

All eyes were on Jack as he punched the numbers into the keypad.

Annabel held her breath as each number appeared on the display. Her husband had lost his life for this, so had Derek and Eliza. She had also been through hell over the past week or so. Her stomach lurched as the thump and grind of catches and bolts slid free from housings; unlocking their destiny.

The door clicked open an inch allowing him to insert his fingers into a ridge at the door's edge. He pulled it towards him, impressed at the smoothness, as the six inch thick slab of steel swung out on its hinges. Lights came on as soon as they pulled the door open to its full extent, they popped as each row came to life. He counted ten, at least four feet apart, exposing a hanger with steel storage running along both sides stacked high with cardboard boxes. But it was the sight of the centre aisle that brought a gasp from Annabel and a low whistle from Riggs. Fixed to pallets in stacks of ten by ten were solid gold ingots covered in a clear cellophane wrap. Five pallets stretching the length of the storage bay. It created a golden glow under the fluorescent lighting.

"Mummy had a hell of a secret." Riggs commented as he followed Jack and the two women down the four stone steps into the room.

"My mother had nothing to do with this." Jayne spoke curtly, objecting to the quip.

"The Nazi's exploited her, made her into an unwitting accomplice for their blood money. There is nothing here of hers except some jewellery and items of sentimental value. It has nothing to do with my family."

Jack prised a gold bar from the first stack and held it up for all to see.

"This might help to explain." He moved closer to the group to show them the markings on top of the ingot, an eagle grasping a wreath of oak leaves surrounding a swastika.

"The Third Reich Parteiadler …the iron eagle." Riggs noted

"Exactly." He pointed to the weight stamp 1KILO.

"In current currency, this is worth around fifty-thousand US dollars. There are at least one hundred gold bars on each pallet. Which would make this…"

"Twenty-five million dollars!" Riggs had worked it out when he first walked down the stairs to the room.

"And all in illegal plunder. Worth even more in the wrong hands." He instinctively looked over to Jayne who returned his gaze impassively.

"Our family has no interest in the gold. I am here to help stop the madness and to protect my mother's name. Now can we get the information we came for before it is too late." She walked to the back of the room to a small safe set into the wall. Following her, Jack couldn't help thinking he may have misjudged her. She seemed determined to thwart her husband's plans. She also interacted well with Annabel, portraying genuine kindness and compassion.

Finally, they had reached the last Russian doll. He stood by the safe next to Jayne. She punched the code from before into the keypad and opened it. The safe was empty except for a sheet of folded paper.

"I hope this makes sense to you." She sounded relieved, passing the responsibility over to someone she hoped, would find the answer. She handed it to Jack.

Written in ink were the coordinates 46°53'59.5'N-9°28'2.5'E. It was an old map of a mine. The name 'Goldene Sonne' written across it, but the location would need to wait.

"This is one for Captain Oberlin." He folded the map carefully and put it into his back pocket.

"Let's get out of here. We need directions to this mine." He led the way out of the vault.

As they passed the gold, Riggs was wondering how easy it would be to smuggle a bar from the complex. He held back carefully prizing out an ingot at waist height to test its weight. As it came free, two more dropped from above causing four more on either side to crumble inwards. They fell to the floor, one landing on his foot causing him to yell out. Everyone turned to see the young American scrabbling around gathering ingots. He placed them back as best he could, hurrying back to the group before any more fell out.

"That is a health and safety hazard." He said as he limped after them.

After closing the door to the vault, Jack and Jayne turned the two keys simultaneously to lock it. The display went blank as Jayne retrieved her key, while Jack pocketed the director's to return when they reached the Keep.

"I guess we should offer to pay for the damage." Riggs commented as he passed the metal table, the etchings of a telephone keypad scratched into its surface.

"I'm sure the director will be fine." Jayne offered. "Johannes is a good man; he will understand."

They all turned to the exit. There was a click and hiss as the door to the reception room began to move. Someone had used the retina scan to gain access.

Standing in the doorway was the dark figure of a man, back-lit from the bright lights of the reception room. He was holding an assault rifle, aiming it at them as he entered the room. Annabel gasped in recognition.

"Father Richards! What are you doing here?" She was too shocked to notice the dog collar had been replaced with black fatigues.

"Hello, Annabel. I would say it is a pleasure, but you will not find it so."

"How did you get past the retina scan?" Jack asked as the gun pointed in his direction. He was dealing with an amateur.

Richards pulled something from his pocket and threw it on the floor. It rolled towards them awkwardly as the tail of the tiny sphere prevented it from rotating. It came to a stop six inches from Annabel's feet, she recoiled in horror, holding a hand to her mouth trying to stop from gagging. Staring at her from the floor, wet and sinewy, was an eyeball trailing optic nerves and tendons behind it.

"You sick bastard." Riggs watched as the rifle aimed at him. A professional would keep a gun trained on one subject while his eyes scanned the group. He could pull the trigger sure of a target should anyone attempt a move. His eyes fixed on Riggs.

"Colin didn't need them anymore." Richards said calmly.

"As I was the one responsible for his remains, I thought I would keep a part of him for a greater cause. I have come for the map."

"And that greater cause is the New World Order I suppose?" The gun moved back to Jack.

"The greater cause is not all about the building of a better world, but a true fight against evil. The evil of religions, creating false prophets and gods to lead the weak like lambs. Lies and corruption are tearing families apart, and heathens who doubt the faith of the one true God. We will bring a true religion to the world. The Gottglaubig will provide the faith needed to bring us closer to God."

He stood looking at the LARA agent waiting for him to challenge his words. But it was Jayne, watching as the gun barrel turned towards her.

"And you think you can change the world by reintroducing the Gottgläubig. The believers in God, using the old Germanic and Nordic rites and beliefs from Nazi Germany. They were nothing more than extremist ideologists, and most of them were mad."

"It's not that…" Jack concluded.

"By destroying the world financially, you destroy independence. Free thinking becomes a thing of the past. If you want to live you conform and will be rewarded and if you don't…."

"You fill the world with concentration camps and give everyone a bar of soap for the showers." Riggs was trying to keep his cool, but this guy made him think of Grandma. Her parents were victims of a concentration camp, he knew more than enough of the horrors of that era. He never thought he would come face to face with a man who had the same ideals as those sadistic Bastards.

"You Monster… I'll fucking kill you." Everyone turned to see Annabel run at the gunman.

She couldn't believe the priest from the tranquil village of Mittand Burrow, and this sadistic creep was the same man. He had defiled her husband's body, not satisfied he was already dead. He had butchered him, and she had thanked him for providing such a lovely service. Her anger boiled over, on top of everything else this had tipped the balance. She avoided Jayne's grasp as she ran past her, ignoring warning shouts or the gun pointing at her chest. She was feet away from him, ready to launch herself forward. She wanted to hurt him.

"Here catch!" Riggs pulled an ingot from inside his jacket and threw it in the direction of the gunman. It landed inches in front of him with a dull thud proving heavier than he had thought, but it served its purpose. Richards reacted to the missile and fired, shifting his balance at the same time as Annabel slammed into him.

He fell backwards hitting his head on the hard floor, the gun sandwiched between his chest and Annabel. She struggled to gain purchase to punch his arrogant face. The bullet ricocheted off the steel walls out of harm's way as Jack pulled her from the fallen priest. Within seconds he drew his Kabar deeply across the priest's throat, severing the jugular and ripping through the carotid artery.

Blood spurted up the wall as Richards twitched and jerked, his heels kicking uselessly along the floor as his brain told him to run. Eventually, all movement ceased, the blood reverting to a trickle as life left him far behind.

He grabbed Annabel, pulling her into the reception room while Riggs ripped the rifle from dead fingers, helping Jayne through the exit.

Jack tried to slam the door shut, but the head of the dead man was half across the doorway preventing it from closing. He stepped back two paces, bounced twice and then drop kicked it shut.

CHAPTER FIFTY-SEVEN
Decision Made

"Here drink this." He gave Annabel a neat single malt as she sat at the table, a comforting arm from Jayne around her shoulders.

Riggs was in the corner placing Erich's jacket over his dead body to hide the slashed throat from view.

"What were you doing with a gold bar?" He asked as the American walked towards him, also accepting a drink.

"Security check. I was going to hand it back to Johannes and tell him to be more careful. But now he has a more serious problem." He looked over at the body lying in the corner.

"I can't believe it." Annabel sat staring straight ahead at nothing. "Why would Father Richards travel to Switzerland to kill us? He was such a nice man, kind, friendly. He was a man of God for Christ's sake!"

"I'm afraid he was far from a nice guy Annabel. Like your father-in-law, he was a plant, doing the bidding of Fabian Brandt. He was primed by the New World Order, for the day of reckoning. I guess Richards was to be part of the New World religion. The death of Colin caused a massive problem for them, due to the entrance protocol of the vault. It would appear your village has an active cell we will need to look into more closely." He wasn't able to do this without his PDA, and he needed to get to the Keep to retrieve it.

There was also something else troubling him, but he couldn't quite put his finger on it. Why go to all the trouble of trying to get the code in the first place? The KVP protocol required a key, a code and a retina scan as a total package? Why kill Colin and attempt to kill Annabel when they knew they were their ticket to the vault? Granted Colin's death was an accident, but with Jayne Langfield missing, now under LARA protection, Annabel was their best chance of success.

The answer was there somewhere, he couldn't see it through the fog of murder, deception and lies. Jack grabbed the handset from the wall. Johannes answered it immediately, and he explained the events over the last few minutes. The phone was silent for several seconds as the Director processed the information.

"It cannot be." He said after a moment.

"You were the only group logged into the vault, we made sure of that. Our last customer left at 9.30 this morning, an hour before your arrival."

"Well, someone got in Johannes. He overpowered Erich and threatened us with his gun." Looking at the fallen guard as he spoke it suddenly came to him. He knew how he had got in unnoticed.

"He dressed in black fatigues, and Erich knew him, Johannes. He was posing as one of your security team. You have been compromised." It explained how he had no trouble getting into the vault. Erich would have thought nothing of it until it was too late.

"Stay where you are, I will come down." The panic in his voice showed that he was a worried man.

"No! We'll come to you, we need our equipment. We'll meet you in the Keep. Get Captain Oberlin to ensure no one has access to the vault until we are safely back in the anteroom." He replaced the handset and faced the group.

"C'mon guys we need to go. You ok Annabel?" They needed to move, but he wanted to make sure he hadn't lost her again. She needed her wits about her until they were away from the bank.

"Damn right I'm ready." She stood up, knocked back the remains of her glass and slammed it down. "Let's get the bastards."

As the doors to the lift opened, they were met by Director Klauss and Captain Oberlin.

"Hey Benny, did you miss me?" Riggs received the usual glare from the ARD officer as he entered the anteroom.

"I cannot imagine how this has happened, Mr Case. All our staff are stringently checked, our enquiries go back to their school days." The Director had gone pale, rubbing his hands together nervously as he tried to come to terms with his security breach. Jack took his Glock from the altar and checked the clip, placing two spares in his pocket.

"Then I expect you will find an anomaly with our gunman, he would have been here for no longer than a few days." He checked his PDA, there was a message from Sara.

"What have you got for me, Sara?" She answered on the first ring.

"Jack, where have you been? This is important. We have intel that Father Richards has left Mittand Burrow bound for Zurich. We discovered his identity during a search of the Brigadier's files, his real name is Heinrich Ullman. He is on the way to intercept you."

"And you would be right, although he is now minus a head in the basement." He confirmed. As expected, there was silence as Sara scolded herself for being too late. He waited for the next piece of information.

"Ok, you are not going to believe this." Sara was hoping this would add something to the mission. "The code is ridiculously simple... it is an ana..."

"An anagram of Dial Magpie... yep done it!"

"Jack! Stop doing that. I have a job to do, and you're not making it easy." He raised his eyes. Was this woman's logic or just Sara being obstinate? He had known her too long to believe it was the latter.

"Ok Sara, go ahead. Tell me something I don't know." Normally he would close his eyes and wait for the barrage, but he didn't have the time or the inclination. They needed to get to the mine and stop all this once and for all.

"Bennett is dead." That did the trick.

"What happened?" Roger Bennett had been a good agent and a friend. They had served together during his military days, Roger being part of Naval Intelligence before joining LARA a year after Jack. He was an expert in surveillance but new to fieldwork.

"He was on a flight to Bangalore tailing Duranichev, he was due to meet Indian intelligence to set up surveillance protocols, he never made it. They poisoned him during the flight. It was one of the stewards who found to be on the Brandt payroll, he didn't stand a chance." All agents risk their lives every time they undertake a mission. But it was never easy to hear when the risk becomes a reality. He closed his eyes and took a moment to say a silent farewell.

"There's more, Jack." He opened his eyes and waited for the rest.

"The story was that BEE had employed Duranichev to ensure the light water reactor at the electronics plant could cope with an increase in production, we now know differently. He was there to work on the extraction of pure uranium from the mox fuel. We found abnormalities in the waste produced from the plant, traces of plutonium." He was listening but not hearing.

"Whoa, Sara what are you saying? Remember, I failed Chemistry." In truth, he failed everything apart from sport.

"In a nutshell Jack, he was extracting highly enriched uranium U235 from waste for the nuclear warheads needed for Brandt's master plan. He was preparing the heart of the bombs."

"But we caught him in time, right?" He could have answered the question himself.

"We raided the plant and shut down the reactor. It was messy with thirty casualties in total, and they weren't going to give up without a fight. But...No, Duranichev is missing along with the uranium. We are not sure how much there is, but we also found a large amount of lead and beryllium missing from the stock inventory. That is likely used for neutron reflectors, more than enough for five missiles." This was getting too predictable.

"They can't have just disappeared Sara. Who was checking for trails?" He was not trying to undermine strategic, but they were missing things. It made being in the middle of it very frustrating.

"They left a hundred trails, Jack. In the week before the raid, they shipped 130 consignments using rail, road, sea and air. We have tracked 80 of them so far, all electronics. We have NATO working with us, and updated regularly. So far there is nothing new to report."

He couldn't do anything about it from where he was at the moment. If they found the gold in the mine, it would put a massive dent in Brandt's plans. That is something he could do.

"Ok Sara, let me know any progress. One more thing, where is Brandt now?" At least knowing the whereabouts of the main man would eventually lead to the weapons. Once they discovered the gold, they would need to move fast. Brandt would be extremely pissed off his master plan was starting to fall apart, a wounded animal at its most dangerous.

"We don't know." Sara's voice came over soft and slow as she hoped he hadn't asked the question.

"Oh, for fuck's sake! Shall we go home and order our' how to speak German' tapes ready for the New World Order to knock on our door?"

"We will find him, he left New York last night. He will turn up, he's only off the radar at the moment." She now wanted Jack to hang up because she didn't want to answer his next question.

"I suppose it's not worth asking about the whereabouts of the Brandt girl and her sidekick Ubermann." The silence was deafening.

"Goodbye, Sara." He cut the call.

They were all looking at him as if waiting for instructions. Captain Oberlin and his three lieutenants stood impassively, while Annabel and Jayne, joined at the hip, stood together with worried looks on their faces. Director Klauss was trying to work out what had happened to his security, while Riggs sat on the altar swinging his legs, bored.

Riggs started the ball rolling as he leapt from his perch and walked towards him.

"So what's next boss?" He cocked his .45 and placed it back into his shoulder holster. He felt better after reuniting with Marilyn.

"First, I would like a word with Captain Oberlin before we decide our next course of action." He looked at the Director waiting for him to take the hint. New events dictated that he would rather keep the map hidden from anyone linked to KVP.

"Oh, yes, of course!" He was an astute man. "I'll be in my office. I will see you before you leave." As he pushed the single release button, the door to the courtyard slid open. Blocking his way was a thick set security guard, dressed in black fatigues like the rest, other than the gold insignia embroidered onto his breast pocket.

"This is Wilhelm Sadel, head of security. He will be your escort until you leave the complex and will remain outside the Keep until you conclude your meeting." The guard nodded his bald pate towards Jack to acknowledge him.

As the Director turned to leave, a bullet took away a part of his head. Brain and bone covered Sadel before he could react. Everyone stood rooted to the spot, the women screamed as Johannes body slumped to the floor. KVP was about to erupt.

Sadel fired towards the battlements hitting two of his own men, they dropped, plummeting into the courtyard. He could not believe his eyes. The director lay slumped at his feet, killed by members of his team. He had shared breakfast with them this morning; they had laughed together. Now he was shooting at them. A bullet bounced off the doorframe above his head, shattering sandstone, showering him in sharp stone shards. A hand grabbed his shoulder pulling him into the Keep.

"Get in, you are too exposed." Jack pulled the guard through the doorway and punched the lock button. The steel door slid into place securing them inside.

"What the hell was that?" Riggs saw exactly what happened, but like the others couldn't believe it.

"My men …" Sadel said as he sat stunned, gripping tightly onto the AK47 that had taken two of them down.

"They are not your men." Jack looked around for a way out.

"Your team have been compromised. Some are part of Brandt's force, we've already met one in the vault. He killed Erich."

Sadel leapt to his feet and flicking open a steel panel in the wall he hit a switch. Suspended over the door was a plasma which sparked to life. It showed an image of the courtyard from above. Cameras fixed to the top of the Keep gave a clear view of the grounds and the carnage taking place. Gunmen from the battlements were shooting at guards in the courtyard as confusion reigned. One of the guards on the ground, hands up, waving, assuming he was waving at friends, fell backwards hit several times before he had a chance to find out.

"It looks like the good guys are at a disadvantage." Riggs said as he went to the door to the east.

"Where do you think you're going?" Jack watched him pull it open.

"Evening the odds." A steel door was blocking the exit.

"Goddammit!" Two of Captain Oberlin's team joined Riggs. Sadel looked at Jack as if for approval. Receiving a nod, he ran to the door and punched the keypad. The steel panel slid away, exposing stone steps leading up. The three men passed through; the door slamming shut behind them.

"We'll take the west." Oberlin set off, taking one of his men with him. "I will have the rest of my men move in from the drawbridge. Is there any way we can get the entrance opened to give them access?"

"I can activate the emergency breakers to open both gates from the Director's office." Sadel said watching them climb the stairs. He ran to the exit door, studying the screen for the best route to the office complex.

"I can use two of the Bentleys for cover and your two cars, giving me only a yard to go." Jack followed Sadel's proposed route, he could cover him from the Keep.

Something caught his eye to the front of the complex, rising above the battlements.

"I think you might want to leave it a minute," Sadel saw the apparition rise in the distance.

A helicopter hovered over the gatehouse, its nose facing directly at them.

"Ladies can I ask you to get behind the altar and duck down as low as you can in the crash position." Annabel and Jayne did as instructed, putting their heads between their knees, covering them with their hands.

"Here it comes." Sadel said as he watched a white puff of smoke release from the rear of the chopper. The missile raced towards them. Both men looked at each other, then in unison dived at the altar, skimming its surface as they leapt for cover.

The whole structure rocked as it hit. Blocks of sandstone fell onto the floor, crashing against the altar. It sent shock waves through their bodies as all four pressed against it for protection. For several minutes, tremors sent loose stone skittering into the anteroom.

As the clouds of dust began to settle, Jack raised his head to see blue sky through a six foot hole, ten foot above them.

"We have to get out of here!" He shouted as gunfire from the courtyard entered the room.

"Good idea!" Annabel agreed as she clambered off the floor

shaking dust from her hair.

They could hear shouts from within the Keep behind them, the guard shift on R&R were still within the accommodation block. They had been oblivious to the gunfire from their soundproofed enclosure.

"Can we lock them in?" He asked Sadel, not knowing who was friend or foe.

"No, I can't and I won't. These are my men, good men, we will need them to help."

"Hang on, chief, you have no idea who is on your side and who will put a bullet in your back."

"Not these." Sadel argued. "They are from the night shift, my most trusted men. I can vouch for them all. Miguel, Hunt, Langher, Moran, Michel, Gordon, Reice, Raisch and Gallatin. They have been with me for many years, and this group together are my best crew. We will need them." Jack checked the screen, the helicopter had moved away. It must be repositioning, one things for sure, it hadn't finished its sortie. He needed Sadel on his side, so against his better judgement he had to concede, but with one condition.

"Ok, get your men, but brief them from here. Let them through one at a time."

He stood facing the door with his gun aimed at each man as they came through. This was utter madness, he had taken the word of a staff member of KVP who he had met only minutes ago. But sometimes trust is pure instinct, and his instinct trusted Sadel.

Once verified and briefed, Sadel issued instructions. Sending three men after Riggs, three assigned to Oberlin, three remained with them. After a final check of the monitor, Jack opened the door. The sound of gunfire filled the anteroom as the battle raged on.

He risked a look above, catching a glimpse of Riggs between the embrasures of the battlements. The additional three men seemed to be helping as they began to move steadily towards the congregation of rogue guards. He watched as one fell through the crenellations and smashed into his hire car. He instinctively winced, that had got to hurt.

Johanne's body was blocking the doorway. Not only would it slow them down, climbing over him to escape, but it also seemed wrong to treat the director in such a way. Sadel and his team lifted him into the Keep, laying him in front of the altar. Each man bowed, signing a cross as a mark of respect, before returning to the door.

Sadel and two of his men ran behind the first Bentley taking Annabel and Jayne with them. Jack with the two remaining guards waited a few seconds before breaking cover to join them. Gunshots thumped into the vehicle as they dived for cover. Glass exploded onto them as bullets rained incessantly on their position. Jack jumped up, returning a burst of fire, sending one man down and three more back into hiding. They used the time before they recovered to run to the next Bentley. He could see the entrance five yards away, the hire cars waiting to provide cover. Sadel moved to the first car taking Annabel and Jayne with no incident, he prepared to move to the second.

"Hold it!" Jack shouted over the noise. The helicopter had returned, hovering over the west wall, facing them.

"Get down." He fell to the floor his face pressed against a wheel, allowing him sight of the hovering menace.

Lights flashed from the base of the chopper, unleashing the .50 caliber twin guns into the east wall. Stray bullets cut down two rogue guards as they ran for cover, they spun several times as they took hit after hit. The bulletproof glass of the office complex popped and shattered; hammered with the constant rain of gunfire. Strafing only feet above them, they could only wait and pray that their cover would hold.

Above, Captain Oberlin and his team had managed to drive the enemy back towards the gatehouse where there was nowhere else to run. He was halfway across as the helicopter unleashed its firepower.

He was no more than twenty feet away, close enough to see the pilot's gritted teeth as he kept his finger on the trigger, relishing the devastation. Oberlin grabbed the assault rifle from his nearest man and aimed at the pilot. He waited a few seconds, following the steady hover of the craft as it rode the thermals. He made sure he was in synch with the gentle sway of his target before he fired.

The pilots head exploded splattering the glass of the cockpit in the dark stain of blood and brain. The aircraft lost its lift, plummeting from view into the base of the castle. The foundations trembled as it erupted into flames.

"Go, go, go!" Jack was up and hustling everybody along, grabbing Annabel and Jayne by their arms, pushing them towards an opening in the glass a yard ahead.

They collapsed exhausted, after rushing the corridor and crashing through the doors to the Director's office.

Annabel flopped onto the regency sofa while Jayne found the chaise longue. They both lay on their backs with their own thoughts, staring blankly at the ceiling. Sadel made for the Dickens desk, moving aside the Rembrandt he opened a steel door containing a bank of switches and a row of keys. He flicked a switch as he looked over to Jack.

"The gatehouse is now open." He announced, checking his weapon before heading towards the door. The Director's office escaped damage, only two ceiling tiles from the ceiling and a broken glass door.

Jack entrusted the women in the care of two of Sadel's men. Inserting a new clip into his Glock, he left to join his comrades.

Sadel was standing by the door staring into the courtyard as he walked up to him.

"It's over." He looked at Jack, unable to hide his despair.

The courtyard was full of bodies in black fatigues, some rogue, some friends and colleagues.

Sadel had no idea who was who, a dilemma which meant he would never mourn completely. He was numb, rooted to the spot, as he tried to make sense of what had happened.

Jack moved past him and entered the courtyard, hearing voices instead of gunfire. The ARD 10 squad had stormed the grounds as soon as the gates rose. The remaining rogue guards, being totally outnumbered, surrendered without another shot fired.

Captors barked orders as they positioned prisoners, seated back to back, shackled together in pairs in the centre of the yard. Captain Oberlin directed his troops, methodically checking everything, from the bindings of the captives to the specific duties of his team. He nodded as Jack entered the courtyard before returning to his task.

"Hey Jack, I hope our next destination is a walk away?" He turned to see Riggs striding towards him with Sadel's men and three prisoners in tow. He was looking at their hire cars as he passed them. One of the vehicles had two legs protruding from the shattered windscreen where one of the rogues had plummeted from the battlements, crashing through the car, using the chassis to break his fall. The second, riddled with bullets, no wheels and two doors short, was going nowhere.

"I have a feeling we will need to use alternative transport."

Riggs followed Jack's gaze to the far side of the courtyard where three undamaged cars were parked.

A grin spread across his face.

CHAPTER FIFTY-EIGHT
Chur

The Bentley cut smoothly through the countryside on the winding A13 towards Chur.

The snow topped mountains dominated the views all around, creating a comfortable yet stunning vista. All three passengers sat in silence as they contemplated the events of the past hour.

Jack was mulling over the disasters of the last week, trying to make sense of everything and coming back with not a lot. It troubled him; he was still missing something.

As events continued to escalate, he kept failing to put all the pieces together. It became compounded when new, more pressing issues joined the mix. His mind kept drifting back to the KVP attack and how the New World Order had upped the stakes. The fact that Brandt had increased his determination to stop their progression was not unexpected, but the extent of the force used was. It was true that Ryker had persuaded some world leaders to help find the evidence needed to halt Brandt. Even NATO had helped monitor global trends of growing aggression. But, the importance of keeping it strictly covert to avoid international incidents, could not be stressed enough.

Brandt's strategy before today had been to use one or two agents, avoiding suspicion, careful to keep his public facade intact. Now he had shown his hand and failed. With the prisoners detained at KVP, it was highly probable plea bargains would be negotiated. An agreement granted on the clear understanding that the evidence leads directly to Brandt.

He knew Wilhem Sadel would be enthusiastic in extracting any information, out of respect for his dead comrades. He wouldn't like to be in their shoes when the balding hulk started on them. Captain Oberlin had left the rest of his team behind to assist on behalf of

Congress. It was highly unlikely that anyone left behind could prevent Sadel from interrogating them his own way.

"So where do we go from here?" Annabel asked from the sumptuous leather surroundings of the rear compartment.

"We won't be attempting the mine until first light. According to Oberlin, the area can be treacherous enough in daylight with the threat of rock falls. In poor light, it would be madness. We will get some rest at the hotel in the meantime."

"Oh good, I could do with freshening up before we go to the mine anyway. Now we have all evening. How wonderful!" The relief was evident in Jayne Langfield's voice as she sank into her seat, relieved at the thought of slowing down after the horrors of the day.

"I'm sorry ladies, but you won't be joining us."

"What? Why? I thought we would all stay together as we are so close to the end?" Annabel felt safe with Jack by her side, the thought of being away from him, even for the shortest time, filled her with trepidation.

" Look what happened the last time I was left alone."

"Yes, I agree." Jayne was equally disappointed. "We are both vulnerable without LARA to protect us. My husband won't stop until he finds me and without your protection, I am dead."

"Ladies, we are arranging protection for you, and you will be perfectly safe. The mines are dangerous, and there are likely to be many confined spaces once we are inside. It will be impossible for us to protect you effectively if we can't manoeuvre around you. We cannot take that risk."

"Then I want a gun." Annabel was not going to be left feeling vulnerable, even though she knew she couldn't use one. He tried hard not to smile as he remembered her attempts with a gun in the sleeper.

"Let us get some rest, we can look at the arrangements in the morning." Nothing will change, but at least giving them the hope, it might mean a restful night for everyone. It was something they all needed.

He was suddenly aware of headlights in the rear view mirror, closing fast. As they got nearer, he recognised the distinctive teardrop headlights of a Porsche. He shook his head as the silver 997 shot past them.

"Yeah… Cmon! I gotta get me one of these!" Anthony Riggs screamed as the throaty 3.6 litre engine tore up the motorway, vibrating through his body like a pneumatic drill.

He looked down at the clock, two-ten kilometres an hour, two twenty, two twenty-five. He floored the accelerator, relishing the force pushing him back into his seat, and the car still had more to give.

"You are aware that we are only borrowing these vehicles?" Captain Oberlin reminded Riggs as he held on for dear life.

"Hey Benny, chill out. I'm only doing what they built this car for … speed!" He was having fun, and he wasn't about to let the Swiss stiff spoil it.

"Then I would suggest you use the brake at this point, our exit is here." He pointed to the sign as it shot past. Exit 16 Chur-Nord.

"Oh, shit!" He slammed his foot on the brake feeling the wheel protest in his hands.

"Right hold on tight Benny, we're about to test this baby to the max!" The exit was almost upon them, and they were travelling too fast.

He pulled up the handbrake pumping the footbrake. Turning into a skid, he sent the rear wheels screeching out towards the central reservation. As the Porsche began to slide sideways on all four wheels, Riggs floored the accelerator, again pulling up the handbrake. The all-wheel drive kicked in, as the tyres spun together, seeking purchase on the unforgiving tarmac. With the assistance of the slide, all four wheels in synch and expert handling, the Porsche wobbled and jumped as it shot forward, hitting the exit ramp's raised verge, before bouncing back in line as it hit the slip road with a crunch.

"Jesus, that was close." Riggs let out a relieved sigh, slowing to a sensible speed as they approached the junction.

"Benny, I wish you would give directions earlier man. Which way now, left or right?"

"Benny?" He looked over to the ARD captain. He was staring through the windscreen, wide eyed and ashen faced.

After a more than satisfying meal, the group relaxed with a selection of fine wines and coffee. They were more than grateful for the chance to unwind in the splendour of the traditional wood panelled restaurant of the Romantik hotel.

"What a wonderful choice of accommodation." Jayne Langfield commented as she tipped her wine glass towards Jack in appreciation.

"I wish I could take all the credit. But I have to put it down to Sara at HQ, she has a knack for it." He had to agree it was the right decision.

The Romantik Stern hotel was a fine example of traditional Switzerland. Dark wood panelling complimented the decor, a mix of original styles of the historic city with modern day design. It created a warm, welcoming environment. The staff, all in traditional dress, added to the authenticity as they served their guests with efficiency. They smiled as they circled the tables, genuine and warm in their manner. Riggs found one waitress particularly appealing. He was using his schoolboy charm and wisecracks in overdrive, although his techniques left a lot to be desired.

Jack knew she was doing her best to be friendly, while politely rejecting his advances.

"I think I'm in there." Riggs winked as Ana left the table after topping up the glasses.

"I think her father would have something to say about that." Captain Benzli Oberlin looked across the table at the American. He had met many people in his life and prided himself on a level of tolerance that was unmatched. Riggs, however, had pushed him close to the edge, he didn't like him.

"Her father owns three farms nearby and is fiercely protective. He has the same attitude when it comes to his family. No man in this area has been brave enough to date her or her sister so far. One of his farm hands, who was sweet on Ana only a year ago has disappeared. The police investigated, checking each farm thoroughly, finding nothing. Rumour has it that he left the area in fear for his life, others say that the pigs grew fat in the weeks afterwards. Did you know that if you cut a man into small enough pieces, a pig will devour bone as well as the meat?" He flicked a glance at Jack as he finished the tale.

"Nya ha! I don't think so, man." Riggs took a larger than usual gulp of his wine, choking a cough, as the heady liquid overpowered his throat. Oberlin smothered a smile, pleased to have planted something in the American's head that would eat at him for the rest of the evening.

The ARD man left his seat, looking towards the restaurant entrance. Five officers dressed in olive green fatigues stood by the doorway studying the diners. Oberlin beckoned them over and introduced them to the group.

"Let me introduce our protection squad from the 70th Infantry and the 12th Mountain Infantry. Their assignment is to ensure our safety while we are here in the Chur region." He passed behind them placing a hand on the left shoulder of each one as he made his introductions.

"Corporals Doris Kinsinger and Anja Joost assigned to Mrs Paxton Thorn and Mrs Langfield. Corporals Jan Fehrman and Daniel Erisman, security detail while we remain at the hotel. Sergeant Jorgan Bircher is our guide to the Goldene Sonne." Each soldier nodded as he announced their name. They sat at an adjacent table where the waitress was waiting to take their order.

Jack explained his decision to Annabel and Jayne. He knew it was the right call to leave them at the hotel until he returned.

"We have got to assume we will be under attack as soon as we reach the mine and we cannot guarantee your safety. We have no idea what we are facing until we get there, leaving it much too late to work an effective contingency plan." He looked at each of them in turn, watching the disappointment on their faces.

"I guess we would be nothing but a burden, anyway." Annabel could see his point. She was fit and had no fears regarding her stamina, but having never experienced pot holing within a cold, dark cave, it didn't exactly appeal to her anyway. But fear was still a driving factor, and the thought of being separated from Jack worried her.

"We will just have to hit the shops." Jayne looked at Annabel and smiled. She had resigned herself to staying behind, deciding retail therapy was a much more pleasurable way of passing the time.

With the first floor secure and everyone tucked away in their rooms, Jack should have been able to rest easy.

But something still troubled him, a gut feeling that he hadn't covered all the bases. It was there scratching at the door of his thoughts, trying to get in. Struggling to move from the far recesses of his conscious mind.

He lay awake staring at the dark beams of the ceiling, surveying every contour in search of answers; none came. He is known to over analyse, this could be another such occasion, but until his gut told him otherwise, he continued to search, his gut had never been wrong. He'd had good news from HQ, Antoine was already up complaining and by now no doubt, well into a pack of twenty. He looked forward to sharing a bottle of Merlot with him when the mission was over.

But there was still no sign of the warheads, Duranichev or the location of the aircraft destined to deliver the chaos planned by the New World Order. Ubermann and Klara had disappeared along with Fabian Brandt, which could only mean one thing. They were preparing for the day of destruction.

LARA was in a race, and they were flagging, unless they picked up the pace, they would be far behind at the finish. The future would be a very different world, one they thought had been left behind seventy years ago.

There was a soft knock on the door. Instinctively grabbing his gun, he peered through the spy-hole. Opening the door, he let Captain Oberlin into the room.

"My apologies for disturbing your rest but I thought you should know this immediately." He walked to the centre of the room turning to face Jack as he closed the door. Oberlin had only one expression, so he had no idea if the news was good or bad.

"I am afraid I have to inform you that all the prisoners captured at Klauss Van Privatbank are dead." It was bad news.

"What happened?" He hoped Sadel hadn't gone to town on them, wiping them out with one sweep of an Uzi.

"They were all put together in the accommodation block, called one at a time for interview. After the cleanup, no more than a few hours, my team entered the block to fetch the first man. All fifteen men were dead. At first, it was assumed they were all sleeping as they found each man to a bunk, but we could not wake them."

"Cyanide." Jack announced. Martyrs to the cause.

"Yes, it is true. Pathology reports confirmed they all died of potassium cyanide poisoning. How did you know?" Oberlin remained impassive, but his tone had changed, it was almost accusatory.

"It was the preferred method used by the Nazis to evade interrogation. It seems it is also used by our friends of the New World Order. They had outlived their usefulness and capture is not an option." It reminded him of the Brigadier, same MO.

"It also means yet again we have nothing to link to Brandt."

Oberlin nodded, relieved that his detail were exonerated of any blame for the mass suicide.

"Will we see more of them at the mine?" He could tell the young Captain was in new territory.

ARD 10, being a peacekeeping force, used aggression only in extreme circumstances, in a neutral country, it was few and far between. Occasional civil unrest, a few robberies, nothing on the scale of where they find themselves now. But he had no doubt in his mind that if called upon, Oberlin and his crew would deliver.

"They appear to have impressive intel locking onto us wherever we go. We should keep our eyes open." Jack was sure there would be a welcome party at some stage. He could guess it would likely be after they found the gold if it was there. The problem will be when they left the mine not when they entered it.

"I will have a detail monitoring us from a position near to our location as we exit the mine. We have notified the 12th Mountain Infantry, and the 70th is monitoring the situation. If we need reinforcements, they are ready." He delivered it as a matter of fact, deliberate and controlled.

Oberlin had thought it through and had come to the same conclusions. For the first time today he felt encouraged.

"I am sorry for keeping you from your rest. I will see you at breakfast." He left the room closing the door quietly behind him.

The contours of the beams provided none of the answers as he returned to the bed and resumed his inspection. Within minutes a calmness flowed through his overactive mind. His eyelids began to feel heavy, closing on their own, forcing him into darkness.

He drifted into a deep sleep for the first time in over a week.

CHAPTER FIFTY-NINE
Cold Comfort

Annabel watched the Hummer pull away from the hotel with a deep sense of unease. Jack was disappearing from view along with her security and peace of mind. She felt alone. The company of Jayne, the two female officers and two corporals gave her no comfort. Jack carried her strength with him, understood her psyche, made her feel safe even in the most deadly of situations. She pushed her muesli aside and swallowed the last of her coffee. Craning her neck by the window, she watched the brake lights extinguish, disappearing as the Hummer drove out of town.

"So, I have been checking, and there is a fine French restaurant on the other side of town. What say we make our way there for lunch?" Jayne had planned the morning for them. Hit the boutiques, break for coffee, more boutiques and a French restaurant for lunch. The woman seemed unfazed by the assigned infantry, oblivious to any potential danger.

Maybe it was bravado for her benefit, knowing how nervous she was or perhaps she felt it was now over for them. Either way, it still made Annabel jittery.

"Right, I'll fetch my handbag and meet you in reception. Shall we say ten minutes?" Jayne left the restaurant with Corporal Anja Joost in tow, leaving her with Corporal Kinsinger, who was staring at her, waiting for a decision.

"Please hurry back Jack." She whispered as she left the table and went to collect her things.

The morning sunshine failed to warm the chill of the alpine air. Jack wore his leather jacket over the wetsuit with a Cordura coat on top, to cope with the elements. It was damned uncomfortable. He was sweating as the Hummer left the motorway, heading through Felsberg onto the winding road of Calanda Mountain. It didn't help that Sergeant Jorgan Bircher had the heater set to warm.

"We will stop halfway at Laschein so we can have a natural break, check our equipment and run through the plan of the mine. There are some things you will need to keep in mind." Bircher had spent years with the 12th Mountain Infantry and was an experienced climber and caver. He had a feeling these agents were ill prepared for this expedition. They would not be entering the mine until he felt confident they were ready.

"It will be great to cool down." Riggs moaned as he unzipped his jacket, struggling to remove it.

"I'm sorry. Are you warm?" Bircher watched him lay the Cordura on his lap. They had climbed to six hundred feet of winding mountain road bordered by tall spruce. It caused the sharp breeze to channel its energy along the track rushing past the Hummer with the force of a wind tunnel.

The Sergeant switched off the heater and pushed the control for the rear passenger window. A blast of freezing air rushed into Riggs' face enveloping him in a fog of ice. He gasped as the chill took his breath away burning his throat and nostrils as it thrust its way into every crevice.

"F-f-f-uck me! Sh-sh-it!" Riggs gasped pulling his coat back around him and pulling the roll neck fleece over his nose. Bircher closed the window smiling as he watched the American in the rearview, slump back shivering in his seat.

He also saw a rare sight from the passenger seat where Captain Benzli Oberlin was sitting.

He was smiling.

CHAPTER SIXTY
Septic Isle

The sun was still beating down on the upper terrace as he watched the Pacific surf crash onto the golden sands. The tropical heat of the early evening burned onto the steel and glass of the palatial superstructure on the island retreat.

He finished the remainder of his vodka as it struggled to maintain a cold temperature, the ice melting within seconds of exposure to the elements. Watching the palms sway in the breeze against the backdrop of the electric blue ocean, should have afforded him some respite. But the thought of his parents brought a wave of unquenchable anger. Something that drove him on to fulfil his destiny. Something that would bring pain to those who had blighted him, those who had destroyed his family, those who made him suffer.

His father, who he had never known, would be so proud of him. He was in touching distance of completing the legacy he was born to fulfil. The Fourth Reich would rekindle the work of his forefathers, creating the world envisioned by the mighty Fuhrer. Many people would pay for their betrayal of the Fatherland. Many more would suffer for the life they had forced him to live from birth. And mother, dear, dear mother, so beautiful and yet destined to live her life in agony and abject misery.

As the Red Army drew nearer to Germany in 1944, his mother was forced to flee with a twelve month old child, seeking refuge wherever she could. His father had disappeared, leaving mother with no one to turn to as the Fatherland began to waver. Their links to the SS made them outcasts amongst their own people. Her beauty was unequalled, and she was forced to whore herself to provide for her and her child wherever she could. The thought of the degradation, the misery she endured while he innocently slept, fuelled the anger inside him. There was worse to come.

At the end of the war, an American soldier found mother and child attempting to escape to Switzerland on a supply truck. Al Rodan, a name that will haunt him until the end of days. Al Rodan the saviour, their knight in shining fatigues. He took mother and child, housing them in a cottage near Freiburg, close... so very close to freedom. Supplies were plentiful, and Rodan gained mother's trust. She gave herself to him, not as payment, with the only thing she had to offer freely, an offer much appreciated at the time. Again he slept through, an innocent two year old, oblivious to the real world and the life awaiting him.

Three weeks was all it took. Three weeks for Rodan to tire of her, to change from the kind hearted hero to the callous American. He was the same as the rest of the scum crawling venomously through the Fatherland. They divided it up as spoils of war along with the British filth, the Russian inbreds and the stinking Polish.

They were rounded up like cattle alongside over thirty-thousand other nationals and transported to a camp in Oksbel, Denmark, the stench of which he could still smell as he remembered his childhood. Mother became ill during the first two years of internment, a parting gift from Rodan... Gonorrhoea. The camp medics and the Danish Red Cross refused medical treatment. They ignored her screams as weeping sores ravaged her skin, seeping internally into her joints. A course of penicillin would have cured her in days. Many died around him as the continued refusal by the authorities to treat refugees led to thousands of deaths. Children he once played with would disappear, never to be heard of again. Whole sections of the camp would be cordoned off as disease spread. Once reopened, the smell of burning, masked unsuccessfully with disinfectant, stayed in the air for weeks.

'Uncle' Heindrich Dolman, a man who had been sent by God as an angel, cared for mother as best he could. He took it upon himself to teach him the ways of the world. An education which included knowledge of his father. Heindrich had known him as a boy. He had been a recruiter of the brownshirts, the Nazi youth, and had mentored father to greatness. Even at the age of sixty, he had the strength of mind to pull them through the hard times, soothing mother's pain as best he could. In 1948, when they transferred to a German refugee camp in Bleidenstadt, mother contracted septic arthritis.

She became wheelchair bound and near incoherent.

Uncle Heindrich managed to procure drugs to help ease the pain, but the madness was beyond any medication. He had no regrets, only sadness when he thought of the night in 1952 when he gave mother her last evening cocoa. Thanks to Heindrich's last drug delivery and his compassionate arguments regarding the quality of life, or the lack of which his mother now faced. Brandt knew what he had to do.

The cyanide took two minutes to work. He held her tightly throughout, felt her tremors as poison coursed through her veins, squeezed her tightly as the convulsions took hold and held her gently as she relaxed in death.

The Order were there for him. They had followed him through his journey, watched him suffer, saw him battle the hypocrisy of the victors of the war.

Victors who condemned the Fatherland for trying to create a perfect world. Yet they had themselves a history of usurping native lands, taking them for their own, killing anyone in their way. They then gained control by denigrating those deemed to be inferior, making them slaves. A hypocrisy that is still there today, but the so called superpowers continue to deny its existence.

The Order nurtured him, conditioned him and in honour of his father ordained him as the ruler of the New World Order. Now he was ready to seek his revenge, fulfil his life's destiny, recover what was once their own. The world would soon be under the control of the Fourth Reich, a New World Order with Fabian Brandt as Fuhrer, leading them to glory.

Walking back into the cool air-conditioned living quarters he gestured for Jai to refill his glass.

"Fetch Ubermann." He instructed as the vodka was given to him, slightly diluted with soda. The servant left the room to find the head of security.

Brandt sat behind his desk, pressing the speed dial on the console set within his burr elm workstation. It was his access to the world.

The six screens allowed him to monitor his entire operation. His production plant in Bangalore, his position on the Dow Jones and his global management accounts. From the island, he could keep an eye on his troops, overseeing their drills at both camps to the north, check the progress of the bombing missions or simply control the air conditioning inside his three storey glass hideaway. Preferring a hands on approach, he could spend the rest of his days behind this desk and remain in complete control.

The call was answered within seconds by a familiar female voice.

"Are we on schedule?" He swivelled his chair to face the ocean, mesmerised as he waited for a response.

"Oh yes indeed, they are on their way to the mine as we speak. We will have our prize in the next hour or so."

"Good, we have a convoy on the way. Make sure they do not leave the mine; it ends here. I want Case and his team dead."

"That is all in hand. We will be in a position to conclude our business with Mr Case as soon as we know they have found the gold."

"Be careful my dear. You know how dangerous he can be." He showed the obligatory concern, but he knew she could take care of herself.

"Oh, don't you worry. Case will have many more things to worry about than me." He could hear the smile in her voice before the call crackled and died.

He took a long swallow of his chilled drink, closing his eyes as the bittersweet liquid soothed him. Excitement rippled through his body, bubbling his stomach and pumping his heart just a little faster, as he thought of his imminent rise to power. Footsteps on the glass spiral staircase announced the arrival of his head of security, Leon Ubermann.

"Sit down Leon." Brandt rose from behind his desk, following his daughter's intended to the L-shaped sofa, placing his vodka on the low gilt glass table. He watched Ubermann take his seat awkwardly as he compensated for his left arm, encased in plaster to the elbow. Two pins and a retaining bar assisted with the healing. Once settled, he rested the cast on his legs.

"How's the arm?" Brandt liked Leon. He was thorough in his work and dedicated to the cause. But more importantly, he treated his Klara well.

"Hurts like hell." Ubermann hated it. A lucky shot and he was in agony, restricted in his movements and feeling less of a man. The hatred he felt for the Paxton bitch was beyond comprehension. He longed for the chance to exact his revenge, instead, he was stuck in the middle of the Pacific Ocean, checking drones.

"Good!" Brandt stared directly into Leon's eyes, satisfied with the anger and hatred he saw in them.

"Pain is good Leon. It teaches us that failure is painful, failure hurts. I want you to embrace the pain, learn from it. We are about to create a world where many of our new subjects have failed in their lives. Failed to understand the difference between right and wrong. They will learn the pain of failure, and I need you to show them the error of their ways. You will be the corrector, possessed with the power to decide who lives and who dies." He leant forward in his seat to emphasise his point.

"You will be the leader of the new Shutzstaffel. Let's just say it will stand for Social Sanitation. I need you to ensure racial purity and absolute loyalty to your new Fuhrer." Brandt collected his glass, draining it before holding it in the air for a refill. Jai was at his side in seconds.

Leon Ubermann looked at his future father-in-law, seeing glimpses of madness in the old man's eyes. It scared him but at the same time excited him. The guy was pushing seventy, and the way he drank he would last no longer than 5 years at the most. He started to envisage the new King and Queen of the Fourth Reich, with Klara at his side they would rule for decades. The pain in his arm began to subside as his senses were drawn to his destiny.

"So, what of the drones? Are we all set?" Brandt cut into his thoughts, pulling him back to the menial task of checking the bomb delivery systems.

"They have all completed test flights and successfully delivered their payload on their targets. Each command console responded smoothly with data response readouts at 99.7%. All warheads are on the way to their destinations and will be primed within the next thirty-six hours. We are ready to go." Brandt took the glass from Jai, sitting back, he took a healthy swallow.

He smiled, raising his glass to his second in command, toasting the future.

CHAPTER SIXTY-ONE
Calanda

Leaving the Hummer at 1200 feet, Jack was worried.

The mountain track had changed from tarmac to natural granite and rock, replenished by the occasional rockfall. The car bounced and rolled up a further 200 metres, stopping at a clearing large enough to park the vehicles away from the track.

The entrance to the mine was somewhere above them through a mixture of mulch, granite and moss, hidden amongst an ample covering of spruce and fir.

Their current position left them open to the elements. Light covering below provided no protection from an assault on their location. Any attack from the air would take them into the trees with the risk of a rockfall sending them over the edge.

"I don't like this." Jack said to Riggs as he scanned their location.

"We are too exposed. Look at it." He pointed to all the areas that put them at risk.

"I needn't worry, Mr Case." Sergeant Bircher grabbed his radio, giving the order.

The earth exploded a yard in front of them, stones and moss sprinkled over their boots. They had no time to react other than dip their heads, which although a natural instinct, was fruitless. Both LARA agents looked at each other, Riggs speechless for the first time in days.

"We have our support teams surrounding the area. Anyone within a hundred yards of this location will be neutralised." His voice was nonchalant, as he opened the back of the Hummer and began to unload the equipment.

"Very impressive, but you can't blame me for checking."

Bircher only shrugged as Jack called Sara.

"What have we got Sara?" Pleasantries ignored, he checked the screen of his PDA as Sara relayed the information through the agents' earpieces.

"There are four of you on the mountain and twelve stationary targets surrounding your location." He counted the red dots confirming Sara's description and received the same number from Bircher. He noticed four more substantial heat sources on the perimeter of the screen.

Bircher filled him in.

"We also have four transport vehicles near Laschein with ground forces awaiting immobilisation... and to transport the gold if we find any." Tourists have been exploring the mine for many years, so the chance of finding gold was unlikely. He felt it would be near impossible, but ready to be proven wrong.

"Ok Sara, we'll report in when we've finished." Jack was happy that the security detail seemed to be on point. He had a feeling they would need to be.

"Jack, before you move out of range." Sara hadn't finished.

"The Navy intercepted a Greek container bound for Holland after a crew member broke ranks and called the coastguard. He was concerned about a shipment putting a section of the hold out of bounds. Rumours were spreading about radiation and contamination. They found a warhead full of uranium. The threat is genuine, Jack."

"Holy shit!" Riggs whispered in his ear.

"One down, four to go." Jack calculated assuming the one discovered must be earmarked for the London attack.

"We have agencies all around the world checking air, land and sea. News channels have agreed on a blackout, which takes the heat off the extra security checks. And for the time being, the Government leaders have agreed to keep it covert. But we have to find the others fast." She was stating the obvious. There was one thing missing though.

"What about the aircraft used in the attacks? There are five locations we were told. A radius of around 700 miles should be enough to shorten the search. Have we anything?"

"No nothing, we thought we had something in Chicago but it was a dead end."

The search for the aircraft was a race against time. Once airborne they would be impossible to stop without the threat of a nuclear explosion. They were no nearer locating the launch sites or the man with his finger over the button. He needed Sara more than ever.

Finding the gold would put a dent in Brandt's aspirations to dominate the financial markets, but it wouldn't stop the devastation he planned. They had to find the maniac. They had to destroy the New World Order. They had to stop the launch.

Sergeant Bircher had finished offloading the equipment, passing it to each man. He handed Jack the replacement for his kitbag. It was a spelunkers backpack.

"Sara got to go. Message me with any updates, I'll retrieve them when I can. But you must focus on the location of the aircraft." He pocketed his PDA and pulled on his harness.

"Let's get this over with." He addressed the group as they donned their equipment.

"Hi Ho Hi Ho it's off for gold we go. With a kraut on the loose, that we'll kick in the caboose, hi ho…"

"I would keep your voice down agent Riggs. There are risks of rockfall in this area, any unnecessary noise could bring it all down on your head."

Bircher forgot to bring a sense of humour with him this morning Riggs thought, as he looked over to Jack, raising his eyes. He couldn't help but smile at him, he was a clown at the most inopportune moment, but it helped to lighten the mood as they climbed gradually towards the mine.

Turning to face them, Bircher went through a final equipment check.

"The mine entrance is just over the ridge. I will take the lead, Captain Oberlin will take the rear. Stay close and follow my instructions."

Riggs saluted and whispered loudly 'Yes sir!' just as Bircher turned. He got the reaction he expected. Bircher stopped for a few seconds, thought better of it, and continued climbing to the ridge.

One day someone would smack Riggs in the mouth, and he wasn't sure he would step in to stop them. Jack slapped him on the back of the head, more for Oberlin's benefit than his own, noticing the Captain's look of disgust.

He preferred the Swiss military on his side for the time being.

She watched them enter the mine through binoculars taken from the dead support soldier. As she recognised Case, hairs rose on the back of her neck, hatred filling her eyes. He was a dead man walking and she would enjoy watching him writhe in agony before he took his last breath. The other guy must be the American, smaller than Case, he would be no trouble, and the Swiss do-gooders were already dead in her eyes.

"They are in." She spoke into her two way. "Get ready on my command." Klara felt exhilarated as she thought of what was to come.

They would recover the gold they needed for their master plan, take care of LARA once and for all, then she would have the bitch. The bitch who damaged her lover, forcing him back to the island. The bitch who had put her sex life on hold, driving her wild. They were meant for each other, now she had lost her connection. They screwed morning, noon and night; not love, not passion, animalistic lust. They hurt each other, a painful ecstasy leaving them exhausted, wanting more. She could feel arousal flood through her, her body throbbing as she thought of her man deep inside her.

She screamed with frustration, smashing the binoculars into the head of the dead soldier, pounding and pounding until her urges passed. Putting the blood soaked binoculars back to her eyes, she checked the entrance to the mine, making sure she had not alerted them with her squeals. She scanned the paths, sweeping slowly until she reached the cave, she was relieved to see the entrance was clear.

Covered in blood Klara lay beside the corpse, taking a few minutes to compose herself before the next part of her mission.

CHAPTER SIXTY-TWO
Target

It took a while to adjust their eyes to the darkness and cramped conditions. Huddled yards from the entrance they studied the map, illuminated by the lamps on their helmets.

"The main tunnel to the east would be the best place to start. It's where one of the main areas of the dig took place over 150 years ago, large enough to be used for storage. The rest were little test digs, only 50 metres long. But as I have said all along, tourists visit this mine regularly. If there was anything here, it would have been found by now." Bircher folded the map and placed it in his pocket. As they faced him, the beams from the helmets danced along the walls and sparkled off the surface.

"Wow, it looks like they stuffed it into the walls." Riggs moved his head along the tunnel watching the light create a kaleidoscope. The surface walls flashed colours across the whole surface; reds, blues, greens, and lot's of gold.

"That's just Calcite, a mineral rife in this mine. It would take years to extract enough gold from it to make one coin. Between 1809 and 1856 when the mine was fully operational, there were only ever 70 gold coins minted from the total of gold extracted. No, if there is a large quantity of gold, it could only have been brought here."

Making their way steadily along the tunnel they had to move past calcite stalagmites growing from the ground like crystal spears. The walls changed shape and size as they progressed, darkness closing all around them. The natural light from the entrance moved further away until it finally disappeared. Riggs felt claustrophobic as the lamp only gave him four feet of visibility. The sparkling stalagmites gave the impression the walls had come alive, reflecting each beam of light as they passed by.

"Are there spiders in here?" He asked, his phobias coming to the surface. He tried to stay away from the wall as much as possible, cringing as he stumbled and grasped it for support.

"No, it's far too cold for spiders, you are more likely to find bats."

"Oh, good!" Riggs mumbled as he crouched down a little, just in case.

Turning right the tunnel narrowed, sloping steeply into total darkness. Their boots struggled for purchase on loose stone, granite and Calcite. They surfed the slope until it levelled out into a wider passage. The shingle following them for a short while, pattering onto the floor like light rain, coming to a stop as the floor levelled out.

It filled the air with a fine dust cloud, dancing around their heads, creating a fog in the beams of light. Bircher and Oberlin pulled their scarves over their noses for protection, leaving the agents to cough through the haze for several yards until they entered a small cavern.

"Thanks for the scarves." Riggs moaned as he sat on one of the timber beams lying across the floor. He cleared his throat, coughed a few times and spat a glob of dust and phlegm at the feet of Bircher.

"Sorry about that, cave ball." He said, looking around the walls to avoid the guide's eyes.

Bircher pulled off his pack and took out an LED lantern, flooding the cavern with light. They were at a junction, used to store equipment and supplies in the old days and a rest area for tourists today. The floor was littered with old timber beams and ironworks, including a section of track used to ferry rubble away in carts. Some of the debris was the result of tourists, crisp packets and food wrappers, coke cans and bottles.

Jack counted four exits. Shining his Maglite into the southern shaft, the light hit a solid wall, no more than ten feet in length. He wandered along it tapping the walls, checking for a difference in the surface. There was no change throughout, and within minutes he had returned to the group.

"We can rule that tunnel out." He walked over to Bircher, checking the map over his shoulder.

"There are three tunnels left in this area; section I, Ia and Ib. Why don't we split up to search the a and b passages, then meet at the intersection, where there seems to be another main tunnel."

Bircher thought for a moment and suggested, as he and Oberlin were familiar with the mine, they would each take an agent. He wasn't surprised when Oberlin agreed to go with Jack Case rather than the egocentric Riggs.

"You shouldn't let Riggs get to you." He said to Oberlin as they began investigating tunnel b.

"In my opinion Mr Case, he does not appear to be the type of person you would be proud of as a representative of your organisation." He continued to tap the walls with his pick, shining the torch at the ceiling and along the floor as he spoke.

"He seems to enjoy upsetting everyone, and he takes risks that endanger lives." There was no doubt Riggs had made an impression on the Swiss ARD 10 officer.

"He can be a bit of a hothead." He conceded as he tapped the wall parallel to Oberlin.

"But he is a good agent, dedicated to his job and an asset in a fight." He was fed up with making excuses for him, but he would stand by his convictions.

Riggs was an essential part of the operation.

After over an hour of fruitless searching, they made their way back to the larger cavern to reassess the map.

"Well, I think Sergeant Bircher might be right, Jack." Riggs took off his helmet and straightened his hair. It was the one thing preventing him from owning a Harley and cruising the open road, helmet hair.

Jack was distant, deep in thought as he concentrated on the east wall. Something caught his eye, and he recalled seeing it the first time they entered. It had floated past his consciousness as the focus was on searching the other tunnels. It was worth checking out.

"Sergeant Bircher, can you switch off the lantern for a second?" He walked to where the sergeant was sitting and stood behind him facing the wall.

"Trouble?" Riggs asked reaching for his gun.

"No, I want to try something. Take a look at the wall; what do you see?" He shone his torch across the surface, from the ceiling running downwards left to right, until reaching the floor. He started again going from floor to ceiling.

"Wait. Stop!" Captain Oberlin held the light three quarters of the way up.

"There, I saw it! Move the light from left to right."

Jack shone the light along a thin seam of calcite running horizontally across the surface. A ragged line glimmering red and gold reflected in the beam. It stopped halfway across for a few feet before appearing again at the same height.

"Well, I'll be damned." Riggs walked towards the line and ran his finger along the seam, stopping where it vanished. Bircher switched on the lamp, bathing the cavern in light once again. The seam mingled with the rest of the surface calcite, virtually disappearing.

"It's more textured than gritty." He said placing his hands against the two sections of the wall, rubbing gently across each surface.

Oberlin took his pick and knocked out a small chipping, rolling it in his fingers and feeling its texture.

"It's clay hardpan." He threw the chip to the floor and hammered some more.

"This is a thick layer of hardpan. It would have taken a while to plug that hole." Riggs said watching Oberlin take chunks out of the wall. Bircher bent down, lifting one end of the wooden beam, he tested its weight.

"Here, take the other end of this." Jack took hold and followed Bircher towards the excavation.

"Hey, hang on!" Riggs moved back. "Watch the whole thing doesn't come down on you." He backed up towards one of the exits.

"Thanks for the support." Jack watched him back away as he moved into position. Sometimes the Yank got to him too.

They crashed the beam against the wall. Calcite and granite fell from the ceiling, showering them in dust. Riggs may have been right to be cautious. He readied himself again once it stopped raining rocks and with Bircher, thrust the beam at the wall. Three attempts later, after more showers from above, a hole appeared in the wall. It was only around six inches in diameter, but it revealed there was something behind it. The work to conceal it had been extensive, the beam had smashed through at least a foot of clay.

"The Nazis must have brought the clay in with them." He wondered how many men it had taken to construct this all those years ago. "This would have taken days to construct."

Within ten minutes the hole was large enough for a man to crawl through. The last two strikes brought the rest of the hardpan crashing into the cavern.

Bircher stepped back staring at their handiwork with his mouth open.

"I don't believe it. It's impossible!" He looked at the map again. "This can't be right, this map is over 150 years old and yet there is no other passage marked on here."

"Well, use your eyes; there's one here now." Riggs had moved away from the exit and made his way to the rest of the group. Sweeping his arm towards the opening and bowing, he looked at the others.

"Shall we?"

CHAPTER SIXTY-THREE
Hidden Treasures

They stood transfixed staring at the sight before them, no one spoke as they took it all in. They had uncovered a narrow stairwell cut into the rock. Eight stone steps led into darkness, taking them into a vast chamber full of objects, their lights showing only shadows of different shapes and sizes. Bircher switched on the LED lamp.

"Oh my God!" Riggs was the first to break the silence.

The chamber was the size of an aircraft hangar, full to the brim. Gold bars, ten pallets wide, were neatly stacked in front of them at a height twice the size of an average man, spread a metre apart. Through the gap was a mountain of coins, ten feet to its pinnacle. Gold standards, statues and irregularly shaped idols stood along the walls.

"We're rich!" Riggs skipped between the stacks to investigate. He disappeared as the light diminished the further he went, a single beam dancing into the distance.

"Wait, Riggs! Get back here. We need to stick together near the light. You have no idea what's back there." He felt as if he was in a tomb, and ancient tombs could mean ancient traps.

"Look over here." Captain Oberlin walked behind the stairwell and pulled a torch from the wall. He stooped down to smell a container positioned below, dipping it inside. Taking his Zippo from his pocket, he lit the soaked material. It caught instantly, an amber flame sparking to life as the oil ignited. The flickering light sent shadows dancing across the chamber.

Setting to work they lit the remaining nineteen torches hanging from the walls. The whole chamber became bathed in an amber glow.

The group separated to investigate each quadrant of the room. They uncovered relics and weaponry from ancient times, portraits and gold items from the middle ages and many more ingots and coins.

"Hey! Look at this." Riggs called them over as he unfurled a roll of fabric, throwing it on the floor in front of him.

It was an intricate woven banner depicting a double-headed eagle with its wings spread wide. Heraldic Shields woven into six unfurled feathers on each wing. Running centrally down the eagle's body was a detailed image of the crucifixion. The image of Christ looking down from a wooden cross.

"The Quaternion Eagle." Bircher recognised it instantly.

"It was the standard of the Holy Roman Empire. The coats of armour represented the Imperial States at the time, fifty-six in all."

They all looked at Bircher, impressed with his knowledge.

"The thesis for my degree was the history of Eastern Europe with Germany heavily involved in my studies. The Holy Roman Empire came after the Roman Empire, founded by Charlemagne, King of the Franks, crowned Emperor in 800AD by Pope Leo III. It revived the Roman Empire in part, and it continued in power until 1806. Officially recognised as the First Reich."

"I guess this has something to do with it as well" Riggs pointed to the far wall at a gold chest set between golden pillars. Two ornate candlesticks stood on its flat surface below an engraving cut into the rock face depicting a two-headed eagle.

"That was behind this rug when I pulled it away from the wall."

"Yes, you are right." Bircher agreed. "That is the Imperial Emblem of the Empire."

"It looks like an altar." He was getting a different perspective on the whole mission and in particular the enemy.

"What if this has nothing to do with the Nazis at all? What if it's all to do with this Holy Roman Empire?"

"How very astute of you, Mr Case."

Jack wheeled around and came face to face with Klara Brandt, an AK47 pointed directly at his body. Six soldiers accompanied her, their weapons trained on the rest of the group.

"It's a pity none of you will be here to see it."

CHAPTER SIXTY-FOUR
Trapped

Relieved of their weapons and packs, the Order soldiers marched them up the stone steps. They shoved them through the opening back into the cavern, where four further gunmen manned each exit.

The prisoners sat in silence as the eleven guards trained their Kalashnikovs on them, offering no chance of escape.

The beam used to open the wall now lay in the centre of the cavern. The captives were positioned along it, a ring of machine guns surrounding them.

"I would like to thank you for returning our property to us. I will be sure to add you as a founder member in our chronicles." Klara paced in front of them with her rifle slung over her shoulder. Her jeans and ski jacket, covered in blood, adding menace to her gait. She theatrically stopped in front of each captive to emphasise her control. She took exaggerated steps, stamping as she stopped, staring down at each of them with disdain. She finished in front of Jack who slowly raised his head and met her stare.

"Your property?" He made sure he looked into her eyes, fixing on the wide pupils, sure he could see the fog of madness there.

"So, the property of the Holy Roman Empire, the Nazis, the Fourth Reich or do you have another name?" A soldier moved forward, his gun butt ready to smash into his head. Klara waved him away.

"We are disciples of the Fatherland and our New World will continue the work of our ancestors. It is our destiny and God's will. The only name you need to remember is Brandt, Leaders of the New World." He needed to keep her talking so he could come up with a rescue plan. With all exits blocked and firepower heavy; he needed to work out the odds.

"So, you are following God's will? As Christians, Catholics,

Muslim or are you creating your own religion?" He recalled Father Richards, back at KVP talking of the Gottglaubig' believers in God'. It was something far beyond his comprehension.

"None, we are Gottglaubig' Believers of God' and will lead our people into righteousness." She was preaching.

"Calvinists." Sergeant Bircher spoke up, explaining his interpretation of the likely path to this new religion.

"Calvinism, a protestant theological system. Practised by both The Holy Roman Empire amongst many of their Imperial States and by the Nazi party to use as a way of control. Based on five principals; total depravity, unconditional election, limited atonement, irresistible grace and perseverance of the saints. In English, it means everyone is a sinner, except the Chosen. The Chosen are forgiven for their sins. The Chosen can choose who lives or dies as it is ordained by God and God accepts all actions of the Chosen as they are seen as the saints of God." His voice became more irascible as he recounted the principals. He spat the last words from his mouth, knowing of the abhorrence this ruling class could subject to all humanity.

"It sounds to me like Sergeant Bircher isn't too keen on change." Klara's voice was mocking in tone; she hadn't finished.

"No matter, you won't be here to see it anyway." Her smile was a mixture of arrogance and mirth.

Bircher leapt from his seat to confront her. Riggs was too slow to react, grabbing and missing his trouser leg in an attempt to pull him back. The butt of a soldier's rifle smashed into the side of his head, sending him crashing down at his feet. Blood trickled down his cheek as Riggs helped him gingerly back onto the beam. He held on to him, resting his head on his shoulder to keep him from falling.

Jack used the diversion to work out the best means of escape, as long as Riggs was on his mettle, it could work. Having Bircher injured had shortened the odds on them all getting out alive, but it was a risk he had to take. Every minute he could stall his captors, the stronger Bircher would get.

"So what are your intentions? Surely you don't intend to remove the gold all at once? You'll be cut down in your tracks." He gambled that before she killed them, Klara would revel in describing their master plan...

He was right.

"We don't have to. We have taken control of the mountain. In three days the world will be ours. There will be far greater issues of global concern than a mountain in Switzerland. Now, thanks to you, we have more than enough to control the world economy. I don't know if you quite realise the value of your contribution."

"This doesn't make sense. If your lot had been using this as a storage facility for centuries, surely you guys could have found it during the seventy odd years you have had to search?" Although he was stalling for time, it was a relevant question.

"Planning is everything, Mr Case. It is no good entering a war without an effective strategy. It has been over sixty years in the making. After the war in 45 there was a major operation, ensuring disciples were safe and transferred to sleeper status. The Directors worldwide continued to mentor and recruit using underground cells to prepare for the day of reckoning."

She began to pace, as Jack thought, she was revelling in the story.

"We kept everything under the radar as our following grew. My father worked through the ranks until he took command in the seventies, his bloodline recognised."

"Bloodline? Don't tell me he was Hitler's love child."

Klara was quick to stop a whack from the soldier stationed behind him.

"Very humorous Mr Case, our ancestry traces back to Otto the First, the first Holy Roman Emperor and King of Germany in 962AD. So you see, this gold is not only our property; it is our inheritance."

"So this leads me to my original question. How come you had no idea where it was until now?" He cleared his throat before saying, "Let's see you get out of that one."

He was hoping Riggs was paying attention as the last sentence was meant for his ears. It worked nicely into the conversation. Riggs sneezed which told him he was onside.

Klara stopped and looked at Jack, narrowing her eyes, wondering if he was playing her.

"Gold has been stored all over Europe through the ages, hidden from enemy factions, relocated regularly. Armies had transporters, specialists in relocating treasures with the locations known only to a few. My grandfather was a transporter, and fearing the Third Reich was failing he was tasked to protect the future. He and Eric Ahlers were the only ones who knew the location on instructions of the Order. The plan was to keep the knowledge to a minimum and limit the risk of betrayal."

"That worked out well. If I've got this right, grandad was topped by his best mate." Jack was risking a beating, but he had to keep her talking.

There was anger in her eyes, she leaned forward. He braced himself for an onslaught, either from the butt of a gun, or from the psycho bitch in front. Neither came, she straightened and seemed to compose herself, he could see it was a struggle. Fighting with every demon controlling her, she took a breath and continued.

"My grandfather was murdered by a traitor, a piece of filth who got what he deserved. Oh, and send Ahlers my regards when you see him in the depths of hell, Mr Case. But that is to come." She was enjoying this.

"Grandfather was revered by both the Reich and the Order. Buried a hero, and now, my father, his son continues the legacy. The New World order has the true lineage to take us to glory." Her expression changed to one of pride, a smile spreading across her face as she watched the captives. Their expressions had changed from one of determination to one of despair. Except for Case, his expression hadn't changed, his ice blue eyes boring into hers. She would soon change that.

She continued with her story.

"After the death of my grandfather and Ahlers, it was the woman, Ahlers' wife Gloria who was the only link to the transporters. She was the only chance we had of finding the location. They assigned Gerald Barth to get close to Gloria, which he did as you know. But then he too died, which was unfortunate."

She slowed her pacing as she came to the end of the tale. They would need to act in the next few minutes.

Looking along the beam, Captain Oberlin seemed resigned to dying, he just sat staring at the wall. Riggs returned Jack's stare with a wink, Sergeant Bircher appeared to be able to support himself, but had he recovered enough? He'd have to risk that he had.

"So the New World Order had no choice but to keep surveillance on Gloria Barth, your father even sought out her daughter. In the meantime, you built your army until you were ready to go. But Gloria died, and your stepmother went AWOL, which led to Colin Thorn etcetera and well… here we are."

Klara stopped near the west exit and looked back, the smile left her face but remained in her eyes.

"Very good Mr Case, bravo! You have it all worked out… well, almost." She walked towards him letting her hips sway provocatively, her eyes fixed on him as she approached.

"My dear stepmother was crazy to think she could make a fool of my father. It was only a matter of time before he caught the slut and like her retard Hugo Dahl, she paid with her life."

All four captives turned towards her, their faces filled with questioning looks. It was only Jack who put the pieces together. He lowered his head closing his eyes and cursed under his breath as it all began to make sense. Klara relished the look on their faces and licked her lips as her sadistic juices started to flow.

"Gentlemen, let me complete your team before you die. I am sure you would like to say your goodbyes."

She turned to the exit and gestured for the soldier to move.

Standing in the opening was a lone figure, a look of despair in her eyes. It was Annabel Paxton-Thorn.

Before any of them had time to register, Annabel was shoved brutally into the cavern, her head snapping back as she stumbled forward. Jack leapt from the beam catching her before she hit the floor. She looked up at him, a small cut across her cheek the only noticeable damage to her face.

"I'm sorry, Jack." Her eyes watered as she put her arms around his neck. Lifting her, he settled her alongside him, ensuring she was on the end of the beam nearest the exit.

"You must stop apologising; otherwise I will start blaming you." He smiled as he wiped a tear from her eye.

"Ah! How very touching." The woman that was Jayne Langfield entered the chamber, armed with a handgun.

"Hello, Claudia." He took the initiative, refusing to give them any further satisfaction. He should have seen this coming.

Claudia Robertson bowed her head and raised her eyes, congratulating him on his correct assumption. She took her place alongside Klara Brandt.

"I would imagine you bear a remarkable resemblance to your sister. You even fooled Johannes Klauss." Jack recalled the warm reception the Director of KVP had given her when they arrived at the bank.

"Oh, it was a simple case of a little hair dye and this god awful red lipstick. We were all but an inch different and similar in build, although I thought Jaynie had a fuller figure." She ran her hands down her body to emphasise her point.

"I'd like to compliment you on your act, but why the elaborate plan? All the wasted lives at Chanteau, your own men! And why involve LARA? Oh … Hang on a minute, of course." It all fitted into place, everything he had been trying to work out, his gut always feeling that something was wrong. Now it all made sense.

"You had to involve LARA because you needed Annabel to get into the vault. Your eyes were not registered, and with Jayne dead, you couldn't use her eyes to get past the scanner. They wouldn't work after her demise, the veins would have altered shape. The priest got lucky with Thorn's eye. What was it? A saline chemical mix to preserve it?" For his own sanity, he wanted to know he'd guessed right. It was a pride thing, tying up loose ends.

"Yes, you are right; the retina scan was a problem. Thankfully Annabel survived the chateau and the attack in the Paris hotel. I'm afraid Leon and Klara get a little enthusiastic when performing their duties. They were supposed to target you only." She emphasised the last sentence and looked at Klara as her voice rose. Suitably rebuked, the younger woman looked away, appearing to sulk.

"We had Jayne's eyes, but they altered as soon as they removed them from her head and we ruined one of Colin's before we found the answer. We were able to produce a solution we were fairly certain would enable the retina to register, but we couldn't risk our entire operation on guesswork. To be on the safe side, I had to infiltrate LARA to ensure Annabel was protected until we opened the vault."

"Once we managed to tighten the leash on those two imbeciles that is, we ensured you had a safe passage to KVP." This time she glared at Klara.

"Now hang on one fucking minute, you cow!" Klara strutted towards Claudia and squared up to her.

"One, we were given instructions to destroy all evidence once we got the key and code from Chanteau. Secondly, we only needed the bitch's eyes as far as I was concerned." Claudia smacked Brandt's daughter around the face so hard it echoed within the cavern. It sounded like a firecracker exploding against the walls. She stumbled back in shock but had no time to recover, Claudia was on her again. This time she grabbed her by the scruff of the neck, pulling her in until they were nose to nose.

"If the pair of you made time to read your messages, even check in occasionally, you would have realised you were supposed to be part of a team. When are you two going to get it through your thick heads that you are not the new Bonnie and Clyde. You would have seen that orders can change during an operation. Do you think I enjoy being here as your father's babysitter?" Klara snapped her arms up, ripping the hands away from her collar, backing away breathing heavily, the hatred in her eyes burned like flames.

"God help the New World with your lot in charge." Jack said looking at Riggs who hadn't taken his eyes off him since he'd given him the signal, any minute now.

Claudia Robertson turned to him and raised her weapon aiming at his head.

"Well, it's a pity you will not…" She didn't finish her threat as a bullet passed through the left side of her head taking the right side with it. Globules of flesh and blood splattered into the face of the gunman positioned at the northeast exit. The one they needed for their escape.

"Bitch!" Klara spat as she watched blood explode from Claudia's head.

Everything then moved at an astonishing pace as the corpse landed on Jack, pushing him backwards.

"Now!" He shouted as he pulled Annabel back with him. Riggs pulled Oberlin and Bircher back at the same time, taking cover behind the beam. Jack pushed the button on his PDA.

The explosion ripped through the cavern. Six soldiers were disabled instantly. The guard stationed by their commandeered bags lost both legs as the blast from the explosive pack cut through him. Flying debris wiped out two others, one collapsing unconscious on top of Klara, pinning her to the floor. He had managed to prise the gun from Claudia's dead hand the moment she had fallen on him. He used it to down two more who collapsed on top of each other. He shot at the last one standing, missing by inches, as he disappeared through the main entrance taking Klara with him.

"Come on, let's go!" He grabbed Annabel and pulled her through the exit. Riggs and their Swiss colleagues following close behind.

"What's the plan, Batman?" Riggs shouted to the front.

"Figuring out how to get out of here!" Jack shouted back.

"We need to get into the main passage so we can see the exit. My guess is they'll be waiting for us."

Armed with one handgun and two Kalashnikovs, the group huddled at the end of the junction between the northwest passage and the main tunnel. They had lost their helmets leaving them reliant on the two Maglites held by the LARA agents.

Jack checked his PDA which displayed a dead signal, they were too deep into the mine.

"See anything?" Riggs whispered.

"No, I can't. Wait here." He left them behind as he entered the main corridor. His recollection of the map told him there was a passage to his right, another on his left, and one further ahead, near the exit. He moved forward at a crouch holding the Ak47 in front of him, ready to fire. The darkness closed in on him as he felt his way along the walls. He tried squinting in search of the smallest light, leaving the torch in his pocket for fear of discovery. Without warning, the corridor was bathed in light and automatic fire filled the air. He dived into the nearest passage as bullets fizzed past his ears, showering him in stone chips.

"Jack!" Annabel screamed.

"I'm OK! Stay where you are!" He shouted back in between bursts of gunfire.

Annabel screamed as more shots resonated from the northeast, Riggs was returning fire as hostiles rushed at them from the cavern. More gunfire erupted further along the corridor, filling the air with stone and dust.

Annabel screamed again. Unable to control her fear, she leapt from her hiding place and ran deeper into the mine. She had to get away from death and destruction.

"Annabel, no! Come back … it's a dead end." Jack sent several shots towards the light, causing their attackers to dive for cover. It gave him enough time to double back and get to the northeast corridor, reaching it just in time as a volley of bullets rattled the walls above his head.

He positioned himself back to back with Riggs. They faced towards the cavern, covering all exits.

"Where are the others?" Although he already knew the answer.

"I dunno." Riggs turned, surprised to see only Jack behind him.

Oberlin and Bircher had gone after Annabel. Swearing under his breath he knew they had to follow them. They had one AK 47, nearly out of ammo, a handgun and no light source. They were sitting ducks.

"We're going after them aren't we?" His resigned tone told Jack he was ready.

"Yep… after three?" He asked.

"After three." Riggs confirmed.

"THREE!" Jack shouted and disappeared. Riggs waited for the gunfire to die down, mentally tracking Jack as he fled into the mine. Bracing himself, he leapt into the corridor, his finger on the trigger, pumping bullets towards the light as he backtracked after the others. Darkness began to envelop him as the firing stopped. Keeping the dim light behind him he turned, walking gingerly in the pitch black, feeling along the walls for any openings. He resisted calling out, in case he gave away his position. He was now in total darkness. He had to risk his torch, pulling it from his top pocket. He felt along its shaft for the switch.

An arm grabbed him and pulled him into the void.

CHAPTER SIXTY-FIVE

Deep Concern

"Jesus Jack! I'm too young to have a heart attack." His heart began to slow as he composed himself.

"Come on." Ignoring the complaints, he pulled him into a passage a few yards ahead, grateful to see the light shining around Annabel, Oberlin and Bircher.

"What was that all about?" Riggs approached Annabel who sat on the floor with her back to the wall, her head rested on her knees.

She looked up at the American as he stood in front of her. Staring at him for several moments she tried to decide the best thing to say. She had no answer; she had just panicked and ran.

"I'm fed up with being shot at." She said finally, not the best answer she could have given, but true.

"Well, I hope you've bought a pick and shovel as it's the only way we can get out now without being shot at. How wide is this mountain Benny?" He looked at the Captain of ARD who was back to his focused self.

"Too wide." He said playing along with Riggs. He also found the woman's action an act of madness.

"Alright guys, what's done is done. We have to make the best of it and work out a way of getting out of here. Sergeant, what does the map say."

Bircher studied it and pointed to an area mark 'dig A'.

"This was the first dig made in the mine before they found the rich seam below. It's a deep cavern with two exits. I'm not sure if there are any alternate routes, but after the discovery earlier on, it wouldn't surprise me."

Stone chips rattled in the darkness behind them. Everyone stopped and turned towards the entrance. Time stood still as they collectively strained to listen, holding their breath for fear of detection. Instinctively, Riggs grabbed the torch and aimed it in the direction of the sound. The LED shone straight into the face of a gunman, crouched less than ten feet away. Dazzled by the beam flashing across his night vision glasses, he had no time to react as Jack sent two blasts into his chest. He fell back a few feet, twitching for a few seconds before laying still. Climbing over the corpse, Jack ripped the glasses from the dead man's face and put them on. It turned the cavern into a rich green haze of rock. Making his way to the edge of the passage, he risked a look along the corridor. It was empty. He looked north just in time to see a booted foot disappear into the passage ahead. It was the entrance to the very cavern they were heading to themselves. Not wanting to alarm the others, he entered the corridor and went after him. Bursts of gunfire forced him back, bad idea. He doubled back and joined the group; they looked up with concern.

"They're using the other entrance. Riggs get yourself over there, I'll cover from here."

"I'll go too." Oberlin offered, taking the torch from Riggs and passing the handgun to Bircher.

"You will need both hands to use the rifle effectively." He said to Riggs as they made their way towards the cavern.

"I'll light the way."

Jack left Bircher and Annabel with the remaining Maglite as he moved along the passage, being careful not to tread on the corpse.

The green hue produced a ghostly malevolence exemplified by the silence, broken only by his footfalls. It was too quiet, and it unnerved him, something was wrong. He heard a sound. It was distant to begin with, a tap, tap, tap getting closer and resonating off the walls. He stopped and readjusted the focus on his glasses, sharpening the area in front of him. He checked the walls, the floor and around his head. His ears strained to the sound as his brain tried to build an image of what he was hearing. Within seconds all became clear as three egg shapes bounced towards him, bright green in the lens of the glasses.

"Shit!" He turned, ran and leapt over the corpse in one go. He hurtled towards Annabel and Bircher, grabbing the woman before the Swiss officer could shout in alarm.

"Move! Let's go!" He pushed Annabel past Bircher before either had a chance to react. Self preservation pushed Bircher to his feet, and he followed closely behind. He still felt a little groggy, but he knew whatever had spooked Jack was behind him. He found his reserves.

The explosion sent the three of them flying forward, landing in a heap as a breeze of dust and stone passed over them.

"Get up! We need to keep moving." Jack pulled Annabel to her feet, Bircher could feel the reasons why through his body.

The floor was vibrating as rock connected to rock as the noise from the explosion died. It changed to a rumble as the earth moved around them. Within seconds the world fell in on them as rock tumbled from the ceiling. Soon small fragments dropped all around them. The sound grew louder as the entire passage caved in on itself collapsing along its length. It was chasing them, a tidal wave of rock and calcite. Jack saw the entrance to the cavern several yards ahead and pushed forward willing it to move closer. Rock fell from the ceiling accelerating towards them, the view through the night vision glasses now useless, a solid green wall of dust and rock. The ceiling gave way and collapsed to the floor. He dived forward hoping he was close enough to clear the passage. Closing his eyes, he sailed through the air waiting to be crushed by falling debris.

Like a cork from a bottle, Jack, Annabel and Bircher popped into the cavern. The expulsion of air as the tunnel collapsed propelled them along the hard rock floor for several yards. They came to a stop, lying still for several seconds, breathing harshly and coughing dust from their lungs.

"Glad you could make it." Jack raised his head to see Riggs sitting on a boulder shining the torch at them. He averted his eyes to avoid being blinded as he looked around the walls. They were on the upper level of a deep excavation, cut into a near perfect circle. The ceiling stretched thirty feet above them with the floor comprising of three ledges spanning the perimeter. The upper ledge ten feet wide, dropped five feet to the second level at fifteen feet, to the lower level of twenty feet. In the centre of the lower level was a bowl of rough-hewn rock where the excavation had ended.

"They blew the other entries too. We didn't even have time to cross the cavern. Damn near shit myself." Riggs, ever one for the literal explanation pointed the light at the far wall. Little dust clouds spiralled into the air, the remnants of another passage collapse.

"So we're trapped in here?" Annabel got to her feet and dusted herself down.

"Sure looks like it." Riggs said waving the torch around the perimeter. "No doors, no tunnels, just rock. Lots and lots of rock."

"Sergeant, are you OK?" He knelt beside Bircher who hadn't moved since they had fallen from the passage. Through his night glasses, the injured man's green face remained still, his eyes closed. He could see a slight movement from his nostrils, a sign he was still breathing. Annabel held the torch to the side of the sergeant's body as she knelt opposite.

"It might be a touch of concussion." She suggested feeling his brow which felt warm to the touch. "That guy hit him pretty hard."

"Stay with him." Jack said as he got to his feet and looked around. "We need to see if there is a way out of here."

He looked down into the base of the cavern.

"Come on Riggs, Captain Oberlin, let's see what we have down there."

Annabel sat with Bircher feeling useless. Had it not been for her stupidity they wouldn't be in this position. She thought to apologise yet again, but this time she knew Jack would have to admit it was her fault. She couldn't handle that right now. Taking off her jacket, she rolled it tightly and carefully placed it under Birchers head. He stirred slightly and coughed. In the dim light, she could see his eyes flicker open.

"What happened?" He whispered hoarsely, the dust scratched at his throat making him cough.

"Sshh …" She felt his forehead, warm but not hot. "The passage caved in. We're all fine. The others have gone below to see if they can get us out of here." He moved to get up, but the walls spun in the light of the small torch; he flopped back onto his makeshift pillow.

"Don't move just yet, let your strength return. There isn't a lot you can do at the moment." She wished she had water to soothe his throat as his coughing was laboured and harsh. They needed to get out of here soon as she was concerned for the man's health. In truth, she was concerned for all of them.

She was no expert on caves, but if all areas were blocked and sealed tight, the air she was breathing wouldn't last forever. Whether it was psychological or real, she found it harder to breathe now than a few minutes ago. Bircher coughed again, this time for longer, a dry wheeze followed by several gasps. He struggled to feed air back into his lungs. He needed medical attention.

"Nothing." Riggs reported as he climbed onto the uneven base of the cavern floor.

"Checked all around. Its solid rock, no cracks or crevices. How are you doing?"

Jack was crouched down, searching along the edge of the basin, feeling for air, looking for a fault. Moving inch by inch trying to find something, anything to give them some hope of escape.

"Same here." He replied as he straightened and tweaked his back, pulling out a knot or two that began to ache.

"Case! Over here." Oberlin crouched opposite, waving his zippo at an area underneath the lower ledge.

The two LARA agents stood by the ARD officer's shoulder, watching the flame flicker slightly.

"Listen." He said, anticipating Riggs would offer some wisecrack and miss his discovery.

They held their breath for a few seconds, cocking their heads towards the flame. They could hear trickling, faint but unmistakably water. With his night vision, Jack could see a tiny fissure in the wall. It was a thin crack running diagonally from the bottom of the lower ledge to the floor. He ran his finger along it, managing to fit his nail inside. Placing his ear against the stone, he blocked the other with his finger. It was definitely running water, quite faint but clear enough to hear there was a lot of it.

"It could be a stream." Oberlin offered as Jack pulled his head away from the gap.

"Mountains develop veins through the years, either through natural subsidence, rock falls or faults. There are glacial streams at the base of most mountains where extreme temperatures result. But it could be quite a distance below, it is difficult to tell."

"Perhaps we could blast through to it." Jack suggested.

"Oh sure, I'll go fetch the dynamite, you set up the detonators. Come on Jack, we're stuck here with two rifles, a handgun and two Maglites. I doubt if we can shoot our way out."

"No, but these might help." He produced two pearl grenades from the inside of his jacket.

"Holy shit!" Riggs shouted. "Where did they come from?"

"I never leave home without them."

He had refused the inner fleece jacket back at the hotel in favour of his leather. It was the tool of his trade, he literally never left home without it. For years now it fitted like a glove. Even when equipped with pearl grenades, Kabar knife, extra clips for his Glock and PDA, the weight was comfortable. It made him feel complete.

He positioned the pearls along the fissure. Placing one on the floor and the other just below the lower ledge, he thrust his Kabar up to the hilt into the crack. He then lay on the top level aiming directly at the higher pearl through the viewfinder of the AK47.

Riggs and Oberlin lifted Bircher to the back of the cavern, moving as far away from the blast as possible. Placing their injured comrade with Annabel against the wall, the two men crouched over them. She could not believe that they were using their bodies as shields to protect them from the blast. If they ever escaped this, Annabel would never forget this act of bravery. It showed her that throughout it all, chivalry was definitely not dead.

"Ready?" He shouted from across the other side of the cavern.

"Ready!" Riggs closed his eyes tightly, waiting for the blast.

Jack lined his sights and placed his finger on the trigger squeezing gently. Careful to keep his aim steady, aware he would need to move away swiftly or risk blinding from the flashback, he pressed home the trigger.

Rolling back he covered his head as the explosion rocked the cavern. With a twenty-five foot clearance, the blast should fall short, hopefully not bringing the roof down on top of them. As the explosion rumbled on, he looked up at the ceiling ready to move if it started dropping chunks of rock. He watched as it appeared to bounce, puffing out layers of dust and tiny shingles of stone and calcite. Nothing more substantial than a pebble rained onto the floor, trickling to an odd tap as the last of the remnants fell.

"Everyone OK?" He shouted across, as the ringing in his ears stopped.

"Yeah, we're fine." Riggs shouted back, surprised they had escaped unscathed.

Rolling onto his front Jack looked down the fifteen feet to the blast zone. As the dust thinned, he could see the fissure had now grown into a hole around four feet in diameter, enough to take a man. He thought he could hear running water and climbed down the three levels to investigate. The grenades had been successful. A yard inside the gaping hole, part of the floor had caved in, and water rushed past, heading south. Both openings could fit a body through, and the vein of water also seemed wide enough. The problem was, where did it end and would it lead to an escape route?

Climbing back to the upper level he joined the others and checked the map, taking a calculated guess on the distance to the main exit

"It's about a hundred and fifty metres to the exit…" A rough estimate, but close.

"… And a further sixty metres at least, to the Rhein, it's the only place it can escape to." Oberlin added.

CHAPTER SIXTY-SIX
Flight

"Are you sure about this?" He was standing next to the excavation, water splashing along the vein below, sounding like a steady downpour. Cold air rushed into the cavern, chilling him as he watched Riggs adjust his wet suit.

"Hey, listen. I was high school swim champion and lifeguard during the holidays, a great way to hit on chicks by the way, and let's face it I am the most athletic." He patted Jack's stomach to emphasise his slimmer frame, which he reluctantly had to concede.

"Remember Riggs, the vein may close to a trickle on its course, it will trap you if that happens. It will be an impossible climb back to us." Oberlin admired the way the American immediately volunteered to recon the stream. But he also knew it was an act of madness, with no way of knowing what he would find.

"Chill Benny, I'll be out of here in no time. I'll have a cold beer waiting for you at the bottom." Riggs had no idea if this would end in disaster, but if he didn't try, they would all die anyway. He knew the risks when he accepted this job and had cheated death several times already. So, he would either succeed, or it was his time. It didn't stop the feeling of trepidation rippling through his gut, twisting it into knots at the thought. He decided it was better to go for it and let the adrenalin take over.

Jack handed him the earpiece.

"Use this when you get out." The signal would be weak, but it should carry, he hoped.

"And take this with you." He handed him a small flip style mobile phone.

"What's this?" He flipped it on, looking at the screen, there was no signal.

"It's Jayne… I mean Claudia's phone. I took it from her pocket when she fell on me. Get Sara to check out the calls, it might tell us where we can find Brandt." He put it into the waterproof bag with the earpiece and thrust it into his wetsuit before zipping it up to his neck.

"Right, well it's been a blast!" Riggs turned from them and eased himself through the floor towards the water below.

It was a yard to the base of the stream, and he was careful to straddle it by placing both feet on either side of the vein wall. It was relatively dry providing some grip. Placing the torch between his teeth he lowered himself into the water.

Jack watched him disappear from view.

It was freezing, and the cacophony of water deafened him as it swept over his shoulders, battling to brush past this new obstruction. It seeped into his suit taking longer than usual to warm to body temperature. Bracing himself, he tried to put air back into his lungs as the icy stream fought to take it away. He eased himself forward using his feet as anchors and his hands for rudders. The light from his torch sparkled through the water as it cascaded into the black void ahead.

Five minutes passed, and he felt as if he had made short work of his descent. His feet were getting sore, as sharp rock fragments battered them. Worse still, claustrophobia strangled him, bringing panicked thoughts of a watery grave. Dark images played with his mind telling him at any minute the vein would narrow, trapping him.

He would be unable to move, waiting for death to take him, the iced water keeping his body perfectly preserved for discovery in a hundred year's time! His right foot slipped, causing his left to buckle as it took his full weight. He just managed to pull it away, preventing it from wrapping around his neck as he let the stream carry him down. He hurtled along like a tobogganist, his body sweeping from side to side as the water took him through the meandering vein. Rock bit into his thighs and elbows as he kept his arms by his side. He was afraid they would break if he attempted to use them to slow down.

The vein dropped a few feet, sending his body crashing to a new level of rock. The torch flew from his mouth, abandoned far behind as he picked up speed.

He crossed his arms, gripping each shoulder and held on tight, hoping for the best. He had lost all feeling in his back as the carpet of water swept him on. His skin could have been torn off by the rocks for all he knew. He watched the ceiling sparkle like tiny stars in a clear night, followed by the grey slate of the rock as he shot by. The vein started to take shape, grey stone and calcite of different colours flashed by him.

He was showered in light. He closed his eyes against the burn of daylight as he flew through the air. He hit the water feet first, the icy blast covered his head sending him down into a new weightless sensation.

His lungs filled with water causing him to cough, but with no way of taking in oxygen. His brain registered he could move his arms, he spread them wide grateful of the release. Sweeping them down, he felt his body rise. Self preservation told him he needed to do this to be able to breathe again. He broke the surface gasping in huge gulps of air before sinking back and taking in more water. Coughing and gasping he waded towards a bank of moss and foliage.

Riggs pulled himself clear of the water and collapsed on his front. Resting his head on welcome dry land, he closed his eyes.

Carrying two waterproof bags full of water and Riggs' fleece soaked from the stream, Jack approached Annabel and Bircher. The Sergeant was sitting up and talking as he approached.

"How are you feeling?" He asked, tearing the corner off the bag and tipping the makeshift carafe into Bircher's mouth.

"I'm fine." His dry throat was now easing. "Slight concussion I would have thought." He got to his feet and steadied himself on the wall. He stared through the blast hole and sighed.

"So we have found an escape route?" The thought of the freezing water filled Bircher with dread but escaping would definitely compensate.

"I'm not sure if it is an escape route. I'm waiting for something back from Riggs."

"We have another problem." Oberlin climbed back from the base and joined them.

"We all have wetsuits under our clothing apart from this young lady." He pointed to Annabel.

"Depending on the time it takes to get down, she could become a hyperthermic before we reach the end."

He hadn't thought of that. It would soak her cotton trousers, woollen jumper and ski jacket within a few feet and she would freeze a few yards later.

His receiver crackled. Putting his finger to the earpiece, he pushed it further into his ear.

"Ja... I'm out... the drop... all clear... final... river..." Even though faint and breaking up Jack knew it was from Riggs. He strained to hear as he repeated the message.

"... ack... out.... only one... op... the vein is... ear... watch... drop... er." It was useless, the signal was too weak... but at least he knew Riggs had got out.

"That was Riggs. He's out." Noticeably buoyed they all got to their feet and prepared themselves.

"We have one problem." He said beginning to disrobe. "If you wouldn't mind turning around Annabel?" He said as she watched him in the dim light of the remaining Maglite.

"Why?... Oh... yes of course!" She swiftly turned her back to him as he pulled his fatigues down from his waist.

Ten minutes later Annabel had changed into his warm but baggy wetsuit. It clung to her skin underneath her clothing, crumpling up in certain places. She convinced herself, although uncomfortable, it was necessary. Jack would risk his thick insulated fatigues and his leather under his ski jacket to protect him.

Oberlin and Bircher went first. They chose to travel in tandem with Oberlin at the front as a brake, Bircher with his feet placed firmly on his shoulders, acting as a breakwater behind.

Giving them five minutes head start, Jack climbed in and waited while Annabel fitted gingerly behind him. She squealed as the icy water crashed around her head. Jack's legs were already numb as they started their steady descent.

"Jack, I'm out. Watch the drop half way down, hurts like fuck but it's all clear to the end. Just watch the final drop into the river; it's a doozy." Riggs repeated it again and again, a dozen times, hoping they had heard him. He assumed if he hadn't called within an hour, Jack would make his own decisions anyway. He just had to wait and watch the tiny waterfall from his vantage point, keeping his fingers crossed that it would spit people out eventually.

CHAPTER SIXTY-SEVEN
Baiting

They sat on the bank beside the Rhein, sipping hot coffee, wrapped in blankets supplied by the 12th Mountain infantry. They had found them thanks to Bircher. He had organised a river squad to look for hostiles appearing from the base of the mountain, somewhere between Felsberg and Tamin. What they hadn't anticipated was the sight of bodies flying clear of the mountains through a waterfall.

"That is something I certainly don't want to experience again anytime soon." Annabel uttered through chattering teeth.

"You and me both." Jack agreed, just beginning to feel his legs again.

The ride had been bumpy, the drop halfway down a painful shock to the system. But they had escaped relatively unscathed.

Bircher had taken a turn for the worse. He was being tended by a medic who had radioed for a chopper to get him to a hospital. Concussion was definitely the diagnosis but a few day's rest would see him back on his feet.

The sound of gunfire from above indicated a fierce battle raging up on the mountain. Information from the infantry told of hundreds of soldiers deployed around the entrance to the mine. Armoured transporters and attack helicopters circled the surrounding area. Explosions could be heard all along the trail. The 70th and 12th infantries were fully deployed and battled forces of the Order, from the entrance of the mine along the descending trails. Reinforcements from British and American troops were on their way from local bases. They would finish it here.

They were out of range and covered by the heavy concentration of trees, but Jack needed to keep moving. He was happy to leave the containment of the Brandt girl and her cronies to the armed forces; he needed to get to the source.

"Any luck with the mobile phone?" He asked Riggs, who was out of his wetsuit and into Swiss army fatigues.

"Sara has it, she knows how urgent it is, and she is confident of getting a fix." He checked his PDA for any messages.

"Fuck that!" He said removing his PDA from the waterproof pack.

"Sara, Jack... what news on the mobile?" It was a frantic request and one she knew needed urgent attention. She gave him what she had so far.

"We have traced several calls to Paris, Switzerland and some to New York, but there are a couple we can't get an effective fix on. It appears to be wavering around the Americas and Asia Jack, I think it's somewhere in the Pacific Ocean, but we can't get a firm trace."

Jack thought a moment, looking at the thirteen digits in question displayed on Claudia's mobile.

"Right set a trace now... I'm dialling it. Send the location to the PDA." He listened to the ring tone as he waited for an answer.

The voice he heard was deep and controlled, with a slight Germanic tinge.

"Darling, did it all go well?" The voice could barely contain his excitement.

"Not quite sweetheart, in fact, I would say it's gone a bit tits up!" He relished the silence. He could imagine Brandt's shock and anger at the man who had dared to speak to him in such a way.

"Now, come on Brandt. All the world's greatest dictators have a rant or two in their locker when the chips are down." He waited for a response, this time holding the mobile in the air towards the sound of gunfire and explosions.

"Hear that? Phase one of your master plan going up in flames. Now that's gotta hurt."

"Mr Case." Finally an answer, controlled and calm.

"You have turned out to be a stubborn thorn in my side. I congratulate you on your ability to stay alive. In different circumstances, I could use a man like you." Jack smiled.

"Well, I would imagine you might need a new head of security" after his hand was nearly blown off by our highly trained housewife!" He shouldn't, but he was enjoying this. He knew if he continued, he could get the man riled, but his aim was to get a signal and hearing the bleep on his PDA, he had, he could now cut the call.

"We're on our way Brandt, put the kettle on."

"Oh, I look forward to our meeting. But I'm afraid by the time you get to me the world will be a different place. You are too late to find all of our planes, and yes I know about London, disappointing but a mere trifle. Believe me Mr Case, we have several contingencies in place, and my people will rise up after the first plane delivers its payload. Fear us, Mr Case, as your time will come." The phone went dead.

He checked the PDA; they had set coordinates, a blinking light in the middle of the Pacific ocean.

"Can you get us out of here and on our way Sara?"

"We have a Chinook on its way, Jack. It will take you to Mollis where a transporter will be waiting for you. We'll take care of Annabel until you get back. Out."

He went to Captain Oberlin.

"Captain, thank you for your help. Without you, we would never have got out of KVP alive." He shook his hand warmly.

"And I thank you, Mr Case, for helping us uncover the underground of evil growing in our country. We will take steps to eradicate it immediately." He returned the handshake with a stiff bow of salute.

Riggs approached and extended his hand to the Captain.

"Thank you, Benny, it's been a blast."

An awkward standoff ensued as they both stared at each other. Different worlds and ideals stood between the two men, who had spent the last few days fighting for the same cause in their own distinct way.

Riggs would generally have a wisecrack or two to break the silence, but the look on Oberlin's face stopped him. He was struggling inwardly to find the right words where none would come. Then he smiled, a warm, friendly smile which looked totally out of place on the young Swiss Captain. He approached Riggs and hugged him, slapping his back.

"Goodbye my friend, that was a brave thing to do. You saved our lives." Riggs held on, not knowing how to react. His eyes began to mist as he realised this was a genuine attempt at affection from a man who found it difficult to smile, let alone hug. He sniffed and spoke softly into the Captain's ear.

"Don't mention it, Benzli. You did your bit at KVP. Saved all of our arses."

Captain Oberlin pulled away and held Riggs by the shoulders. He returned to his usual stern, austere self, staring into his eyes for several seconds.

Finally, he opened his mouth to speak.

"Call me Benny."

He broke into a smile, laughing to himself as he walked away.

CHAPTER SIXTY-EIGHT
New Coordinates

The giant Chinook set down near the tiny hangar of Mollis airport. A disused military airbase set between a range of mountains to the south of the ski resort. As tourism soared, the government moved the base 100 kilometres away from prying eyes.

The twin-prop remained active as the passengers disembarked, heads bowed to combat the heavy downdraft. Medics rushed in and carefully lifted Bircher into an ambulance. The helicopter took to the skies, while the ambulance rushed to the local hospital.

Jack, Annabel and Riggs watched as a limousine approached through the ramshackle service bays, parking a few yards ahead of them. The doors opened, and two men left the vehicle, both smartly dressed and instantly recognisable.

"Dad!" Annabel ran across the tarmac and met Major Paxton halfway as he ran to meet her. Taking her in his arms she buried her head in his neck. He stroked her hair as she sobbed, her body shaking as she let her emotions flood out.

The other man, ignoring the emotional reunion, walked towards the two LARA agents.

"Jack, Tony everything OK?" Ed Ryker's concern was their fitness to continue the mission. It was paramount.

"We're fine, sir." He delivered a formal response, aware Riggs was with him.

"You took a risk making that call Jack. But it looks like we were lucky."

"We had to locate the bastard, sir. The only way to stop this is to stop it at the source. We'll find him."

"We have a Hercules due within the hour. Let's get you cleaned up, kitted out, and you can be on your way."

After changing into dry clothes, the agents joined the others for a light meal. Jack's leather jacket was still damp, so he hung it on a chair to give it a chance to dry a little more. He helped himself to the ham and eggs on offer and joined the others at the table.

"Jack, I haven't had a chance to thank you for looking after my daughter." The Major was around the table in a flash. He had just enough time to place his plate down before his hand was grabbed in a vice-like grip and shaken vigorously.

"No problem Major, she did pretty well herself." He looked over to Annabel who sat quietly, head lowered, toying with a plate of pasta. She seemed to have had the stuffing knocked out of her. He sat opposite as the Major returned to his seat.

"Well, it's a rum business and no mistake." The Major continued to dominate the conversation as they ate.

"Who'd have thought Jayne Langfield wasn't Jayne Langfield after all, but her sister! It's amazing she got away with it for so long. She even fooled you didn't she Ed?" He shovelled several slices of ham in his mouth and chewed noisily as he stared over at the LARA chief, waiting for his answer.

"Either by design or through careful manipulation, Claudia became a recruit to the detriment of her real family. Brandt and the organisation before him had planned well. All IDs and background information well prepared, it allowed detection near on impossible. Take the Brigadier for instance. We can trace him back to his birth, and yet we now know he was not who he claimed to be. He was born as Thorn, but his father was Gerd Haas. Through indoctrination and God knows what else, he became a disciple for this Future World, New World Order, Fourth Reich or whatever it is they want to call themselves." Ryker had to admit that they had deceived LARA, despite their technology, they had failed to uncover the deception.

"It would appear the catalyst was the death of Gloria Barth. Whether a coincidence or a strategy built around her estimated life span, as soon as she passed away, they pressed 'go' button. That was when they discovered a problem."

"My Colin…" Annabel joined the conversation. " So it was the real

Jayne Langfield who appointed the practice to manage the estate. She then realised there was something wrong." She was beginning to piece it all together.

"Exactly…" Ryker agreed.

"We assume that Jayne Langfield was killed shortly before Colin died. It was the real Jayne who visited KVP along with him, to create the initial retina signature several months before. Jayne escaped from her husband's clutches before the death of her mother, risking everything to see her until it became too dangerous. After her sister's death, Claudia resurrected Jayne to gather the information they needed to put their plan in motion." It was still sketchy, but enough for them to base a lot of the assumptions on fact.

"So the Jayne Langfield Colin left the house for that day was Claudia?" Annabel said, trying to understand.

"Yes, but we must assume there was never going to be a meeting. They needed to lure Colin from the house so they could get to him and make it look like an opportunist robbery. From what we now know from the Brigadier, he should not have met his death. They simply wanted the code, unaware of the retinal scan at the time. The intention wasn't to kill him, it was to gather information. The gunman miscalculated the shot, panicked and ransacked the house to find the code. That was when your father contacted LARA, and everything began to go wrong for them."

"Wait, what about Eliza Winch and Derek Gant? They had nothing to do with this." Annabel pushed her plate away failing to build an appetite, however much she played with it.

"Derek was also killed for the code." Jack took up the story. "He was coming from the bank when he was attacked. Again, they used the same poison to disable him. My guess is he either caught sight of the attackers or had enough to identify them should he remain alive. Eliza was due to meet us on our way back from Oxford. She had come across something important relating to the Barth case. We can only assume it would have pointed us in the direction of the New World Order, so they had to stop her."

Annabel lowered her head, thinking of the devastation inflicted on her beautiful village.

"The rest we know." Jack summarised the story so far.

"It became apparent that the only person remaining who could open the vault was Annabel. So the elaborate plan to bring Jayne Langfield back from the dead was more important than ever. What they didn't count on was the devil child Klara and her psycho boyfriend Leon Ubermann. Before Brandt was aware of the need for living eyes to get past the scanner, he wanted to tidy up any loose ends. Annabel's kidnap was meant to draw me to them to gather the code before blowing up the chateau, making that the end of it."

"Realising Brandt needed to keep Annabel alive, he sent word to Klara and her sidekick. But they had gone rogue, failing to pick up messages or report in. The blood lust was too strong for them to deviate from their initial instructions. It forced Claudia to pose as Jayne, allowing her to infiltrate LARA to help safeguard Annabel. Brandt could see no other way of protecting her from Klara and Ubermann, they were a law unto themselves. The rest, as they say, is history."

"They are a disorganised mess at the moment, with a man at the helm consumed with the need for power. His lieutenants have failed him by being hell bent on death and destruction. It has now put the whole operation on a critical path as, like a wounded animal, they are more dangerous than ever. We have to finish it now."

Ryker looked towards Jack for the confirmation that his man was still up for the job. The questioning look from the LARA chief was acknowledged by a nod; he was ready and willing.

Towards the end of their meal, the steady drone of an aircraft drifted through the restaurant. He recognised the sound of a Hercules coming in to land.

Their transport to the Pacific had arrived.

Annabel watched the giant aircraft lift into the skies. Its four propellers cut through the air, throwing vapours over its wings as it moved away from Mollis. She stared transfixed as it continued to climb, getting smaller by the second, until it disappeared into a grey blanket of cloud.

She feared she had seen the last of him. Her vulnerability returned, knowing he was no longer nearby.

She would find it impossible to trust anyone again after her experiences of the past few weeks. The deception by Claudia Robertson, posing as Jayne Langfield, was still fresh in her mind.

They were having coffee after a few hours of shopping, acting like tourists. Giggling at some outfits they tried on, enjoying each others company. They had even arranged weekends together once they got home. Annabel felt sure she had found a new friend, one who would fit within her circle. She was horrified when she felt a gun thrust into her side as they moved away from the cafe.

She was bundled into a military vehicle, amongst a group of heavily armed soldiers. She was then told by her 'friend' that she would have her fingers broken if she cried out. She had no idea what had happened to their protection detail. They had just disappeared. She suspected that they had ended up like so many others during this conflict. What was happening to the world? It was beyond comprehension that any one person could try to take it for his own. Yet, here she was, watching a man fly away to stop that very thing from happening.

"He'll get him you know." Annabel jumped as Ed Ryker appeared by her side.

"Jack is our best agent and a man like no other. He does the job his own way, but he always gets it done. I wouldn't worry about him, he will be back." He looked skywards and hoped he was right. He never doubted Jack, or he had never had to before. But before all of this started, before the murders in the village, Jack had voiced concerns. He was tired, feeling burnt out. Ryker had a feeling this would either be the resurgence of Jack Case or heaven forbid, his last mission.

"Come on, Annabel, let's get you and your father back to LARA HQ. You can relax until this is all over; Sara is keen to meet you."

The limousine passed through the airfield, taking the mountain roads as it made its way out of Switzerland.

CHAPTER SIXTY-NINE
Long Journey ahead

Commander Ryan Campbell handed the aerial photographs to the LARA agents. They sat together on the webbed seats, against the fuselage walls of the Hercules, the seats swayed matching the pitch and yaw of the aircraft. It wasn't the most comfortable seat but offered a smoother ride.

"After several reconnaissance flights over your grid references we came up with these."

The images showed an island covered with vegetation. A jagged oval with two small stretches of sandy beach to the north and south. There was a natural rock formation dominating the east-west perimeters, dividing the island in two as it traversed its centre.

"Known as Atra Island, it was once protected, used to conserve and study some rarer wildlife and flora of the Pacific. The island is the home of Nenes and Hawksbill turtles mainly. But around ten years ago research ceased as migration took them away. The BEE corporation funded it."

"So Brandt took possession of the island." Jack studied the different images.

"It was abandoned" Campbell explained.

"An uninhabited island in the northeast quadrant of the Pacific, with no real ECO or financial interest. Brandt made a case for continuing the research, maintaining an ecological strategy. He vowed to preserve the land in its natural state. The US and Republic of the Marshall Islands, with the help of a 100 million dollar donation approved it."

"So technically, he owns it." He took the nod from Campbell as affirmative.

"Well, that's good news at least." They both looked at Riggs.

"We won't upset any country in particular when we blow it out of the water."

He studied one of the close-up images, noticing something within a clearing. The image blurred of any detail but looked out of place amongst the natural features. Along the centre of the southern edge of the rock formation, cutting a swathe through the island, was a strip of white, a few yards long. It started from the east, curving out slightly before disappearing to the west.

"Any ideas of what this is?" Jack moved it closer to focus better before moving it away again to get a perspective.

"Yes, it's a building cut into the rock." He took the photographs from him, rifling through them until he found what he was looking for. He handed them back with the selected image on top.

"This is the best we could get without bringing too much attention to ourselves."

He was looking at an angled shot taken as the spotter plane was performing a turn. It clearly showed a wall of glass, curving out from the rock face. Obscured by a well placed grove of palms and fauna, he was able to make out the blurred edge of a swimming pool.

"It looks like we have Brandt's island hideaway." He felt a rush of exhilaration; they were in the right place.

"That's not all, take a look at the next two shots. It is why NATO felt you might need some help."

Jack flipped to the next shot. Again at an angle, it was off the east side of the island. Along the promontory of rock was a dense cluster of trees and fern growing close to the water's edge. A darker area of shading within the covering appeared to show what looked like an opening. Squinting to get a better perspective, he saw the unmistakable shape of the bow of a boat, the tiny dark circle above it made him look at the Commander.

"Is that a gunboat?" The circle above the bow could only be a gun barrel.

"Sure is. It's a corvette by the shape of the front, which means he has surface-to-air and underwater warfare weapons at his disposal. Something you wouldn't have on an island paradise unless you were planning on using it as a military base. Which brings me to the last shot, take a look at this." Campbell nodded at the photographs, prompting him to turn to the next picture. It was of the north side, zooming in on a clearing among the foliage. Unnoticeable from a distance, the zoomed image showed camouflaged canopies. The green tones perfectly blended with the tree cover. Black shapes dotted around its edge and squinting, he could make out several figures.

"Soldiers?" He again made his own assumption.

"Exactly, and a lot of them. The spotter picked out many instances of what were clearly military exercises. He's got a whole army on there."

"And I'm guessing, four nuclear warheads." He kept a bird's eye snap of the island. Shuffling the rest into a neat pile, he handed them back.

Commander Campbell left his seat.

"It's a long journey, another sixteen hours. Come and join us when you are ready or use one of the litters if you want to get your head down for a while. They are more comfortable than they look." He left them, joining his team towards the front of the cargo bay

They had fitted twenty airline seats behind the flight deck for the journey. Eight stretchers fixed into the centre of the compartment gave the men a chance to rest if they preferred.

They had been joined on board by a special forces Bravo team, code named Echo. NATO had assigned Commander Ryan Campbell and his team of 12 commandos to provide LARA with the support needed to finish the job. Although he preferred working alone or at most with a trusted partner like Riggs, looking at the photographs, he was happy to have them along.

Riggs exaggerated a yawn and stretched his arms high above his head.

"I think I'll get my head down." He walked to the nearest litter and turned back the covers. Belting himself in and pulling a blanket over his chest, he sank into the pillow closing his eyes.

The steady drone of the Hercules hummed a melody that swirled around his ears and bringing sleep to him in an instant. Jack joined the task force choosing to sit next to Dregs, a beast of a man who was sleeping soundly. His head was slumped onto his chest, rising and falling in rhythm with his deep breaths. Staring at the photograph, he studied the perimeter. He worked each area millimetre by millimetre, searching for the best way to approach unobserved.

With miles of open water in all directions clearly, there were none at all.

CHAPTER SEVENTY
D Day

Anatoly Duranichev and his two technicians Saval and Dimitri worked in silence in the subterranean island laboratory.

They stared transfixed through the viewing window of the hermetically sealed cell, as the robotic arm positioned the warhead against the bomb casing. Anatoly checked the condition of both the room and the bomb on three screens. He carefully monitored for fluctuations in heat radiation and static. Any rise on any screen could cause a chain reaction, which would mean trouble.

Saval controlled the arm using a tiny joystick at his console, careful to ensure smooth movement as the warhead moved ever closer to the casing. Dimitri looked on, poised at his station waiting for the connection. Both halves of the bomb contained a subcritical mass of uranium 235. Once connected, it was a detonation away from nuclear fission, causing an explosion far deadlier than Hiroshima.

He positioned the warhead carefully, sending it into the housing until a ping from the console registered connection. Pushing the button on top of the joystick caused the jaws to twist a few millimetres as it screwed the warhead home. It clicked into place. Moving the arm away from the completed bomb, Dimitri took the next procedure over. At his console he controlled the two arms gripping the bomb casing in place to accept the warhead. Pressing a switch, he watched as the floor split open to reveal an underground track. The unmanned combat aerial vehicle, a small craft, eight foot long with wings retracted into its body, was positioned directly below the opening.

Dimitri moved the controls forward, lowering the bomb past the open floor until it rested on the back of the waiting craft. Four small clamps appeared from its body, gripping the missile in place. Once it was secure, it disappeared with its payload. Another craft moved into position awaiting its delivery. The floor slid back into place as Dimitri grabbed another bomb casing from the holding pen. He repeated the painstaking operation of placing it ready for Saval to position another warhead.

The intercom came to life at Anatoly's console.

"Progress report?" Two simple words, barked by the unmistakable voice of Fabian Brandt.

"UCAV One is on its way to the launch tube." Short and sweet, the way Brandt preferred his reports.

"Good. How far away from completion?"

"I expect we will load all launch tubes within the next eight hours." The process took around ninety minutes, from preparing the bomb to the craft reaching its launch position. Adding additional time for errors or malfunctions, it was a reasonable conservative estimate.

"Excellent! Keep me informed." The intercom clicked ending the call, silencing the lab once more.

Anatoly returned to his monitors watching as the process began again.

Fabian Brandt moved away from the intercom and finished his vodka. Slamming his glass onto the veneer work surface, a slither of ice escaped. It slipped along the tabletop disappearing over the edge. It was elation, not anger that coursed through his body, an excitement he was finding hard to control. He was smiling; the day had come.

Jai, hearing the clatter on the desk, appeared from another room and rushed in to replenish his drink. Brandt waved him away, pushing himself back and rising from his seat.

"Set the fires burning Jai; I am in need of contemplation."

He bowed subserviently and left the room, his sandals slapping on the glass stairwell as he made his way to do his Master's bidding.

Everything was in place, and Brandt was feeling the excitement grow. His heart was fluttering, his skin tingling with expectation. It had been a lifelong quest, one started by his forefathers. They had left a legacy, for far too long driven underground and dismissed. They were foolish to discount the New World Order as nothing more than far right extremists, cultist obsessives or misguided fanatics. It had taken time, but he would show the world they had used the time well. Brandt was ready to rise up and take back a world that had belittled them, scorned them and attempted to crush them. Today the world would pay.

The console buzzed as a call came from somewhere in the complex.

"Brandt." He answered curtly as he was pulled from his reverie.

"You have a visitor." It was Leon Ubermann, unimpressed by Brandt's tone, responding with a bored monosyllabic tone of his own. "It's the bishop."

Brandt raised his eyes and smiled. He was earlier than expected, he must have it with him. Keeping his voice calm and being careful to keep his youthful exuberance at bay, he put the question to Leon.

"Has he brought anything with him?"

"A box, and by the way he was carrying it, I would say quite heavy. I sent him to the chapel."

"Excellent. Meet me there, you will want to see this." He cut the call and headed for the stairs.

CHAPTER SEVENTY-ONE
Coronation

Fabian Brandt resisted the urge to run along the marble corridor as he headed towards the three doors ahead of him. His heart was fluttering with excitement as he knew what he was about to see. Every detail had been planned meticulously to ensure the New World would be commemorated in such a way that it would never be forgotten. It would be known as the day of reckoning.

He pushed his fob against the reader and entered through the central door. It opened into a tunnel of natural granite, left untouched from the original hillside excavation. Crudely lit flames from ancient torches illuminated the stone flagstones leading the way to the chapel. The medieval passageway was precisely to his specification and in keeping with the room at the end.

He turned the large ring handle of the 14th century oaken door; the clack echoed through the corridor as it swung open. He moved forward a pace and let it slam shut.

Brandt was pleased with his creation. He spent a moment to take it all in, smelling the history, embracing the power. He stood in a rough-hewn cavern, the flagstone floor aged to add authenticity. Three backlit stained glass windows adorned the walls, creating the impression of the chapel bathed in the natural light of a summer day. Each window held the intricate designs important to the scriptures of the New World Order. The first, of the Madonna, her head bowed looking serenely at the child in her arms. The second, an image of the crucifixion, Christ looking down from the cross. The final, and most significant, was that of Charlemagne. He was Resplendent in the national dress of the Franks, red flowing gown adorned with jewels. The Imperial crown of the Holy Roman Empire sat imperiously on his head.

Dominating the centre of the floor sat a monolithic stone structure. Five steps ascended to a square throne of marble, an exact replica of the throne of Charlemagne. The two braziers burning either side caused it to shimmer, creating an aura, a sense of power.

Past three rows of wooden pews, to the rear, an altar of marble and gold glimmered in the light of the candles surrounding it on all sides. Standing prominently between various idols and images, stood the six foot golden statue of the sacred heart of Jesus.

Three life-sized portraits wholly covered the wall behind. They each emanated power and malevolence, an echo of their living persona.

To the left, Charlemagne in imperial red, holding the golden sword and orb in his hands. A flag of the quaternion eagle of the Holy Roman Empire hung imperiously above. In the centre, Kaiser Wilhelm the First in his highly decorated military uniform. A flag of black, white and red of the Second Reich hung above his head. To the right, Adolf Hitler in military brown, standing to attention in a perfect pose. The Nazi flag, blood red with the black swastika enclosed in a white circle, draped menacingly overhead.

It denoted the entire history of the New World Order. Brandt's eyes hovered over the display for several minutes as he envisaged his own image amongst his peers.

He lowered his gaze to the solitary figure dressed in black, kneeling before the altar in silent prayer. Brandt cleared his throat to announce his presence, annoyed that his initial entrance had not attracted his attention.

Bishop Marcel Donaretti crossed himself and backed away from the wooden crucifix. He was careful to concentrate on the image of Christ, ignoring all other pictures and insignia surrounding the altar. He turned and faced the man who had deliberately announced himself in a way designed to interrupt his prayer.

"Your Eminence, good to see you again." Brandt walked forward, taking hold of Donaretti's hand turning it palm down to expose the Amethyst ring. Kneeling on his left knee, he kissed the cold stone.

Bishop Donaretti, being the youngest bishop in office at 49, was uncomfortable with the genuflection. He preferred not to offer the ring, it was a sycophantic submission that was neither warranted or necessary. In his eyes, a modern opinion that had caused much consternation amongst his peers. He allowed Brandt's indulgence purely for the Church and the assurances they had given him.

"Fabian, good to see you and it is your Excellency if you insist on using an official address, as well you know." It wasn't the first time he had corrected him on the issue.

"But we all know your true vocation, and in a few days, you will no longer be in pectore. The Pontiff will reveal you as one of his most trusted cardinals and my chief advisor."

Even though he did not want to admit it, it was enticing. The thought of working within the Holy See, close to the Pontiff, allowed him to achieve his life's work many years ahead of schedule. As one of the few secret cardinals appointed by the Pontiff, he had a trust offered to very few in the Vatican. He was aware many saw him within the Holy See as a protege who needed to be watched. The speed of his elevation had put many on their guard, they had even excluded him from some gatherings.

"How is Rome?" Brandt now standing, studied the man in front of him as he prepared his answer. He was a young looking forty-nine with a smooth complexion and soft features, perfect for a man of the cloth. He wore black trousers with black clerical shirt open at the neck, preferring to remove his collar when not on official business. With his Latin features and neatly cut blue black hair, he was striking in appearance, a real lady killer.

"There is a divide within the Diocese of Rome." His deep soft voice belied his stature, and in the confines of the cavernous chapel, it echoed serenely in the air. "Many admit the Church has suffered over the past few years. Because of the scandals uncovered throughout the world, the faith of many is being tested. The opportunity of reform is attractive, but there are some who are concerned as to the real cost."

"And what of his Holiness?" Brandt searched the bishop's eyes for a reaction. This was why he was paid handsomely. He was a man with the ear of the head of the most powerful of all churches, a church who would lead the faith of the New World Order.

"The Holy Father is monitoring the situation and will act accordingly on the outcome." An excellent diplomatic response, Brandt had to concede, but it was not good enough.

"That is not quite the reaction I need your Excellency!" Using the title of his current office gave Donaretti no doubt Brandt needed answers.

"Fabian, all I can tell you is the Holy Father is aware that the Church requires reform. He is also aware his influence is waning, and an opportunity to rebuild the faith, returning the Church to its former glory is attractive. But he is not about to show any allegiance at this stage."

Brandt stood for a moment, pensive as he considered the bishop's answer. He needed Rome onside, and he had been meticulous in his recruitment of disillusioned clergy, with the help of Donaretti as the main protagonist. He was an ambitious young priest, enough of a zealot to be bought easily.

He smiled, accepting the answer for now.

"So, I believe you have a package for me?"

"I put it over there." Donaretti pointed to the throne.

Unable to contain himself, Brandt followed the bishop's gesture. He bounded up the steps to a leather box positioned on the seat. He released the clip and taking a deep breath, carefully raised the lid.

As he removed the object, it reflected the flames of the braziers, bathing the throne in a golden hue, mesmerising Brandt with its beauty. It was an octagonal shaped Crown, made of eight hinged plates rounded at the top, linked by strips of iron fixed by gold rivets to hold it together. Each plate was twenty-two carat, studded with pearls, sapphires, amethysts and emeralds, all were sparkling vividly in the moving light of the flames. Etched on the plates were scenes from the bible. Christ enthroned between two cherubim, the prophet Isaiah addressing King Hezekiah, King Solomon holding a scroll, and an image of King David. An arch of gold ran from front to back over the centre, holding a jewelled cross above at its centre.

Brandt raised it above his head and marvelled at the gems as they seemed to glow and sparkle from within.

He felt a tear escape his eyelid, gradually running down his cheek.

eventually dripping from his chin onto the floor.

"What have you got there?" Brandt, so wrapped in the aura of the spectacle in his hand, failed to notice Leon Ubermann enter the chapel.

His head of security looked up with curious fascination as he watched his future father-in-law stand transfixed. The way he held the crown in the air, unmoving, unblinking, he looked frozen in time.

"This Leon…" Brandt spoke without taking his eyes from his prize. "… Is the Imperial Crown of the Holy Roman Empire."

"The Crown of Charlemagne."

"How did you manage to get hold of that?" Leon knew of Brandt's acquisitions because he had been responsible for organising the shipment or installation of most.

The Sacred Heart of Jesus had been a particular challenge when removing it from the Church of the Sacred Mother in Verona. It had cost the life of the Pastor. He tried to intervene when his team of four had broken in at the dead of night, another occasion when Dolf Stollman had used his brawn rather than his brains. He chose to pummel the old man to death rather than restrain him.

Thankfully, the idiot is now feeding the fish at the bottom of the ocean. But the golden crown was something else. Solid gold and covered with every conceivable precious stone he could think of. Surely it would be missed?

"You can thank his Eminence for this" Brandt gestured to Donaretti, who bowed his head as he recalled his act of betrayal. Bishop Donaretti stood still for a moment before raising his eyes towards Ubermann.

"There are copies held at the Frankfurt Museum, during the renovation of the Hofburg in Vienna, Frankfurt sent a copy. We placed it in a temporary wing, storing the original in the vaults. Upon completion, they tasked me to take the copy back to Frankfurt. I was to return the original to prepare for the celebration of the crown's return in 90 days. Mr Brandt supplied the security team who transported the original back to Hofburg." Donaretti voiced regret at the betrayal of the Church, but it was a decision he had to make. He was struggling with his own demons, and on occasions, they won.

"They performed the switch, giving me the original crown along with an identical leather box full of lead. The box of lead is now in the vaults of the museum." His voice ended close to a whisper as he confessed. He knew that no amount of punishment would atone for his heinous act.

"So this is the original?" Ubermann was impressed.

"Of course it is the original!" Brandt spat. "And from tomorrow it will be mine by right. This magnificent piece is the reason for all of this." He waved his arms around the chapel.

"Almost seven billion people will be witness to the greatest day in history when the new Emperor of the Holy Roman Empire is crowned. We have to ensure we give them the greatest show on earth." He looked over to Donaretti. "Are you ready, your Eminence?"

Donaretti walked to the stone structure and climbed the steps towards Brandt, who had seated himself on the throne. He had placed the crown carefully on the floor beside him.

"Take a seat Leon and witness the coronation. After all, practice makes perfect."

Donaretti reached Brandt and looking into his eyes started to recite.

"Almighty everlasting God… your servant…."

Leon Ubermann stood passive as he stared at the man before him. He was fascinated by Brandt's face, a face now entirely under the spell of the bishop as he spoke the words of God. He felt the hairs rise on the back of his neck as he watched the ceremony unfold. As Bishop Donarreti placed the crown onto Brandt's head, he felt a sense of pride, of passion and with it, an excitement never felt before. It was going to happen.

They were about to take over the world.

CHAPTER SEVENTY-TWO
Strategy

The patrol boat cut engines allowing the waves of the Pacific Ocean to caress its hold, rising and falling in a rhythmic dance of nature.

Jack looked all around but saw nothing but darkness, hearing only the gentle splash of water as it pushed into the boat. The heavy cloud cover gave no quarter for the moon to glow, only a bright pool of mist high in the sky gave any indication it was even there at all.

"The island is about two klicks north of our current position. We will use the Zodiacs from here." Commander Campbell answered his questioning look as he passed, heading towards the bridge.

The Hercules had touched down two hours ago on the small runway at Majuro Airport, a strip of land along the narrow arm of Majuro Island. They joined up with a team of twelve navy seals, headed by Adam Strong. They had been waiting just offshore aboard two special operations patrol craft. They would transport them the rest of the way.

After seventeen hours on the plane and a further two hours on the boat, Jack felt fatigue trickle into his muscles. He hoped the sea air would clear his head a little, but the warm moist breeze of the early hours just added to his lethargy. The crew and most of the Echo team were preparing the rubber inflatables, as he followed the leader to the bridge, finding Campbell and Strong swapping notes.

He passed Riggs who was standing against the port side looking into the distance. The American leant forward as if he noticed something, stretching as far as he could while both hands gripped the handrail. He then released the contents of his stomach into the undulating ocean. He patted him on the back as he passed by.

"Get yourself ready Tony, we're leaving."

Riggs turned from his vantage point, clearing his throat. He slumped to the floor taking a swig from his water bottle, gasping as the refreshing drink eased his burning throat.

"God, I hate boats." He moaned and spun back to grab hold of the handrails as his stomach lurched and burbled, ready for a new attack.

Jack made his way to the small bridge of the special ops craft to find Campbell and Strong poring over an aerial shot of the island.

"We'll take the northwest." Strong pointed to a clearing where small oblong huts could be seen clearly from the blown up exposure.

"This is where the main concentration of military activity seems to stem from."

Commander Campbell studied the map, passing an eye over all quadrants. He stopped to explore the central area of concentration. He pointed to the eastern section of the island. It revealed a sheer wall of mountainous rock with a dark blemish rising a quarter of the way up from the ocean surface

"We'll circle to the east and take a closer look at this cave entrance where we believe there is a gunboat. Whatever it is we will immobilise it and see if we can land on the island from there."

Noticing him arrive, Campbell brought him into the conversation.

"Jack, you'll go with Dregs, Digger and Leggit in the CRRC, they'll get you to the south beach. They're a good lethal force team, I have a feeling you might need them."

"Sure, that's fine." He wasn't about to turn down three good men. "Set your receivers to 19600 so we can patch you in to Sara. She's on point for this operation and can monitor aggressor movement."

"Consider it done." Strong nodded to one of his men standing by. He saluted, before leaving to broadcast the instructions to the rest of the team.

"Thanks to the low cloud cover we have a chance of getting into position before first light." Campbell checked his watch. "We have around an hour, so I suggest we get started."

He called through to LARA, switching to hands-free he waited for the call to engage. Within seconds the familiar, slightly husky tones of Sara filled the bridge.

"Jack, I have you stationary three miles out and... hang on... yes, thirty-six green lights over two crafts. Does that compute?"

Campbell and Strong nodded to confirm their team, plus a crew of eight over two boats, adding the LARA agents, amounted to thirty-six.

"That's affirmative Sara, what else do you have?" By identifying the friendlies, he knew it would enable Sara to pinpoint any threats in the area.

"Nothing immediate, Jack but ..." He knew Sara well enough to know she was concerned about something and he couldn't help thinking. 'Here we go again, there was always a but.'

"... The island is crawling with personnel. To the north, over one hundred that we can see free of cover, and active movement from at least twenty in and around the beach area to the south."

He closed his eyes momentarily, it was never easy. He had a feeling that an island at least five miles in diameter would house more than one single madman and a few housekeepers. But with an entire team of twenty-eight against such a large number of trained military, it was going to be a challenge. There was nothing they could do until they had gathered enough intel on the nuclear threat. If he was right, he would find the answer here. But if he was wrong, and they called in the military to storm it, millions of lives could be lost.

It was imperative they took Brandt quickly before he could release the missiles, so an element of surprise was the best course of action. Once they had him, Strong could bring in his seal team to neutralise the force to the north. Trying to keep battle hardened specialists at bay was a task in itself, but they had no real choice but to wait.

"Sara, you are on point on this one. I need you to keep us informed on the activity at all locations around the island. Keep it tight, and we should get a result."

"That's a roger, Jack, we have a US carrier stationed 1500 miles due west of Hawaii. We can get air support to you in fifteen minutes if you need it." He hoped he could manage with the team he had, but it was reassuring.

"I'll let you know if it's needed Sara, thanks." Jack pocketed the PDA. He looked over to the two commanders. He could tell they were ready for action.

"Shall we, gentleman?" He gestured towards the deck. It was a go.

CHAPTER SEVENTY-THREE
Rough Seas

The Combat Rubber Raiding Craft cut through the ocean surface, its fifty-five horsepower two-stroke engine reaching a top speed of eighteen knots in a matter of minutes.

Riggs welcomed the spray fizzing into the inflatable. It was a relatively smooth ride, which eased his nausea. Occasionally it hit a swirl, kicking them into the air a few feet. As they crashed back, they collected a couple of centimetres of ocean water each time. It swirled around their feet, splattering them as they hit another swirl. The spray cooled him, settling his stomach, he was almost feeling human again. Watching Leggit as he controlled the outboard engine, he was impressed at how he handled the craft. Even with lousy visibility and no help from the natural moonlight, he felt his way through the worst of the waves, while still maintaining a steady heading towards the island.

He had once owned a small Campion power boat in his early twenties. He used to coast the shores of Miami and always thought he could handle it like a pro, powering the 320 horsepower to the max. But he couldn't match this guy and to top it all, Leggit was steering from the rear of the craft.

Riggs hadn't had much of a chance to get to know the three guys accompanying them, as he had spent most of his time staring at the ocean, barfing for the cause. But he managed to get the lowdown on most of them from one of the team, Flipper, back at the Hercules. He was a friendly Eastender and was the only one open to conversation amongst a group of relatively stoic men.

They appeared happy in their own company, preferring to sleep through the long flight. During the conversation with Flipper, however, Riggs learnt all about the nicknames they answered to. Each had his own, specific to his personality, and they were aptly named. Flipper was so called on account of his prowess in the water. He was a competent swimmer, who once represented England in the Commonwealth games some years ago. He had a silver medal to show for it.

Leggit, the CRRC pilot, earned his name due to his speed on the ground during recreation and manoeuvres. He was one of the smaller members of the team and being slight of frame helped with his agility. Even geared up he had been known to outrun many unarmed colleagues in a straight race over 100 yards.

Dregs, who was twice the size of Leggit, was known for a different type of prowess. He could drink anyone under the table, and by the end of the night, once everyone had had their fill, he would finish theirs off too. In army terms he was a rich man, scooping fortunes from the gullible or anyone up for a challenge.

The last team member Digger, a tall well built man, was an explosives expert. He was more comfortable on his stomach in the middle of a minefield than in an amphibious craft surfing the ocean. His favourite position was in front of a land mine with dagger poised, ready to dig out the deadly threat.

Continuing through the darkness, Riggs watched Jack's silhouette as he sat stock still at the bow, looking for any signs of life. He got to thinking of a suitable nickname for him and came up with Maverick, Nomad or The Lone Ranger… all very appropriate. He couldn't help smiling at the last one as that would make him Tonto.

"Case, do you read?" The electronic voice through the earpiece broke the monotony of the roar from the outboard. It was Commander Campbell, reporting from the patrol boat. Leggit immediately cut the power to the motor, slowing down while still holding the craft on course.

"Go ahead." He sat up and placed a finger on his earpiece as he focused on the information.

"We've entered the cave to the east, and there is a small docking platform, but no boat. Be careful, Jack, keep your eyes peeled, it's out there somewhere. We've also come across an armoured door leading deeper into the mountain. I suspect it leads into the complex, but there's no access from our side so we will need to blow it. I'll position three of my men here, and they can blast it on your signal. The rest of us will travel north to provide the seals with some support. We'll hold off until you go."

"That's a roger, Commander…"

Suddenly the small inflatable was bathed in white light. The crew covered their eyes as the beam seared into their faces, growing painfully brighter as it continued to advance on them. As the light grew, they heard the unmistakable chug of an engine.

"I think we've found the gunboat." Jack announced to anyone still listening.

It blinded all on board as the beam eclipsed them. Someone had to take evasive action, and Leggit was the first to move. He swung his AK47 into position and aimed at the light. If he could extinguish the beam, they could assess the threat and even up the odds. A heavy volley of gunfire exploded through the glare and cut Leggit down instantly. He collapsed with a neat line of red holes, spraying jets of blood across his chest.

With no time for the shock to register, the rest of the crew bailed. Jack dived head first over the bow, swimming downwards as fast as the pack on his back would allow. He felt the sudden rush of water fly past him as stray bullets whizzed by. Dregs and Digger followed suit. Experience had taught them to dive underneath the submersible, making the most of the protective cover of the bulletproof deck plates. Riggs was not so lucky. To avoid the gunfire and Leggit's falling body, he was forced towards the rear of the craft.

He had no choice but to dive clear from where he stood, over the large outboard motor. As he grabbed his pack and took flight, a strap caught on the tiller arm pulling him into the hard casing of the engine. He felt his senses leave him as he plummeted into the ocean, his pack thrown into the air. He lost consciousness as soon as he hit the water.

Jack stayed submerged as long as he could, treading water and holding his position some fifteen feet below the surface. Looking up, he could see the searchlight as it scanned the area looking for movement. The light emitted a beam strong enough to cut into the water a few feet below the surface, illuminating the arena with a pale indigo hue. It was enough to enable him to see a short distance ahead, noticing two figures close to the base of the CRRC as it bobbed unmanned on the ocean surface. They were kicking lazily beneath the craft, maintaining a fixed position a few feet below the hull.

Spirals of water like crystal spears passed them by as the machine gun continued to strafe a wide area surrounding the inflatable. Bullets cascaded past them like lead rain.

He felt the pressure on his lungs as they burned in protest at the lack of oxygen, but he dare not surface as he would be picked off instantly. If they didn't move soon, he would have no choice.

Relief washed over him as the hull of the gunboat changed direction and moved away.

The bullets stopped as the water churned beneath the craft as they fired the engines into life. It sent plumes of pressured ocean tumbling through the wash. It travelled only a few yards before cutting the engines, allowing it to drift towards what looked like debris. He watched as two arms and two legs came into view, dangling down amongst it. Seconds later a whole body appeared as a pole, a grappling hook at its end, caught part of the clothing and roughly yanked it out of the water and away. The pole appeared again grasping at a piece of debris, sinking momentarily as the hook took hold. It was a mission pack.

The body dragged into the boat was Riggs. Jack knew it was his partner. The unmistakable army issue boots were still kicking below the surface as two soldiers maintained their position below the CRRC.

The body he had just watched fished from the surface was wearing trainers, Rigg's preferred footwear. Was he still alive? He would have to wait for the answer as the propeller of the gunboat powered into life again. He watched helplessly as the vessel sped away.

As his head broke the surface, he gasped in several gulps of air, coughing as a spray of seawater filled his mouth. He was greeted by Digger and Dregs who had surfaced earlier, gripping the tie ropes on the side of the CRRC.

"Everyone OK?" Jack asked, realising once he had said it that their colleague was lying dead inside the submersible.

Both men stared at him for a moment before Dregs gave him a cursory nod. Digger ducked back under the water before launching himself out and over the side, sliding effortlessly into the boat. He leant over and pulled Dregs in alongside him. They hauled Jack in next and dumped him on his back, still wearing his mission pack. He rocked slightly back and forth, before rolling over onto his knees. He came face to face with the dead eyes of Leggit, staring past him to the heavens that had now claimed him as their own.

The sky had taken on the light grey of dawn, revealing a deep red stain covering the front of Leggits fatigues, soaking him from his chest to his thighs. The water in the craft's base had turned a translucent red as it swirled around the body. Dregs moved alongside him, leaning over his fallen comrade he pulled open a compartment below the tiller, grabbing a field blanket and a small black box. Draping the camouflage sheet over the body, making sure it covered his face, he opened the box. He pulled out a wad of fabric, tightly folded into something resembling a large pack of cards. Unfurling the stack, he moved across to the starboard side of the CRRC; the side that took most of the damage. Part of the wall had collapsed causing gallons of seawater to pour in at each ebb and flow of the ocean. Dregs made his way along the fortified rubber, checking for tears an inch at a time. Pulling a black patch from the fabric strip, he plugged each hole as he found them.

Jack and Digger looked on in silence as they pressed against the port side. They provided enough weight together to lift the damaged wall clear of the water. Once satisfied, Dregs returned to the compartment, taking an aerosol bottle attached to a small air hose. Fixing the nozzle to one of five adaptors he pushed the trigger. Within a few minutes, it inflated the starboard wall to its fullest, keeping the ocean at bay.

"This won't last forever." Dregs said once he was satisfied it would hold. "But it will stay up long enough for us to get the bastards."

Jack looked starboard at the gunboat. It was cruising away from them in the distance.

"That's easier said than done." Jack offered. "They'll cut us down before we get within fifty yards."

So much for the element of surprise, he thought as he studied the look on Dreg's face.

Digger looked over at him.

"You haven't done many amphibious assaults have you?" He said disparagingly. He was about to reel off his several sorties as commander of the SBS, but now wasn't the time to measure their manhood.

Both men moved over to Leggit's body and secured the blanket entirely around the corpse, pulling straps around the ankles, waist and chest. Once it was enclosed entirely in fabric, they lifted it port side and eased it into the water. All three watched as the corpse bobbed away from them further into the Pacific, soon to be taken below to rest in peace. An honourable burial, unsanctioned, an oath within the Echo team to look after their own.

As Digger checked the weapons and ammo stocks, Dregs fired up the motor and with a quick flick of the tiller, arrowed the CRRC towards the gunboat.

CHAPTER SEVENTY-FOUR
Entombed

It was dark, and his head hurt, but at least there was no blood. Riggs was proud of his pain threshold, but embarrassed by the light headed need to vomit when seeing the sight of his own blood. He had killed many in his time, in his job blood was an inevitable consequence, he had no problem with anyone else's. With his own, he had a phobia he had never shaken.

They had bound his hands to the front with cable ties. It allowed him to feel the lump pulsing on his forehead, after his clumsy exit from the submersible. He remembered nothing after hitting the water, he must have blacked out. He awoke with a jolt as they unceremoniously dumped him onto the deck of the gunboat. Before he had time to get his bearings, they bundled him into the cargo hold, crammed into a space with only enough room for three quarters of his height. He could shift sides enough to avoid cramping, but apart from being able to move his shackled arms, it wedged him in from head to his waist. Attempts at pushing the ceiling to test the hatch proved hopeless. He was stuck fast. He was thankful for some air circulation, but it was far from pure. Mixed with the smell of oil and gasoline together with the undulation of the hull, he was struggling to fight the nausea.

His eyes began to adjust to his dark enclosure, he could see his outline as small rays of light from the advancing dawn poked through a vent near his feet. Feeling the cable ties wrapped tightly around his ankles, he felt like a trussed up chicken.

His ear began to crackle and pop. Then he heard a familiar voice.

"Riggs, do you copy?" Static whistled and creaked through the earpiece, but it was unmistakably Jack Case, thank God. His spirits rose as he realised the earwig had stayed in place, his captors had missed it. He had a way out.

"Jack, I read you. Get me out of here." Again the voice sounded in his ear.

"Riggs! Do you copy?"

"Jack, hello? It's me, Riggs, can you hear me?" He waited for confirmation; nothing came. A short while passed before his ear came alive again.

"Riggs, do you copy?" What was up with this thing? Riggs began to hit his head gently against the wall of the hold, careful not to dislodge it but hoping he could jolt the bud to life.

"Jack... Jack ... It's me, Riggs, can you hear me... Over?" He lay in silence for several minutes with only the hum of the engine for company. Had they given up hope of rescuing him and reverted back to the mission, convinced he was dead? Riggs couldn't blame them, he would have done the same under the circumstances, but it didn't stop panic coursing through his veins. He pressed his knees against the hatch and pushed with all his might. It didn't move... trying again... this time flattening his hands and straining to use all the strength he could muster... it moved, only a millimetre or so, but enough for him to double his efforts. Using every muscle, every joint, every sinew trying to force the hatch open, he roared in frustration. He could feel the lump on his forehead pulse so hard it felt like it was ready to burst. He slumped back down as he realised this would not work.

Laying back and closing his eyes, tears squeezed through his eyelids falling down his face, partly through disappointment, but mainly through fear.

"Riggs, do you copy?" His earwig came alive again.

"Yeah, I hear you, Jack and I would definitely copy if this fucking thing worked." He said more to himself, resigned to the fact he had damaged the transmitter and it was inoperable.

"Riggs! Thank God! Repeat your last message, you're coming in weak... Over."

Rigg's heart bounced in his chest and forgetting where he was he tried to sit up, falling back as he hit his head on the hatch door. Jack had heard him!

"Jack, Jack... It's me! I'm here, can you hear me? Over."

"Yeah, I've got you, Tony. Are you OK?" Confidence flowed through him. He was saved.

"Yeah, just great Jack! I'm inside a cargo hold, can't see a thing, bound hand and foot, have a lump the size of a baseball on my head and my arse has gone numb. But apart from that, I'm absolutely fine!"

"Hang in there, Tony. We're coming up behind you. Tell me... and this is very important. Is your pack in there with you?" Rigg's new found confidence was mixed with a feeling of confusion and anger. Why, at this moment in time, would Jack want his pack? Here he was, encased in a box on his way to be tortured or killed, his head hurt, and he needed these shackles removed. Why would Jack want his pack, he had enough ammunition and support to bring down a small country... what else could he...

Then he knew.

"Hang on Jack, you wouldn't?" He thought communication had broken down again as there was silence for what seemed an eternity. Then Jack replied.

"Listen Tony. We can't let them get back to the island. Is your pack with you?" It was turning into a nightmare. He had gone through every emotion a body could take, and he much preferred the feeling of elation. But now he reverted back to fear and panic. He moved his arms around as far as he could, feeling the smooth side walls of his tomb. Above him was no different and looking down towards his feet he could make out the same smooth surface as the rest of his enclosure. But in his current position, he could not check what was underneath him. He could feel tarp by the rustle it made against his fatigues, but what was below was anyone's guess. If it wasn't his pack, could it be an ammunition store? He was on a gunboat for fuck's sake.

"Jack, I can't be sure. When I fell in, I was all over the place. But I'm laying on something, and I can't tell if it's my pack, ammo, beans... I dunno... it could be anything." He waited for a response. He knew this time the silence was down to Jack weighing up the options and thinking things through.

"Listen Tony." Riggs could tell he had more work to do.

"The only way to stop them reaching the island is to disable the boat." Again a pause... Both men were going through options, Riggs definitely drew a blank. There was only one thing he was sure of; he didn't want to die.

"They hoisted you in towards the rear of the vessel. Can you recall the position of the hold before you landed in it?" Riggs closed his eyes and tried to think.

He remembered waking as they bound his hands, the cable ties pulled tight, cutting into his wrists. He could see the face of the man methodically applying the shackles. Bulbous nose flaring with exertion as he made sure his prisoner would not escape his restraints. His fat lips pursed as he concentrated on the job in hand, his dark eyes never leaving his own, relishing the wincing as he pulled them overly tight.

Things came back to him. He remembered hearing a command shouted from a distance. It was in German which was a language he didn't know, but it must have been an instruction to throw him into the hold. He saw the one who gave the order. He couldn't pick him out in a lineup, but he saw the man barking orders from a doorway to the bridge, a good thirty feet away. He caught just a glimpse, but he was almost sure he was holding something by his side, something bulky. It must have been his pack. He tried to concentrate. Did he see the man holding something? Was he holding his pack? Did he actually see it or was it wishful thinking? He wasn't sure ... but he had to get out of here. He thought for a moment more before he spoke.

"Jack! They put me into the hold to the rear of the boat. The captain shouted orders from the bridge. He was about thirty feet away, and I can't be sure..." He hoped he was right, "... But I think he was holding my pack."

Silence again. He was getting used to being part of Jack's thought process, weighing everything up before deciding. It came quicker than he expected.

"Right Tony, cover yourself as much as you can! Don't worry, we'll get you out. Now after three!"

"One..." Riggs tensed and pulled his hands to his face, his shackles just allowing his fingers to splay enough to cover his eyes.

"Two…" Riggs could feel his heart pummelling his chest. The lump on his forehead pulsing in rhythm … Then he remembered something…Something important.

"Err … Jack!" He tried to shout, but as tense as he was, all that came was a whimper.

"Three!"

Too late!

CHAPTER SEVENTY-FIVE
Woken

Today was the day, and Fabian Brandt was dozing. He gave clear instructions not to be disturbed under any circumstances. He needed to rise naturally refreshed and ready to greet his public. The devastation would impact on the world's financial districts, and the rest of the globe would be desperate for news, reassurance and sanctuary.

The New World Order would offer a fresh start, a world where they could all be someone, be an essential part of the New World. Many would die, but only as collateral damage, necessary to allow the re-modelling of the planet. There would be doubters, rebels against the cause, but only to be expected. They would eradicate them before they could cause any real damage. It was a framework to provide freedom to all, with only one ruler, one administration and one voice, Fabian Brandt. New rules would govern each area, no more elections, no corruption, no alternatives. It would be a simpler time with only one fundamental way to a happy, fulfilling life, comply or die; it was so simple.

Rome was ready to head the religious order, an order that would embrace change, a new beginning, a revitalisation of the old ways. A chance to go hand in hand with the New World Order, to rework and re-model the very thinking of the people. A new Roman Empire.

Brandt sank further into his pillow, drifting in and out of sleep. So much to be done, but with all the time in the world to do it. As first light crept through the window, he drifted again. He could feel the comforting sensation of floating as sleep once again smothered his thoughts, cleared his mind, soothed his body and carried him away.

Jack pushed the button on his PDA, watching as the gunboat erupted in flames.

Moments later the explosion reached their ears crashing like thunder over their heads. The cacophony amplified tenfold in the silence of the Pacific dawn.

The CRRC bounced over the waves created by the aftershock, lurching precariously as Dregs fought with the tiller arm to keep it on course.

"Jesus!" Digger shouted as the deafening boom made him duck.

"Well, that's definitely stopped them." Dregs offered as he watched the thick black smoke spiral from the crippled craft. They were only two hundred yards from the boat, Dregs not letting the speed drop below top.

"Oh, shit!" Jack shouted as he watched a plume of smoke drift into the air and the rear of the boat rise above the surface. They were by now only twenty yards from the stricken vessel. He watched mesmerised as the hull came into full view before descending, sinking slowly into the ocean. The slide was unrelenting until it disappeared.

The explosion had cut the ship in two as the water flooded into the wreckage, finding any opening it could, the two halves filling in seconds as the sea claimed them for its own. Dregs slowed as they entered the space where the boat used to be, crashing through debris still clinging to the ocean's surface. Some of the debris was human. A hand touched the side of the submersible, they made no attempt to grab hold as it was only attached to a shredded forearm. The skin fanned out behind it like a gruesome jellyfish rippling along, carried by the current. There were empty life belts and deflated life jackets bobbing around them, their use futile to the unfortunate crew. They could see nothing else other than small fragments of the hull and splintered crates; there was no sign of life.

Jack didn't hesitate, he knew time was against him as he dived headlong into the ocean kicking hard as soon as he was fully submerged. He immediately caught sight of the rear of the craft as it continued its slow descent. He had to reach it before it sank much deeper, he hoped his partner was still inside the hold, and prayed that he was holding his breath.

Pumping for all his worth, he pushed on and saw the aft closing in as he cut through the clear water. After a few more feet he managed to grab hold of the handrail. Moving hand over hand, he edged his way along the port side of the vessel, peering over to scan the ruined deck. He saw the hatch almost instantly, still intact and secured by two ring handles nestled into domed recesses. His lungs were screaming as the pressure squeezed his chest, trying to force the last of the captured air from his body. He could see tiny spots exploding in front of him. He felt light headed.

Swinging himself at the deck which was now vertical, a vast wall of steel making its way down to rest on the seabed. He gripped the handrail trying to grab one of the handles by stretching across the hold, but he was several feet away. Frantic now, he sidled further down the rail until he was a good six feet below it. He looked up and concentrated on the handle to his right. This would be his only chance. If he missed he would need to surface as his senses were becoming cloudy, he could black out at any moment. Only his experience and years of aquatic training allowed him to stay submerged this long, but it was now or never.

He let go of the handrail.

As the hold raced towards him, Jack grabbed for the ring handle, wrapping three fingers of his left hand around it. His momentum kept his body moving towards the surface while the vessel continued its slow descent. Hanging on for dear life, his body swung around 180 degrees, until he was now above the hold looking down. The ring started to cut into his fingers as he held on.

Steadying himself, he extended his right hand, grabbing the second ring and in one movement, he twisted both handles.

What happened next he could not account for.

The hold door came free in his hands leaving him holding onto the rings as the deck of the gunboat continued to slide past him. Deeper and deeper towards its final resting place. He had failed. He dropped the door and watched it float away before being forced to ascend. He was careful to release the small pockets of air still left in his lungs, as he kicked dejectedly to the surface.

CHAPTER SEVENTY-SIX
Sunk

The explosion made Brandt sit up with a start. Had he been dreaming?

Had he been dreaming of a warhead crashing into Wall Street, or The Docklands or the Pudong district of Shanghai? It had been so realistic he had even felt the impact. He looked at the large sash windows, at the blinds gently swaying unaided by any breeze, he hadn't dreamt it. Lifting his Rolex from the bedside cabinet, he looked at the golden dials … 5 AM, far too early.

There was a frantic rapping on his door. Sliding from the silk sheets, he covered his night clothes with a shimmering purple robe tied at the waist with a gold braid. He opened the door to the trembling figure of Jai. He had leapt from his bed and hastily dressed before waking his master. Although he was bowed to cover his face, Brandt could see he was unkempt and still half asleep.

"Master, please forgive my impertinence at this early hour… but boat … it gone." Jai's mastery of the English language was passable when calm, but when nervous, it was all over the place.

"What do you mean gone? What happened Jai?"

"Someone has attacked the gunboat and blown it out of the water; that's where it's gone." Leon Ubermann hurried past Brandt's room. He was already dressed and occupied with checking his gun clip before chambering it and replacing it into his shoulder holster.

"Get Anatoly to meet me at the lab!" He shouted to Leon as the head of security bounded down the stairs towards the command centre.

"Jai, I want coffee! Bring it to me in the lab." The little manservant ran down the marble corridor, his flip-flops slapping an echo along its length. He self consciously tucked his black tee shirt into his trousers, then tried to smooth down an unruly tuft of hair as he scuttled towards the kitchen.

Brandt closed the door and rested against it, closing his eyes, taking time to gather his thoughts. No one would spoil his day. No one. Snapping his eyes open he stormed towards his walk-in wardrobe throwing open the door. He screamed with rage as he ripped a shirt from its hanger.

As Jack's head broke through the waves, he tried desperately to gasp for breath, but nothing came. He tried again, but he couldn't inhale, when he attempted to his lungs refused to move. Water entered his throat causing him to gag. He coughed, reflex helped him draw a breath; it was a scream like inhale as his throat constricted. It allowed only a small amount of air into his lungs, with a lot more seawater. He frantically splashed his arms to lift himself out of the water, hoping to capture clean air. He was failing, the exertion sapped his energy, so he stopped flapping and sank back. He was too weak to push anymore, and he resigned himself to let the ocean decide his fate.

He was grabbed by the collar and hauled out of the water. He landed on his back on the hard deck of the CRRC. Coughing and spluttering he was able to take large gulps of beautiful clean air. He was staring into the face of Dregs who was leaning over him, glaring into his eyes.

"You fucking idiot!" He bellowed at the floundering man lying in front of him.

"You nearly killed yourself!" He could only stare at the face shouting down at him. His words a distant echo as his ears were still emptying ocean from the canals.

"It was also a hell of a thing to do for a colleague though." Dregs smiled.

"I've never seen anything like it and I sure as hell don't know anyone who would do the same. There's a lot about you we don' know, I guess." He grabbed him by the arms and pulled him into a seated position.

He immediately vomited salt water, clearing his system in seconds. Sitting with his head between his legs, getting used to breathing again, he felt his senses sharpen, and the strength return to his muscles. But his mind remained on Riggs.

He had let him down, had promised him he would be fine, that Jack Case would get him out alive. The pack should have had enough explosive to neutralise anyone within a range of around ten feet. If they were lucky, it may have disabled the steering mechanism, not blow it out of the water. Riggs must have packed several pearl grenades and ammo, overcompensating as usual for the battle ahead. He had failed to ask the question.

If he had known he would have thought of an alternative, another way around it. He could have called Campbell to turn back and intercept them. It would have been the logical course of action, what with the CRRC approaching from the rear. The two pronged attacks would have overpowered them easily.

But no … The great Jack Case had to risk the life of his colleague. He had also announced their presence with an explosion loud enough to wake a country. All he had achieved was to endanger everyone assigned to support him. Doubts again flooded his mind. He wasn't as good as everyone thought he was and this self-doubt was chipping away at his psyche. He was burnt out. He had to pull himself together, this attitude would do nothing to help anyone, least of all himself. He had a job to do, and for the sake of millions of lives, he would ensure they completed it because this one was for Riggs.

Mentally slapping himself, he looked around to get his bearings.

An island dominated the horizon to the north. It was a large mountainous rock covered in vegetation, looking uninhabitable.

Sheer rock wall covered most, rising vertically from the ocean before levelling out several hundred feet above sea level. As he scanned the base, he noticed a bluff to the east and behind it, the beginnings of an inlet of sand. It was too far away to study fully, but instinct told him it was where they needed to go.

Something was wrong … He scanned the small sixteen foot CRRC, so deep in thought, he hadn't noticed it at first. He turned to Dregs.

"Where's Digger?" Failing to notice immediately he put down to exhaustion, as he realised he only had one companion in the submersible.

Dregs watched him impassively for a few moments and then smiled as he saw something over his shoulder. Jack wheeled around and looked to the west. Twenty yards away, swimming towards them was Digger, he was pulling a body behind him, still shackled. It was Riggs.

His heart leapt as he jumped to his feet and dived overboard. All signs of exhaustion left him, replaced with a boost of adrenalin and relief. He reached them within a few strokes, passing behind Digger to help lighten his load.

The American, his head back staring at the blue sky, turned to look at Jack. He was smiling.

"I forgot to mention." Riggs managed to speak, moving his head constantly to avoid gulping mouthfuls of water. "I had packed my bag full of grenades just in case. Probably not a good idea to blow it up."

He turned his head back towards the sky as a wave sent sea water rolling over his mouth.

CHAPTER SEVENTY-SEVEN
Loyalty

Brandt watched as the final warhead descended through the floor and attached itself to the drone. As it moved away to take its position in the launch tube, he looked at Anatoly Duranichev and marvelled at how the man had aged over the past few days. He was in his early sixties, a thin man with a face that always seemed to be in turmoil and had taken on a stooped, withered appearance since arriving at the laboratory. Brandt was five years his senior, but the scientist could easily pass as the billionaire's father. It was incredible how forty-eight hours with no sleep can affect a man.

"I assume everything is in place and fully tested." It wasn't a question.

The Russian raised his head on his tired neck looking at the man in front of him. The hard stare he received in return sent a chill up his spine. Brandt was in no mood to be messed with. They had all heard the explosion, and it was apparent they were under attack.

It had taken all of his persuasive powers to persuade Saval and Dimitri to stay, as the young technicians were ready to flee at any moment. He could just as easily have told them Brandt would kill them if they attempted to leave, but he needed them to complete their work. He chose instead to remind them of countless riches and the high esteem coming their way.

"Yes, Fabian, everything is ready."

Brandt looked at all three in turn.

"Excellent!" He said, a smile crossing his face.

"Exceptional work, all of you. You will be rewarded for your loyalty." He looked over to Saval and Dimitri.

"You look tired, rest now for a few hours. I have arranged for a helicopter to take you to Hawaii this afternoon, where you can relax and enjoy yourselves for a few weeks at my expense. A token of my appreciation for your hard work over the past few days. I will call for you once our administration is in place, in the meantime make the most of your time in Hawaii. Leave us now, I need a word with Anatoly in private."

The two technicians thanked him as they left for their accommodation suite to pack.

Once they were alone, Brandt walked towards Duranichev and grasped his hand, shaking it warmly.

"My friend, you will go down in history as one of the founders of the New World Order. The man who cleared the way for the new administration. Anatoly, you have shown your loyalty, and in return, you will have earned riches beyond your wildest dreams. You are now a very wealthy man."

Anatoly bowed his head in appreciation, although inside he didn't feel like celebrating. Brandt's over familiarity was disconcerting, and he was unsure right now if it wasn't worse than one of his rages. Either way, he feared the man more than anyone he had ever met in his life.

The billionaire was a double-edged sword, each side as deadly as the other.

"It is important however Anatoly, that you build a loyal team around you. I need to know I can trust each and everyone in my administration and it includes any staff employed within my inner circle."

Brandt leant across and switched on a monitor, showing a stylishly decorated accommodation suite.

It composed of two plush beds with small storage units either side and a low soft seating area complete with low tables. A large screen TV fixed to the wall hung above a well stocked drinks cabinet. They could see Dimitri packing his clothes neatly into his holdall. Sava helped himself to a cola as he flicked through the channels, stopping at a 49ers - Redskins NFL re-run.

Anatoly looked on for a moment or two as Dimitri cleared out his sock drawer and Saval sank into the sofa to watch the game. He turned to Brandt, confusion etched on his tired face.

Brandt leant over again and flicked on another monitor, this time of the lab. The feed was from earlier, just after the explosion. Duranichev was trying to calm Dimitri as he remonstrated with him, placing a reassuring arm on the young man's shoulder. Saval was on the far side of the lab. He was trying to leave for the accommodation suite, pushing frantically at the release switch. A switch disabled, until the task had completed. Giving up, he stormed towards Anatoly to join Dimitri. They both stood shouting profanities, violently animated in their remonstrations. The old man moved away as they poked at his chest only stopping once they had backed him to a wall. Brandt switched off the screen.

Anatoly's eyes were drawn to the accommodation suite in time to see Saval suddenly jump up from his seat and drop the remote control. His cola followed, the glass bouncing twice along the floor before shattering. The young Frenchman began to claw at his throat, his mouth wide open as if in song. His eyes moved around the room, frantically searching for something. He watched as the young man's chest rose and fell. He forced his head forward as he searched for air, opening and closing his mouth, desperate to find life-giving oxygen. Eventually, his shoulders began to spasm, his arms flopped down by his side, and he toppled headlong into the drinks cabinet sending bottles in all directions. He came to rest on the floor, twitched for a second or two and was still.

The screen then filled with the terrified face of Dimitri. He was staring into the camera, screaming for help from anyone watching. Horror filled eyes unnaturally wide, blood-filled tears pouring down his face. His mouth was opening and closing as he tried to call out, tried to breathe, tried to scream. His pupils rose into his head, exposing haemorrhaging veins amongst the white of his eyes. He then sank from view.

Brandt moved closer to Duranichev, who was still transfixed on the horror before him and whispered into his ear.

"Be careful in your choice of assistants my friend. As I said, I demand loyalty." As he turned and left the room, his chief scientist could not move, staring silently at the monitor.

CHAPTER SEVENTY-EIGHT
Beach Head

As the sun sparkled off the pool within the small beach alcove, Jack, Riggs, Digger and Dregs hid behind a small outcrop of rock behind a clump of palms. It was an ideal vantage point to view the vast complex before them. Jack's first impression was that Fabian Brandt had used Gerry Anderson as the architect of this outlandish structure.

From the beach, they gained access through a small gap in a low curtain wall of marble pillars, decorated with flowering vines. A tiled pool area running the length of the grounds dominated the courtyard. It finished just before the marble steps led fifteen feet up to the impressive balcony. To the west, a waterfall fell twenty foot from an outcrop of rock into a clear natural pool surrounded by exotic plants of many varieties and colours. The tables and chairs with colourful umbrellas created a welcoming oasis.

The ground level of the building, stylishly modelled on a Mediterranean villa, was an expanse of white marble and beige stucco in a Grecian style of columns, statues and decorative pots, spaced evenly along its front. A twelve foot iron gate secured the entry within a marble archway. The emblem of FB with a flaming phoenix, mirroring the one seen at the chateau, fixed to its centre.

Four gunmen armed with M16's patrolled the balcony, turning regularly towards the beach as part of their patrol. The uniform of choice was a white tee shirt and white trousers, ideally suited to the tropical climate.

Above the marble facade was a massive three level structure of curved glass. It resembled a large bay window cut into the mountain either side, taking the overall structure to well over 100 feet. Polished aluminium rails bordered each balcony level, giving the impression of the teeth of a giant mythical beast, grinning in the morning light.

"Fuck me! That's one hell of a holiday villa." Riggs whispered, now fully recovered from his recent drowning.

He had been lucky. As the broken hull of the gunboat had started to sink, the hold had filled only halfway, providing an air pocket that kept his head above water. Once Jack removed the hatch the water rushed in, and he popped out. Thankfully, Digger had followed to assist in the rescue. As Jack moved away having run out of oxygen, he was there to grab him and pull him safely back to the surface.

But he was worried about Jack. His perceived lack of judgement culminating in the near fatal loss of his colleague hit him hard. It also seemed that the exertion of the rescue had taken a lot out of him physically. His only words had been to give orders so far.

He would need to keep an eye on him for all their sakes.

In the distance came the distinct rat-a-tat of a helicopter, the sound growing louder by the minute. All four searched the skies for a sighting. It was difficult to pinpoint the exact location, due to the confines of the bay and the high walls of the mountainous rock. Then, from above the building, rising majestically over the mountain ledge high above, a black gunship roared into view. Swooping down once it had cleared the peak, it powered across the pool, over the beach, slowing as it reached the ocean.

All four watched as it came to a stop, hovering twenty feet above the surface. It started to rotate until it was facing back towards their position.

With palms to the north and the rock formation to the south, they were well concealed. They kept their eyes on the black threat as it swayed gently, riding the thermals from the ocean. Gunfire sounded in the air as the flying menace released its cannons to the east of their position.

The CRRC exploded into a fireball as bullets ripped through the gasoline powered motor. The remaining pearl grenades in Jack's pack intended for their escape, blew the craft to smithereens.

"Well, it looks like we're staying." He said as he stated the obvious.

"Yes, but I don't think we can stay here for much longer." Dreg said as he pointed back towards the building. They all turned to se the guards running around the pool towards them. The iron gate swung open, several gunmen passed through, pouring down the marble staircase.

Very clever, he thought. They knew their general whereabouts. Having the chopper cover the beach from the south, using the guards to pincer from the north; they were being flushed out. They had to think fast.

"Riggs! You get to the west of the curtain wall, I'll get to the east side. You two remain where you are and cover us. Join us on my signal." He looked over at him. "Ready?" Riggs nodded and zeroed in on the west wall.

"Go!"

Both LARA agents ran from cover, using the element of surprise to cut down three of the advancing guards before any had time to retaliate. Within seconds the bay was full of noise as every man opened fire. The chopper, spotting Jack and Riggs, sent a volley of bullets after them. Sand kicked high into the air creating a thick fog of war, it helped to provide cover as they advanced. Jack weaved from side to side heading towards the curtain wall, diving behind a boulder just as a bullet ricocheted off it. Scrambling to a safer position he sent a shell into the throat of a gunman as he leapt from the poolside towards him. He crumpled in a gurgling fit, blood spraying into the air as the severed carotid artery emptied his body pint by pint, seconds later he was dead.

He looked over to Riggs who had reached the curtain wall taking one guard down before huddling behind the low pillars. He readied himself, waiting for the right moment to move. Dregs and Digger used their AK47's to good effect, cutting down half a dozen gunmen with supporting fire.

It had worked so far. The guards stopped advancing, favouring the cover of the balcony instead. They fired from the safety of the marble walls, instead of the slippery tiled floor of the poolside.

The bay, naturally moulded from the jagged rock of a mountain was peppered with several ruts and outcrops. It gave ample cover to assist in their advance on their target. Riggs, seeing a suitable spot, straddled the low wall, running behind the nearest recess. He released several rounds to accompany Digger and Dregs, keeping return fire at a minimum. The American danced and zigzagged across the ground, finding an outcrop of rock, tucking himself in as far as he could go.

Jack signalled to Riggs to provide cover. He received a nod in acknowledgement and signalled back to the two special forces ops to advance. First Dregs and then Digger burst from cover, shooting forward as the LARA agents kept the guards busy. They too zigzagged towards the pool avoiding the cannon fire from the chopper sending a volley after them. Both reached the curtain wall unscathed.

The gunship, seeing the enemy move out of range, pushed its nose down and advanced, descending straight at them. The side of the chopper opened revealing a gunman straddling a static machine gun, his legs dangling just above the landing skids.

"Get over here!" He shouted at Dregs who was closest. Riggs beckoned Digger to do the same. Covered by the LARA agents, the two specials split, raced across to their colleagues, diving to safety to avoid a hail of gunfire. Bullets rained down on them as the guards continued to fire from the safety of the balcony making it difficult to counterattack. They showed themselves only briefly to shoot a round or two before ducking out of sight again. But after hitting two of them, the shooting suddenly stopped.

Sand began to lift off the floor and swirl around them, the sound of an engine drawing nearer and nearer off to the south. The sand stung their faces as it began to fly all around them hitting them hard from all sides. The harsh, gritty dust rattled against rock, like a torrential downpour, it constantly rained on them, making it difficult to see or hear. All four covered their faces the best they could as they continued to get battered and stung.

Squinting through the storm, Jack could make out the nose of the black gunship as it hovered into view no more than ten feet above them. The gunmen had ceased fire to watch the scene unfold from their vantage point. The sound of the helicopter as it emerged further into the enclosure of the bay was deafening. The vibration of the rotors sent tremors through the earth sending more shale on top of them.

As it advanced over the curtain wall towards Brandt's hideout, the sand cleared allowing them to watch as it hovered over the pool. It was rotating slowly until the machine gunner came into view. It stopped side on to its adversaries.

"Everyone get down!" He shouted through his earwig. They all followed suit making themselves as small as possible. Jack and Dregs crouched low behind a boulder, Riggs and Digger pressed back as hard as they could within the cover of the recess. The machine gun came to life strafing across both locations giving no quarter to return fire. All four cowered in their hiding places, bombarded with debris as bullets sprayed large chunks of rock on top of them.

As the gun's chamber emptied, the chopper lifted several feet into the air while the gunner fitted a new clip. It gave them the chance to return fire. It proved futile, the craft was too high to have any effect. Their bullets ricocheted harmlessly off the landing skids and the steel underbelly. There had to be another way.

The guards broke cover, sending a volley of bullets towards them. They were getting overwhelmed. Dividing their time between the two targets, breaking to reload, but they failed to land one shot.

Moving back into cover as the chopper descended again, the machine gun refreshed, resumed its onslaught. Forced back yet again as the attack continued as ferocious as the first, Jack had to think fast.

There was no way of advancing further without eliminating the chopper. The problem was, they had very little chance from their current position. He could think of one way, it was a considerable risk, and if he failed, all would be lost. But he had to do something. He pulled a pearl grenade from his jacket and held it ready to prime.

"Riggs!" He screamed through the earwig again. "If you can hear me I need you to cover me on my go!" He looked across at Dregs knowing what Jack was about to do, gave him the thumbs up.

"Roger!" came the bellowing response from Riggs.

The machine gun stopped as another chamber exhausted.

"Go!" He shouted as he ran from cover.

His three colleagues emptied their guns at the balcony keeping the guards at bay. By alternating reloads, they managed to hold them back, giving him time to focus.

Everything was down to timing. One misjudgement and he could put the whole operation and the lives of his companions in jeopardy.

Priming the grenade as he ran, Jack held it tightly in his left hand with his Glock grasped tightly in his right. The helicopter started to rise again. He leapt onto the curtain wall and launched himself at the landing skids. The gunner looked below at the madman leaping towards him. He had no time to react as a bullet entered his chin and hurtled through his brain, exploding out of the top of his head.

Jack caught the skid at the joint of his right forearm and bicep, wrapping his arm around the steel plate. He kept hold of the Glock although it was now uselessly dangling from his right hand as the gunship continued to rise to twenty feet. With his left hand, he tossed the pearl grenade into the cabin. The chopper spun as the pilot saw it clatter across the flight deck. Jack tried to shake it loose, but the body of the gunman was blocking the only exit. Swinging underneath the craft, he pulled his left arm over the skid to avoid being thrown clear, looking down to survey his options. He had seconds left to decide … thirty feet.

The pool was his only choice as it began to shrink away directly below him. How deep was it? Would the downdraft of the rotor throw him off course and send him into the building, the tiles, into the mountain? He had no time to decide …

He let go …

The gunship exploded. Glass blew out on all sides drifting down like sharp rain, the rotor split in two, the blades arrowing to the earth.

The tail split from the body toppling away, the rear rotor blades spinning wildly out of control. The cockpit, now nothing more than a distorted flaming hulk of molten metal, careered towards the waterfall. It filled the bay with carnage as the debris fell all around One of the rotor blades landed on the lower balcony where the gunmen had taken refuge. Two of them were cut in two instantly Blood covered several feet of the stucco, a red stain of death. The tail crashed into the first floor balcony, rotors cutting through the rails shattering the enormous pains of glass. It continued to tear into the first floor, sending brick and metal on top of a section of the guard detail retreating from the devastation. It came to rest, swaying precariously above the pool.

Steam erupted by the waterfall as the cockpit splash landed. Large chunks of the west wall broke loose from above as it shook the very foundations of the mountain. Rocks cascaded down, bounced across the forecourt and decimated the tiled poolside. By the time they came to rest the curtain wall to the west was no more.

He plummeted into the water on his back and kept going, bracing himself for the impact as he sank towards the bottom. Thankfully, it was deeper than he thought as his back only kissed the tiled base, and he began to rise. He rolled onto his front kicking to the surface. But then, pausing his ascent, he started treading water, remaining submerged in the centre of the chlorine filled pool. He circled a full 360 degrees as he studied the construction and in particular the transparent walls. Having seen enough, he kicked to the surface aiming for the side nearest the curtain wall. His hand broke through first, feeling for the pool's edge.

Grabbed by the wrists as he was about to break the surface, he was pulled out with a strength that surprised him. Before he had time to react, he was lying on the tiles staring up at two faces. They belonged to Digger and Dregs.

"You are one hell of a crazy bastard!" Dregs said as he crouched down checking the LARA agent for any injuries. He stood shaking his head as he found none and offered his hand. Jack took it gratefully and was pulled to his feet, soaking wet but unharmed.

He pulled the PDA from his pocket, shook the water from it and dialled.

"Sara, send troops to the north of the island. Get them to help Campbell and Strong. But no air strikes, I repeat no air strikes."

"Roger Jack. There are hostiles in your vicinity. Do you need support at your location?"

He looked at Digger and Dregs next to him, then at Riggs, standing near the crushed archway entrance to the building. They were alert, focussed, Riggs looking all around, his gun at the ready to cut anyone down who approached.

"No, Sara, we'll be fine."

"Jack, one other thing. We have taken Calanda Mountain. Troops have neutralised the area and secured the gold. Task force casualties were light, but Brandt's forces took severe damage. Jack, they wouldn't stop, they fought to the death, even greatly outnumbered they kept fighting. A handful of prisoners were taken and only then because they were severely injured. It was madness."

"And the Brandt girl?" He had seen the madness in Klara Brandt first hand and knew surrender was never an option for her.

"We haven't found her yet. But we have search parties throughout the area. We'll find her." He wasn't so sure.

"OK Sara, keep me informed. One more thing … Get a message to NATO and every security service involved in the operation and get them to close in on the enemy cells. Tell them that there is no localised nuke threat. Take them down."

Sara was silent for a second or two as she digested the last request.

"Are you sure of this Jack?"

"Oh yes, I'm very sure." He confirmed looking at his three companions who were all in earshot, intrigued by what they heard.

"We are standing above the launch site. The missiles are here."

He placed the PDA back into his jacket. They had work to do.

The once picturesque bay was now a mass of destruction. Rocks from the west wall completely covered the terrain up to the main pool's edge, the decorative curtain wall now a mass of rock, clay and sediment. There was nothing left of the Mediterranean marble and stucco facade apart from one window. Its frame was still attached to the only remaining section of the wall still standing. A part of the archway supporting the tilting iron gate hung desperately to the last hinge still functioning. As the chopper broke apart, most of the debris hit the structure, wiping away the balcony. The landing skids took several of the concealed guards with it. The rotors had taken care of a further section of the guard detail, continuing on to burrow into the brickwork. It transformed three quarters of the building to rubble. As the devastation began, the gunmen who were lucky enough had retreated deep into the complex.

Digger, Dregs and Riggs could watch it all unfold from the safety of their cover, picking off Brandt's men as they broke for the entrance

Jack's spectacular manoeuvre had given them clear access to the building.

"So wait, let me get this right. Are you saying all the missiles are launched from here?" Riggs called from his position by the entrance.

"Yes, this island is the launch site. I thought as much, but I couldn't be sure until now."

"Hang on." Dregs held his hand up dismissively. "That's impossible, they couldn't reach half of the destinations without refuelling. London is what ... 8500 miles? Frankfurt 8000? New York 7500? Even with a decent tailwind, a bomber could hope at best for 6000 miles, and the island isn't capable of hiding a runway ... we've seen the aerials, nothing."

"UCAV." He said simply.

"Drones?" Digger sounded surprised. "That is a complex operation, and they need a command centre to control them over such a distance."

Unmanned Combat Air Vehicles, used throughout modern warfare and designed to deliver weapons to their targets without the need of onboard pilots. But they had to be flown real time by a 'pilot' controlling them from a land-based command centre.

"Are we sure the command centre is here?" Digger knew they could position it anywhere in the world as long as communication with the drones is set correctly. Whatever happened, they could not stop the missiles without disabling the command consoles. He had to admit it was a fair question, and he didn't have the answer.

"I think we should get going and find out." He tried to sound as positive as he could as he made his way around the pool towards Riggs.

He felt a vibration first, a soft hum through the balls of his feet. He watched the ground as the tremors increased, small pieces of rubble danced across the tiles, bouncing into the pool. The water rippled in time to the movement, slight undulations bubbling from the south, developing into thin waves as they swept northwards. Jack stopped by the poolside his eyes drawn to the southern edge.

"You have got to be kidding me!" He stood watching as the pool split from the tiled surround to the south.

He was joking earlier when he referenced Gerry Anderson as the architect of the island complex. As he watched the pool sliding away underneath the ruined villa, he expected Thunderbird One to launch into the sky at any moment. The group watched, weapons aimed at the growing cavernous hole as the pool continued to disappear beneath their feet. Digger crouched close to the edge to look inside.

"I think we've found what we were looking for." He stood up as the contents of the opening became clear.

Below them, moving into view were five white conical noses set vertically within five chambers in a large cylinder. It resembled a giant revolver loaded with bullets and ready to fire.

"Jesus!" Dregs gasped as the missile silo came into view. "This guy means business. What can you see Digger?" Being the explosives expert he had heard this question many times before, but on this occasion, he just gave Dregs a contemptuous glare.

"I'll give you a clue. The white rocket things are the UCAV's and strapped to their backs with the little red hats are the nuclear missiles. By the look of them, big enough to flatten a city and more."

"See, I knew you were in the right job." Dregs gave him a slap on the back that nearly sent Digger into the hole. He forced a foot forward to stop from falling.

"For fuck's sake..." Digger turned to confront his colleague. Dregs was smiling his most stupid of smiles.

"Now, now, ladies!" Jack cut in. "I think we need to do something about this don't you."They both looked over to him, the spat forgotten.

"Digger, do you think with the help of Dregs, you can detach those missiles from the UCAV's, providing we can get to the command centre and disable them?" Digger looked at the missiles, working out in his head how it could be done, dismantling them in his mind. He then looked up at Dregs who returned his gaze, face now serious expressionless. He poked his tongue out and wiggled it at the explosives expert. Digger choked a laugh and smiled.

"Yeah, we'll be fine." He confirmed.

Jack nodded and turned to leave with Riggs, climbing up the rubble that had once been a marble staircase towards the gate to the complex.

Suddenly, the silo filled with white smoke and the ground

trembled.

"Oh bollocks!" Dregs backed away from the poolside.

"Get down!" Digger shouted.

All four hit the deck, Digger instinctively diving on top of Dregs while Jack and Riggs flattened against the rubble. With a roar as the thrusters ignited, one of the conical noses rose from its chamber, heat and smoke from the silo filled the bay.

A UCAV rose into the air picking up speed, clearing the trees in seconds. They looked to the skies and watched as the rocket sprouted wings from within its body. Accelerating to an astonishing speed, it arced out of its upward trajectory and headed away across the Pacific Ocean.

CHAPTER SEVENTY-NINE
Inner Sanctum

They bolted through the entrance onto the sandstone tiled floor of the lower level living accommodation. They had to find the control room before any more missiles were released and find it fast. Sprinting along the passage, passing several rooms in keeping with the style of the exterior. The summer floral furniture and the yellows and blues adorning the walls flashed by in a blur as they hurtled past, so far without incident. They came to a flight of stone stairs cut into the far wall leading to the upper levels. Riggs reached them first.

"Riggs. No!" He turned just as Jack caught him in the midriff and pushed him clear of the stairwell. Bullets shattered tiles by their feet sending ceramic shards into the air. He looked him in the eye, waiting for the penny to drop, before stating the obvious.

"We need to be aware of the guards. They are here to stop us remember." Riggs looked over Jack's shoulder, and much to his chagrin closed his eyes.

Ten yards away, lying halfway out of one of the side rooms, was the body of a guard. His white tee shirt red with blood from his sliced throat. Jack had taken him down while Riggs concentrated all his efforts on reaching the stairs.

"Oh, shit!" He was mortified at his schoolboy error, putting it down to fatigue. Jack consoled him by patting him on the shoulder. "Come on then. Let's get them shall we?"

Positioned either side of the stairwell, Jack crouched, gun at the ready, while Riggs remained standing. Two different targets to occupy their assailants. Mouthing one, two, three, Jack turned into the stairs and fired six quick rounds. Riggs fired after three shots and caught a guard in the shoulder as he returned fire. More bullets followed shattering even more of the floor as the agents moved back into cover.

They needed to get up the stairs and time was running out. It was messy, but it was all he could think of to give them an advantage. He pulled a pearl grenade from his jacket and in one smooth movement primed it, tossing it underarm into the stairwell. He moved back sharply to shelter behind the wall. The explosion, followed by a rolling plume of smoke filled the surrounding corridor. Debris crashed down, collecting in a pile at the foot of the stairs. Using the smoke as cover, Jack bounded up the steps two at a time, gun raised, ready to fire. He found no threat as he entered the utilitarian corridor. He signalled for Riggs to join him.

The corridor was a total contrast from the decor of the lower level. Black marble tiles replaced the sandstone ceramics, the walls a 21st century mixture of glass and steel.

Four gunmen lay motionless around the stairwell, two had missing limbs, soaked in blood while a third was laying in such a contorted state, his back must have snapped at every vertebra. He was, like his two colleagues, very dead.

The fourth guard who had been furthest from the grenade moaned as he shifted his body to look at the man who had arrived. His white clothing was now a deep red; his body ripped apart. His left leg shattered, an oozing bloody limb, it had taken most of the blast stripping his trouser leg and most of the skin away. A metal strut had peeled away from one of the stair balustrades and pierced his stomach. He was holding it with his left hand, unsure whether to pull it free.

"Sie sterben vor dem tag" He growled at Jack as he approached.

"Sorry mate, not a language I know. Sprechen sie Englisch?" That was the full extent of his German, asking if he could speak English.

"Deine Mutter ist eine Hure du stück Scheisse." The guard spat at him as he approached.

"Nope means nothing I'm afraid."

"It might mean nothing to you, but your mother wouldn't be too happy." Riggs had taken his time to join him as he checked around for more guards, not wishing to get caught out again.

"He just called her a whore." Riggs didn't know much German, but he'd heard the phrase many times.

"Did he now?" He crouched next to the man and looked up and down his prone body. He tutted and shook his head as he surveyed the extent of his injuries. He finished by staring into his searing eyes filled with anger, pain and deep-rooted hatred.

"Where is the control room?" Jack fixed his gaze on the chiselled features of the German.

"Wo ist der Kontrollraum?" Riggs tried his best college German knowing he was stuffed if the conversation developed any further. The guard remained motionless apart from the rapid rising and falling of his chest as pain wracked his body. He was a big man, huge biceps stretched the sleeves of his tee shirt to ripping point. His neck, veined and tense, was the same width as his head, a square hard, threatening face with a broken nose and piercing eyes staring defiantly at them.

"Fuck you … You sons of dogs … You will not win … You will die before the day is done." He spoke through gritted teeth, broken English full of venom.

"My guess is that you'll beat us to it." Jack finished with a sarcastic smile.

The eyes closed as the Germans' hand holding the protruding balustrade began to shake. Slowly and deliberately he pulled it from his gut, one inch at a time.

"Holy shit!" Riggs backed away as he watched another inch slide free from the wounded man's stomach.

He made no sound as he continued to pull the steel rod from the wound. Three inches … four … it came free. His body relaxed for a moment as he fought with the trauma and then with a superhuman effort he rose.

It was Jack's turn to back away as he watched him make his way shakily to his feet.

"You don't want to do this." They watched as the big German hobbled towards him, his ruined leg dragging behind him. It reminded Riggs of a zombie movie as the wounded man moved nearer, drops of blood following him like a snail trail. He fixed his eyes on Jack the whole time, hatred flowed from every sinew. When he had reached within a few feet, the hulk raised the balustrade above his head. He roared a blood chilling curse, knowing it would be his last and launched at them.

He crashed in between them, dead before he hit the floor, felled by the fresh fatal wound of a bullet hole in the centre of his forehead. Stepping away from the corpse as it landed, they avoided the spray of blood and brain from the gaping hole in the back of the head, as it crashed into the ground.

"C'mon, we haven't got time for this." Jack walked the corridor checking each room as he passed.

He stopped at one, devastated by the tail of the gunship as it crashed through the building. It was a kitchen. Stainless steel units, bent and mangled, filled the room. It had cut the central marble island in two with debris crumpled all around it. He walked to the rear tail section where he spotted a body.

It was a native of the area, a slight man in his early thirties. His black tee shirt, torn away from his torso, lay shredded either side of his exposed innards. The tail rotor had ripped apart his chest as it landed on top off him, blades slicing continuously until the motor wound to a stop. A flip-flop hung from one of the rotor blades

He left him where he lay. He had bigger fish to fry.

At the end of the hallway, they came to a flight of stairs and a set of three steel doors. Which first?…

An explosion came from the kitchen, blowing through the corridor The walls shuddered and marble tiles vibrated under their feet. It emanated from the pool, the sound carrying through the broken windows. They had launched another UCAV. Jack touched his earwig activating the transmitter.

"Digger… Do you read?" The sound dissipated as the missile moved away from them allowing his ear to come to life.

"Yeah, we're here Jack, that was bloody close though, we were ready to enter the silo! What's taking so long in there? Over." His relief was palpable in his response. Digger and Dregs were fine.

"Thank God… Stay away from the silo until we signal. We're making progress, but we've had a couple of obstacles to deal with."

"Well, you should be on your own from now on. Campbell has arrived. We are holding the south of the island, it is pretty quiet here and Strong with the NATO ground forces are sweeping through the north. These missiles are a worry though, and we can't get to them until you disable the command centre. if you make it in time, you should also be able to recall the two in the air." Digger was right, they had to work fast.

"Leave it to us. We're nearly there … Out."

He looked at the situation again. Three doors with one set of stairs leading up, it made sense the command centre would be behind closed doors so they would start there.

He looked at Riggs. "You take the left, I'll take the middle. Shout if you find it, and I'll come running and vice versa." He would leave the control room to Riggs, he was a trained pilot and far more used to using technology in the field. All he needed was a gun and a mobile phone, the thought of technology taking over his life was a scary thought. He was in charge, he didn't need to be controlled by a microchip.

"Oh, bollocks!" He couldn't believe he was eating his words just moments after taking a swipe at technology. The door had no handles, no hinges and sat snugly in its steel frame. There was a black panel set in the wall alongside each entry waiting for an electronic key. Together both agents used their PDA's, placing them onto the plates, making a selection on the keypad. The screen came alive with binary code.

1111100011001100010101001010000101000 flashed across the screen, a luminescent mix of red and green, a jumble of ones and zeros flicking across the display. After a few seconds, both doors clicked, sliding aside into their steel frames exposing corridors leading deeper into the complex.

Nodding across to each other they entered. The doors closed and sealed them in.

CHAPTER EIGHTY
False Prophet

After a short walk along the aluminium corridor, Riggs came to another steel door, normal this time, pulling down on the handle he entered the room. There was a little hiss as the controlled air of the laboratory escaped.

At first, he felt a rush of excitement thinking he had found the control centre. But he realised, looking closer, that the three consoles positioned around a glass cubicle were used for a different discipline. He was ready to leave to continue his search when he spotted two legs poking out from under the furthest console as he did a final sweep of the room. It was the prostrate figure of an old man, his white coat splayed around him where he fell. From the initial inspection, Riggs couldn't see any apparent cause of death. He turned the body over. The corpse flopped on its back, it sighed as the last of the air in the non-functioning lungs escaped through its mouth. Almonds … He looked at the frozen expression of horror as the effects of the cyanide had taken hold. The old man would have realised too late that it wasn't the painless death they had promised him. He recognised the face of Anatoly Duranichev from the photo images sent to his PDA.

Leaving the corpse where it lay he looked over the console at the glass cubicle beyond. It was an airtight room with a frame mechanism of a clamp and grapple arm. The floor had a seam in between a red line stretching the length of the room, at the wall to the rear, a neat row of shell casings. This was where they put the nukes together, below the floor must be the transport mechanism to the silo. An impressive operation Riggs thought. His eyes moved to the live monitor facing him as he got to his feet. It showed the image of a body sprawled on the floor in amongst bottles and broken glass. He must have fallen where he stood as only part of a drinks cabinet remained fixed to the wall, its shelves smashed, both doors laying nearby. Pressing a bank of switches on the console changed the view on the monitor. He switched from the sleeping accommodation to an office, a large black desk with several monitors fixed to its surface. The camera position focused on the empty chair positioned behind it. It must be Brandt's desk, placed in a way that his image would fill the screen. A President addressing the nation he thought, switching to another camera. The scene now was the pool area, raised high enough to take in the whole of the south beach and beyond into the ocean. That was how they were spotted earlier, their stealth operation had been in full view of the inhabitants of Brandt's complex at all times. He could see the special forces guys scanning the area, AK47's at the ready. Digger and Dregs were deep in conversation with Campbell who was over at the poolside looking into the silo. He switched again and found what he was looking for.

Five consoles dominated the scene, each had one thirty inch monitor, two small data screens and set within the desktop a large joystick. Sitting at one of the desks, his plastered limb visible resting on the seat arm for support, gripping the controls was Leon Ubermann.

"Jack, I've found the command centre and Ubermann. What's your position ... over?" He waited for the response ... none came.

"Jack? Do you read... over?" The silence was tangible; something was wrong.

"Jack?"

Jack entered the corridor feeling as if he had transported back six hundred years. The floor was smooth, but the walls and ceiling were left crudely hewn. Flaming torches dotted along the walls lit the tunnel, giving a sinister feel to the surroundings, by the time he reached the heavy oak door, he expected to find Dr Frankenstein on the other side.

Gun raised he twisted the heavy iron ring, surprised when it didn't creak as he entered the room.

"Come in Mr Case, we have been expecting you." He didn't know whether to rub his eyes to ensure they weren't playing tricks on him or pinch himself to wake up. He was in a temple, dimly lit by burning braziers. Artificial light flowed from intricately designed stained glass windows, the colours giving the room a reddish hue.

Flags and insignia decorated the east wall. He found himself drawn to the Swastika, the black symbol sharp and malevolent within a white circle, surrounded by the blood red of the flag. Even in the 21st century it still sent a chill through the spine. But the eeriest sight of all was the man who had spoken as he first entered the room. Fabian Brandt was sitting on a throne at the top of a set of stone steps. He wore a flowing red robe, trimmed with gold, and on his head a crown of gold and jewels. It took Jack several minutes to compose himself as it was all too surreal. Finally, he found his voice.

"Give it up Brandt, it's over. We have the island surrounded. All of your troops have surrendered, and we have disabled the missiles."

"Make it easy on yourself and come down from there." His gun remained trained on Brandt at all times, and although some of what he had said was far from the truth, it was only a matter of time.

He had to get the man down and into custody. Once banged up, the world's media could reveal the truth, convincing the zealots still awaiting a call to arms that it was over. It would make mopping up a lot easier. Sometimes the media really could help.

But the man on the throne just continued to look back at him, unmoving. They kept staring at each other with only the crackle of the flames from the brazier breaking the silence. What was he waiting for?

"I would say that it was far from over." Brandt said finally.

His senses screamed at him, recalling the welcome from Brandt as he walked into the room 'We have been expecting you'… We…?

His head exploded in pain as he was struck from behind, his legs and arms useless as he toppled forward, crashing to the ground.

He felt no pain as his forehead smashed onto the stone floor.

CHAPTER EIGHTY-ONE
Amen

Jack remained conscious as he fell, but his head was full of noise. He could hear the blood rushing through his temples, pass by his ear canal and along his carotid arteries. The sparks and stars covering his vision blinded him, and his head hurt like hell. He could hear words, but they were too confused and muffled to understand. As he tried to gather his senses, he could feel blood dripping from his neck onto the stone floor. His forehead throbbed where it had hit the ground, splitting the skin as he landed. He needed time to get his faculties back, but he was in such a bad way he could only lay still, hoping his head cleared fast.

"Is he dead?" The voice came from behind, clearer now but not enough to reveal the speaker. He assumed it was Brandt.

"I'm not sure, his eyes are open, but I can't tell if he's breathing." The new voice sounded above him a little way to the left.

He kept his eyes still, zeroing in on the Glock thrown from his grip as he fell. It was laying five feet away.

"Well, check him dammit!" The voice was clear, he knew it was Brandt.

Two black shoes came into view. They were civilian soft-soled shoes, not military, and the voice sounded soft, unsure, scared. He was not one of Brandt's henchmen. Jack could feel his strength returning, seeing only faint pops in his vision as the world came into focus again. He was still in a lot of pain, but he could cope with that, as long as there was no concussion. If he lifted his head and the world began to spin, any advantage of surprising his assailant would be lost. He had one shot at this.

Bishop Marcel Donaretti was terrified. He was hoping he had killed the man using all his strength when he hit him with the sceptre.

The way he fell must have caused serious damage, and the blood, it turned his stomach as it trickled from his shaved head. He still felt concerned about checking the body. He saw the gun on the floor, dropped by the man as he fell. He was not an expert on firearms, but he would feel better if he was holding it while he checked him over. He bent down and picked it up.

Jack took his chance. Remaining on the floor he whirled around, sliding in a circle with his legs outstretched. Rolling onto his back he windmilled towards the stooping man. His six foot frame gave him enough length to shorten the distance. His right foot caught the ankle of his assailant just as he was rising with the gun.

The weapon flew in the air as Donaretti's legs went from under him, his right ankle searing with pain as he fell onto his back.

Having no time to break his fall his head cracked against stone. Dazed and confused he scrambled to his feet, kicking frantically to get a grip so he could move away from the floor and his current position. He stopped and sat down with a bump … looking straight ahead, coming face to face with Jack Case who was sitting a few yards away from him, his legs splayed in front to support his weight.

The agent was holding something in his hand, pointing it at him. It was only slight, but there was smoke rising from the object in his hand, a thin stream of blue smoke, quite beautiful. His saliva felt strange, and it was filling his mouth at a fast rate, a metallic taste not unpleasant, but when he tried to swallow, he found he couldn't. Choking, he felt the saliva leave his mouth and roll down his chin. Instinctively he wiped it away, embarrassed that he was dribbling like a baby. He saw the blood smeared over his hands and wiped his chin again, more blood. He wasn't quite sure what was happening, confusion reigned, his head filled with the need to sleep. Everything can wait, he wasn't sure what everything was, but it can't have been important. He needed to sleep. He closed his eyes and fell backward letting life float away from him.

He was dead before he hit the floor.

Jack watched the man in black stumble as a bullet hole appeared in the middle of his chest. He was still a little light headed, but he had recovered enough to catch the Glock as it fell from the bishops grip. He had managed to grab it, find his target, steady his aim and send a bullet into his torso. He watched mesmerised as the man sat with a bump, wiped his mouth and keeled over ... Dead.

The exertion made him dizzy, he felt nauseous as he struggled to clear his vision. His head was thumping but had receded to a manageable state, the blood had now dried. He blinked several times; it helped a little. He then remembered the other man in the room and pointed his gun in the throne's direction. Brandt had disappeared.

Climbing gingerly to his feet he stood for a second as another wave of nausea passed over him. Moving to the door, pulling it open, he squinted along the gas lit corridor for any sign of the madman. He was nowhere to be seen, he hadn't gone this way. To prove it to himself, he moved back into the room and let go of the door. It swung shut on its own, closing automatically with a bang, a noise he knew he hadn't heard at any time since he had arrived. Brandt must still be here.

The temple wasn't large, and within a few minutes, even in his less than coherent state, he had searched it thoroughly. The stained glass windows offered no route for escape. The pews were moveable, but throwing them aside revealed no trap door and pulling all the flags from the east wall showed only rock.

He stood staring at the throne, how had he escaped? Climbing the few steps he lifted the crown from the seat. Brandt had left it behind along with the gown as he fled. Sweeping the fabric aside to examine the seat properly it became stuck fast at the base. He pulled again following the seam and saw half of the gown trapped underneath the throne. So that was how he did it. He managed to get his fingers marginally underneath the marble, but it wouldn't budge. He felt along the sides, it was smooth and moving around to the rear proved a similar fruitless exercise. He was stumped, how had he managed to move it?

He sat on the marble seat, looking around for any clues, feeling along the arms, the seat, around the base. He searched the floor for a difference in the steps. A depression, a change in texture or shape, but found nothing.

Flopping back into the seat he closed his eyes tilting back his head to relieve the ache, staying there a while taking deep breaths as he tried to think. After a moment he opened them, staring at the ceiling, watching silhouettes and shadows dance across the stone, fuelled by the flames of the braziers. It seemed to ease his head just a little, relaxing him and clearing the fog that had clouded his vision since the attack. As he leant forward, he looked over at the brazier glowing hot beside him. He followed the ornate decoration of the gold stand as it weaved its way to the floor. Kneading his neck, feeling for the knots developing above his shoulder, he turned to look at the other brazier. Identical and decorated with the same swirls of gold. Nothing out of the ordinary there.

Lifting the crown, examining the precious stones as they flickered in the light of the flames, he found it hard to see how a mass murdering megalomaniac could attribute any religion to the New World Order. Yet all around him the symbols, statues and insignia collected to create a place of prayer, contemplation and worship were clear evidence to the contrary.

His eyes moved to his attacker. He hadn't seen it before, but he now noticed the clothing. Dressed in black, his knee length jacket had opened as he fell revealing a plain black shirt with a distinct collar open at the neck, a clerical shirt. He'd killed a priest. He usually left his kills where they lay, too engrossed on the mission at hand. But this time he descended from the throne and knelt next to the body. He had no religious leanings, to an extent he was an agnostic. To believe in anything he needed proof.

He saw the church as a meeting place for people to practice a faith that in reality no one on earth could prove even existed. The bible was a book written by thousands of people, all with different views, interpretations and preconceptions. It was nothing more than a book of ideas with no hard and fast rules. A way in the old days of controlling people, and unfortunately it still does today. He preferred to trust his own judgement, create his own destiny, choose his own way to live.

But he still felt a sense of regret as he closed the priest's eyes, shutting his already sightless view of this world. He was a man in his early forties, soft features, without a blemish on his skin. His pallor and the dried blood staining his chin clearly indicated death, but his expression was of a sleeping man, serene and at peace. Even more unsettling was the way he had fallen. He had thrown his arms wide to break his fall, outstretched as they were with his legs straight and together, he created the symmetrical pose of a crucified man.

"I'm sorry about this Father." He spoke to the corpse as he checked the jacket pockets. He pulled out a heavy object wrapped tightly in a thick chain. Unfurling it, he held it up to the light. It was a pectoral cross of gold inset with jewels with an enamel image of Christ at the centre. At the top of the cross sat a mitre complete with a ring, allowing the heavy chain of gold to pass through. His priest was a bishop of high religious order. From the inside pocket, he pulled out a silver card holder and studied the business card. Bishop Marcel Donaretti. 00120 Via del Pellegrino. Citta del Vaticano. He was a bishop of the Vatican. It was a powerful find, a revelation that could have implications worldwide, even after the defeat of Brandt and his forces.

It would need to wait for now as he had spotted something else while kneeling next to the body. He pocketed the cross and business card as he walked over to the brazier on the right. Black specks were surrounding the base, a heavy concentration to one side, the side furthest from the throne. He checked the other brazier; the area surrounding this base was clean. With his strength returning he pushed up the steps and standing in front of the throne he pushed the bowl of the left brazier away from him. It tilted a few inches and stopped with a click. In one smooth action the base lifted, and the throne fell back coming to a rest at 90 degrees exposing a steel ladder attached to the stone wall of a shaft. Brandt had gone underground.

As he touched his earwig to let Riggs know of his discovery, his finger went straight into his ear. He had dislodged it.

"Damn". His curse echoed around the temple as he bolted down the steps checking the floor as he went. It must have dislodged when hit over the head, which made him realise just how hard that had been. He had to find it as he needed support to secure the perimeter to prevent Brandt's escape. There was no time to make his way out of the complex to warn the others, he had to get after him. He already had a head start. Damn technology, this was when it came back around and bit you on the arse. He pulled out his PDA. At least he had a direct link to Riggs. He could get a message to the others.

"Riggs … do you copy." Jack listened to the static in response.

"Riggs … do you read … over?" Static again.

Where was he?

"Riggs?"

CHAPTER EIGHTY-TWO
Fight for the Air

Riggs raised his gun and prepared to open the door. As with the first door, he held the PDA to the keypad and waited for the binary code to match. Maintaining radio silence for fear of alerting Ubermann, made his concern for Jack worse. He hadn't heard from him for well over fifteen minutes, and it worried him. The door clicked and slid clear revealing the command centre control room. He stood in the relative safety of the corridor for a moment as he cast his eyes over the five consoles. Ubermann was not there.

Gun at the ready he thrust his head into the room ducking in left and then right before pulling back. It was clear. He moved cautiously into the room, checking for any signs of movement.

The space was only forty feet square and housed the control consoles, a few storage units and a free vend drinks and snack machine. There was no sign of the German. His eyes focused on the monitors, in particular, the first two which showed images from the directional cameras of the airborne UCAVs. They were live feeds of clouds hurtling past as they flew towards their destinations.

Below the main screen were two smaller monitors. One showed reams of data, sending information on the current state of the UCAV, its performance, airspeed and ETA. The second screen showed a map, a small crosshair blinking on a particular area in the centre of the screen. Threadneedle Street, London and Wall Street, New York highlighted on the two live screens. They were starting with the big ones. Riggs studied the equipment, comfortable with the setup. He was sure he could take control and divert them away from their destinations. Another screen hanging on the wall drew his attention, he hadn't noticed it before, his eyes drawn to the UCAV consoles instead. It was a security screen, split into six sections. The first showed an image of the north of the island, an area full of activity. There were NATO forces all over the place supported by the Seals rounding up insurgents and loading them into waiting boats. The second showed the south, now held by the UK special forces guarding the silo and patrolling the beach perimeter. The rest of the screens were made up of interior rooms, offices, corridors and utility rooms. One, in particular, took his interest, it was of the laboratory where he had just been. He could see the body of Duranichev laying on his back, exactly as he had left him not ten minutes since. It took a moment for realisation to dawn as he studied the next image. He was looking at a room full of consoles with a man staring off to the right. It took him seconds to register the man on the screen was actually him and a millisecond later to process there was someone behind him.

It was the millisecond that saved his life. Riggs swung around, stepping back in one movement, his senses attuned just in time to reduce the full force of the knife. He suffered a glancing blow to his right arm as he held it up to defend himself. The blade sliced through his jacket, biting into his flesh. It was only a nick, and he felt no pain as he stumbled back, catching the back of a control chair as he crashed to the floor. His gun flew from his hand, spinning underneath the bank of consoles, wedging itself between the frame of the first and second machine. Ubermann stumbled forward, taken by surprise as Riggs diverted his attack, and greeted by an American boot to his stomach. He flew up in the air, the boot propelling him over Rigg's prone body. He landed on the restraining bar protruding from the plaster cast of his left arm, the pins pushed into bone sending a sharp pain through his body, his agonising screams echoed around the room. Angered and in severe pain, the German roared as he pulled his gun from his waist and fired at the scrambling figure. Rigg managed to dive for cover behind a console. Three shots hit the wall tearing through the stone. Shards of dust and rubble exploded everywhere.

He would finish him now, he had to get the other missiles in the air as the island had been breached. He needed to do this urgently enabling him to make his escape and avoid capture.

He heard the sound of a plastic cup dropping from the machine and a steady whine and trickle as it filled with liquid. The American was near the vending machine.

Ubermann moved behind the bank of consoles which would bring him out facing the machine. He crawled past tall storage units arriving at a pillar standing between him and the open area facing it. He winced as a sharp pain shot up his left arm from the trauma of the fall. He had to stop to take a few deep breaths to ease it.

"I bet that hurts like shit." He snapped his head around.

The American was standing behind his left shoulder; he had been duped. His pain and anger had caused a lapse of concentration which enraged him even more. Amateurish, he should have known better.

Before the German could react, Riggs grabbed the restraining bar sticking out of the arm. He felt it give in his hand as he strengthened his grip. Plaster fell away from the cast and Ubermann squealed in torturous agony. Using it as a handle, he swung the man across the room.

As he pulled, the restraining bar ripped through the plaster, bringing with it pins and bone fragments. The cast shattered before Ubermann hit the floor. His screams were mixed with Germanic curses as he held his shattered arm close to his chest. In a rage now out of control, Leon Ubermann rose to his feet, a moan escaped him at very exhalation of breath.

Blind with fury he pulled his Kabar from the sheath and rushed at the American who stood a few yards from him, enjoying his pain. He launched at him; the blade glinting in the air as he held it high, intending to bury it into his enemy's head. He would keep stabbing and cutting, enjoying the screams as he sliced into his flesh. He would not stop until the screams died. Riggs watched as the German got to his feet and lumbered towards him. He waited until he was within striking distance before blasting him with three body shots sending him sprawling back.

He collapsed in a heap, the second shot blowing his heart apart, forcing him to lay still forever.

CHAPTER EIGHTY-THREE
Double Back

He let out a sigh of relief as he looked down at the German's gun in his hand, the gun Ubermann had dropped as he was being swung around by his arm. He hadn't had time to check if it was loaded, he just hoped for the best. With no time to lose he crouched, pulled his gun free from under the consoles and ran around to take a seat at the first one. He tried his earwig again.

"Jack … It's Riggs can you hear me … over?" There was silence again.

"Digger … can you read … over?" He thought to try another route but was greeted with more of the same. He pulled the transmitter from his ear and threw it across the floor, it must have given up the ghost from all the water it had taken in. He grabbed his PDA preparing to call Jack when he noticed he had missed eight calls. He took the handset off silent, rebuking himself for putting it on in the first place, and made the call. He had a thing about ring tones; he hated them, preferring the vibrate function and the use of the earwig at all times. He loved that bit of kit; it made him feel so cool.

"Riggs, where the hell have you been?" He could hear a mixture of anger and relief as he took the call.

"Had a slight problem with a one armed German." He replied as he checked the heading of the London bound missile and prepared his strategy to divert. "Anyway, where were you? I got the same lack of response too."

"Had a problem with a priest, don't ask… Now listen Riggs, get hold of Campbell and let him know Brandt has escaped. There's an underground tunnel leading to an exit, God knows where. Get them to circle the island, look for any routes out."

"Got it!" Riggs knew how he could do this without the earwig. He grabbed a headset from the console and switching the frequency to 19600 called out to Campbell. He got through instantly and relayed the message to the Special Forces Commander who went into action.

"All done Jack, they're getting a few boats to circle now, they'll find him."

"Great, you are in the control room I guess?" He was already on to the next item as he continued to scan the floor with no luck. There was only one place it could be.

"I am, and I have the two missiles under control. One was heading for London and the other for New York."

Jack placed the PDA on the floor switching to hands-free as he shuffled his fingers under Donaretti's body and turned him on his side. The corpse had covered the earwig. Brandt had indeed had divine intervention to aid in his escape.

"What are you planning on doing with them?" He asked, as he placed the transmitter into his ear.

"I'm bringing them back." Riggs said feeling pleased with himself.

"I would be careful with that tactic." It was Digger. "The UCAVs have no landing mechanism and here's the good bit... They are rigged to explode on landing." The explosives expert had a good look at them from the poolside vantage point. He was able to see the small incendiary devices fixed onto the belly of each craft. If they tried to land, the explosion would provide enough of a jolt to trigger the nuke.

"Then I'll send them to the Arctic, freeze the bastards!" Rigg moved the map screen to the north in search of whiter climes.

"Nope, you can't do that." Digger again offered his knowledge of the effects of a nuclear fallout.

"It would be catastrophic to the ECO system and the globe itself if you release them anywhere near the poles." Thinking as he explained there had to be another way.

"Not only would the fallout destroy everything for several thousand miles, but the caps would melt like an ice cube in a hot cup of tea. The tidal surge would cover half the land above sea level."

Jack made his way down the walls of the shaft listening to the conversation as he took the rungs one careful step at a time. Wall lights provided perfect visibility as he descended.

"Right." Riggs started to think. "Then I'll fly them as high as I can and press this red button that blows the nuke to smithereens, well out of harm's way."

"And kill many more than a city strike Einstein! Have you never heard of black rain? The nuke would disperse into the atmosphere, catch the wind and rain down God knows where. We would do a better job at wiping out the world than Brandt." Riggs thought of suggesting the water, but to save further embarrassment, he left it alone. Impact at high speed is the same as hitting concrete. So the incendiary device would go off, blowing up the nuke and destroying sea life around the world … he got it now.

"So what do you suggest Digger?" He would leave it to the expert.

"Bring them back for now… I have an idea. But I need to think about it a little more. In the meantime, we have three men in the silo underneath the remaining UCAVs. Can you activate the clamps and release the warheads? At least if we get these off the island, we can breathe a little easier."

"Ok, give me a couple of minutes, I'll get back to you … Out."

Riggs manoeuvred the joystick, watching as the bearing changed. Using the keyboard to fine tune the destination on the map screen, he moved the crosshairs to the centre of the island. Happy the UCAV was on its way back he followed the same procedure for the other craft. The ETA was 40 minutes and 45 minutes, respectively.

Riggs then moved to console three and switching on the rear view camera of the UCAV saw two biohazard suits looking up at him.

"OK, brace yourself. Number three coming up. 3… 2… 1… Go!" He pressed the release button.

The clamps holding the warhead retracted and the sixty-four kilogram missile pulled away from the UCAV. The specials, encased in their hazmats carefully placed it in a leather canopy attached to a winch system, rigged up to help with the extraction. It raised to the surface where two other operatives transported it to a waiting submersible. It sat in the water ready to transport the nukes away and into a waiting frigate two kilometres away. As the last warhead was removed safely from the silo, Riggs took his place back at the first console. ETA was 20 minutes and 25 minutes.

"Right." Digger began … "This is what we will do." He listened to the instructions, his eyes opening wide as he heard the proposal for bringing the warheads back to earth.

"Are you fucking mad! That's suicidal."

"It's our only option and it'll work. Don't worry; I'll come up, we can work out the finer details together. In the meantime … Sit tight."

Riggs flopped back in his chair. He was too young to die.

CHAPTER EIGHTY-FOUR
Countdown

Letting go of the rungs he looked both ways, deciding the best route to take. He stood in silence listening for footsteps. Apart from a trickle of water echoing in the enclosed space as it dripped into an ever expanding puddle, he heard nothing.

He was in a purpose built oval tunnel smoothed out and finished in white. The bright inset lights dotted along the ceiling offered near daylight vision. A channelled drain cut into the centre of the floor carried a small stream north to south. He followed the direction of the water figuring it would end in the open sea.

After a hundred yards he could hear the distinctive sound of the ocean emanating from the tunnel as it took a sharp turn to the left. Following the route he drew his Glock, as ahead the tunnel opened up into a vast underground dock. Built inside an existing cavernous inlet of rock, the dock rose forty feet high, stretching sixty foot across. Waves crashed against the small quay with a deafening boom as it reverberated around the enclosure.

Jack crossed to the observation rails, looking down at the fifteen foot drop to the water's surface. To the west it ended where erosion had created a rock platform. It was stacked high with oil barrels. Looking east the cavern opened into the sea, offering a gleaming vista of blue as ocean met clear calm skies. The quayside stretched east towards the exit before dropping away to what he could only assume was a slip dock sloping down towards the water's edge. He walked over to verify his theory. He stopped short as he noticed a wet print on the concrete floor six inches away from a puddle. Brandt had been here.

Edging back, gun raised, he eased himself along the rough wall of the cavern reaching the point where the slip dock began its descent. He peered over the edge. Machine gun fire cracked all around him, sharp shards of rock stinging his face as he dived from view. Remaining on his front he crawled to the edge of the platform and risked a glance. He saw enough before they drove him back with more gunfire ringing off the metal rail. One of Brandt's guards was shooting at him from the main hatch of a mini submarine. Rolling onto his back, he ejected a clip and reloaded before rolling again, preparing for his next move. He had seen enough to gauge the angle between his position and the hatch. He shuffled his knees under his body to add to his speed of attack, jumping up he aimed a volley at the sub. His bullets harmlessly bounced off the closed hatch and rear of the steel body as the craft floated away.

"Damn it!" He ran down the slip dock firing all the way. It was useless as he watched the sub sink from view. He used the PDA. "Sara I need you to look for signs of a small craft moving away from the island, I think I am facing southeast. Brandt has escaped."

"I'm on it, Jack ... nothing yet ... I'll report to the patrol ships when it comes into view."

"Hang on Sara ..." He stopped her short as a klaxon sounded ringing around the cavern hurting his ears. A deep automated voice accompanied it.

"Warning! This is not a drill, evacuate the island immediately. Detonation in T minus 20 minutes ... Warning! This is not a ..."

"Sara, I'll get back to you ... Stop that sub!" He closed the call and looked around the slip dock.

On the wall directly behind his position was a display showing an electronic timer in hours, minutes and seconds, and a keypad, red switch and conventional lock set in the wall below. That is where Brandt had set the countdown. The dial read 00:19:35; the seconds counting down. He set his PDA timer, synchronised it with the readout and ran. He sprinted along the quay and launched into the tunnel heading back to the temple.

"Riggs, we need to get out! The island's going up in twenty minutes. Campbell, get your guys to clear up and get off as quickly as you can. We need to get out of here."

He followed the tunnel round to the main corridor and set off for the steps.

"I know Jack, I can hear it. What have you done now?" Riggs was perplexed, first because of Digger and now this. How were they going to get this to work?

"We can't leave. We need to bring down the nukes."

"What are you talking about?" He screamed through the earwig.

"Digger has a plan, and I think it will work. It's a risk, we need a large slice of luck, but we can do it." He knew he was right. The nukes needed to be stopped, or millions would die, and the ECO system around the Pacific would be devastated for years.

"Ok Riggs, how long have we got?" Jack pulled himself clear of the shaft and walked down the steps from the throne. The countdown continued. '… Detonation in T minus 16 minutes.'

"Ten minutes…" Riggs said. Great, that should give them enough time with a fast boat on standby he thought.

"… And fifteen minutes!" Oh shit! He threw open the oak door and printed along the medieval corridor on his way to the control room.

CHAPTER EIGHTY-FIVE
Regroup and Rewind

The sub cruised into open waters and levelled out at 200 feet below sea level at a steady 20 knots. The hollow beep of the sonar cutting through the silence as the three inhabitants kept to themselves. Lucien used his instruments to keep the heading constant and was hopeful they would dock in fifteen minutes. He could then let Brandt off and be rid of him. It had all gone wrong, and he didn't want to be associated with the master plan anymore. He would go back to his scuba diving business, return to normal life and hopefully escape from any investigation. Christian sat at the rear, resting his M16 on his lap, thinking of the future. The boss had left Leon Ubermann behind and set the island to explode. It meant the man was either dead or excluded from the revised plans of Mr Brandt. He had aspirations, he could see himself taking the role as head of security. He was experienced, committed and now with Ubermann out of the picture, one of the very few staff members who Brandt confided in. It was his big chance. Even though the mood was sombre, and the boss was in no mood for conversation, he couldn't help smiling to himself.

"How close are you?" Brandt sat in the centre of the bridge on a rather recliner fitted explicitly for his use.

They designed the sub to hold six people at its maximum capacity. But since the refit, it allowed only one support passenger to the rear, one pilot and Brandt. They had transformed the centre of the bridge into a luxury lounge area. There was a stocked drinks cabinet to the left of his chair and a console to the right. Brandt used the console.

"We will be in position in ten minutes, Mr Brandt." The reply was official and succinct.

"Good, be prepared to move as soon as I am on board. Do you have the crew ready?"

"That's affirmative sir!" Again the response was official, just as he liked it. Brandt had called upon The Endeavour, his luxury yacht, to assist in his departure. He refused to see it as an escape. He wasn't escaping, he only needed time to regroup.

The speed in which the authorities had discovered his plans had been disconcerting. LARA had been the catalyst for that. He had to admire the tenacity of Jack Case, he could do with a man like him alongside, although he knew it would never happen. He would eliminate him along with his organisation. It was his next task, and once they were out of the way, he would announce a call to arms.

The New World Order would once again rise, and this time he would not fail.

CHAPTER EIGHTY-SIX
No Time

ack joined Riggs and Digger in the control room. Riggs positioned at he first console alongside Digger at the second. Both were concentrating on the monitors, while their hands worked the joystick and keyboard.

"And you are sure this is going to work?" He asked as they briefed him on their strategy to bring the nukes back to earth.

"It has to, or we are toast." Digger continued scanning the data as he tried to reassure him they had thought it through.

"So let me get this right. You'll send the UCAV to the south of the island. Before it hits the beach, you are going to release the missile and hope the sand will slow it down enough to stop it hitting the building." He still could not believe what he was hearing.

"That's correct, we have Dregs and Commander Campbell on the beach ready to load them onto the CRRC and once the second one loads we run like hell." He looked at the screen on the east wall showing a single CCTV image of the beach. It enlarged enough to see the two special forces operatives in their bio-suits looking in the direction of the cameras. They were waving after hearing their names mentioned by Digger. He smiled, he was with a group of crazy bastards, and to be honest; he was glad they were here.

"We have a good chance." Digger continued. "The nukes have to detonate to work. They either have to impact on a hard enough surface to force the two uranium sections to hit one another or by remote control." He pointed to the red button on the top of the joystick currently locked behind a transparent cover.

"The beach is man made. With very fine grains to give it the soft luxurious beach look. We have checked the depth to about fifteen feet so we have a cushion waiting for them."

"… T minus 7 minutes and 30 seconds." The voice continued to count down around them. They had disabled the control room speaker, Riggs had blown it to pieces with a well aimed shot. It had drilled into their heads. They could hear the countdown perfectly well from the one down the hall.

"Here it comes!" Campbell announced, seeing a speck in the air a few miles in the distance.

"Yep, I can see us." Digger saw the island come into view from the forward camera of the UCAV. "Brace yourselves, ladies!"

He pushed the joystick forward, watching the UCAV tilt towards the ocean. The readout showed 10,000 feet. Campbell and Dregs moved to the edges of the bay hugging the walls of the mountain. There was nowhere to run, and thoughts of death were not far from their minds. If it went up, there was nothing they could do about it, the only comfort was they wouldn't feel a thing. It was more important to be close enough to grab the nuke if it landed where they hoped, as a few minutes later they would need to be ready for the next one. Dregs had never seen himself as a God botherer, but he recited the Lord's Prayer as he watched the craft descend and level it's flight towards them. He looked over to Campbell and raised his thumb; the gesture returned immediately. They had bought into this and they were ready.

5000 feet, 4000 feet, 3000 feet, 2000 feet … Digger kept the descent constant never taking his eyes from the instruments. No one spoke as the UCAV continued on its path. 500 feet, 400 feet … Jack wondered how Dregs and Campbell must be feeling as they saw the missile arrow towards them. From his own vantage point, he felt as if he was watching a scene from a movie. He experienced a surreal fascination as they flew the nuclear warhead straight at themselves. Digger levelled the UCAV at six feet, slowing the speed to twenty miles an hour, just enough to keep the craft in the air. The sun shone over the white casing creating a mirrored image on the surface of the ocean, gleaming blur of destruction. If it hit turbulence or a down draught now, it would be over. But the weather was calm, and he trusted his calculations. Digger watched as the beach moved towards him. He had to release at just the right moment, around twenty yards from the sand, an area where the waves were relatively light. The sea should deep enough to support the missile's trajectory.

50 yards, 40 yards, 30 yards … He hit the release button, forcing the joystick full forward pushing the UCAV towards the ocean surface. The clamps retracted, and the missile came free, continuing along in a straight line heading for the beach.

The UCAV hit and exploded, sending spray twenty feet in the air, a mist of sea water mushroomed across the surface peppering down like light rain. The missile continued to hurtle towards the bay skimming the ocean, keeping its trajectory straight ahead. As it approached the beach a small wave flicked it as it made its way towards the waiting sand. It hit the ground with a whoomp and burrowed into the soft grains slowing as it scraped towards the silo and the rock fall lying in front of it.

They held their breath as they watched the bomb cut a swathe through the sand. Dregs and Campbell decided to go for it and leapt from their cover running towards the red tipped target. The missile came to a stop.

"Come on, you beauty!" Digger shouted, high fiving the agents, all breathing heavy sighs of relief as they watched their plan come together. Digger and Campbell scooped the missile up in their arms and carried it carefully towards the submersible banked at the damp edge of the beach.

Placing it securely into a lead-lined box, they ran back to their positions and waited for the next one. Looking across open seas, they could see it as a speck in the distance.

"Jack can you read…. Over?" it was Sara.

"Go ahead, Sara." He kept his eyes on Riggs as he brought in the second UCAV.

"The sub has surfaced three miles southeast of your location. Satellite images show it has docked with a yacht. Shall we get them picked up?"

"No!" It was Riggs. He had brought the UCAV down to 100 feet and was reducing its speed. "Three miles is not safe enough for us to intercept. Keep monitoring its movement, we can get them later … if we survive this."

"Survive what?" Sara hadn't realised they were still in danger. She thought it was over.

"... T minus 3 minutes 30 seconds."

"T minus what? Jack, what's going on?" Riggs was at ten feet and closing.

"Not now Sara I'll get back to you in a few minutes."

"But Jack..."

"Sara! Not now ... Out!" He pushed the earwig to break the connection.

"Here we go!" Riggs announced as he levelled the UCAV at six feet and aimed it at the beach.

"Now remember as soon as you release the nuke let's get out of here." He looked over to Digger and touched Riggs shoulder hoping he had heard. They would have very little time to escape.

50 yards, 40 yards, 30 yards ... Riggs pressed the release on the panel and pulled the joystick back sending the UCAV up into the air accelerating as he did so. The missile followed its intended route towards the bay.

"What are you doing Riggs?" He shouted as he watched the screen turn sky blue rather than the crackle of interference as the UCAV exploded. He was flying the thing!

"C'mon, let's go!" Digger moved out of his chair and headed for the exit.

"Riggs come on." Jack stood and touched his shoulder again gripping it this time and pulling gently.

Riggs shrugged his hand off, maintaining his concentration on controlling the craft.

"No Jack, let's finish this." He realised what Riggs was doing and decided to stay. Digger was on the same wavelength and returned to his seat.

They watched the screen as the missile raced towards them. Riggs kept his eyes on the forward camera of the UCAV, focussing on searching the ocean landscape in front of him.

The missile headed towards the beach skimming the surface as before. It was perfectly horizontal and speed identical. They kept their fingers crossed for the same result.

As it hit the beach, it caught a divot from the channel made by the first nuke. Flipping ten feet into the air it sailed towards the rocks. landed back on its belly and kept moving. The additional air time created an injection of speed sending it coursing forward faster than they had calculated. This time it wasn't going to stop. They braced themselves for the impact as the nuke, now only twenty feet away was still travelling.

From the corner of the screen, a figure ran into shot, clad in his bio suit but with the cumbersome headgear discarded. Dregs pumped his legs for all his worth, the sand biting around his ankles and pulling at his calves. He dived full length, his arms outstretched, grabbing at the fins of the missile. His right hand caught, and he heaved his weight towards it, pulling his left arm across to catch hold of the body. Nuke and man came to a halt within two feet of impact.

"T minus 1 minute 40 seconds…" the speakers announced.

"Well, I'll be fucked!" Digger shouted before collapsing into fits of laughter, giggles and a demented roar he would never admit to when he recalled the story.

Dregs got to his feet, bent double with his hands on his knees breathing heavily. He couldn't remember the last time he had run so fast and his whole body told him it would be a long time before he did again. He was joined by Campbell who gave him a slap of congratulations on the back. It made him stumble a foot from his position. Seeing the condition of his colleague, Campbell lifted the missile and staggered towards the CRRC. He arched his back as far as he could to support the ten stone weight in his arms. Within a few yards, Dregs joined him and together they secured the nuke. They pulled the submersible into the sea, riding it to safety while they waited for the others.

Jack stood over Riggs and watched the screen. He had found the yacht, gleaming white in open water it was an easy target, but still at least a mile away.

"T minus 1 minute 20 seconds."

"Riggs let's go, buddy, we'll go after him once we're clear of the island." He ignored him.

"Riggs! Come on! It's over, we can round him up as soon as we get clear of the explosion."

"No Jack, we can stop this now! I need to make sure we don't miss. I want to land right on top of the bastard." Riggs wasn't going to move.

"T minus 1 minute."

"Can I suggest something?" Digger leant past Rigg's left shoulder and pressed a button marked TLM. A crosshair appeared on the monitor and Riggs aimed it at the yacht which was now only half a mile in the distance.

The crosshair bleeped and flashed green as soon it came into contact with the cruiser. The word 'locked' flashed next to it as the Target Locking Mechanism took control.

"T minus 50 seconds."

All three men sprinted through the door, running the length of the corridor at breakneck speed.

"T minus 40 seconds."

Reaching the stairs they automatically reverted to single file jumping down four steps at a time.

"T minus 20 seconds."

They raced through the Mediterranean decor of the lower level homing in on the door to freedom. Climbing the debris that was once a marble staircase, they hit the warmth of the midday Pacific sun. Clearing the silo, leaping over the rocks to land on soft sand they felt a rumble through their feet growing stronger with each step. The building exploded without warning, sending all three men flying onto the damp sand by the ocean's edge.

They didn't look back as they ran splashing through the waves reaching the submersible together and diving in headfirst. With legs still being pulled into the craft Dregs fired the throttle and swung the tiller towards open waters.

Fabian Brandt pulled himself onto the deck of The Endeavour with the help of two of the crew helping with the last step, their M16's strapped to their backs. Christian Voltz climbed up behind.

"Right, let's go!" Brandt shouted across to the bridge as he walked to the accommodation level to pour himself a drink.

"Err, Mr Brandt." Christian called to his boss as he looked toward he skies. Brandt turned, irritated at the interruption he glared at Christian. Following the young German's gaze, a UCAV came into view high above, it was heading straight towards them. He stared in disbelief. How?

"Get us out of here!" Brandt screamed at the bridge.

He could have saved his breath as the captain had already pushed the throttle lever to ahead full, forcing the yacht to lurch forward. The propellers cut through the water picking up speed as all eyes watched the sky. Some of the crew jumped overboard as it became clear the UCAV was matching their course, homing in and closing fast.

Brandt looked around, searching for an escape. He ran into the accommodation deck looking for somewhere to hide, checking the window in a panic, every second the aircraft moved ever closer. Brandt was frantic; what should he do? He opened cupboards, ran to the window, opened the cabinets again, then back to the window. Running to the bathroom, a strange mewling escaped from his mouth, a pathetic cry for help. As fear enveloped him and with nowhere to go, he allowed it to take over his body. His senses scrambled as his brain ceased to function. He was no longer scared; he felt at peace as the electrons in his head shut down receptors, and his body went into motor neurone autopilot.

He walked calmly to the cocktail cabinet and poured a vodka. Taking a seat by the window, he watched the approaching craft, no more than a few hundred yards away.

"I'm sorry father I have failed you." Fabian Brandt took a mouthful of vodka.

He didn't get the chance to swallow.

CHAPTER EIGHTY-SEVEN
Bouyant

Dregs kept the throttle on full, speeding as far away from the island as possible. The submersible bounced over choppy waters as the waves grew stronger, propelled by the tremors from the explosion. Campbell laid by the lead container trying to hold it steady, riding every undulation. After untangling their arms and legs from each other, the LARA agents faced towards the southeast. They were just in time to see the flash of an explosion colour the horizon. They couldn't hear it over the blast coming from behind, but by the size of the flames, it had been a big one.

Turning to face the island they watched the destruction unfold. There was no sign of the building from the beach as it was now completely buried by the mountain as it collapsed in on itself. A mushroom cloud of smoke and dust grew steadily larger as other areas collapsed and imploded. It blackened the air as it rolled outward blotting the clear blue sky. Explosions erupted all over the island. Fragments of steel and rock flew in every direction falling into the sea before sinking out of sight.

"Great catch out there in the field man." Riggs was the first to speak as he turned to Dregs congratulating him on his quick thinking as he dived on the missile. "You'd make a great linebacker back home."

Dregs smiled.

"I prefer Rugby … you know, American Football for men. Same rules, same ball, no suit of armour." He winked a smile.

"It was all I could think of doing. That sucker wasn't going to stop, and I was close enough to get a hold of it." His modesty didn't wash with the rest of the passengers. They all knew it had been a superhuman effort, one that had saved all their lives.

"We can slow down a little now, don't you think?" Campbell continued to hold on to the missile, but he was feeling the strain as he concentrated on keeping it from bouncing overboard. He was gritting his teeth as he tried to ride every bump. Dregs cut the throttle and brought the craft to a slower speed, the waves carrying them onwards to the waiting frigate. Campbell let go and gratefully shook the stiffness from his arms.

Jack sat with his thoughts, aware of a job well done. He couldn't help feeling however that world intelligence had failed to gather any inte on potential global destruction. Too many times agencies like LARA are appointed to clear up the mess created by governments who fai to realise any threats until they were already out of control.

It paid the bills and kept him employed, but the menace was growing. With insurgent groups and religious zealots, creating new factions of fanatics and wackos, becoming stronger throughout the globe, there could be another Fabian Brandt just around the corner.

"So, where do we go from here?" Riggs brought him back from hi dark reverie. He turned and looked at the confident grin of the American, his sparkling veneers gleaming under the midday sun.

"Because I don't know about you, I am off on a long vacation straight after the debrief." He thought again for a moment, narrowing his eyes.

"Mind you; I will stay on the mainland. Islands worry me."

The CRRC pulled up alongside the waiting frigate and Campbell and Digger grabbed the lines to keep them steady. Dregs caught the rope ladder as it rolled down to him.

"We're home!" Dregs announced holding it steady as Riggs began his climb to the deck.

CHAPTER EIGHTY-EIGHT
The Patio

The sun shone warmly in a clear blue sky. It brought alive the fusion of colours in the garden of the Manor House in the tranquil village of Mittand Burrow.

"More juice Jack?" Annabel proffered the jug of fresh orange towards his nearly empty glass as he nonchalantly circled it in his hands.

"Uh!… Oh… No thank you; I'm fine." He smiled at her as he snapped back from his muse.

He was looking over at the Grecian style pool house, studying the row of small circular windows running evenly between the eaves of the sloping roof. He took a particular interest in the last one on the right, newly repaired, the window that started it all. Colin Thorn had been the unwitting victim of a plot which could have changed the very fabric of the world as we know it today. A plot involving so many people, had taken so many innocent lives, and had ended with more questions than answers.

"Are you Ok?" Annabel leaned over and touched his arm.

He looked into her sparkling eyes unable to repress the fluttering inside as they drew him in. She looked as beautiful as ever and more relaxed than he could remember seeing her. The pastel pink blouse and figure hugging white trousers gave her a summery glow, enhanced by the sunlight creating a haze around her. Her dark shoulder length hair framed her face creating a sultry look that oozed sexual intimacy.

"Yeah, I'm fine." Jack turned towards her and finished his glass, placing it on the table.

"You look well, Annabel. How have you been?" He watched her relax back into her chair flicking back her head to move her fringe aside.

"Oh, I'm fine." She smiled. "Everyone has been marvellous, and it appears the village is back to how it was before Colin…" She stopped for a moment and lowered her head.

Time is a great healer, but not enough had passed yet since Colin's death to look back warmly on their life together. There was still so much hurt, so much anger, so much pain.

"… I mean Mittand Burrow is back to normal. An ordinary country village where people live their daily lives in peace and tranquillity. It is so nice to be a part of it." Again she looked over to him, her eyes probing his. But there was something behind them now. He had seen the same in Paris, on the train to Zurich and again at the mine.

"Jack…" She wanted to ask, but he could see her inner struggle as she feared the answer. She took a deep breath.

"… Is it really over?" He smiled, relieved by the question. That one was easy.

Last night had been awkward as he politely declined her advances. He had arrived late, and they sat together enjoying a drink or two catching up. Before they knew it, they had polished off three bottles of wine and were comfortably halfway through a bottle of single malt. An intimacy developed they both wanted and probably needed. But as the kissing began, tender and warm, he pulled away and as gently as he could he changed the mood by suggesting coffee.

They carried on talking until she eventually dozed and they retired to separate rooms. There was an attraction that he couldn't deny, but his feelings for Annabel conflicted with his professional need to ensure her safety. She was too high profile now. She had been seen on news programmes around the world, guesting on chat shows, both sides of the Atlantic. She was also the woman of the moment in most of the glossies. He was not prepared, because of his line of work, to put her at risk. There were too many people in the world who were out to get him, and he wouldn't put her in danger by having some maniac target her to get to him. Under normal circumstances, he would not have hesitated, but it was hard to explain it to her. She would never understand.

"Yes, Annabel … It's over." He could tell by her expression; she needed more than that.

"Two weeks ago we captured the last cell in China. A group of sixty sleepers all prepared to jump when the order came. It turns out most of them were just anarchists along for the ride headed by two ex-military commanders with a beef against the government."

"In truth, the whole New World Order was full of Anarchists, Anti Capitalists and Neo-Nazis, intent on following the Brandt dream purely for the money and a chance to create chaos. The true disciples of the cause came to no more than two hundred, and it included Brandt's own security staff." He watched as relief registered in her eyes. She noticeably relaxed as he finished his account.

"It was true many held a historical hatred for the free world in favour of the Nazi dream, but they had no voice, no trigger. Like the Brigadier and his father, they were two war criminals who had melded into society and stayed hidden from the authorities. Brandt offered them the ammunition, and they were easy to recruit. Bringing the idea of a Fourth Reich based on the history of Germany and the link to the Roman Empire just fuelled the indoctrination. It is easy to brainwash those who already had a malleable mind."

He omitted the corruption and influence of the Vatican as that would never be released to the world. After the extraction of those implicated in Brandt's scheme, the church agreed to work with the authorities. They allowed a full investigation in return for a news blackout. The announcement of a reconstitution of the diocese with the coming and going of cardinals, bishops and priests was broadcast officially as the church embracing modern society, seen as a new age where more clergy would be rewarded for their faith. An announcement welcomed globally.

"I tell you what Mrs Paxton-Thorn, you make one hell of a good croissant." Antoine Valois came out of the kitchen, his mouth full of pastry, balancing a plate full of croissants, a plate of mini jams and a cereal bowl.

"Don't you ever stop eating?" Jack watched the Frenchman carry his booty precariously across the patio, wincing as he put them on the table and missed. The conserves clattered across the marble top, one pot of strawberry jam rolled over the edge and crashed onto the concrete.

"Sacré bleu! I apologise Mrs Paxton-Thorn I will clear it up right away." Antoine moved around the table to see to the mess.

"It's Ok Mr Valois, let me." Mrs Claridge came up behind him carrying a dustpan and brush in one hand and a plate of warm toast in the other, which she handed to him. She then went to work scraping gooey glass into the dustpan.

He took a bite from his toast as he walked over to them, sitting back in his wheelchair.

"Antoine, you really don't need that chair. You are fine." He had recovered fully from his stab wound. He was now back on active duty. When he received a call from Annabel inviting him to the Manor House for a long weekend, by way of thanks, he took sick leave, an option open to him. When he first arrived in a wheelchair with a young nurse in tow, Annabel was shocked fearing he had been paralysed from the attack. But, whenever the nurse left the room, and he started to move around freely she realised he had an ulterior motive. He was unbelievable, but she agreed to cover for him. Finishing his toast, taking only two bites per slice to eat it, Antoine stood to grab another croissant from the table.

"Monsieur Valois!" A young blonde woman who was extremely well endowed appeared at the rear doors. Her high heels clicked across the slabs as she went to the aid of her patient. Antoine, hearing her, stooped down and became unsteady on his legs. She reached out placing her slender arms around his waist and helped him back to his seat. Easing him gently down until she was happy he was comfortable.

"Thank you, Marianne, I was just after a little breakfast." He looked at her pathetically as he accepted her admonishment. She bent towards him helping him to sit correctly in his seat. He didn't move his eyes from her ample cleavage other than a glance at Jack who looked on with suspicion. Marianne wiggled towards the table placed a croissant on a clean plate and returned to him, placing it on his lap.

"Wait, a moment Monsieur Valois, there is no strawberry jam." She skipped back to the house. Antoine watched her go, admiring her long legs barely covered by her skirt.

Jack narrowed his eyes.

"What's going on here you fraud?" Antoine rested back in his chair, a satisfied grin across his face. He was pleased his crazy French comrade had lightened the mood, but he still had to wonder after all these years if he was for real.

"All part of my recuperation." Antoine explained. "My sickness benefit covers me for physiotherapy until I am back to full fitness. All the expenses are covered and, as you know, I am not as young as I used to be. It will take a little while yet."

"Ah… So she is a physiotherapist then is she?" He was beginning to understand.

"Well, a medical student actually." Antoine confessed. "but very good!" He fixed Jack with a knowing stare.

"I see." He tried to stop smiling, but he was finding it hard to keep a straight face. "And which hospital is she from?"

"Shh … shh … shh!" Antoine sat back in his chair as Marianne came out of the kitchen and made her way towards him.

"Here is your jam. Now, why don't we take this to your room, it is time for your morning massage." She walked to the back of the wheelchair and kicking the brake free, pushed him towards the house. As they watched him being pushed across the paving, Annabel giggled, and Jack shook his head. Just before she tipped the wheels to lift him over the step, Antoine looked back at Jack from his chair.

"The Moulin Rouge." He answered.

They disappeared into the house to sounds of laughter from the garden.

EPILOGUE

BARBADOS

he watched the fisherman cast into the black slick floating within the
tranquil turquoise of the Caribbean sea, marvelling as he walked back
to the beach with a net full of sardines. Breakfast would be ready in
an hour. It was 7 AM, and the temperature was already into the
eighties, another hot day in Barbados.

There was a knock on the door. Covering her bikini with a
patterned silk sarong, she tied it loosely at her shoulder and crossed
the tiled floor. A Bajan waiter stood with a tray of beautiful fruit,
prepared and ready to eat, surrounding a pot of hot coffee.

"Good morning Miss Davenport, I hope you slept well? Please
accept this with the compliments of the management. We appreciate
your patronage of the Coconut Creek Hotel."

She let him in and followed him out to her first floor terrace. She
watched as he arranged the colour co-ordinated fruits across her
breakfast table. By the time he had finished, the presentation was
perfect; it seemed a shame to eat it. There were mangos; strawberries,
kiwi, banana, melon, berries and several fruits she had never seen
before. They all looked mouth watering. A coconut with a straw
poking through one eye was the centrepiece of the whole creation.

"Why thank you, Alfred, you are so kind." She went to her purse
and gave him a 100 dollar bill. He accepted it gratefully and bowed as
he pushed it into his hand.

As soon as the waiter left, she pulled the tie of the sarong letting it
fall to the floor. She would take advantage of the early morning sun
and enjoy her sea view terrace for an hour or two.

Settling into a plushly padded recliner, she breathed deeply, drawing in the fresh, sweet aroma of Alfred's masterpiece. She poured the hot aromatic coffee into a cup and put a strawberry in her mouth enjoying the delicious juicy experience as it tantalised her taste buds. Settling back she sipped at her coffee and studied the breathtaking view.

In the distance two cruise liners made their way across the horizon transporting their guests through paradise. They travelled at such a slow pace they appeared to be at a standstill. Only when she turned back to them again, she could see they had changed position slightly. A pirate ship came into view just off the coast moving at a much faster speed. It was the Jolly Roger, the local Barbados party boat. Its role was to pick up passengers from all over the island and provide a booming reggae propelled rum cruise. It was on its way back to base to replenish supplies for another day of fun and frolics.

It was not for her, perhaps fifteen years ago in her early twenties but not now. Not that she was opposed to a party or two, but she was used to a more refined affair. Events that required an afternoon to prepare an outfit, perfect the makeup and allow her hairdresser to choose a style to suit the theme. She smoothed her hair further back into her scrunchy, her red locks falling onto her neck as she felt the sun on her face. She lowered her sunglasses, pushed her head back and closed her eyes.

"Beautiful isn't it?" A male voice interrupted the peace and calm. She remembered seeing a glimpse of him yesterday. He had moved back into his room from the adjoining balcony just as she came out to relax and read her book.

"Yes, it is beautiful." She agreed, remaining reclined, her eyes closed letting the warmth bury deep into her pores.

"It's such a shame…" The man said. That was all, nothing more.

She could hear the waves rippling on the private beach below. From above the birds were waking, their excited cries creating a chorus as they began their patrol around the resorts in search of tidbits. But she was aware the man was still standing on his terrace, his last statement still hung in the air, unfinished. It pushed the whole sensory experience of the idyllic location to the background. It nipped at her, irritated her and as the seconds ticked by, really annoyed her.

Shame about what?

She raised her glasses onto her head as she sat up and looked over at the man leaning on the adjacent wall. Her eyes grew wide as she recognised his rugged features. The stubble following the contours of his strong jaw, meeting the blue shadow of his close cropped, near balding scalp. But it was the ice blue eyes boring into her she remembered most.

"Hello, Klara." The silencer popped once, leaving a neat hole in her forehead.

She stared for a moment more, before crashing forward onto the table, spraying the patio with an exotic, fruity aroma.

Jack Case placed the Glock into his kit bag and left the room. He had a plane to catch.

END

THE EAGLE LEGACY ©

Book one of The Case Files

45180322R00327

Printed in Poland
by Amazon Fulfillment
Poland Sp. z o.o., Wrocław